CAMILLA LÄCKBERG

Born in 1974, Camilla Läckberg graduated from Gothenburg University of Economics, before moving to Stockholm where she worked for a few years as an economist. However, a course in creative crime writing triggered a drastic change of career. Her first six novels all became Swedish No 1 bestsellers. She lives in a suburb of Stockholm.

Also by Camilla Läckberg

The Ice Princess

CAMILLA LÄCKBERG

The Preacher Ff 2

Translated from the Swedish by
Steven T. Murray

from Andrew

HARPER

Harper
An imprint of HarperCollins*Publishers*
77–85 Fulham Palace Road,
Hammersmith, London W6 8JB

www.harpercollins.co.uk

This paperback edition 2010
1

First published in Great Britain by
HarperCollins*Publishers* 2009

Copyright © Camilla Läckberg 2004
Published by agreement with Bengt Nordin Agency, Sweden
English translation © Steven T. Murray 2008

Camilla Läckberg asserts the moral right to
be identified as the author of this work

A catalogue record for this book is
available from the British Library

ISBN: 978-0-00-725394-4

Set in Meridien by Palimpsest Book Production Limited,
Grangemouth, Stirlingshire

Printed and bound in Great Britain by
Clays Ltd, St Ives plc

Mixed Sources
Product group from well-managed
forests and other controlled sources
www.fsc.org Cert no. SW-COC-1806
© 1996 Forest Stewardship Council
FSC

FSC is a non-profit international organization established to promote the
responsible management of the world's forests. Products carrying the FSC
label are independently certified to assure consumers that they come
from forests that are managed to meet the social, economic and
ecological needs of present and future generations.

Find out more about HarperCollins and the environment at
www.harpercollins.co.uk/green

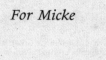

For Micke

1

The day was off to a promising start. He woke up early, before the rest of the family, put on his clothes as quietly as possible, and managed to sneak out unnoticed. He took along his knight's helmet and wooden sword, which he swung happily as he ran the hundred yards from the house down to the mouth of the King's Cleft. He stopped for a moment and peered in awe into the sheer crevice through the rocky outcrop. The sides of the rock were six or seven feet apart, and it towered up over thirty feet into the sky, into which the summer sun had just begun to climb. Three huge boulders were solidly wedged in the middle of the cleft, and it was an imposing sight. The place held a magical attraction for a six-year-old. The fact that the King's Cleft was forbidden ground made it all the more tempting.

The name had originated from King Oscar II's visit to Fjällbacka in the late nineteenth century, but that was something he neither knew nor cared about as he slowly crept into the shadows, with his sword ready to attack. His father had told him that the scenes from Hell's Gap in the film *Ronja Rövardotter* had been filmed inside the King's Cleft. When he had watched the film himself, he felt a little tickle in his stomach as he saw the robber chieftain Mattis ride through.

Sometimes he played highwaymen here, but today he was a knight. A Knight of the Round Table, like in the big, fancy-coloured book that his grandmother had given him for his birthday.

He crept over the boulders that covered the ground and made ready to attack the great fire-breathing dragon with his courage and his sword. The summer sun did not reach down into the cleft, which made it a cold, dark place. Perfect for dragons. Soon he would make the blood spurt from its throat, and after prolonged death throes it would fall dead at his feet.

Out of the corner of his eye he saw something that caught his attention. He glimpsed a piece of red cloth behind a boulder, and curiosity got the better of him. The dragon could wait; maybe there was treasure hidden there. He jumped up on the rock and looked down the other side. For a moment he almost fell over backwards, but after wobbling and flailing his arms about he regained his balance. Later, he would not admit that he was scared, but just then, at that instant, he had never been more terrified in all six years of his life. A lady was lying in wait for him. She was on her back, staring straight up at him with her eyes wide. His first instinct was to flee before she caught him playing here when he wasn't supposed to be. Maybe she would force him to tell her where he lived and then drag him home to Mamma and Pappa. They would be so furious, and they were sure to ask: how many times have we told you that you mustn't go to the King's Cleft without a grown-up?

But the odd thing was that the lady didn't move. She didn't have any clothes on either, and for an instant he was embarrassed that he was standing there looking at a naked lady. The red he had seen was not a piece of cloth but something wet right next to her, and he couldn't see her clothes anywhere. Funny, lying there naked. Especially when it was so cold.

Then something impossible occurred to him. What if the lady was dead! He couldn't work out any other explanation for why she was lying so still. The realization made him jump down from the rock, and he slowly backed towards the mouth of the cleft. After putting a few yards between himself and the dead lady, he turned round and ran home as fast as he could. He no longer cared if he was scolded or not.

Sweat made the sheet stick to her body. Erica tossed and turned in bed, but it was impossible to find a comfortable position. The bright summer night didn't make it any easier to sleep, and for the thousandth time she made a mental note to buy some blackout curtains to hang up, or rather persuade Patrik to do it.

It drove her crazy that he could sleep so contentedly next to her. How dare he lie there snoring when she lay awake night after night? She gave him a little poke in the hope that he'd wake up. He didn't budge. She poked a little harder. He grunted, pulled the covers up and turned his back to her.

With a sigh, she lay on her back with her arms crossed over her breasts and stared at the ceiling. Her belly arched into the air like a big globe, and she tried to imagine her baby swimming inside of her in the dark. Maybe with his thumb in his mouth. Although it was all still too unreal for her to be able to picture it. She was in her eighth month but still couldn't grasp the fact that she had another life inside her. Well, pretty soon it was going to be very real. Erica was torn between longing and dread. It was difficult to see beyond the childbirth. To be honest, right now it was hard to see beyond the problem of no longer being able to sleep on her stomach. She looked at the luminous dial of the alarm clock. 4.42 a.m. Maybe she should turn on the light and read for a while instead.

Three and a half hours and one bad detective novel later, she was about to roll out of bed when the telephone rang shrilly. As usual she handed the receiver to Patrik.

'Hello, this is Patrik.' His voice was thick with sleep. 'Okay, all right. Oh shit, yeah, I can be there in fifteen minutes. See you there.'

He turned to Erica. 'We've got an emergency. I've got to run.'

'But you're on holiday. Can't one of the others take it?' She could hear that her voice sounded whiny, but lying awake all night hadn't done much for her mood.

'It's a murder. Mellberg wants me to come along. He's going out there himself.'

'A murder? Where?'

'Here in Fjällbacka. A little boy found a woman's body in the King's Cleft this morning.'

Patrik threw on his clothes, which didn't take long since it was the middle of July and he only needed light summer clothes. Before he rushed out the door he climbed onto the bed and kissed Erica on the belly, somewhere near where she vaguely recalled she once had a navel.

'See you later, baby. Be nice to Mamma, and I'll be home soon.'

He kissed her quickly on the cheek and hurried off. With a sigh Erica hoisted herself out of bed and put on one of those tent-like dresses which for the time being were the only things that fit her. Against her better judgement she had read lots of baby books, and in her opinion everyone who wrote about the joyful experience of pregnancy ought to be taken out in the public square and horsewhipped. Insomnia, sore joints, stretch marks, haemorrhoids, night sweats, and a general hormonal upheaval – that was closer to the truth. And she sure as hell wasn't glowing with any inner radiance. Erica muttered to herself as she slowly made her way downstairs in pursuit of the day's first cup of coffee. Maybe that would lift the fog a bit.

By the time Patrik arrived, a feverish amount of activity was already under way. The mouth of the King's Cleft had been cordoned off with yellow tape, and he counted three police cars and an ambulance. The techs from Uddevalla were busy with their work and he knew better than to walk right into the crime scene. That was a rookie mistake which didn't prevent his boss, Superintendent Mellberg, from stomping about amongst them. They looked in dismay at his shoes and clothing, which at that very moment were adding thousands of fibres and particles to their sensitive workplace. When Patrik stopped outside the tape and motioned to his boss, Mellberg climbed back over the cordon, to the great relief of the Forensics.

'Hello, Hedström,' said the superintendent.

His voice was hearty, bordering on joyful, and Patrik was taken aback. For a moment he thought that Mellberg was about to give him a hug but thankfully, this turned out to be wrong. Nevertheless, the man appeared completely changed. It was only a week since Patrik had gone on holiday, but the man before him was really not the same one he'd left sitting sullenly at his desk, muttering that the very concept of holidays ought to be abolished.

Mellberg eagerly pumped Patrik's hand and slapped him on the back.

'So, how's it going with the brooding hen at home? Any sign that you're going to be a father soon?'

'Not for a month and a half, they say.'

Patrik still had no idea what had brought on such good humour on Mellberg's part, but he pushed aside his surprise and tried to concentrate on the reason he'd been called to the scene.

'So what have you found?'

Mellberg made an effort to wipe the smile off his face and pointed towards the shadowy interior of the cleft.

'A six-year-old boy sneaked out early this morning while his parents were asleep and came here to play Knights amongst the boulders. Instead he found a dead woman. We got the call at 6.15.'

'How long have Forensics had to examine the crime scene?'

'They arrived an hour ago. The ambulance got here first, and the EMTs were immediately able to confirm that no medical help was needed. Since then they've been able to work freely. They're a bit touchy . . . I just wanted to go in and look round a bit and they were quite rude about it, I must say. Well, I suppose one gets a little anal crawling about looking for fibres with tweezers all day long.'

Now Patrik recognized his boss again. This was more Mellberg's sort of tone. But Patrik knew from experience that it was no use trying to alter his opinions. It was easier just to let his remarks go in one ear and out the other.

'What do we know about her?'

'Nothing yet. We think she's around twenty-five. The only piece of fabric we found, if you could call it that, was a handbag. Otherwise she was stark naked. Pretty nice tits, actually.'

Patrik shut his eyes and repeated to himself, like an inner mantra: *It won't be long until he retires. It won't be long until he retires . . .*

Mellberg went on obliviously, 'The cause of death hasn't been confirmed, but she was beaten severely. Bruises all over her body and a number of what look to be knife wounds. And then there's the fact that she's lying on a grey blanket. The medical examiner is having a look at her, and we hope to have a preliminary statement very soon.'

'Has anyone been reported missing around that age?'

'No, nowhere near it. An old man was reported missing about a week ago, but it turned out that he just got tired of being cooped up with his wife in a caravan and took off with a chick he met at Galären Pub.'

Patrik saw that the team round the body was now preparing to lift her carefully into a body bag. Her hands and feet had been bagged according to regulations to preserve any evidence. The team of forensic officers from Uddevalla worked together to get the woman into the body bag in the most efficient way possible. Then the blanket she was lying on also had to be put in a plastic bag for later examination.

The shocked expression on their faces and the way they froze instantly told Patrik that something unexpected had happened.

'What is it?' he called.

'You're not going to believe this,' said one of the officers, 'but there are bones here. And two skulls. Based on the number of bones, I'd say there are easily enough for two skeletons.'

2

SUMMER 1979

She was wobbling badly as she pedalled homewards in the bright midsummer night. The party had been a bit wilder than she'd expected, but that didn't matter. She was grown-up, after all, so she could do as she liked. The best part was getting away from the kid for a while. The baby with all her shrieking, her need for tenderness and demands for something she couldn't give. It was because of the baby, after all, that she still had to live at home with her mother, with the old lady who hardly let her go a few yards away from the house, even though she was nineteen years old. It was a miracle that she'd been allowed to go out tonight to celebrate Midsummer's Eve.

If she hadn't had the kid she could have had her own place by now; she could be earning her own money. She could have gone out whenever she liked and come home when she felt like it, and nobody would have said a word. But with the kid that was impossible. She would have preferred to give her up for adoption, but the old lady wouldn't hear of it, and now she was the one who had to pay the price. If her mother wanted to keep the kid so much, why couldn't she take care of her alone?

The old lady was really going to be furious when she came rolling in like this in the wee hours of the morning. Her breath stank of alcohol, and she would surely be made to pay for that later. But it was worth it. She hadn't had this much fun since the brat was born.

She bicycled straight through the intersection by the petrol station and continued a bit up the road. Then she turned off to the left towards Bräcke but lost her balance and almost went into the ditch. She straightened out the wheel and pedalled harder to get a little head start up the first steep hill. The wind riffled through her hair, and the light summer night was utterly quiet. For a moment she closed her eyes and thought about that bright summer night when the German had got her pregnant. It had been a wonderful and forbidden night, but not worth the price she finally had to pay.

Suddenly she opened her eyes as the bike hit something. The last thing she remembered was the ground rushing towards her at great speed.

Back at the station in Tanumshede, Mellberg was sunk in uncharacteristically deep thought. Patrik didn't say much either as he sat across from him in the lunchroom, pondering the morning's events. It was actually too warm to be drinking coffee, but he needed something stimulating, and alcohol was hardly suitable. Both men absentmindedly flapped their shirts up and down to cool off. The air-conditioning had been broken for two weeks now, and they still hadn't had anyone out to fix it. In the morning the temperature was usually tolerable, but around noon the heat began to climb to unbearable levels.

'What the hell is this all about?' said Mellberg as he scratched cautiously at the nest of hair that was coiled on top of his head to hide his bald pate.

'I have no idea, to be honest with you. A woman's body was found lying on top of two skeletons. If someone hadn't actually been killed, I would have thought it was some sort of prank. Skeletons stolen from a biology lab or something. But there's no getting round the fact that the woman was murdered. I heard a comment from one of the Forensics as well – he said the bones didn't look fresh. Of course that could be due to where they've been lying. They might have been exposed to wind and weather or they might have been

11

protected. I hope the ME can give some estimate as to how old they are.'

'All right, when do you think we can expect the first report from him?' Mellberg frowned anxiously.

'We'll probably get a preliminary report today, then it will take a couple of days for him to go over everything in more detail. So for the time being we'll have to work on whatever evidence we've got. Where are the others?'

Mellberg sighed. 'Gösta is off today. Some damn golf tournament or something. Ernst and Martin are out on an investigation. Annika is on some Greek island. She probably thought it was going to rain all summer again. Poor thing. It can't have been fun to leave Sweden right now with this great weather we're having.'

Patrik gave Mellberg another surprised look and wondered at this unusual expression of sympathy. Something funny was going on, that was for sure. But he couldn't take the time to worry about it now. They had more important things to think about.

'I know you're on holiday for the rest of this week, but would you mind coming in and helping out on the case?' Mellberg asked. 'Ernst isn't imaginative enough and Martin is too inexperienced to lead an investigation, so we could really use your help.'

The request was so flattering to Patrik's vanity that he found himself saying yes on the spot. Of course he would catch hell for it at home, but he consoled himself with the fact that it would take no longer than fifteen minutes to get home if Erica needed him in a hurry. Besides, they'd been getting on each other's nerves in the heat, so it might be a good idea for him to be out of the house.

'First I'd like to find out whether any woman has been reported missing,' said Patrik. 'We should check a fairly wide area, say from Strömstad down to Göteborg. I'll ask Martin or Ernst to do it. I thought I heard them come in.'

12

'That's good, a great idea. That's the right spirit, keep it up!' Mellberg got up from the table and cheerfully slapped Patrik on the shoulder. Patrik realized that he would be the one doing the work, as usual, while Mellberg once again took all the credit. But he no longer got upset about that; it wasn't worth it.

With a sigh he put both of their coffee cups in the dishwasher. He wasn't going to need to put on any sunblock today.

'All right, everybody up! Do you think this is some sort of bloody boarding-house where you can lie about all day long?'

The voice cut through thick layers of fog and echoed painfully against his temples. Stefan cautiously opened one eye but closed it the instant he saw the blinding glare of the summer sun.

'What the hell . . .' Robert, his older brother by one year, turned over in bed and put the pillow over his head. It was abruptly yanked out of his grasp and he sat up, muttering.

'Can't I ever sleep in a little at this place?'

'You two slackers sleep in every single day. It's almost noon. If you didn't stay up late gadding about every night and doing God knows what, maybe you wouldn't have to sleep half the day. I actually need a little help around this place. You live here for free and you eat for free too, and both of you are grown men. I don't think it's too much to ask for you to give your poor mother a helping hand.'

Solveig Hult stood with her arms crossed. She was morbidly obese, with the pallor of someone who never goes outside. Her hair was filthy, framing her face with straggly, dark locks.

'You're almost thirty years old and still living off your mother. Yeah, you're real he-men, all right. And how can you afford to run around partying every single night, if I may ask? You don't work and I never see you contributing anything to the household expenses. All I can say is that if your father were still alive, he'd put a stop to this behaviour. Have you heard anything from the Job Centre yet? You were supposed to go down there week before last!'

Now it was Stefan's turn to put the pillow over his face. He tried to block out the endless nagging; she was like a broken record. But his pillow was yanked away too. He sat up, hung over, his head pounding like a marching band.

'I put away the breakfast things long ago. You'll have to find something in the fridge yourselves.'

Solveig's huge posterior waddled out of the little room that the brothers still shared, and she slammed the door behind her. They didn't dare try to go back to sleep, but took out a packet of cigarettes and each lit a fag. They could skip breakfast, but the fag lifted their spirits and gave them a nice burn in the throat.

'What a fucking blast last night, eh?' Robert laughed and blew smoke rings in the air. 'I told you they'd have great stuff at home. He's a director of some company in Stockholm. Thank God guys like that can afford the best.'

Stefan didn't answer. Unlike his big brother, he never got an adrenaline rush from the break-ins. Instead he went about for days both before and after a job with a big cold lump of fear in his stomach. But he always did as Robert said; it never occurred to him that he could do anything different.

Yesterday's break-in had given them the biggest payday they'd had in a long time. Most people had grown more wary of leaving expensive things in their summer houses; they used mainly their old junk that they would have otherwise thrown out, or finds from jumble sales that made them feel they'd made a coup even though the items weren't worth a shit. But yesterday they'd got hold of a new TV, a DVD player, a Nintendo, and a bunch of jewellery belonging to the lady of the house. Robert was going to sell the stuff through his usual channels, and it would bring a pretty penny. Not that it would last them very long. Stolen money always burned a hole in their pockets, and after a couple of weeks it would be gone. They spent it on gambling, going out and treating their friends, and other necessary expenses. Stefan looked at the pricey watch he was wearing. Luckily their mother couldn't recognize anything valuable when she saw it. If she knew what this watch cost, the nagging would never stop.

Sometimes he felt trapped like a hamster on a wheel, going round and round as the years passed by. Nothing had really changed since he and his brother were teenagers, and he saw no possibilities now, either. The one thing that gave his life meaning was the only thing he had ever kept secret from Robert. An instinct deep inside told him that no good would come of confiding in his brother. Robert would only turn it into something dirty with his rude remarks.

For a second Stefan allowed himself to think about how soft her hair was against his rough cheek, and how small her hand felt when he held it between his own.

'Hey, don't just sit there daydreaming. We've got business to take care of.'

Robert got up with his cigarette dangling from the corner of his mouth and headed out the door first. As usual, Stefan followed, which was all he knew how to do.

In the kitchen Solveig was sitting in her usual place. Ever since Stefan was a little boy, since that incident with his father, he had seen her sitting on her chair by the window as her fingers eagerly fiddled with whatever was in front of her on the table. In his earliest memories his mother was beautiful, but over the years the fat had accumulated in thicker and thicker layers on her face and body.

Solveig looked as if she were sitting there in a trance; her fingers lived their own life, incessantly plucking at things and then smoothing them out. For almost twenty years she had messed about with those fucking photo albums, sorting and resorting them. She bought new albums and then re-arranged the photos and news clippings. Better, more elegantly. He wasn't so stupid that he didn't understand that it was her way of holding on to happier times, but someday surely she would see that those days were long gone.

The pictures were from the days when Solveig was beautiful. The high point of her life had been when she married Johannes Hult, the youngest son of Ephraim Hult, the noted Free Church pastor and owner of the most prosperous farm in the region. Johannes was handsome and rich. Solveig may have been poor, but she was the most beautiful girl in all of Bohuslän; that's what everyone said at the time. And if further proof were needed, the articles she had saved from when she was crowned Queen of the May two years in a row would suffice. It was those articles, and the many black-and-white photos of herself as a young girl, that she had carefully preserved and sorted every day for the past twenty years. She knew that the girl was still there somewhere beneath all the layers of fat. Through the photos she could keep the girl alive, even though she was slipping further and further away with each passing year.

With a last look over his shoulder, Stefan left his mother sitting in the kitchen and followed Robert out the door. As Robert said, they had business to take care of.

Erica considered going out for a walk, but realized that it probably wasn't such a good idea right now, with the sun at its peak and the heat most intense. She'd done splendidly throughout her entire pregnancy until the heat wave set in. Since then, she went about like a sweaty whale, desperately trying to find a way to cool off. Patrik, God bless him, had come up with the idea of buying her a table fan, and now she carried it about with her like a treasure wherever she went in the house. The only drawback was that she had to plug it in, so she could never sit further from an outlet than the cord would reach, which limited her choices.

But on the veranda the outlet was perfectly placed, and she could settle down on the sofa with the fan on the table in front of her. No position was comfortable for more than five minutes, which made her keep shifting to find a better position. Sometimes she felt a foot kicking at her ribs, or else something that felt like a hand punching her in the side. Then she was forced to change position again. She had no idea how she was going to stand another month of this.

She and Patrik had only been together for half a year when she got pregnant, but oddly enough it hadn't upset either of them. They were both a little older, a little more certain of what they wanted, and they didn't think there was any reason to wait. Only now was she starting to get cold feet, at the eleventh hour, so to speak. Perhaps they'd not shared enough everyday life before they embarked upon this pregnancy. What would happen to their relationship when they were suddenly presented with a tiny stranger who required all the attention they'd been able to devote to each other before?

The crazy, blind infatuation of their early days together had faded, of course. They had a more realistic, everyday foundation to build on now, with better insight into each other's good and bad sides. But after the baby was born, what if only the bad sides were left? How many times had she heard the statistics about all the relationships that fizzled out during the first year of a baby's life? Well, there was no use worrying about it now. What's done is done, and there was no getting around the fact that both she and Patrik were longing for the arrival of this child with every fibre of their bodies. She hoped that sense of longing would be enough to get them through the turbulent changes ahead.

Erica gave a start when the telephone rang. Laboriously she struggled to get up from the sofa, hoping that whoever was calling had enough patience not to hang up.

'Yes, hello? . . . Oh, hi, Conny . . . Oh, I'm fine, thanks, it's just a little too hot to be fat . . . Drop by? Sure, of course . . . Come on over for coffee . . . Spend the night? Well . . .' Erica sighed inside. 'Of course, why not? When are you coming? Tonight? Well no, it's no problem at all. You can sleep in the guest room.'

Wearily she hung up the receiver. There was one big drawback to having a house in Fjällbacka in the summertime. All sorts of relatives and friends – who hadn't uttered a peep during the ten colder months of the year – would pop up out of the blue. They weren't particularly interested in seeing her in November, but in July they saw their chance to live rent-free with an ocean view. Erica had thought that they might be spared this year, when half of July passed without a word from anyone. But now her cousin Conny said he was on his way to Fjällbacka from Trollhättan with his wife and two kids. It was only for one night, so she supposed she could handle it. She'd never been that fond of either of her two cousins, but her upbringing made it impossible to refuse to take them in, even when that was what she wanted to do. In her opinion, they were both freeloaders.

Yet Erica was grateful that she and Patrik had a house in Fjällbacka where they could receive guests, invited or not. After her parents died, her brother-in-law had tried to effect a sale of the house. But her sister Anna finally got fed up with his physical and mental abuse. She'd divorced Lucas, and she and Erica now owned the house together. Since Anna was still living in Stockholm with her two kids, Patrik and Erica were able to move into the house in Fjällbacka. In return they took care of all the expenses. Eventually they would have to make more permanent arrangements regarding the house, but for the time being Erica was just glad to have it. And she was thrilled to be living there year-round.

Erica looked around and saw that she'd have to get busy if she wanted the house to be relatively tidy when the guests arrived. She wondered what Patrik would say to the invasion, but then shrugged her shoulders. If he was willing to leave her alone here and go off to work in the middle of their holiday, then she could certainly decide to have guests. She'd already forgotten that she had been thinking it was rather nice not to have him underfoot all day.

Ernst and Martin had come back to the station from the call they'd been on, and Patrik decided to start by getting them up to speed in the case. He called them into his office, and they sat down in the chairs in front of his desk. He couldn't help noticing that Ernst was beet-red with anger because a younger detective had been assigned to lead the investigation, but Patrik chose to ignore it. That was something Mellberg would have to handle. In the worst-case scenario Patrik could manage without Ernst's help if his colleague refused to work with him.

'I assume you've already heard about what happened.'

'Yes, we heard it on the police radio,' said Martin. Unlike Ernst, he was young and enthusiastic and sat bolt upright in his chair with a notebook in his lap and his pen poised.

'A woman was found murdered in the King's Cleft in Fjällbacka. She was naked and looks to be somewhere between twenty and thirty. *Underneath* her were found two human skeletons of unknown origin and age. Unofficially, Karlström in CSI told me that they weren't exactly fresh. So we seem to have been given a lot on our plate, besides all the usual pub fights and drink-drivers we're up to our necks in. And both Annika and Gösta are on holiday, so we'll have to roll up our sleeves and get busy. I'm actually on holiday this week as well, but I agreed to come in and work. Mellberg has asked me to lead this investigation. Any questions?'

This was aimed primarily at Ernst, who chose not to confront him. No doubt he would grumble about things behind his back instead.

'What do you want me to do?' Martin was like a restless horse, now impatiently circling his pen above his notebook.

'I want you to start by checking with the Schengen

19

Information System for missing-persons reports about women who've disappeared during, let's say, the past two months. It's better to expand the time interval until we hear more from the forensic medicine lab. Although I suspect that the time of death is much more recent, maybe just a couple of days ago.'

'Haven't you heard?' asked Martin.

'Heard what?'

'The database is down. We'll have to forget about SIS and do things the good old-fashioned way.'

'Damn. Great bloody timing. Well, according to Mellberg we don't seem to have any missing-persons reports outstanding from before I went on holiday. So I suggest that you ring round to all the nearby districts. Start with the closest districts and work your way out. Understood?'

'All right. How far out should I go?'

'As far as you need to until we find someone who matches. And ring Uddevalla right after the meeting to get a preliminary description of the victim to use in your enquiries.'

'So what should I do?' The enthusiasm in Ernst's voice was not exactly contagious.

Patrik glanced over the notes he had jotted down after his conversation with Mellberg.

'I'd like you to start by talking to the people who live near the entrance to the King's Cleft. Find out whether they saw or heard anything last night or early this morning. The Cleft is full of tourists in the daytime, so the body, or the bodies if we're going to be precise, must have been transported there sometime during the night or early morning. We can assume that the remains were brought there via the larger entrance; they could hardly have been carried up the steps from Ingrid Bergman's Square. The little boy discovered the woman at about six o'clock, so you should focus on the hours between nine at night and six in the morning. I thought I'd go down

20

to the archives and take a look myself. There's something about those two skeletons that is tugging at my memory. I have the feeling that I should know what it is, but . . . can you think of anything? Isn't there something that jogs your memory?'

Patrik threw out his hands and waited with raised eyebrows for an answer, but Martin and Ernst just shook their heads. He sighed. Well, there was nothing to do but go to the catacombs . . .

Wondering whether he might be in disfavour, and not sure whether he even would have known if he'd had time to ponder the matter, Patrik sat deep in the bowels of the Tanumshede police station and dug through old documents. Dust had settled on most of the folders, but thank goodness they still seemed to be in good order. Most of the files were archived in chronological order, and even though he didn't know exactly what he was looking for, he knew that it had to be there somewhere.

He sat on the stone floor with his legs crossed and methodically went through box after box. Decades of human fates passed through his hands, and after a while it struck him how many people and families kept reappearing in the police registers. It was as if a life of crime were being passed down from parents to children and even to grandchildren, he thought when he saw the same family names popping up again and again.

His mobile phone rang and he saw from the display that it was Erica.

'Hi, darling, is everything all right?' He knew what the answer was going to be. 'Yes, I know that it's hot. Just sit by the fan, there isn't much else to be done . . . Erica, we've got a homicide on our hands here, and Mellberg wants me to lead the investigation. Would you be very upset if I came in and worked a couple of days?'

Patrik held his breath. He knew he should have rung her earlier to say that he might have to work, but like a typical man he had evaded the issue, trying to put off the inevitable. On the other hand, she was well aware of the demands made by his profession. Summertime was the most hectic season for the Tanum police, and they had to take turns going on holiday. It was never guaranteed that they could even take a few days in a row; it all depended on how many drunks, fights, and other side-effects of tourism the station had to handle. And homicide, of course, took precedence over everything else.

Erica said something that he almost missed.

'Coming to visit, you say? Who? Your cousin?' Patrik sighed. 'No, what can I say? Sure, it would have been nicer if we could be alone tonight, but if they're already on the way . . . They're just staying for one night, I hope? Okay, then I'll pick up some shrimp to serve them. Something simple, so you won't have to cook. I'll be home around seven. Kiss, kiss.'

He stuck the phone back in his pocket and continued going through the contents of the boxes in front of him. A file marked 'Missing' caught his interest. Some ambitious person had at one time collected all the missing-persons reports resulting from police investigations. Patrik knew that this was what he'd been looking for. His fingers were filthy from all the dust, so he wiped them on his shorts before he opened the thin file. After a few minutes' reading, his memory received the jog it required. He should have remembered this straight away, considering how few people in the district had actually gone missing without being found again. His age must be starting to take its toll. At least now he had the relevant reports in front of him, and he had a feeling that it was no coincidence that two women were reported missing in 1979 and were never seen again. Then two skeletons turn up now in the King's Cleft.

He took the file with him upstairs to the daylight and placed it on his desk.

The horses were the only reason she stayed. With a practised hand she curried the coat of the brown gelding with steady strokes. The physical labour acted as a safety-valve for her to get rid of some of her frustration. It was shit to be seventeen years old and not have any say about your own life. As soon as she came of age she was going to get the hell out of this hole. Then she'd accept the offer she'd received from the photographer who'd come up to her when she was walking about in downtown Göteborg. When she became a model in Paris and was making tons of money she would tell them all where they could stuff their fucking education. The photographer had told her that with each passing year her value as a model decreased. A whole year of her life would be wasted before she ever got the chance to model, just because the old man had education on the brain. It didn't take much education to strut down the runway. Later, when she was around twenty-five and starting to get too old, she'd marry a millionaire. Then she could laugh at the old man's threat to cut her out of his will. Someday she'd be able to go shopping and spend the equivalent of his entire fucking fortune.

Her marvellous bloody brother didn't make matters any easier. It was better to live with him and Marita than at home, but not much. He was so damned reliable. Nothing he did ever went wrong, while she always got the blame for everything.

'Linda?'

Typical, even here in the stall she couldn't be left in peace.

'Linda?' The voice was more urgent. He knew that she was here, so there was no use pretending she didn't hear him.

'Don't be such a bloody nag. What is it?'

'You really don't need to speak to me in that tone of voice. I don't think it's too much to ask that you show a little courtesy.'

She muttered a few curses in reply, but Jacob let it pass.

'You're actually my brother, not my father, did you ever think of that?' she told him.

'I'm well aware of that, but as long as you're living under my roof, I actually do have a certain responsibility for you.'

Just because he was almost twice her age, Jacob thought he knew everything. It was easy for him to get on his high horse because he was comfortably off. Father had said many times that Jacob was certainly a son to be proud of, and that he would take good care of the family estate. Linda assumed that her brother would inherit the whole lot one day. Until then he could afford to pretend that money wasn't important, but Linda saw right through him. Everyone admired Jacob because he worked with young people at risk. At the same time they knew full well that eventually he would inherit both the estate and a fortune. Then it would be interesting to see how much longer he continued this idealistic work.

Linda couldn't help giggling. If Jacob knew that she was sneaking out at night he'd go nuts, and if he knew who she was meeting, she'd get the lecture of her life. It was fine to talk about having compassion for the less fortunate, as long as they weren't on your own front porch. Besides, there were other, more deeply rooted reasons for Jacob to hit the roof if he found out that she was seeing Stefan. He was their cousin, and the feud between the two branches of the family had been going on since long before she was born – even before Jacob was born. She had no idea why. That was just the way things were. So she had extra butterflies in her stomach whenever she sneaked out to meet Stefan.

Linda had a good time with him. He was very considerate, but he was much older, after all, so he had a self-confidence that boys her own age could never muster. It didn't bother her that they were cousins. Nowadays cousins could even get married. That wasn't really part of her long-term plans, but she had nothing against exploring one thing or another with him, as long as it remained a secret.

'Did you want something, or were you just planning to hover?' she said now.

Jacob gave a deep sigh and put a hand on her shoulder. She tried to shrink away, but his grip was strong.

'I don't really understand where all this aggression is coming from. The kids I work with would give anything to have a home like yours and be brought up the way you were. A little gratitude and maturity would seem appropriate, you know. And yes, I did want something. Marita has finished cooking and we're ready to eat. So hurry up and change your clothes. Then come and eat with us.'

He loosened his grip on her shoulder and left the stable, heading up to the manor house. Muttering, Linda put down the curry-comb and went to change. In spite of everything, she was very hungry.

Once again Martin's heart had been broken. He'd lost count of how many times it had happened before, but the fact that he was used to it didn't make the sting any less. Like all the times before, he'd thought that this woman resting her head on the pillow next to his was the right one. Of course he was fully aware that she was already taken, but with his usual naïveté he thought that he was more than just a diversion and that her boyfriend's days were numbered. He had no idea that, with his innocent face and almost sweet-as-pie openness, he was like a lump of sugar to a fly for women who were a little older, more mature and living in an everyday rut with their respective husbands. Men they had no intention of leaving for a nice 25-year-old cop, though they thought nothing of having it off with him when the urge or the need for affirmation had to be satisfied. Not that Martin had anything against the physical aspects of a relationship – and he was especially talented in that area – but the problem was that he was also an unusually sensitive young man. Love affairs found a willing participant in Martin Molin. That's why his little flings always ended in tears and gnashing of teeth on his part, when the women thanked him and then went home to their own lives, that might be boring but were steady and familiar.

Martin sighed heavily as he sat at his desk, but he forced himself to focus on the task at hand. The calls he had made so far had been fruitless, but there were still plenty of police districts to ring. The fact that the database had crashed just when he needed it most was probably his usual luck. Now he had to sit here looking up one telephone number after the other, trying to find someone who fit the description of the dead woman.

Two hours later he leaned back and flung his pen at the wall in despair. No one had been reported missing who matched the description of the murder victim. What were they going to do now?

It was so damned unfair. He was older than that snot-nosed kid and should have been the one to lead this investigation, but the world was filled with ingratitude. For several years now he had assiduously kissed up to that bloody Mellberg, but nothing ever came of it. Ernst took the curves at high speed on the way to Fjällbacka. If he hadn't been driving a police car he certainly would have seen plenty of raised middle fingers in his rear-view mirror. Just let them try it, those fucking tourists, then they'd have the devil to pay.

Go and ask the neighbours. That was an assignment for a rookie, not for a cop with twenty-five years of experience. That whippersnapper Martin could have handled the task, leaving Ernst to make some calls to his colleagues in the nearby districts and get a chance to shoot the breeze.

He was seething inside, but that had been his natural frame of mind since he was a kid, so it was nothing out of the ordinary. A choleric disposition made him ill-suited to a profession that required so much social contact. On the other hand, the hooligans showed him respect because they instinctively knew that Ernst Lundgren was not someone to be trifled with if they valued their health.

As he drove through the town there were rubberneckers everywhere. They followed him with their eyes and pointed, and he knew that the news had already spread all through Fjällbacka. He had to drive at a crawl across Ingrid Bergman's Square because of all the cars parked illegally. He saw to his satisfaction that a number of patrons rushed from Café Bryggan's sidewalk tables to move their cars. A smart thing to do. If the cars were still there when he came back he had nothing against spending some time upsetting the holiday mood of people who had parked illegally. Make them blow into the breathalyser a little, maybe. Some of the drivers had been downing a cold beer when they saw him drive by. If he was lucky he might even be able to confiscate a couple of driving licences.

There wasn't much room to park on the short strip of road outside the King's Cleft, but he squeezed into a space and began Operation Door-Knocking. As he expected, nobody had seen a thing. People who would normally notice if their neighbour farted in his own house seemed to go deaf and blind when the police wanted to know something. Although, Ernst had to admit, maybe they actually hadn't heard anything. In the summertime the noise level was so loud at night, with drunks staggering home at dawn, that people learned to block out the noise from outside so they could get a good night's sleep. But it was still damned irritating.

He didn't get even a nibble until the last house. Not a big catch, of course, but at least it was something. The old man in the house farthest from the entrance to the King's Cleft had heard a car drive up around three in the morning, when he was up taking a piss. He narrowed the time frame to a quarter to three. He said he hadn't bothered to look out, so

27

he could say nothing about either the driver or the car. But since he was a former driving school instructor and had driven many types of cars in his day, he was quite certain that the vehicle wasn't a newer model but had a few years on it.

Great, the only thing Ernst had got out of two hours of knocking on doors was that the murderer had probably driven the body here around three o'clock and that he may have been driving an older model car. Not much to cheer about.

But his mood rose a few notches when he drove past the square again on his way back to the station and noticed that new scofflaws had parked in the spots vacated by the previous drivers. Now he'd have them blowing into the breathalyser till their lungs popped.

An insistent ringing of her doorbell interrupted Erica as she was laboriously running the vacuum cleaner over the carpets. Sweat was copiously pouring out of her, and she pushed back a couple of wet strands of hair from her face before she opened the door. They must have driven like joyriders to arrive that fast.

'Hey, fatty!'

A bear hug caught her in a firm grip, and she noticed that she wasn't the only one sweating. But with her nose deeply buried in Conny's armpit she realized that she smelled like roses and lilies of the valley in comparison.

After extracting herself from his embrace she said hello to Conny's wife Britta, politely shaking hands since they had only met a few times. Britta's handshake was damp and limp and felt like a dead fish. Erica shuddered and fought back an impulse to wipe her hand on her slacks.

'What a belly on you! Have you got twins in there or what?'

She really hated hearing people comment on her body that way, but she'd already begun to realize that pregnancy seemed to give everyone a free pass to make comments on your shape and touch your belly – it was altogether too familiar. Complete strangers had even come up and started pawing at her stomach. Erica was just waiting for the obligatory patting to begin, and within seconds Conny was running his hands over her swollen stomach.

'Oh, what a little football star you have in there. Obviously a boy, with all that kicking. Come here, kids, feel this!'

Erica didn't have the strength to object, and she was attacked by two pairs of little hands sticky with ice cream that left handprints on her white maternity blouse. Luckily Lisa and Victor, six and eight years old, soon lost interest.

'So what does the proud father have to say? Is he counting the days or what?' Conny didn't wait for an answer, and Erica recalled that dialogues were not his strong suit.

'Yes, damn it, I can remember when these two little rascals came into the world. A hell of an intense experience. But tell him to forget about watching it down there. It'll make him lose the urge for a long time to come.'

He chuckled and elbowed Britta in the side. She just gave him a surly look. Erica realized that this was going to be a long day. If only Patrik would come home on time.

Patrik knocked cautiously on Martin's door. He was a bit jealous of how neat things were in there. The desk was so clean that it could have been used as an operating table.

'How's it going? Have you found anything?'

Martin's dejected expression told him the answer was negative even before he shook his head. Damn. The most important thing in the investigation right now was to be able to identify the woman. Somewhere people were worried about her. Surely somebody must be missing her.

'What about you?' Martin nodded towards the folder Patrik was holding in his hand. 'Did you find what you were looking for?'

'I think so.'

Patrik pulled up a chair so he could sit next to Martin.

'Take a look at this. Two women disappeared in the late Seventies from Fjällbacka. I don't know why it didn't occur to me at once, it was front-page news back then. Anyway, here's what's left of the investigative material.'

The file he placed on the desk was very dusty, and he saw that Martin's fingers were itching to wipe it off. A stern look from his colleague made him refrain. Patrik opened the folder and showed him the photographs lying on top.

'This is Siv Lantin. She disappeared on Midsummer's Day in 1979. She was nineteen.' Patrik pulled out the next photo. 'This is Mona Thernblad. She disappeared two weeks later and was eighteen years old. Neither of them has been seen since, despite an enormous effort with search parties, dragging the waterways, and everything you can think of. Siv's bicycle was found in a ditch, but that was the only thing that was found. And they found no trace of Mona except for a running shoe.'

'Yes, now that you mention it, I do remember those cases. There was a suspect, wasn't there?'

Patrik leafed through the yellowing pages of the report and pointed to a typed name.

'Stefannes Hult. It was his brother, Gabriel Hult, of all people, who called the police and reported that he'd seen his brother with Siv Lantin on the way to his farm in Bräcke the night she vanished.'

'How seriously was the tip taken? I mean, there must be something behind it if you turn in your own brother as a suspect in a murder case.'

'The feud in the Hult family had been going on for years, and everyone knew about it. So the information was received with some scepticism, I think. It still had to be investigated, and Johannes was brought in for questioning a couple of times. But there was never any evidence besides his brother's testimony. It was one brother's word against the other's, so Johannes was released.'

'Where is Gabriel today?'

'I'm not sure, but I seem to recall that Johannes committed suicide shortly after. Damn . . . if Annika were here she could have put together a more updated account of this in no time. As I mentioned, the material in the folder is meagre to say the least.'

'It sounds like you're quite sure that the skeletons we found are these two women.'

'I wouldn't say that. I'm just basing my guess on the law of probability. We have two women who disappeared in the Seventies, and now two skeletons turn up that seem to have a few years on them. What are the odds that it's only a co-incidence? Although I'm not positive, of course – we won't be until the ME submits his report. But I intend to see to it that he has access to this information right away.'

Patrik glanced at the clock. 'Damn, I'd probably better get going. I promised to be home early today. Erica's cousin is visiting, and I have to fix some shrimp and things for supper. Could you make sure that the ME gets this information? And check with Ernst when he comes in, in case he's turned up anything useful.'

The heat struck Patrik like a wall when he left the police station, and he hurried to his car so he could get back into an air-conditioned environment. If this heat was sapping his energy, he could only imagine what it was doing to Erica, the poor dear.

It was unfortunate that they were having visitors just now, but he understood that it was hard for her to say no. And since the Flood family were leaving tomorrow, it was only one evening wasted. He turned up the cool to max and headed for Fjällbacka.

'Did you talk to Linda?'

Laine was nervously rubbing her hands together. It was a habit that Gabriel had learned to detest.

'There isn't that much to talk about,' he said. 'She'll do as she's told.'

Gabriel did not even look up but calmly continued what he was doing. His tone was dismissive, but Laine wasn't about to shut up so easily. Unfortunately. For years he had wished that his wife would choose to be silent more often. It would do wonders for her personality.

Gabriel Hult himself had the personality of an accountant to his very core. He loved to match credits against debits and figure the balance on the bottom line; he loathed with all his heart everything that had to do with emotions and not logic. Neatness was his motto, and despite the summer heat he was wearing a suit and tie, of a more lightweight fabric of course, but nonetheless very proper-looking. His dark hair had thinned over the years, but he still combed it back and made no attempt to hide the bald patch in the middle. The pièce de résistance was the pair of round spectacles that rested on the tip of his nose so that he could look over the rims with disdain at whoever he was talking to. What's right is right – that was the motto he lived by, and he only wished that other people would do the same. Instead it seemed as if they spent all their energy upsetting his perfect equilibrium and making life hard for him. Everything would be so much easier if they just did as he said rather than thinking up a bunch of foolishness on their own.

The big disturbance in his life at the moment was Linda. Jacob had never been as difficult in his teenage years. In Gabriel's ideal world, girls were calmer and more compliant than boys. Instead they had a teenage monster on their hands who contradicted them at every turn and in general was doing her best to ruin their lives in the shortest time possible. He didn't put much store in her idiotic plans to become a model. There was no doubt that the girl was cute, but unfortunately she'd inherited her mother's brain and wouldn't last an hour in the harsh world of professional modelling.

'We've had this discussion before, Laine, and I haven't changed my opinion. It's out of the question. I won't allow Linda to traipse off and have her picture taken by some sleazy photographer who just wants to get her naked. Linda has to get an education, and that's all there is to it.'

'Yes, but she'll be eighteen in a year, and then she'll do whatever she wants anyway. Isn't it better for us to support her now instead of running the risk of losing her for good a year from now?'

'Linda knows what side her bread's buttered on, so I'd be very surprised if she ran off without securing some financial support. And if she keeps studying that's exactly what she'll get. I promised to send her money every month if she keeps on with her studies, and I intend to honour that promise. Now I really don't want to hear any more about this matter.'

Laine kept on rubbing her hands, but she knew when she was beaten, and she left his office with her shoulders slumped. She carefully closed the sliding doors after her and Gabriel heaved a sigh of relief. This nagging was getting on his nerves. She ought to know him well enough after all these years together to see that he wasn't one to change his mind once it was made up.

His sense of satisfaction and calm returned as he went back to writing in the book he had before him. The modern computer accounting programs had never won him over, because he loved the feeling of having a big ledger in front of him, with neatly written rows of figures that were summed up on each page. When he was finished he leaned back contentedly in his chair. This was a world he could control.

For a moment Patrik wondered whether he was in the right house. This couldn't be the calm, peaceful home that he'd left this morning. The noise level was far above what was permissible in most workplaces, and the house looked like someone had tossed a grenade into it. Belongings he didn't recognize were strewn everywhere, and things that should have been in a certain place were missing. Judging by Erica's expression, he should have come home an hour or two earlier.

In amazement he counted two kids and two extra adults, and he wondered how in the world they could sound like a whole day-care centre. The Disney channel was blaring full blast on the TV, and a little boy was running about chasing an even smaller girl with a toy pistol. The parents of the two little devils were sitting peacefully on the veranda. The big lug of a man waved happily to Patrik but didn't bother getting up from the sofa or tear himself away from the tray of pastries.

Patrik went out to the kitchen to find Erica, and she collapsed in his arms.

'Take me away from here, please. I must have committed some unpardonable sin in a former life to be saddled with all this. The kids are little demons in human form, and Conny is . . . Conny. His wife has hardly said a peep and looks surly enough to curdle milk. Help, they've got to be on their way!'

Patrik patted his wife sympathetically on the back and felt that her blouse was sopping wet with sweat.

'You go and take a shower in peace and quiet, and I'll take care of the guests for a while. You're soaked through.'

'Thanks, you're an angel. There's a pot of coffee ready. They're into their third cup already, but Conny has started to drop little hints that he wants something stronger, so you might want to check what we have available along that line.'

'I'll fix it. Now get going, dear, before I change my mind.'

Erica gave him a grateful kiss and then waddled up the stairs to the bathroom.

'I want some ice cream.' Victor had sneaked up behind Patrik and was aiming his pistol at him.

'Sorry, we don't have any ice cream in the house.'

'Then you'll have to go and buy some.'

The boy's contrary expression drove Patrik crazy, but he

tried to look friendly and said as gently as he could, 'No, I'm not going to do that. There are biscuits on the table outside, you can have some of those.'

'I want ice creeeeeeam!!!' The boy whined and jumped up and down, and now his face was bright red.

'We don't have any, I tell you!' Patrik's patience was starting to wear thin.

'ICE CREAM, ICE CREAM, ICE CREAM, ICE CREAM . . .'

Victor wasn't going to give up easily. But he must have seen from Patrik's eyes that a limit had been reached, because he quieted down and slowly backed out of the kitchen. Then he ran crying to his parents who were sitting out on the veranda, ignoring the tumult in the kitchen.

'PAPPAAA, Uncle Patrik is mean! I want some ICE CREEEAM!'

With the coffee pot in his hand Patrik tried to turn a deaf ear and went out to greet his guests. Conny stood up and held out his hand. When Patrik greeted Britta he too experienced her cold-fish handshake.

'Victor's going through a phase right now,' she said. 'He's testing the limits of his own will. We don't want to hamper his personal development, so we're letting him find out where the dividing line runs between his own wishes and those of other people.'

Britta gave her son a tender look, and Patrik remembered Erica telling him that she was a psychologist. But if this was her idea of raising children, then psychology was a profession that little Victor would be in close contact with when he grew up. Conny hardly seemed to notice what was going on, and he shut his son up by stuffing a good-sized piece of cake in the boy's mouth. Judging by Victor's rotundity, this was a frequent tactic. But Patrik had to admit that it was effective and appealing in all its simplicity.

By the time Erica came downstairs, freshly showered and with a much more alert expression on her face, Patrik had set the shrimp and other dishes on the table. He'd also managed to fix the children each a pizza after realizing that it was the only way to avoid a total catastrophe at dinner.

They all sat down and Erica was just about to open her mouth to say 'bon appetit' when Conny dug into the bowl of shrimp with both hands. One, two, three big fistfuls of shrimp landed on his plate, leaving barely half of the original amount in the bowl.

'Mmm, delicious. Now I'm a guy who knows how to eat shrimp.' Conny proudly patted his stomach and dug into his mountain of shrimp.

Patrik, who had put in the serving bowl fully two kilos of ruinously expensive shrimp, merely sighed and took a small handful that hardly took up any space on his plate. Erica without a word did the same and then passed the bowl to Britta, who morosely took the rest.

After the unsuccessful dinner they made the beds for their visitors in the guest room and excused themselves early, on the pretext that Erica needed to rest. Patrik showed Conny where the whisky was and escaped in relief upstairs to peace and quiet.

When they finally got into bed, Patrik told Erica what he'd been doing all day. He had long since given up trying to keep his police activities a secret from Erica, but he also knew that she kept her mouth shut about what he told her. When he got to the episode with the two missing women, he could see that she pricked up her ears.

'I remember reading about that. So you think they might be the ones you found?'

'I'm fairly sure of it. It would be too big a coincidence otherwise. But as soon as we get the report from the ME we can start investigating the matter properly, but for the time being we have to keep as many options open as possible.'

'You don't need any help digging up background material,

do you?' She turned eagerly towards him and he could see the gleam in her eyes.

'No, no, no. You have to take it easy. Don't forget that you're actually on sick leave.'

'Sure, but my blood pressure was back down at the last check-up. And I'm going stir crazy being at home all the time. I haven't even been able to start writing a new book.'

The book about Alexandra Wijkner and her tragic death had been a big seller, and in turn had brought Erica a contract for another true crime book. The writing had demanded enormous effort on her part, both in research and emotion, and after sending it off to the publisher in May she hadn't felt like starting a new project. High blood pressure followed by sick leave had tipped the scales against her, so she had reluctantly postponed all work on a new book until after the baby arrived. But it wasn't in her nature just to sit at home and twiddle her thumbs.

'Annika is on holiday, so she can't do it. And it isn't as easy as you might think to do research. You have to know where to look, and I do. Can't I just take a quick peek – '

'No, out of the question. Hopefully Conny and his wild bunch will leave early in the morning, and then you can take it easy. Now be quiet so I can talk to the baby a minute. We have to get started planning his football career – '

'Or hers.'

'Or hers. Although then it would probably be golf instead. There isn't any money in women's football yet.'

Erica just sighed, but obediently lay down on her back to facilitate the conversation.

'Don't they notice when you sneak out?' Stefan was lying on his side next to Linda and tickling her face with a straw.

'No, because Jacob "trusts" me.' She frowned, mimicking her brother's serious tone of voice. 'It's something he picked up from all those courses on how to create good contact with young people. The worst thing is that most of the kids seem to lap it up; for some of them Jacob is like God. Although if you've grown up without a father you probably take whatever you can get.' Annoyed, she slapped away the straw Stefan was tickling her with. 'Cut that out.'

'What's the matter, can't I tease you a little?'

She could see that he was offended, and she leaned over and kissed him, as if putting a plaster on a cut. It just wasn't a good day today. She'd got her period that morning, so she wouldn't be able to make love with Stefan for a week. And then it was getting on her nerves to be living in the same house with her splendid brother and his equally splendid wife.

'Oh, if only the year would be over fast so I could leave this fucking hole!'

They had to whisper so they wouldn't be discovered in their hiding place in the hayloft, but she slapped her hand on the boards to punctuate her words.

'Do you wish you could leave me too? Is that what you want?'

The hurt expression on Stefan's face deepened, and she bit her tongue. If she ever got out in the wide world, she would never look at someone like Stefan. As long as she was stuck here at home he was amusing enough, but that was all. But he didn't need to know that. So she curled up like a cuddly little kitten and snuggled closer. When she got no response, she took his arm and put it around her. As if of their own accord his fingers began to wander over her body, and she smiled to herself. Men were so easy to manipulate.

'You could come with me, couldn't you?' She said this knowing full well that he would never be able to tear himself away from Fjällbacka, or rather from his brother. Sometimes she wondered whether he even went to the toilet without asking Robert's permission.

He didn't answer the question. Instead he said, 'Have you

talked to your father? What does he say about your idea of leaving town?'

'What can he say? In a year he won't be able to tell me what to do. As soon as I turn eighteen he'll have fuck-all to do about it. And that will drive him crazy. Sometimes I think he wishes that he could enter us in one of his fucking account books. Jacob debit, Linda credit.'

'What do you mean, debit?'

Linda laughed. 'Those are financial terms, nothing you need to worry about.'

'I just wonder how things would have been if . . .' Stefan fixed his gaze somewhere behind her as he continued to chew on a straw.

'How things would have been if what?'

'If Pappa hadn't lost all the money. Then maybe we would have been the ones living in the manor house, and you'd be in the cabin with Uncle Gabriel and Aunt Laine.'

'Oh yeah, that would have been a sight. Mamma living in a shabby cabin. Poor as a churchmouse.'

Linda tilted her head back and laughed so loud that Stefan had to shush her so she wouldn't be heard over in Jacob and Marita's house, only a stone's throw from the barn.

'Maybe Pappa would have still been alive today, in that case. And then Mamma wouldn't spend her days poring over those sodding photo albums,' said Stefan.

'But it wasn't because of the money that he – '

'You don't know that. What the hell do you know about why he did it?' His voice rose an octave and turned shrill.

'Everybody knows.'

Linda didn't like the turn the conversation had taken, and she didn't dare look Stefan in the eye. The family feud and everything connected with it had always been off limits, by tacit agreement.

'Everybody thinks they know, but nobody knows fucking

39

shit,' Stefan went on. 'And there's your brother, living on our farm – that's too fucking much!'

'It's not Jacob's fault things turned out the way they did,' said Linda. It felt odd to defend the brother she usually showered with abuse, but blood was thicker than water. 'He got the farm from Grandpa, and besides, he's always been the first to defend Johannes.'

Stefan knew that she was right, and his anger drained out of him. It was just that sometimes it hurt so damn much when Linda talked about her family, because it reminded him of what he himself had lost. He didn't dare say it to her face, but he often thought that she was pretty ungrateful. She and her family had everything, and his family had nothing. Where was the justice in that?

At the same time he could forgive her for everything. He had never loved anyone so intensely, and the mere sight of her slim body next to his made him burn inside. Sometimes he couldn't believe it was true. That an angel like Linda would waste her time on him. But he knew better than to question his good fortune. Instead he tried to ignore the future and enjoy the present. Now he pulled her closer and shut his eyes as he inhaled the scent of her hair. He unbuttoned the top button of her jeans, but she stopped him.

'I can't, I've got my period. Let me instead.'

She unbuttoned his jeans and he lay back in the hay. Behind his closed eyelids heaven flickered past.

Only a day had passed since the dead woman was found, but impatience was already plaguing Patrik. Somewhere somebody was wondering where she was. Pondering, worrying, letting their thoughts run along ever more anxious paths. And the terrible thing was that in this case the worst misgivings had come true. He wanted more than anything else to find out who the woman was so he could inform her loved ones. Nothing was worse than uncertainty, not even death. The work of grieving could not commence until they knew the reason for their grief. It wasn't going to be easy to be the one who delivered the news – a responsibility that Patrik had already shouldered in his mind – but he knew that it was an important part of his job. To facilitate and offer support. But above all, to find out what had happened to the loved one.

Martin's fruitless phone calls the day before had demonstrated the task of identification would be more difficult. She had not been reported missing anywhere in the local area, so the search field had to be expanded to all of Sweden, perhaps even to other countries. At the moment the task seemed impossible, but he quickly dismissed that thought. Right now they were the unknown woman's only advocates.

Martin knocked discreetly on the door.

'How would you like me to proceed? Widen the search radius, or start with the big-city districts, or . . . ?' He raised his eyebrows in an enquiring gesture.

At once Patrik felt the weight of the responsibility for the investigation. Actually there was nothing pointing in any direction, but they had to start somewhere.

'Check with the big-city districts. Göteborg has been taken care of, so start with Stockholm and Malmö. We should be getting the preliminary report from Forensics soon, and if we're lucky they might be able to come up with something useful.'

'Okay.' Martin slapped the door on his way out and headed for his office. A shrill signal from the front hall made him turn on his heel, and he went to let in the visitor. That was usually Annika's job, but while she was gone they just had to help each other out.

The young woman looked upset. She was thin, with two long blonde braids and an enormous pack on her back.

'I want to speak to someone in charge,' she said in English.

She spoke with a thick accent, and he guessed that she was

German. Martin opened the door and motioned her to come in. He called down the hall, 'Patrik, you have a visitor.'

Too late it occurred to him that maybe he should have asked what her business was first, but Patrik had already stuck his head out of his office and the young woman was headed in his direction.

'Are you the man in charge?'

For a moment Patrik was tempted to send her on to Mellberg, who was technically the chief, but he changed his mind when he saw her desperate expression and decided to spare her that experience. Sending a good-looking girl into Mellberg's office was like sending a lamb to the slaughter, and Patrik's natural protective instincts won out.

'Yes, how can I help you?'

He motioned for her to come in and sit down in the chair in front of his desk. With surprising ease she slipped off the enormous backpack and carefully leaned it against the wall by the door.

'My English is very bad. You speak German?'

Patrik ransacked his ancient knowledge of school German. His answer depended on how she defined 'speak German'. He could order a beer and ask for the check, but he suspected that she wasn't here in the capacity of waitress.

'Little German,' he replied haltingly in her mother tongue, wobbling his hand in a 'so-so' gesture.

She seemed pleased to hear this and spoke slowly and clearly to give him a chance to understand what she was saying. To Patrik's surprise he found that he knew more than he'd thought at first, and even though he didn't understand every word, he got the gist of it.

She introduced herself as Liese Forster. Apparently she had been in a week earlier to report her friend Tanja missing. She had spoken with an officer here at the station, who told her that he would contact her when he knew more. Now she'd been waiting a whole week and still hadn't heard a peep.

Anxiety was writ large across her face, and Patrik took her story seriously.

Tanja and Liese had met on the train on the way to Sweden. They were both from northern Germany but hadn't known each other before. They got along well at once, and Liese said that they became like sisters. Liese had no fixed plans about where to go in Sweden, so Tanja had suggested that she come along with her to a little town on the west coast called Fjällbacka.

'Why Fjällbacka exactly?' asked Patrik with his clumsy German grammar.

The answer came with hesitation. Liese admitted that she didn't really know why. It was the one topic that Tanja had not discussed cheerfully and openly with her. All Tanja had told her was that she had some business to take care of there. When it was done, they could continue their trip through Sweden. But first there was something Tanja needed to find. The subject seemed sensitive and Liese had not pursued it. She was just glad to have a companion on her travels and she happily tagged along. It didn't really matter to her why Tanja had to go there.

They had been staying at the Sälvik campground for three days when Tanja disappeared. She had set off in the morning, saying that she had something to take care of during the day and that she would come back towards afternoon. Afternoon passed and then it was evening, and Liese's anxiety had increased as the hours had ticked away. The next morning she went to the tourist bureau on Ingrid Bergman's Square and asked for directions to the nearest police station. The report was taken and now she wondered what had been done.

Patrik was shocked. As far as he knew, they hadn't received any missing-persons report. He felt a heaviness gathering in his gut. When he asked what Tanja looked like, his fears were confirmed. Everything Liese had told him about her friend matched the dead woman in the King's Cleft. With a heavy heart he showed Liese a photograph of the body, and her sobs told him what he already suspected. Martin could stop making phone calls, and someone would have to be called to answer for not reporting Tanja's disappearance correctly. They had wasted many precious hours for nothing, and Patrik had little doubt where to find the guilty party.

Patrik had already driven off to work when Erica awoke from a sleep that for a change had been deep and dreamless. She looked at the clock. It was nine, and there was not a sound from downstairs.

Soon she had the coffee on, and she started setting the breakfast table for herself and her guests. They trickled into the kitchen one by one, each more bleary than the last, but they came round quickly when they began helping themselves to the breakfast she had prepared.

'Weren't you all heading for Koster next?' Erica's question was polite, but she was anticipating getting rid of them.

Conny exchanged a swift glance with his wife and said, 'Well, Britta and I talked it over a bit last night, and we thought that since we're here, and the weather's so fine, we might run out to one of the islands here today. You do have a boat, don't you?'

'Well, yes, we do,' Erica admitted reluctantly. 'Although I'm not sure Patrik is terribly anxious to lend it out. Considering the insurance and all that . . .' The thought that they would stay even a few more hours than planned made her bones tingle with frustration.

'We thought that you might be able to give us a lift to some nice spot, then we can ring you when we want to come back.'

Conny took the fact that Erica was speechless at this suggestion as tacit agreement on her part. She called on higher powers for patience and persuaded herself that it wasn't worth a confrontation with the family just to spare herself a few more hours of their company. Besides, she would get out of being with them during the day, and maybe they would decide to drive on before Patrik came home from work. She had already decided to fix something special for dinner and have a cosy evening at home. After all, Patrik was supposed to be on holiday. And who knew how much time they would have for each other once the baby arrived – it was best to take advantage of their time together.

After much shilly-shallying the whole Flood family finally packed up their sun gear, and they set off for the boat dock. The little blue wooden boat was low and hard to step into from the dock at Badholmen. It took a good deal of effort to squeeze her pregnant body down into the boat. After cruising about for an hour searching for a 'deserted rock, or preferably a beach' for the guests, she finally found a tiny cove that other tourists miraculously had seemed to miss. Then she headed for home. Getting up onto the dock without help proved impossible. Feeling humiliated, she had to ask some passing beachgoers for assistance.

Sweaty, hot, exhausted, and furious she drove home but changed her mind just as she was passing the sailing society's clubhouse. She made a sharp left turn instead of driving straight ahead towards Sälvik. She took the right-hand curve around the hill, past the sports field and the Kullen apartment complex, and parked outside the library. She would go completely insane if she had to sit at home all day with nothing to do. Patrik could protest all he wanted later, but he was going to get help with the investigation whether he wanted it or not!

When Ernst entered the police station he headed reluctantly towards Hedström's office. As soon as Patrik rang him on his mobile and with granite in his voice ordered him to come to the station at once, Ernst knew that he was in trouble.

He ransacked his memory to try and work out what he might have been caught doing, but he had to admit that there were too many possibilities to make an educated guess. He was the de facto master of short cuts, and he had made fiddling about an art form.

'Sit.'

He docilely obeyed Patrik's command, then put on a defiant expression to meet the approaching storm.

'So what's the big hurry? I was in the middle of something. Just because you happened to be put in charge of an investigation, you can't just boss me about . . .'

A good offence was usually the best defence, but judging from Patrik's ever-darkening expression it was absolutely the wrong way to go.

'Did you take a report about a missing German tourist a week ago?'

Damn. He had totally forgotten about that. The little blonde girl had come in right before lunch, and he got rid of her in a hurry so he could be on his way and go eat. Most of those reports about missing friends never amounted to anything. Usually the person was dead drunk in some ditch, or else she'd gone home with some guy. Shit. He knew now that he was going to pay for this. He couldn't imagine why he hadn't connected it with the girl they found yesterday, but hindsight was 20-20. The important thing was to minimize the damage.

'Yes, well, I suppose I did.'

'You *suppose* you did?' Patrik's usually calm voice resounded like thunder in the little room. 'Either you took the report or you didn't. There's nothing in between. And if you did take it, where in the . . . where is it?' Patrik was so furious that he was stumbling over his words. 'Do you realize how much time this has cost the investigation?'

'Well, it's obviously unfortunate, but how was I supposed to know – '

46

'You aren't supposed to know, you're supposed to do what you're assigned to do! I hope I never hear about something like this again. Right now we have precious hours to make up.'

'Is there anything I can . . .' Ernst made his voice as submissive as he could and tried to look contrite. Inside, he was cursing at being addressed like a whippersnapper, but since Hedström now seemed to have Mellberg's ear it would be stupid to aggravate the situation any further.

'You've done enough. Martin and I will continue with the investigation. You'll take care of any other incoming reports. We received one about a burglary in Skeppstad. I talked to Mellberg and got the go-ahead for you to handle that on your own.'

As a sign that the conversation was over, Patrik turned his back on Ernst and began typing so frenetically that the keyboard jumped.

Ernst left the room grumbling. How serious could it be to forget to write up a single little report? At the proper time he would have a talk with Mellberg about the suitability of having someone with such an unstable personality in charge of a homicide investigation. Yes, damn it, that's what he would do.

The pimply-faced youth sitting before him was a study in lethargy. Hopelessness was written all over his face; the meaninglessness of life had been pounded into him long ago. Jacob recognized all the signs, and he couldn't help looking on it as a challenge. He knew that he had the power to turn the boy's life in a completely different direction. How well he succeeded depended only on whether the boy had any desire to be steered onto the right path.

Within the religious community Jacob's work with young people was well-known and respected. So many broken souls had entered the farm only to leave as productive members of society. The religious aspect was toned down for the rest of the town, since the state subsidies were rather precarious. There were always people with no faith in God who cried 'sect' as soon as anything diverged from their conventional view of what religion involved.

It was on his own merits that he had won the greater part of the respect he enjoyed, but he could not deny that some of it could also be attributed to the fact that his grandfather was Ephraim Hult, 'the Preacher'. Of course his grandfather had not belonged to this same congregation, but his reputation was so widespread along the coast of Bohuslän that it resonated within all the free-church groups. The Lutheran state church in Sweden naturally viewed the Preacher as a charlatan. On the other hand, all the pastors who chose to settle for preaching to empty pews on Sundays did the same, so the freer Christian groups took little notice.

The work with the outsiders and addicts had filled Jacob's life for almost a decade, but it no longer satisfied him the same way it had done before. He had been involved in planning programmes at the rehabilitation centre in Bullaren, but the work no longer filled the vacuum he had lived with all his life. Something was missing inside him, and the search for this unknown something frightened him. For so long, he had believed that he stood on solid ground but now he felt it trembling precariously beneath his feet. He dreaded the abyss that might open and swallow him whole, both body and soul. So many times, secure in his faith, he had sententiously observed that doubt is the primary tool of the Devil, not knowing that one day he would find himself in that same predicament.

Jacob got up and stood with his back to the boy. He looked out of the window facing the lake, but saw only his own reflection in the glass. A strong, healthy man, he reflected sardonically. His dark hair was cut short, and Marita, who cut his hair at home, actually did a very good job. His face was finely chiselled, with sensitive features without being unmasculine. He was neither delicate nor particularly power-fully built; he was the very definition of a man with a normal physique. Jacob's biggest asset were his eyes. They were a piercing blue and had the unique ability to seem both gentle and penetrating at the same time. Those eyes had helped him convince many people to take the right path. He knew it, and he exploited it.

But not today. His own demons were making it hard for him to concentrate on anyone else's problems. It was easier to take in what the boy was saying if he didn't have to look at him. Jacob looked away from his reflection and instead peered out across Bullar Lake and the forest that spread out for miles and miles before him. It was so hot that he could see the air shimmering above the water. They had purchased the big farm cheaply because it had been so dilapidated after years of mismanagement. After countless hours of toil they had renovated it to the condition it was in now. The place was not luxurious, but it was neat, clean and comfortable. The district's representatives were always impressed by the house and the lovely surroundings. They enthused about what a positive influ-ence this would have on the poor maladjusted boys and girls. Previously the farm had never had any problems in getting subsidies, and their work had progressed well during the ten years they had been in operation. So the problem was all in his head . . . or was it in his soul?

Perhaps the temptation of daily life was what had pushed him in the wrong direction at a decisive fork in the road. He had not hesitated to take his sister into his home. Who else would be able to soothe her inner turmoil and calm her rebel-lious temperament? But she had proven to be his superior in the psychological battle, and as her ego grew stronger day after day, he felt the constant irritation undermining his whole foundation. Sometimes he would catch himself clenching his fists and thinking that she was a stupid, simple girl who deserved it if her family washed their hands of her. But that was not the Christian way of thinking, and such thoughts always led to hours of soul-searching and devout Bible study in the hope of finding renewed strength.

Outwardly Jacob was still a rock of security and confidence. He knew that the people around him needed him; he was the one they could always lean on. And he was still not prepared to give up that image of himself. Ever since he vanquished the illness that for a time had ravaged him so fiercely, he struggled not to lose control over his life. But the mere exertion of maintaining the façade taxed his last resources, and the abyss was inexorably drawing nearer. Once again he reflected over how ironic it was that after so many years things had come full circle. The news had made him for a second do the impossible – he had succumbed to doubt. The doubt lasted only a moment, but it had created a tiny little crack in the strong fabric that held his life together, and that crack was expanding.

Jacob banished those thoughts and forced himself to focus on the young man in the room and his pitiful existence. The questions he asked came automatically, like the smile of empathy that he always had ready for a new black sheep in the flock.

Another day. Another broken soul to mend. It never ended. But even God had a chance to rest on the seventh day.

After going to collect her relatives, now as pink as pigs, out on the skerry, Erica was eagerly waiting for Patrik to come home. She was also searching for signs that Conny and his family would start packing their things, but it was already half past five and they had made no move to leave. She decided to wait a while before thinking up some subtle way to ask whether they were going soon. The kids' shrieking had given her a splitting headache, so she wouldn't wait long. With relief she heard Patrik coming up the steps and went to meet him.

'Hi, honey,' she said, standing on tiptoe to kiss him.

'Hi. Haven't they left yet?' Patrik spoke in a low voice as he glanced towards the living room.

'No, and they don't seem to be making any moves in that direction, either. What on earth are we going to do?' Erica replied in an equally low voice, rolling her eyes to show her displeasure at the situation.

'They can't expect to stay another night without asking, can they? Or can they?' said Patrik, looking nervous.

Erica snorted. 'If you only knew how many guests my parents used to have during the summer over the years. People who were just going to be here a night or two and then stayed for a week, expecting to be waited on, expecting free meals. People are crazy. And relatives are always the worst.'

Patrik looked horror-stricken. 'They can't stay for a week! We have to do something. Can't you tell them they have to leave?'

'Me? Why should *I* have to tell them?'

'They're your relatives, after all.'

Erica had to admit that he had a point. She was just going to have to bite the bullet. She went into the living room to hear about their plans, but never got a chance to ask.

'What's for dinner?' Four pairs of eyes turned expectantly towards her.

'Well . . .' Erica was speechless at their sheer audacity. She quickly went over the contents of the fridge in her mind. 'It's spaghetti with meat sauce. In an hour.'

Erica felt like kicking herself when she went back to Patrik in the kitchen.

'So, what did they say? Are they leaving?'

Erica couldn't look Patrik in the eye. She said, 'I don't really know. But we're having spaghetti with meat sauce in an hour.'

'Didn't you say anything?' Now it was Patrik's turn to roll his eyes.

51

'It's not that easy. Try it yourself, you'll see.' Annoyed, Erica turned away and started banging pots and pans as she took them from the cupboard. 'We're going to have to grit our teeth for another night. I'll tell them tomorrow. Start chopping some onions, will you? I can't make dinner for six all by myself.'

In oppressive silence they worked together in the kitchen until Erica couldn't keep quiet any longer.

'I was at the library today,' she said. 'I copied some material that you might be able to use. It's on the kitchen table.' There was a neat stack of photocopies lying there.

'I told you that you shouldn't – '

'No, no, I know. But now it's done, and it was really fun for a change instead of sitting at home staring at the walls. So don't complain.'

By this time Patrik had learned when he should shut up, and he sat down at the kitchen table and began going through the material. They were newspaper articles about the disappearance of the two young women, and he read them with great interest.

'Damn, this is great! I'm going to take this stuff to the office tomorrow and go through it more carefully, but it looks fantastic.'

He went over to stand behind her at the stove and put his arms around her swollen belly.

'I didn't mean to complain. I'm just concerned about you and the baby.'

'I know.' Erica turned to face him and put her arms round his neck. 'But I'm not made of porcelain, and if women in the old days could work in the fields until they pretty much gave birth on the spot, I can certainly sit in a library and turn pages with no ill effects.'

'Okay, I know.' He sighed. 'As soon as we get rid of our lodgers, we can pay more attention to each other. And promise me that you'll tell me if you want me to stay home. The station knows that I've volunteered to work during my holiday and that you take precedence.'

'I promise. But now help me get the dinner ready and maybe the kids will calm down.'

'I doubt it. Maybe we should give them each a shot of whisky before dinner, so they'll fall asleep.' He gave her a wink and then laughed.

'Ooh, you're terrible. Give one to Conny and Britta instead, then we'll at least have them in a good mood.'

Patrik did as she suggested, casting a mournful glance at the hastily dropping level in the bottle of his best single-malt. If Erica's relatives stayed another couple of days, his whisky supply would never be the same.

3

She opened her eyes with great caution. The reason was a splitting headache that produced shooting pains to the very roots of her hair. But the strange thing was that there was no difference in what she saw when she opened her eyes. It was still the same dense darkness. In a moment of panic she thought that she had gone blind. Maybe there was something wrong with that homebrew she had drunk yesterday. She'd heard stories about that stuff – young people who went blind drinking home-made rotgut. But after a few seconds her surroundings hazily began to emerge, and she understood that there was nothing wrong with her eyesight; she was somewhere with very little light. She looked up to check whether she could see a starry sky, or maybe some moonlight if she were lying outdoors somewhere, but she realized immediately that it never got this dark in the summertime. She should have been able to see the ethereal light of a Nordic summer night.

She touched the surface she was lying on and picked up a fistful of sandy soil, which she let run between her fingers. There was a strong odour of humus, a sickly sweet smell, and she had a sense of being underground. Panic set in. Along with claustrophobia. Without knowing how big the space was she had an image of walls slowly closing in on her. She clutched at her throat when it felt like the air was running out, but then forced herself to take some calm, deep breaths to keep the panic at bay.

It was cold, and she understood all at once that she was naked except for her knickers. Her body ached, and she shivered, wrapping her arms round herself and drawing her knees up to her chin. The first wave of panic now gave way to a terror so strong that she could feel it gnawing at her bones. How had she got here? And why? Who had undressed her? The only thing her mind told her was that she probably didn't want to know the answers to those questions. Something evil had happened to her but she didn't know what — that in itself multiplied the terror that was paralysing her.

A streak of light appeared on her hand, and she automatically raised her eyes towards its source. A little crack of light was visible against the velvet-dark blackness. She forced herself to her feet and screamed for help. No response. She stood on tiptoe and tried to reach the source of the light but wasn't even close. Instead she could feel water dripping on her upturned face. The drops became a steady trickle and she realized at once how thirsty she was. Without thinking she opened her mouth to drink. At first most of it ran down her face, but soon she discovered the proper technique and drank greedily. Then a mist seemed to settle over everything, and the room began to spin. After that, only darkness.

Linda woke up early for a change but tried to go back to sleep. It had been a late night with Stefan, and she felt almost hung over from lack of sleep. But for the first time in months she heard rain on the roof. The room that Jacob and Marita had fixed up for her was just under the roof-ridge, and the sound of the rain on the roof tiles was so loud that it seemed to echo between her temples.

At the same time, it was the first morning in ages that she had woken up to a cool bedroom. The heat had been constant for almost two months, breaking records for the hottest summer in a hundred years. At first she had welcomed the blazing sunshine, but the pleasure of novelty had vanished several weeks ago. Instead she had begun to hate waking up each morning to sweat-drenched sheets. So the fresh, cool air that now swept in under the roof-beams was all the more enjoyable. Linda threw off the thin covers and let her body feel the pleasant temperature. Contrary to habit, she decided to get up before someone chased her out of bed. It might be nice not to eat breakfast by herself for a change. Downstairs in the kitchen she could hear the noise of breakfast being prepared, and she pulled on a short kimono and stuck her feet in a pair of slippers.

In the kitchen her early arrival was met with looks of surprise. The whole family was assembled: Jacob, Marita, William and Petra, and their muted conversation stopped short when Linda flung herself down on an empty chair and began buttering some bread.

'It's nice that you want to keep us company for a change, but I'd appreciate it if you put on some more clothes when you come downstairs. Think of the children.'

Jacob was so bloody sanctimonious that it made her sick. Just to irk him further, Linda let her thin kimono slip open a bit so that one breast could be seen through the opening. His face turned white with rage, but for some reason he didn't take up the fight and let the matter drop. William and Petra looked at her in fascination. She made faces at them, causing them both to erupt in spasms of giggles. The children were actually quite sweet, she had to admit, but Jacob and Marita would ruin them soon enough. When the kids were done with their religious upbringing they wouldn't have any joy left in life.

'Now you children settle down. Sit up straight at the table when you're eating. Take your feet off the chair, Petra, and sit like a big girl. And close your mouth when you eat, William. I don't want to see what you're chewing.'

The laughter vanished from the children's faces and they sat up straight like two tin soldiers with empty, vacant eyes. Linda sighed to herself. Sometimes she couldn't believe that she and Jacob were actually related. No siblings were more unlike than she and Jacob; she was convinced of that. It was so damned unfair that he was their parents' favourite, always praised to the skies, while he did nothing but pick at her. Was it her fault that she had arrived unplanned, long after they had decided to leave their baby-rearing years behind? Or that Jacob's illness so many years before she was born had made them unwilling to have another child? Naturally she understood the seriousness of the fact that he almost died, but why did she have to take the blame for it? She wasn't the one who had made him sick.

All the coddling they had showered on Jacob had just continued on, even after he had completely recovered. It was as if their parents regarded each day of his life as a gift from God, while her life caused them only trouble and difficulty. And then there was the relationship between Grandfather and Jacob. She certainly understood that they had a special bond, after what Grandfather had done for Jacob, but that shouldn't mean that there wasn't any room for his other grandchildren. Of course, Grandfather had died before she was born, so she never had to face his indifference, but she knew from Stefan that he and Robert had landed in Grandfather's disfavour and they saw all the attention focused on their cousin Jacob. Surely the same thing would have happened to her if Grandfather were still alive.

The injustice of it all made hot tears well up in her eyes, but Linda forced them back as she had so many times before. She did not intend to give Jacob the satisfaction of seeing her tears or allow him another opportunity to act as saviour of the world. She knew that his fingers itched to get her life onto the right path, but she would rather die than be a doormat like him. Nice girls might get to Heaven, but she intended to go much, much farther than that. She would rather come down to earth with a crash of thunder than live her life a milksop like her big brother, secure as he was that everyone loved him.

'Do you have any plans today? I could use a little help around the house,' said Marita.

She was buttering several slices of bread for the children as she directed her question to Linda. She was a motherly woman, slightly overweight and with a plain face. Linda had always thought that Jacob could have done better. An image of her brother and her sister-in-law in bed popped into her mind. She was sure that they did it dutifully once a month, with the lights off and her sister-in-law wearing some concealing, ankle-length nightgown. The image made her giggle, and the others gave her a quizzical look.

'Hey, Marita asked you a question. Can you help her around the house today? This isn't a boarding-house, you know.'

'All right, all right, I heard her the first time. You don't have to nag. And no, I can't help out today. I have to . . .' She searched for a good excuse. 'I have to check on Scirocco. He was limping a little yesterday.'

Her excuse was received with sceptical looks, and Linda put on her most contentious expression, ready for a fight. But to her astonishment no one felt like challenging her today, despite the obvious lie. The victory – and yet another day of loafing – was hers.

The desire to go outside and stand in the rain, with his face turned up to the sky and the water streaming over him, was irresistible. But there were certain things that an adult could not permit himself, especially if he was at work, and Martin had to restrain his childish impulse. But it was wonderful. All the oppressive heat that had held them captive the past two months was flushed away in one good downpour. Through the open window he could smell the rain in his nostrils. Rain came splashing onto the part of his desk closest to the window, but he had moved all the papers so it didn't matter. It was worth it to be able to smell the cool air.

Patrik had called in to say that he'd overslept, so Martin had been the first one in for a change. The mood at the station had been low after yesterday's revelation of Ernst's serious mis-judgement, so it was nice to be able to sit here in peace and quiet and collect his thoughts surrounding the latest develop-ments. He did not envy Patrik the task of notifying the woman's relatives, but even he knew that learning the facts was the first step in the healing process of grief. They probably didn't even know that she was missing, so the news would come as a shock. Now the most important thing was to locate the family, and that was one of Martin's tasks for the day: to contact his German colleagues. He hoped he'd be able to talk to them in English, otherwise he'd have a problem. He remembered enough school German that he didn't regard Patrik's German as much of an asset, after hearing his colleague stammer through the conversation with Tanja's friend.

He was just about to pick up the receiver and dial Germany when the phone rang. His pulse sped up when he heard that it was Forensics in Göteborg, and he reached for his notepad covered in scribbles. Actually the person on the line was supposed to report to Patrik, but since he hadn't come in yet Martin would have to do.

'Things certainly seem to be heating up out there in the sticks.'

Forensic doctor Tord Pedersen was referring to the autopsy he had done a year and a half ago on Alex Wijkner, which led to one of the very few homicide investigations that Tanumshede police station had ever conducted.

'Yep, we're starting to wonder whether it's something in the water. Pretty soon we'll be catching up with Stockholm in the murder statistics.'

The light, bantering tone was a way for them – and many other professionals who often came in contact with death and misfortune – to handle the pressures of their daily work. It was not meant to detract from the gravity of their profession.

'Have you already finished with the autopsy? I thought people were killing each other faster than ever in this heat we've been having,' Martin went on.

'Well, you're actually right about that. We can tell that people have a shorter fuse because of the heat, but things have actually slowed down the past few days. So we were able to get to your case sooner than we thought.'

'Let's hear it.' Martin held his breath. Much of the progress of an investigation depended on how much Forensics had to offer.

'Well, it's clear that you're not dealing with a pleasant fellow. The cause of death was easy to determine: she was strangled. But it's what was done to her before she died that's really remarkable.'

Pedersen paused, and Martin pictured him putting on a pair of glasses.

'Yes?' Martin couldn't hide his impatience.

'Now let's see . . . You'll be getting this by fax as well . . . Hmm,' said Pedersen, apparently skimming the report. Martin's hand began to sweat from his tight grip on the receiver.

'Yes, here it is. Fourteen fractures to various parts of the skeleton. All inflicted before death, judging from the varying degrees of healing that had taken place.'

'You mean – '

'I mean that somebody broke her arms, legs, fingers, and toes over the course of about a week, I would reckon.'

'Were they broken on a single occasion or on several? Can you tell that?'

'As I said, we can see that the fractures show a varying degree of healing, so my professional opinion is that they occurred sporadically over the entire period. I've made a sketch of the order in which I think the fractures occurred. It's included in the report I faxed to you. The victim also had a good number of superficial incisions on her body. Also in varying stages of healing.'

'Good God!' Martin couldn't help blurting out.

'I'm inclined to agree with that opinion.' Pedersen's voice sounded dry over the telephone. 'The pain she experienced must have been unbearable.'

For a moment they contemplated in silence how cruel people could be. Then Martin pulled himself together and continued, 'Did you find any evidence on the body that might help us?'

62

'Yes, we found semen. If you find a suspect, he could be tied to the murder with DNA. Naturally we're searching our database as well, but it's rare that we get any hits that way. So far, the register is just too small. We can only dream of the day when we'll have the DNA of every citizen in a searchable database. Then we'll be in a totally different position.'

'Dream is probably the right word. Complaints about infringing on the freedom of the individual and all that will probably stop that plan cold.'

'If what this woman went through can't be called restricting an individual's freedom, then I don't know what can . . .'

This was uncharacteristically philosophical for the normally prosaic Tord Pedersen. Martin realized that for once he had actually been moved by the victim's fate. This was usually not something a pathologist could allow if he wanted to sleep well at night.

'Can you give me an estimated time of death?'

'Yes, I got the results from the samples that the techs took on-site, and then I supplemented them with my own observations, so I can give you quite a reliable time interval.'

'Let's hear it.'

'In my estimation she died sometime between six and eleven o'clock, the evening before she was discovered in the King's Cleft.'

'You can't give me a more exact time than that?' Martin sounded disappointed.

'It's standard practice here in Sweden never to give a narrower interval than five hours in such cases, so that's the best I can do. But the interval's probability is 95 per cent, so at least it's very reliable. However, I can confirm what you must have suspected: that the King's Cleft is the secondary crime scene. She was murdered somewhere else and lay there for a couple of hours after death, which is evident from the *livor mortis*.'

'Well, that's something, anyway.' Martin sighed. 'What about the skeletons? Did they give you anything? You got the message from Patrik, I suppose, about who we think they might be.'

'Yes, I did. And on that we aren't really clear yet. It isn't quite as simple as you might think to obtain dental records from the Seventies, but we're working on it as fast as we can. As soon as we know more we'll let you know. But I can say that they are two female skeletons, and the age seems to be about right. The pelvis of one women also indicates that she had borne a child, and that agrees with the information we have. The most interesting thing of all is that both skeletons have fractures similar to the recent victim's. Between us I would even venture to say that the fractures are almost identical on the three bodies.'

Martin dropped a pen on the floor from pure shock. What had actually landed in their laps? A sadistic murderer who let twenty-four years pass between his evil deeds? Martin didn't even want to think about the alternative: that the murderer might not have waited twenty-four years, and they simply hadn't found the other victims yet.

'Were they also stabbed with a knife?'

'Since there is no soft-tissue material left, that's more difficult to say, but there are some scrape marks on the bones that might indicate they were subjected to the same treatment, yes.'

'And the cause of death for them?'

'The same as for the German woman. Bones that were compressed at the throat correspond to injuries resulting from strangulation.'

Martin was rapidly taking notes during the conversation. 'Anything else of interest you can give me?'

'Just that the skeletons were probably buried. There are traces of dirt on them, and we might be able to get something out of them in the analysis. But it isn't clear yet, so you'll have to be patient. There was dirt on Tanja Schmidt and the blanket she was lying on also, so we'll be comparing that to the samples from the skeletons.' Pedersen paused. 'Is Mellberg leading the investigation?'

There was some apprehension in his voice. Martin smiled to himself, but he could set the pathologist's mind at rest on that point.

'No, Patrik has been given the case. But who will get the credit once we solve it is quite another matter . . .'

They both laughed at the remark, but it was a laugh that at least on Martin's part stuck a bit in his craw.

After saying goodbye to Tord Pedersen, he went to collect the pages that had arrived in the station's fax machine. When Patrik came to work a while later, Martin had done his homework well. After Patrik heard a summary of the forensic report he was just as depressed as Martin. This was developing into a hell of a case.

Erica's sister Anna let the sunshine bake into her skin as she lay stretched out in a bikini in the bow of the sailboat. The children were taking their afternoon nap in the cabin below, and Gustav was at the tiller. Tiny drops of salt water splashed over her each time the bow hit the water's surface, and it was wonderfully refreshing. If she closed her eyes she could forget for a moment that she had any cares in the world and convince herself that this was her real life.

'Anna, phone for you.' Gustav's voice woke her from her meditative state.

'Who is it?' She shaded her eyes with her hand and saw that he was waving her mobile.

'He wouldn't say.'

Damn it all. She knew right away who it was, and feeling hard little knots of anxiety in her stomach she cautiously made her way over to Gustav.

'Anna.'

'Who the hell was that?' Lucas hissed.

Anna hesitated. 'I told you I was going out sailing with a friend.'

'So now you're trying to fool me into thinking that the guy is just a friend,' he snapped. 'What's his name?'

'That's none of your – '

Lucas cut her off. 'What's his *name*, Anna?'

The resistance inside her was breaking down more with each second she heard his voice on the phone. Quietly she replied, 'Gustav af Klint.'

'Oh, right. How posh can you get?' His voice switched from scornful to low and threatening. 'How dare you take my children on holiday with another man.'

'We're divorced, Lucas,' Anna said. She put her hand over her eyes.

'You know as well as I do, that doesn't change a thing, Anna. You're the mother of my children, and that means you and I will always belong together. You are mine and the children are mine.'

'So why are you trying to take them away from me?'

'Because you're unstable, Anna. You've always suffered from weak nerves, and to be honest, I don't trust you to take care of my children in the manner they deserve. Just look at how you live. You work all day and they're at day care. Do you think that's a good life for the children, Anna?'

'But I have to work, Lucas. And how were you planning to solve the problem if *you* took care of the children? You have to work too. Who would take care of them then?'

'There is a solution, Anna, and you know what it is.'

'Are you mad? Do you think I'd go back to you after you broke Emma's arm? Not to mention everything you did to me?' Her voice rose to a falsetto. Instinctively, she knew at once that she had gone too far.

'It wasn't my fault! It was an accident! Besides, if you hadn't been so stubborn and kept fighting me, I wouldn't have needed to lose my temper so often!'

It was like talking to thin air. There was no use. After all her years with Lucas, she knew that he believed what he said. It was never his fault. Everything that happened was someone else's fault. Every time he hit her he had made her feel guilty because she couldn't be understanding enough, loving enough, submissive enough.

Drawing on previously hidden reserves of strength, she had finally managed to divorce him. That had made her feel strong, invincible, for the first time in years. Finally she would be able to regain control of her own life. She and the children would be able to start over from scratch. But everything had gone a little too smoothly. Lucas had actually been shocked that he had broken his daughter's arm in a fit of rage, and he had been uncharacteristically amenable. His busy bachelor life after the divorce had also meant that he had let Anna and the children live in peace, while he was making one conquest after another. But just when Anna had felt that she had managed to escape, Lucas had begun to tire of his new life, and once again he turned his gaze to his family. When he had no luck with flowers, gifts and entreaties for forgiveness, the silk gloves had come off. He demanded sole custody of the children. To support his claims he had a multitude of baseless accusations concerning Anna's unsuitability as a mother. None of it was true, but Lucas could be so convincing when he turned on the charm that she still trembled at the possibility that he might succeed in his attempt. She also knew that it really wasn't the children he wanted. His business life would not function if he had custody of two small children, but his hope was to frighten Anna enough to make her come back. In weaker moments she was prepared to do just that. At the same time she knew that it was impossible. It would destroy her. So she steeled herself.

'Lucas, it does no good to have this discussion. I've moved on since the divorce, and you should too. It's true that I've met a new man, and that's something that you'll just have to learn to accept. The children are doing fine and I'm doing fine. Can't we try to deal with this like adults?'

Her tone was entreating, but the silence on the other end was impenetrable. She knew that she'd crossed the line. When she heard the dial tone and realized that Lucas had simply hung up, she knew that he was going to make her pay in some way. And dearly.

4

The hellish ache in her head made her dig her fingers into her face. The pain of her nails tearing long gashes in her skin was almost satisfying compared with the splitting headache, and it helped her to focus.

Everything was still black, but something had made her wake from her deep, dreamless torpor. A tiny crack of light appeared above her head, and while she was squinting upwards it slowly widened. Unused to light as she was, she did not see but rather heard someone come through the crack that had widened to an opening and climb down the stairs. Someone who came closer and closer in the dark. The confusion made it hard for her to decide whether to feel fear or relief. Both feelings were there, mixed together. First one prevailed, then the other.

The last footsteps coming towards her, where she lay curled up in a foetal position, were as good as soundless. Without a word being spoken, she felt a hand stroke her over the forehead. Perhaps that gesture ought to have been soothing, but the simplicity of the movement made terror take a tight grip on her heart.

The hand continued its way along her body, and she trembled in the darkness. For a second, it occurred to her that she ought to

69

put up some resistance against the faceless stranger. The thought vanished as rapidly as it appeared. The darkness was too overwhelming, and the strength in the hand that caressed her penetrated her skin, her nerves, her soul. Submission was her only option, she knew that with a terrifying insight.

When the hand changed from caressing to prising and twisting, pulling and tearing, she was not at all surprised. In a way she welcomed the pain. It was easier to handle the certainty of pain rather than the terror of waiting for the unknown.

The second call from Tord Pedersen had come just a couple of hours after Patrik spoke with Martin. They had a positive ID on one skeleton. Mona Thernblad, the second girl who disappeared in 1979, was one of the bodies found in the King's Cleft.

Patrik and Martin sat together and went over the information they had gathered during the investigation. Mellberg was conspicuous by his absence, but Gösta Flygare was back on the job after an excellent performance in the golf tournament. He hadn't won the competition, of course, but to his great surprise and joy had made a hole-in-one and was invited for champagne at the clubhouse. So far Martin and Patrik had heard in great detail about how the ball went straight into the hole with one stroke on the 16th hole. They had no doubt they would hear the story several more times before the day was over. But that didn't matter. They didn't begrudge Gösta his joy, and Patrik let him have an hour before they involved him in the investigative work. So for the moment Gösta was ringing round to all his golf buddies to tell them about the Big Event.

'So it's some devil who breaks the girls' bones first before he murders them,' said Martin. 'And cuts them with a knife,' he added.

'I'm afraid that's what it looks like. If I were to guess, I'd say there was certainly some sexual motive behind it. Some sadistic fuck who gets off on other people's pain. The fact that there was semen on Tanja's body indicates that as well.'

'Are you going to talk to Mona's relatives? Tell them that we found her, I mean?'

Martin looked uneasy, but Patrik calmed his fears by taking on the task himself.

'I thought I'd drive out and see her father this afternoon. Her mother died years ago, so her father is the only one left to notify.'

'How can you be so sure? Do you know them?'

'No, but Erica was at the library in Fjällbacka yesterday looking up everything that was written in the press about Siv and Mona. Their disappearances have been reviewed periodically, and there was even an interview with the families a couple of years back. Only Mona's father is still alive, and Siv only had her mother when she went missing. There was a little daughter as well, so I thought I'd talk to her too – as soon as we've got confirmation that Siv is the second woman.'

'It would be a devil of a coincidence if it was someone else, don't you think?'

'Well, we'll assume that the skeleton is Siv's, but we can't say that for certain yet. Stranger things have happened.'

Patrik rummaged through the photocopies that Erica had brought home for him and fanned some of them out in front of him on the table. He had also laid out the file that he had dug out of the archive in the cellar, intending to put together all the information they had about the disappearance of the two girls. There was a good deal in the newspaper articles that was not included in the investigative material; both sources were necessary to give them a complete picture of what was known so far.

'Look here. Siv vanished on Midsummer's Eve in 1979, and then Mona disappeared two weeks later.'

In order to clarify and give some order to the material, Patrik got up from his desk chair and wrote on the whiteboard on his wall.

'Siv Lantin was last seen alive as she was bicycling home after a party with friends. The very last witness described how she turned off the main road and rode towards Bräcke. It was two in the morning, and she was seen by a driver who passed her on the road in his car. After that no one saw or heard from her again.'

'If you disregard Gabriel Hult's information,' Martin added.

Patrik nodded in agreement. 'Yes, if you ignore Gabriel Hult's testimony, which I think we will for the time being.' He went on: 'Mona Thernblad went missing two weeks later. Unlike Siv, she vanished one afternoon in broad daylight. She left her house around three to go out jogging but never came home. One of her jogging shoes was found by the road along her usual route, but nothing more.'

'Were there any similarities between the girls? Besides the fact that they were about the same age.'

Patrik couldn't help smiling a little. 'I can see you've been watching that *Profiles* programme. Unfortunately I have to disappoint you. If we're dealing with a serial killer, which is what I assume you're fishing for, there are no obvious external similarities between the girls.' He fastened two black-and-white photographs to the whiteboard.

'Siv was nineteen years old. Small, dark and curvaceous. She had a reputation for being rather difficult, and she created something of a scandal in Fjällbacka when she had a baby at the age of seventeen. Both she and the baby lived with her mother, but according to what the newspapers claim, Siv liked to go out partying and wasn't very fond of staying home. Mona, on the other hand, was described as a real family girl who did well in school, had a lot of friends and was generally popular. She was tall and blonde and worked out a good deal. Eighteen years old but still living at home because her mother was sickly, and her father couldn't take care of her by himself. Nobody seemed to have anything negative to say about her. So the only thing these girls had in common was that they disappeared without a trace from the face of the earth over twenty years ago. And now they've appeared as skeletons in the King's Cleft.'

Martin was leaning his head on his hand, pondering. Both he and Patrik sat in silence for a while, studying the newspaper clippings and the notes on the whiteboard. They were both thinking of how young the girls looked. They would have had so many years left to live, if something evil hadn't crossed their paths. And then Tanja, who they didn't yet have a photo of while she was alive. She was a young girl too, with her whole life ahead of her. But now she was dead too.

'A massive investigation was launched.' Patrik took a thick stack of typed pages out of the folder. 'Friends and family of the girls were interviewed. Officers knocked on every door in the area, and known hooligans were also questioned. A total of about a hundred interviews were done, as far as I can see.'

'Did they produce anything?'

'No, not a thing. Not until they got the tip from Gabriel Hult. He rang the police himself and told them that he saw Siv in his brother's car the night she disappeared.'

'And? That could hardly have been enough to make him a murder suspect, could it?'

'No. When Gabriel's brother Johannes was questioned, he denied having spoken to her or even seeing her, but in the absence of any other leads the police chose to focus on him.'

'Did they make any progress?' Martin's eyes were wide with reluctant fascination.

'No, nothing else came out. And a couple of months later Johannes Hult hanged himself in his barn. So the trail went very cold, you might say.'

'It seems odd that he took his life so soon afterwards.'

'Yes, but if he was guilty then it must have been his ghost that murdered Tanja. Dead men don't kill people.'

'And what was the deal with his brother calling in and reporting his own flesh and blood? Why would anybody do that?' Martin frowned. 'Wait, how stupid can I be? Hult – our faithful old servant in the thieves' fraternity. He must be related to Stefan and Robert.'

'Yes, that's right. Johannes was their father. After reading about the Hult family, I actually have a little more understanding of why Stefan and Robert visit us so often. They were no more than five or six years old when Johannes hanged himself, and Robert was the one who found him in the barn. You can only imagine how that must have affected a six-year-old boy.'

'Yes, good Lord.' Martin shook his head. 'You know, I need a cup of coffee before we go on. My caffeine level is about to reach empty. Would you like a cup?'

Patrik nodded, and a couple of minutes later Martin returned with two cups of steaming hot coffee. For once the weather was right for hot drinks.

Patrik continued his summation. 'Johannes and Gabriel are the sons of a man named Ephraim Hult, also called the Preacher. Ephraim was a well-known, or you might say notorious, free-church pastor in Göteborg. He held big meetings at which he had his sons, who were small then, speak in tongues and heal the sick and the lame. Most people considered Ephraim a charlatan and swindler, but even so he hit the jackpot when one of the ladies in his faithful congregation, Margareta Dybling, died and left everything she owned to him. Besides a considerable fortune in ready cash, she left a large forested estate and a magnificent manor house in the vicinity of Fjällbacka. Ephraim suddenly lost all desire to spread God's word. He moved here with his sons, and the family has been living on the old lady's money ever since.'

The whiteboard was now covered with notes, and there were papers spread all over Patrik's desk.

'Not that it isn't interesting to have a little family history, but what does this have to do with the murders? As you said, Johannes died more than twenty years before Tanja was murdered, and dead men don't kill people, as you so eloquently expressed it.' Martin had a hard time hiding his impatience.

'True, but I've gone over all the old material, and Gabriel's testimony is actually the only interesting thing I found from the old investigation. I'd also hoped to be able to talk with Errold Lind, who was in charge of the investigation, but unfortunately he died of a heart attack in 1989, so this material is all we have to go on. Unless you have some better suggestions, I propose that we start by finding out a bit more about Tanja, as well as talking with Siv and Mona's surviving parents. After that we'll decide whether it's worth having another talk with Gabriel Hult.'

'Sure, that sounds sensible. What should I do first?'

'Start with the investigation about Tanja. And make sure you put Gösta to work on it as of tomorrow. His halcyon days are over.'

'What about Mellberg and Ernst? What are you going to do about them?'

Patrik sighed. 'My strategy is to keep them out of it as best I can. That will mean a bigger workload for the rest of us, but I think we'll come out ahead in the long run. Mellberg will just be glad to get out of doing anything, and besides, he's basically sworn off this investigation. Ernst will have to keep on doing what he's been doing, handling as many of the incoming reports as he can. If he needs help we'll send Gösta. As far as possible, I want the two of us to be free to run this investigation. Understood?'

Martin nodded eagerly. 'Yes, boss.'

'Then let's get going.'

After Martin left, Patrik sat facing the whiteboard, deep in thought with his hands clasped behind his head. It was an enormous task they were undertaking, and they had hardly any experience in homicide investigations. His heart sank with a sudden feeling of apprehension. He sincerely hoped that what they lacked in experience they could make up for with dedication. Martin was already on board, and damned if he wasn't going to wake Gösta Flygare out of his Sleeping Beauty sleep as well. If they could just manage to keep Mellberg and Ernst away from the investigation, Patrik thought they might have a chance to solve the murders. But the odds were against them, especially considering that the trail for two of the murders was so cold that it was almost in a deep freeze. He knew that the best chance they had was to concentrate on Tanja. At the same time his instinct told him that there was such a strong and clear connection between the murders that they would have to be investigated simultaneously. It was not going to be easy to shake some life into the old investigation, but they would have to try.

He grabbed an umbrella from the stand, checked an address in the telephone book, and headed off with a heavy heart. Certain duties demanded more of him than he could humanly bear.

The rain drummed persistently on the windowpanes, and under different circumstances Erica would have welcomed the coolness it brought. But fate and importunate relatives made her feel otherwise, and she was slowly but surely being driven to the brink of madness.

The kids dashed about as if they were going crazy in their frustration at having to stay indoors, while Conny and Britta had begun to turn on each other like cornered dogs. It had not yet escalated to a full-fledged fight, but their bickering had now reached the level of hissing and snapping. Old sins and injustices were being dragged up, and all Erica wanted to do was go upstairs and pull the covers over her head. But once again her good upbringing stood in her way, wagging its finger and forcing her to try to behave in a civilized manner in the midst of a war zone.

She had gazed longingly at the door when Patrik went off to work. He hadn't been able to conceal his relief at being able to escape to the station, and for a little while she had been tempted to test his promise to stay at home whenever she asked. But she knew that it wouldn't be right to do it just because she didn't want to be left alone with 'the fearsome four'. Instead, like a dutiful little wife, she waved to her husband from the kitchen window as he drove away.

The house was not big enough to keep the general disarray from reaching catastrophic proportions. She had taken out some games for the kids, but the only result was that alphabet blocks now lay strewn all over the living room in a glorious mess along with Monopoly houses and playing cards. Laboriously she bent down and gathered up the tiny game pieces, trying to bring a little order to the room. The conversation out on the veranda where Britta and Conny were sitting grew more and more heated, and she began to understand why the kids had not acquired any manners. With parents who quarrelled like five-year-olds it wasn't easy to learn respect for others and their belongings. If only this day would be over! As soon as it stopped raining she would send the Flood family packing. Never mind good manners and hospitality – she would need to be Saint Birgitta herself not to have a fit if they stayed much longer.

The bombshell dropped at lunch. With aching feet and a pain in her lower back she had stood at the stove for an hour, making a lunch that would suit Conny's voracious appetite as well as the children's finicky tastes, and in her own estimation she had succeeded rather well. Falun sausage *au gratin* with macaroni would satisfy all takers, she thought. But she soon learned that she had been dreadfully mistaken.

'Yuck, I hate Falun sausage. Gross!'

Lisa demonstratively shoved away her plate and crossed her arms with a sullen expression.

'That's too bad, because that's what we're having.' Erica's voice was firm.

'But I'm hu-u-u-ungry. I want something else.'

'There isn't anything else. If you don't like Falun sausages then you can eat the macaroni with ketchup.' Erica was making an effort to keep her tone of voice steady, even though she was boiling inside.

'Macaroni is gross. I want something else. Mam-ma-a-a-a!'

'Could you possibly get her something different?' Britta patted her little whiner on the cheek and was rewarded with a smile. Confident of victory, Lisa's cheeks took on the glow of triumph as she gave Erica a defiant look. But now the line had been crossed. Now it was war.

'There isn't anything else. Either you eat what's in front of you or go hungry.'

'But dear Erica, I think you're being unreasonable,' said Britta. 'Conny, explain to her how we do things at home, what our policy on childrearing is.' But she didn't bother to wait for a reply. 'We don't force our children to do anything. That would stunt their development. If my Lisa wants something different, we think it's her right to have it. I mean, she *is* an individual with just as much right to express herself as the rest of us. And what would you think if somebody tried to force you to eat food that you didn't like? I don't think you would accept it.'

Britta lectured in her best psychologist voice, and Erica suddenly knew this was the last straw. With icy calm she took the girl's plate, raised it over Britta's head, and then turned it over. The shock when the macaroni ran down over her hair and inside her blouse made Britta stop in the middle of a sentence.

Ten minutes later, they were gone. And would most likely never return. In all probability she would now be blacklisted by that side of the family, but no matter how hard she tried Erica couldn't say that she had any regrets. She wasn't ashamed either, even though her behaviour could at best be called childish. It had felt fantastic to find an outlet for the aggressions that had built up over their two-day visit, and she had no intention of apologizing.

The rest of the day she planned to spend on the sofa on the veranda with a good book and her first cup of tea of the summer. All at once life seemed much brighter.

Although it was small, the dazzling greenery in his glass veranda could compete with the best of gardens. Each flower was tenderly cultivated from seed or a cutting, and thanks to the hot weather this summer the air was now almost tropical. In one corner of the veranda he raised vegetables, and there was nothing to compare with the satisfaction of going out to pick tomatoes, squash, onions, and even melons and grapes that he had grown himself.

The little row-house stood on Dinglevägen, near the entrance to Fjällbacka from the south. It was small but functional. His veranda stuck out like a green exclamation mark among the more modest plantings of the other row-house residents.

It was only when he sat out on the veranda that he didn't miss the old house. The house where he had grown up and later created a home together with his wife and daughter. They were both gone now. The pain of their absence had intensified until one day he realised that he needed to say goodbye to the house too and all the memories that clung to its walls.

Of course the row-house lacked the character that he loved about the old house, but it was also the impersonality of his new lodgings that made it possible to ease the pain in his breast.

By now his grief was mostly like a dull rumble constantly heard in the background.

When Mona disappeared he thought that Linnea would die of a broken heart. She was already sickly, but she proved to be of tougher stuff than he thought. She lived for ten more years. For his sake, he was sure. She didn't want to leave him alone with the grief. Every day she struggled to continue a life that for them was only a shadow existence.

Mona had been the light of their life. She was born when they had both given up hope of ever having a child, and there were never any more. All the love they had was embodied in this bright, happy creature, whose laugh had ignited small fires in his breast. It was utterly inconceivable that she could just disappear like that. Back then it had felt as though the sun should have stopped shining. As though the sky should have fallen. But nothing happened. Life went on as usual outside their sorrowful abode. People laughed, lived, and went to work. But Mona was gone.

For a long time they lived on hope. Maybe she was still alive somewhere. Maybe she was living a life without them and had decided to disappear of her own accord. At the same time they both knew what the truth was. The other girl had disappeared just before Mona, and it was just too great a co-incidence for them to be able to fool themselves. Besides, Mona wasn't the type of girl who would deliberately cause them such pain. She was a nice, lovable girl who did every-thing she could to look after them.

On the day that Linnea died, he received final proof that Mona was in Heaven. The illness and the grief had reduced his beloved wife to a shadow of her former self, and as she lay in the bed and held his hand, he knew that this was the day he would be left alone. After hours of keeping vigil she had squeezed his hand one last time, and then a smile spread across her face. The light that was ignited in Linnea's eyes was a light that he had not seen in ten years – not since the last time she had looked at Mona. She fixed her gaze somewhere behind him and died. Then he knew for certain. Linnea died happy because her daughter was the one who met her in the tunnel. In many ways it made the loneliness easier to bear. Now, at least, the two people he loved most were together. It was only a matter of time until he would be reunited with them. He looked forward to that day, but until then it was his duty to live his life as best he could. The Lord had little patience with quitters, and he didn't dare do anything to risk his place in Heaven, where he would join Linnea and Mona.

A knock on the door interrupted his melancholy thoughts. Slowly he got up from his easy chair and ploughed through the greenery, leaning on his cane. He made his way down the hall to the front door. A serious-looking young man was standing outside, with his hand raised to knock again.

'Albert Thernblad?'

'Yes, that's me. But I don't need anything you're selling.'

The man smiled. 'No, I'm not selling anything. My name is Patrik Hedström, and I'm with the police. I wonder if I might come in for a moment?'

Albert said nothing but stepped aside to let him in. He led the way out to the veranda and showed the policeman to a place on the sofa. He hadn't asked what this was about. He didn't need to. He had been waiting for this visit for more than twenty years.

'What amazing plants. It certainly takes a green thumb.' Patrik gave a nervous laugh.

Albert said nothing as he regarded Patrik with his gentle eyes. He understood that it wasn't easy for this policeman to bring him the news, but he needn't have worried. After all these years of waiting, it was good to find out the truth at last. He had already done his grieving.

'Well, the thing is, we've found your daughter.' Patrik cleared his throat and started over. 'We've found your daughter, and we can confirm that she was murdered.'

Albert merely nodded. At the same time he felt a peace of mind. Finally he could lay her to rest. Have a grave to visit. He would bury her next to Linnea.

'Where did you find her?'

'In the King's Cleft.'

'The King's Cleft?' Albert frowned. 'If she was buried there, why wasn't she discovered sooner? So many people go there, after all.'

Patrik told him about the German tourist who was murdered, and that they had presumably found Siv as well. They believed that someone had moved Mona and Siv there at night, but that they had been buried somewhere else all these years.

Albert didn't go into town much any more, so unlike the rest of Fjällbacka he hadn't heard about the murder of the young German woman. The first thing he felt when he heard about her fate was a lurch in his stomach. Somewhere someone was going to experience the same pain that he and Linnea had felt. Somewhere a father and a mother would never see their daughter again. That overshadowed the news about Mona. Compared with the dead girl's family he was lucky. For him the grief had grown blunt and dull. But they had many years ahead of them before they reached that point, and his heart ached for them.

'Do you know who did this?'

'No, unfortunately, we don't. But we're going to do everything in our power to find out.'

'Do you know if it's the same person?'

Patrik hung his head. 'No, we don't even know that for sure, not as things stand right now. There are certain similarities, but that's all I can say at this point.'

He looked uneasily at the old man sitting before him. 'Is there anyone you'd like me to call? Someone who could come and keep you company?'

Albert's smile was kind and fatherly. 'No, there's no one.'

'Should I ring and hear whether the pastor can come over?'

Again the same kind smile. 'No thank you, I don't need a pastor. Don't trouble yourself. I've lived through this day over and over again in my thoughts, so it doesn't come as a shock. I just want to sit here in peace among my plants. I have everything I need. I may be old, but I'm tough.'

He placed his hand over Patrik's, as if he were the one offering consolation. And perhaps he was.

'If you don't mind, I'd like to show you a few pictures of Mona and tell you a little about her. So that you'll understand how she was when she was alive.'

Without hesitation the younger man nodded, and Albert hobbled out to fetch the old albums. For about an hour he showed Patrik photographs and told him about his daughter. It was the best hour he had spent in a long time, and he realized that it had been far too long since he'd allowed himself to retreat into memory.

When they said goodbye at the door, he pressed one of the photos into Patrik's hand. It showed Mona on her fifth birthday, with a big cake and five candles in front of her and a smile stretching from ear to ear. She was delightfully sweet, with blonde locks and eyes that glittered with the joy of life. It was important for him that the police have this picture in their mind's eye as they searched for his daughter's murderer.

After the policeman had left, Albert sat down on the veranda again. He closed his eyes and inhaled the sweet scent of the flowers. Then he fell asleep and dreamed about a long, bright tunnel where Mona and Linnea were waiting for him like shadows at the end. He thought he saw them waving.

The door to Gabriel's office flew open with a bang. Solveig stormed in, and behind her he saw Laine come running, her hands fluttering helplessly.

'You shit! You fucking dick!'

He grimaced automatically at the choice of words. He had

84

always found it extremely embarrassing when people showed strong feelings around him, and he had no patience for such language.

'What's going on? Solveig, I really think you should calm down and not speak to me that way.'

Too late he realized that the critical tone of voice, which came so naturally to him, only made things worse. She seemed about to fly at his throat, and for safety's sake he retreated behind his desk.

'Calm down? Are you telling me to calm down, you fucking prick? You limp dick!'

He could see that she was enjoying seeing him flinch at each sexual epithet. Behind her Laine was turning more and more pale.

Solveig lowered her voice a bit, but the tone was even more venomous. 'What is it, Gabriel? Why do you look so dejected? You used to like it when I whispered dirty words in your ear. It used to turn you on. Do you remember, Gabriel?' Now Solveig was hissing the words as she approached his desk.

'There's no reason to rehash the past. Do you have something to tell me, or are you just drunk and disagreeable as always?'

'Do I have something to tell you? Yes, you can bet your arse I do. I was down in Fjällbacka and you know what? They've found Mona and Siv.'

Gabriel gave a start. Shock was written all over his face.

'They've found the girls? Where?'

Solveig leaned over the desk, supporting her weight on her hands so that her face was only a couple of inches from Gabriel's.

'In the King's Cleft. Along with a young German girl who was murdered. And they think it's the same killer. So for shame, Gabriel Hult. Shame on you, accusing your brother, your own flesh and blood. And he had to bear the blame in people's eyes,

85

despite the fact there was never a shred of evidence against him. It was all the pointing and whispering behind his back that broke him. But maybe you knew that was how things would go. You knew that he was weak. That he was sensitive. He couldn't deal with the shame and hanged himself. I wouldn't be surprised if that was exactly what you had counted on when you called the police. You never could stand the fact that Ephraim loved him more.'

Solveig jabbed him so hard in the chest that he lurched backwards with each blow. By now he was standing with his back to the window seat and couldn't get any farther away from her. He was trapped. With his eyes he tried to signal Laine to do something about this unpleasant situation, but as usual she just stood there and stared, completely at a loss.

'My Johannes was always more loved than you, by everyone. And you couldn't stand it, could you?' She didn't wait for an answer to her assertions masked as questions. She just continued her diatribe. 'Even when Ephraim cut Johannes out of his will, he still loved him more. You got the estate and the money, but you could never win your father's love. Despite the fact that you were the one who worked the farm while Johannes lived a carefree life. And then when he stole your fiancée, that was the last straw, wasn't it? Was that when you began to hate him, Gabriel? Was that when you started to hate your brother? Sure, it may have been unfair, but you still had no right to do what you did. You destroyed Johannes's life, and mine and the children's too, for that matter. Don't you think I know what the boys are up to? And it's all your fault, Gabriel Hult. Finally people are going to see that Johannes didn't do what they've been whispering about all these years. Finally the boys and I will be able to walk with our heads held high again.'

Her anger seemed to be ebbing away, and in its place came

tears. Gabriel didn't know which was worse. For a moment he had seen in her wrath a brief glimpse of the old Solveig. The lovely beauty queen that he had been proud to have as his fiancée, before his brother came and took her, precisely the way he had taken everything else he wanted. When her anger was replaced by tears, Solveig deflated like a punctured balloon, and he once again saw the fat, slovenly wreck who spent her days wallowing in self-pity.

'May you burn in hell, Gabriel Hult, along with your father.' She whispered the words and left as abruptly as she'd come. Then Gabriel and Laine were alone. Gabriel felt shell-shocked. He sat down heavily on his desk chair and stared mutely at his wife. They exchanged a complicit look. They both knew what it meant that old bones had resurfaced.

With great zeal and confidence Martin took on the task of finding out all about Tanja Schmidt, which was the full name in her passport. Liese had turned in all of Tanja's things at their request, and he had gone through her backpack with a fine-toothed comb. At the very bottom he had found her passport looking practically unused. There was actually only one stamp from when she entered Sweden from Germany. Either she had never been outside Germany before, or the passport was new.

The photo was surprisingly good, and he decided that she had been nice-looking though a bit plain. Brown eyes and brown hair, a little longer than to her shoulders. Height five foot five, normal build, whatever that meant.

Otherwise her backpack had produced nothing of interest. Changes of clothes, some worn paperbacks, toiletries, and some wrappers from sweets. Nothing personal, which he found rather odd. Wouldn't she at least have a photo of her family or boyfriend with her, or an address book? Although they *had* found a handbag near the body. Liese had confirmed that Tanja owned a red handbag. Apparently that's where she had kept her personal belongings. Now they were gone, in any case. Could it have been a robbery? Or had the killer taken her personal items as souvenirs? Martin had seen a programme on the Discovery Channel about serial killers, that apparently it was common for them to save things from their victims, as part of the ritual.

Martin checked himself. There was nothing to indicate that they were looking for a serial killer, not yet. He did his best not to get stuck in that line of thinking.

He began writing down notes about how he was going to handle the investigation into the Tanja case. First, contact the German police authorities, which he had been about to do when he was interrupted by the call from Tord Pedersen. Then he had to talk with Liese again, and finally he thought he'd get Gösta to drive out to the campground with him and ask around. See whether Tanja might have spoken to anyone there. Or perhaps it would be better to ask Patrik to assign that task to Gösta. In this investigation Patrik, not Martin, had the authority to give orders to Gösta. And things had a tendency to go much more smoothly if protocol was followed to the letter.

Once again he began to dial the number of the German police, and this time he got through. It would have been an exaggeration to say that the conversation flowed smoothly, but by the time he hung up he was relatively sure he had succeeded in laying out the relevant details correctly. They promised to get back to him as soon as they had more information. At least that's what he thought the person on the other end had said. If there was going to be a lot of contact with their German colleagues they would have to bring in an interpreter.

Considering the time it might take to get information from abroad, he sincerely wished that he had an internet connection in front of him that was as good as the one he had at home. But because of the risk of being hacked, the police station didn't even have a lousy dial-up modem. He made a mental note to do a search for Tanja Schmidt in the German telephone directory, if it was accessible on the Net. Although if he remembered correctly, Schmidt was one of the most common German surnames, so there was little chance that it would produce anything.

Since he couldn't do much else than wait for information from Germany, he decided to get started on the next task. He had got hold of Liese's mobile number, and he rang her first to make sure that she was still in town. Actually she had no obligation to stay, but she had promised not to leave for another couple of days so that they would have a chance to talk to her again.

Her trip must have lost all of its charm by now. According to her testimony to Patrik, the two girls had grown very close in a short time. Now she sat alone in a tent at the Sälvik campground in Fjällbacka knowing her travelling companion had been murdered. Maybe she was in danger too. That was a scenario that Martin hadn't thought of earlier. Maybe it would be best to talk to Patrik about it as soon as he came back to the station. It could be that the murderer had seen the girls at the campground together and had then focused on the two of them for some reason. But how did Mona and Siv's bones fit into the picture? Mona and *possibly* Siv, he corrected himself at once. One should never regard anything as certain if it was merely *almost* certain, as an instructor at the police academy had once said. It was a maxim that Martin tried to live by in his police work.

On closer reflection he did not believe that Liese was in any danger. Once again they were dealing with probabilities, and the odds were that she had been drawn into something simply because of an unfortunate choice of travelling companion.

Despite his previous misgivings, Martin decided to do some fast talking to rope Gösta into a little concrete police work. He walked down the hall to his office.

'Gösta, may I interrupt?'

Still waxing poetic about his hole-in-one, Gösta was talking on the phone. He hung up guiltily when Martin stuck his head in the door.

'Yes?'

'Patrik has asked us to drive down to Sälvik campground. I have to meet with the victim's travelling companion, and you're supposed to ask questions around the campground.'

Gösta uttered a grunt but didn't question the validity of Martin's statement as to how Patrik had assigned the tasks. He grabbed his jacket and followed Martin out to the car. The downpour had changed to a light drizzle, but the air was clear and fresh to breathe. It felt as though weeks of dust and heat had been flushed away, and everything looked cleaner than usual.

'Let's hope that this rain isn't here to stay, or else my golf game is going to go to hell,' Gösta muttered crossly as they sat in the car. Martin thought that he was the only person who didn't think it was good to have a little break from the summer heat.

'Well, I think it's quite nice. That sweltering heat was about to kill me. And just imagine Patrik's wife. It must be rough to be eight months pregnant in the middle of summer. I could never handle it, that's for sure.'

Martin chattered on, well aware that Gösta had a tendency to be a bit taciturn when there was talk of anything other than golf. And since Martin's knowledge of golf was limited to the fact that the ball was round and white and that golfers were usually identified by checked clown trousers, he decided to carry on the conversation all by himself. That's why he hardly heard Gösta's muttered comment.

'Our boy was born in early August, one hot summer like this.'

'Do you have a son, Gösta? I didn't know that.'

Martin searched his memory for comments about Gösta's family. He knew that his wife had died a couple of years ago, but he couldn't recall hearing anything about a child. In surprise he turned to look at Gösta seated next to him.

His colleague did not meet his gaze, but kept staring at his hands in his lap. Without seeming to be aware of it, he was twisting the gold wedding band that he still wore. He didn't seem to have heard Martin's question. Instead he went on in a monotone: 'Majbritt put on sixty-five pounds. She was as big as a house. She could hardly move in the heat either. Towards the end she just sat in the shade, panting. I brought her one pitcher of water after another, but it was like watering a camel. Her thirst never seemed to quit.'

He laughed, a strange, introspective, slightly tender laugh. Martin realized that Gösta was so far down memory lane that he was no longer talking to anyone else.

'The boy was perfect when he arrived,' Gösta went on. 'Plump and splendid he was. The spitting image of me, everyone said. But then it all happened so fast.' Gösta turned his wedding ring faster and faster. 'I was visiting their hospital room when he suddenly stopped breathing. There was a terrific commotion. People came running from every direction, and they took him away from us. We never saw him again until he lay in his coffin. But it was a fine funeral. After that we just didn't feel like trying to have any more kids. What if things went wrong again? Majbritt wouldn't have been able to stand it, and neither would I. So we had to make do with each other.'

Gösta gave a start as if waking from a trance. He gave Martin a reproachful look, as if it were his fault that all those words had poured out.

'It's not something I talk about any more, of course. And it's not something any of you need to sit and babble about during coffee breaks, for that matter. It's forty years ago now, and nobody else needs to know.'

Martin nodded. But he couldn't stop himself from giving Gösta a light pat on the shoulder. The old man grunted, but Martin still felt that at that moment a fragile bond had formed between them, whereas before there had been only a mutual lack of respect. Gösta still might not be the finest example of a police officer that the corps could produce, but that didn't mean he didn't have experience and knowledge, and Martin could learn something from him.

They were both relieved when they reached the campground. The silence that followed the sharing of confidences could be oppressive, as the last five minutes had been.

Gösta slouched off with his hands in his pockets and a downhearted expression on his face, in search of campers who might answer his questions. Martin asked for directions to Liese's tent and was surprised to find that it was scarcely bigger than a handkerchief. It was jammed between two larger tents, which made it look even smaller in comparison. In the tent to the right of hers some children were playing noisy games; in the tent to the left a beefy bloke about twenty-five years old was drinking beer beneath an awning that stuck out from the tent. All of them gave Martin inquisitive looks as he approached Liese's tent.

Knocking was not an option, so he called her name a bit hesitantly. The tent zipper opened and Liese's blonde head appeared in the opening.

Two hours later the two police officers drove off without having found out anything new. Liese had nothing more to contribute than what she had already told Patrik at the station, and none of the other campers had noticed anything of interest regarding Tanja or Liese.

But something else had caught Martin's attention and was

hovering at the back of his mind. He feverishly searched through the sensory impressions from his visit to the campground but remained puzzled. There was something he'd seen that should have registered. Annoyed, he drummed his fingers on the steering wheel, but he finally had to give up trying to pin down the elusive memory.

They rode home in silence.

Patrik hoped that he would be like Albert Thernblad when he got old. Not as alone, of course, but just as stylish. Albert hadn't let himself go after his wife's death, as so many older men did who ended up living alone. Instead he was well-dressed in both shirt and vest, and his white hair and beard were well-groomed. Despite his difficulties walking, he moved with dignity, with his head held high, and from the little Patrik got to see of the house it seemed that it was kept neat and tidy. He was also impressed by the way Albert handled the news that his daughter had been found. He seemed to have made peace with his fate and was living his life as best he could under the circumstances.

Patrik had been deeply moved by the photographs of Mona that Albert had shown him. Like so many times before, he had realized that it was all too easy to view the crime victims as just another statistic, or to label them 'the plaintiff' or 'the victim'. It didn't matter whether the person had been robbed or, as in this case, murdered. Albert had done the right thing by showing him the photographs. He'd seen Mona progress from the maternity ward to chubby baby, from schoolgirl to student. Then he'd seen her as the happy, healthy girl she was just before she disappeared.

But there was another girl that he needed to find out more about. Besides, he knew the town well enough to realize that rumours were already flying with the speed of lightning through the community. It would be best to head them off and have a talk with Siv Lantin's mother, even though they had no confirmation of Siv's identity as yet. For safety's sake he had checked on her address before he left the station. It had been a little harder to locate Siv's mother, since Gun was no longer called Lantin. She must have married, or re-married, as the case may be. After a little detective work he had discovered that her surname was now Struwer and that there was a summer house registered to Gun and Lars Struwer in Norra Hamngatan in Fjällbacka. The name Struwer sounded familiar, but he couldn't quite place it.

He was in luck and found a parking place on Planarna down from the Badrestaurant, and he walked the last hundred metres. There was one-way traffic along Norra Hamngatan in the summertime, but in the short stretch he walked he saw three idiot drivers fail to read the road signs. He had to press himself up against the stone wall as they tried to squeeze past the oncoming traffic. The terrain was apparently so rugged where they lived that they felt the need to drive a big four-wheel-drive Jeep. That type of vehicle was far too common among the summer visitors. Patrik surmised that in this case the Stockholm region was considered rugged terrain.

He had a good mind to whip out his badge and read them the riot act but refrained. If the police spent their time trying to teach all beachgoers common sense they wouldn't get much else done.

Patrik finally reached the right residence, a white house with blue trim on the left side of the street, across from the red boat-houses that gave Fjällbacka its characteristic silhouette. The owners of the house were busy unloading a couple of huge suitcases from a gold-coloured Volvo V70. To be more precise, an older gentleman in a double-breasted suit was lifting the suitcases out with a groan, while a short, heavily made-up woman stood by and gesticulated. They were both tanned, verging on sunburned, and if the Swedish summer hadn't been so sunny Patrik would have guessed that they'd been on holiday abroad. This year the rocky skerries of Fjällbacka could have served as a tanning parlour.

He walked up to the couple and hesitated a second before he cleared his throat to attract their attention. Both of them stopped what they were doing and turned.

'Yes?' Gun Struwer's voice was a touch too shrill, and Patrik noticed a peevish expression on her face.

'My name is Patrik Hedström and I'm with the police. Could I have a few words with you?'

'At last!' She raised her hands with the red-manicured nails and rolled her eyes. 'To think that it would take so long. I don't understand what our tax money is going for. All summer we've been reporting that people have been parking illegally in our parking spot, but we haven't heard a peep from the police. Are you finally going to do something about this nuisance? We paid a lot of money for this house, and think we have the right to use our own parking place. But maybe that's too much to ask!'

She put her hands on her hips and squinted at Patrik. Behind her stood her husband, looking as though he'd like to sink into the ground. Apparently he didn't think the matter was quite so important.

'Actually, I'm not here about a parking infraction,' said Patrik. 'But first I have to ask you: was your maiden name Gun Lantin? And do you have a daughter named Siv?'

Gun fell silent instantly and put her hand to her mouth. No other reply was necessary. Her husband was the first to gather his wits and accompanied Patrik to the front door, which was standing open. It seemed a bit risky to leave the bags out on the street, so Patrik grabbed two of them and helped Lars Struwer carry the luggage inside. Gun hurried into the house ahead of them.

They sat down in the living room, Gun and Lars next to each other on the sofa, while Patrik chose the easy chair. Gun was clinging to Lars, but his comforting pats seemed almost mechanical, something that he knew the situation required of him.

'What's happened? What have you found out? It's been over twenty years. How can anything have come out so long afterwards?' she babbled on nervously.

'I have to emphasize that we don't have a positive identification yet, but it's possible that we may have found Siv.'

Gun's hand flew up to her throat and for once she seemed speechless.

Patrik went on, 'We're still waiting for the medical examiner to make a positive identification, but it seems most likely that it's Siv.'

'But how, where . . . ?' she stammered. The questions were the same ones that Mona's father had asked.

'A young woman was found dead in the King's Cleft. The remains of two other victims were found with her. Mona Thernblad, and probably Siv.'

Just as he had explained to Albert Thernblad, Patrik told Gun that the girls had been transported to the site and that the police were now doing all they could to find out who could have committed the murders.

Gun leaned her face against her husband's chest, but Patrik noticed that she was sobbing with dry eyes. He got the impression that her expressions of grief were largely play-acting, but it was just a hunch.

When Gun had pulled herself together she took a little hand mirror out of her purse and checked her make-up. Then she asked Patrik, 'What happens now? When can we claim our poor little Siv's remains?' Without waiting for his reply she turned to her husband. 'We have to have a proper funeral for my poor darling, Lars. We could have coffee and refreshments for the guests afterwards in the ballroom at the Grand Hotel. Perhaps even a three-course sit-down dinner. Do you think we should invite . . .' She mentioned the name of one of the bigwigs in the business community.

Patrik happened to know that he owned a house down the street.

Gun went on, 'I ran into his wife at Eva's early this summer, and she said we should really get together sometime. I know that they would appreciate being invited.'

An excited tone had crept into her voice, while a disapproving frown had appeared on her husband's face. All at once Patrik recalled where he had heard their surname before. Lars Struwer was the founder of one of the biggest grocery chains in Sweden, but he'd been retired for many years, and the chain had been sold to a foreign company. No wonder that they could afford a house in this location. The guy was good for many, many millions. Siv's mother had certainly moved up in the world since the late Seventies when she lived in a little summer cabin year-round with her daughter and grand-daughter.

'Dear, shouldn't we worry about the practical matters later? You need some time to let the news sink in first.'

He gave her a reproachful glance and Gun lowered her eyes, remembering her role as grieving mother.

Patrik looked round the room. Despite the sad nature of his visit he had to stop himself from laughing. The place was a parody of the tourist homes that Erica liked to ridicule. The whole room was decorated like a sailboat cabin in a marine colour scheme, with navigational charts on the walls, light-house lamps, curtains with seashell patterns, and even an old rudder as a coffee table. A good example of the fact that a lot of money and good taste didn't necessarily go hand in hand.

'I wonder whether you could tell me a little about Siv. I've just been to visit Albert Thernblad, Mona's father, and he showed me some photos from her childhood. Would it be possible to see a few pictures of your daughter?'

Unlike Albert, who had brightened up at the prospect of talking about the apple of his eye, Gun squirmed self-consciously on the sofa.

'Well, I don't really see what purpose that would serve. The police asked lots of questions about Siv when she disappeared. All that stuff is probably in the police archives . . .'

'I know, but I was thinking a little more on the personal level. What sort of girl she was, what kind of things she liked, what she wanted to be, and so on.'

'Wanted to be? That really wasn't an issue. She got knocked up by that German boy when she was seventeen. After that I saw to it that she didn't waste time on studies any more. By then it was too late anyway, and I certainly had no intention of taking care of her baby myself, that's for sure.'

Her tone was scornful. Patrik saw Lars look at his wife, and he thought to himself that no matter what the man's picture of Gun had been when they first married, there was not much left of his illusions. There was a weariness and resignation in Lars's face, which was also marked by disappointment. It was obvious that the marriage had reached a point where Gun no longer made much effort to hide her true character. Lars may have felt that it was true love to begin with, but Patrik suspected that the attraction for Gun had been all those beautiful millions in Lars Struwer's bank account.

'What about Siv's daughter? Where is she now?' Patrik leaned forward, curious as to the answer.

Once again, crocodile tears. 'After Siv disappeared I couldn't take care of her by myself. I wanted to, of course, but times were a bit tough, and taking care of a little girl was simply out of the question. So I made the best of the situation and sent her to Germany, to her father. Well, he wasn't very happy to have a kid descend on him out of the blue, but there wasn't much he could do about it. He was the girl's father, after all, and I had papers to prove it.'

'So she lives in Germany today?' A glimmer of an idea appeared in Patrik's mind. Could it be that . . . ? No, that would be hard to believe.

'No, she's dead.'

The idea vanished as quickly as it had come. 'Dead?'

'Yes, in a car crash when she was five. But the German didn't bother to ring me with the news. I got a letter telling me that Malin had been killed. I wasn't even invited to the funeral, can you imagine? My own granddaughter and I couldn't go to her funeral.' Her voice quavered with indignation.

'He never answered the letters I wrote to him when the girl was alive. Don't you think he should have helped out the grandmother of his poor motherless child a little? I was the one who saw to it that his kid had food on the table and clothes on her back the first two years of her life. Don't you think I had the right to some compensation?'

Gun had now worked herself into a rage over the injustices she thought she'd been subjected to, and she didn't calm down until Lars put a hand on her shoulder. He gave her a kind but firm squeeze, which was his way of admonishing her.

Patrik refrained from answering. He knew that any reply he made would not be appreciated by Gun Struwer. Why in the world did she think the child's father should send her money? Couldn't she see how unreasonable she was being? Apparently not. He saw her suntanned, leathery cheeks turn crimson with wrath, despite the fact that her daughter had now been dead for more than twenty years.

He made one last attempt to find out something personal about Siv. 'Might there be some photographs?'

'Well, I didn't take that many pictures of her, but I should be able to find something.'

Gun left the room, leaving Patrik alone in the living room with Lars. They sat in silence for a few moments. Then Lars said something, but in a voice so low that Gun wouldn't be able to hear it.

'She's not as cold-hearted as she seems. Gun has some very fine qualities.'

Yeah right, Patrik thought. He would call that statement a fool's defence. But Lars was probably doing what he could to justify his choice of a wife. Patrik estimated that Lars was about twenty years older than Gun, and it wasn't too far-fetched to surmise that his choice had been made with a part of his body other than his head. Although Patrik had to admit that perhaps his profession was making him a bit cynical. Maybe it really was true love. How would he know?

Gun returned, not with a thick photo album like Albert had produced, but with a single little black-and-white photo which she morosely handed to Patrik. It showed a sullen teenaged Siv holding her newborn daughter in her lap. Unlike the pictures of Mona, in this photo there was no joy in the girl's expression.

'Well, we must get busy straightening up the house. We've just returned from Provence, where Lars's daughter lives.' From the way Gun said the word 'daughter' Patrik could hear that there was no love lost between her and her step-daughter.

He also realized when his presence was no longer desired, so he thanked them for their help.

'And thank you for lending me the photo. I promise to return it in good condition.'

Gun waved her hand dismissively. Then she remembered her role and contorted her face into a grimace.

'Please let me know as soon as you're positive. I would so dearly like to be able to bury my little Siv.'

'I'll come back as soon as I hear anything.'

Patrik's tone was unnecessarily curt, but he had found the entire histrionic show quite distasteful.

When he was back out on Norra Hamngatan, the skies opened up. He stood still for a moment and let the down-pour rinse away the cloying feeling he had from his visit with the Struwers. He needed to get home and hug Erica and feel the life pulsing inside when he put his hand on her belly. He needed to feel that the world wasn't as cruel and evil as it sometimes seemed. It simply couldn't be.

5

It felt as if months had passed. But she knew that it couldn't possibly be that long. And yet each hour down here in the dark was like a lifetime.

There was far too much time to think. Far too much time to feel how the pain was twisting every nerve. Time to ponder everything she had lost. Or would lose.

By now she knew that she would never get out of here. No one could escape such pain. And yet she had never felt softer hands than his. No hands had ever caressed her with such love, and it made her hunger for more of that touch. Not the horrible or painful touch, but the soft touch that came afterwards. If she had ever felt such a touch before, everything would have been different, she knew that now. The feeling when he ran his hands over her body was so pure, so innocent, that it reached all the way to that hard core inside her, the one no one before had been able to reach.

In the darkness he had become her everything. No words had been spoken, but she fantasized about how his voice would sound. Fatherly, warm. But when the pain came she hated him. Then she wanted to kill him. If only she could.

Robert found him out in the shed. They knew each other so well, and he knew that's where Stefan went when he was worried about something. When he saw that the house was empty he went directly to the shed, and quite rightly found his brother there, sitting on the floor with his knees drawn up and his arms wrapped tightly round his legs.

The two of them were so different that Robert found it hard to believe they were brothers. He himself was proud that he never spent a minute of his life pondering anything or trying to predict the consequences. He simply acted and let things turn out as they may. Whoever survives will see what happens – that was his motto, and he saw no reason to worry about things he couldn't control. Life blew you one way or another, that was simply the way things were.

Stefan, on the other hand, thought far too much for his own good. For a brief moment Robert felt a pang of regret that his little brother had chosen to follow in his crooked footsteps, but maybe it was for the best. Otherwise Stefan would have felt disappointed. They were the sons of Johannes Hult, and it was as though a curse had settled on their whole bloody branch of the family. There was no chance that any of them would succeed at anything they attempted, so why even try?

He would never admit it, even under torture, but he loved his brother more than anything in the world. It pained him to see Stefan's silhouette in the gloom of the shed. His brother's thoughts seemed to be miles away, and there was a sadness about him that Robert occasionally glimpsed. A cloud of melancholy seemed to hover over Stefan's psyche, forcing him into a dark, ugly place for weeks at a time. Robert hadn't seen any sign of it all summer, but now he felt its physical presence as soon as he stepped through the door.

'Stefan?'

He got no reply. Robert quietly walked farther into the darkness. He squatted down beside his brother and put his hand on his shoulder.

'Stefan, are you sitting in here again?'

His younger brother only nodded. When Stefan turned his face Robert saw to his surprise that it was swollen from crying. That's not what usually happened during one of Stefan's moods. Robert felt suddenly uneasy.

'What is it, Stefan? What's happened?'

'Pappa.'

The rest of the sentence was drowned in sobs, and Robert strained to hear what he was saying.

'What are you saying about Pappa, Stefan?'

Stefan took a couple of deep breaths to calm himself down and then said, 'Everyone's going to realize now that Pappa was innocent. That he didn't make those girls disappear. Don't you see? People will finally know that it wasn't him!'

'What are you raving about?' Robert shook him, but could feel his heart skipping a beat.

'Mamma was in town and heard that they'd found a girl murdered, and along with her they found the girls who

106

disappeared. Don't you see? A girl was murdered *now*. So nobody can claim that it was Pappa who did it, right?'

Stefan laughed. He sounded slightly hysterical. Robert still couldn't fully take in what he was saying. Ever since he had found his father on the floor of the barn with a noose around his neck he had dreamed and fantasized about hearing the words that Stefan was now spouting out.

'You're not screwing with me, are you? Because you'll have hell to pay if you are.'

Robert clenched his fist, but Stefan merely kept laughing hysterically, and the tears ran down his face. Robert now understood they were tears of joy. Stefan turned and hugged his brother so hard that he could hardly breathe. When it dawned on Robert that his brother was speaking the truth, he hugged him back as hard as he could.

Finally their father would be vindicated. Finally they, and Mamma too, would be able to hold their heads high without hearing the whispers behind their backs and without seeing the fingers pointing in their direction when people didn't think they were looking. Now all those people would be sorry for everything, those damned gossipmongers. For twenty-four years the town had discredited their family, but now everyone else would feel the shame.

'Where's Mamma?'

Robert pulled away from his brother and gave him an enquiring look. Stefan began to giggle uncontrollably. He said something incoherent as he laughed.

'What did you say? Calm down and speak up. I asked you where Mamma is.'

'She's with Uncle Gabriel.'

Robert's face clouded over. 'What the hell is she doing with that old bastard?'

'Telling him the truth, I think. I've never seen Mamma as mad as when she came back and told me what she'd heard.

She went right up to the farm to give Gabriel a piece of her mind. That probably kicked some life into him. You really should have seen her. With her hair sticking straight up and smoke practically coming out of her ears.'

The image of their mother with her hair sticking straight up and puffs of smoke coming out her ears now made Robert snicker too. She had been a shambling, mumbling shadow as long as he could remember, so it was hard to imagine her as a raging fury.

'I would have loved to see Gabriel's face when she came storming in. And can you imagine Aunt Laine?'

Stefan did a spot-on imitation of her worried expression as she wrung her hands. In a shrill voice he declaimed, 'But Solveig, really! My dear Solveig, you shouldn't use such language!'

Both brothers collapsed in convulsions of laughter on the floor.

'Do you ever think about Pappa?' asked Stefan. His question drew them back to seriousness again, and Robert was quiet for a moment before he replied.

'Yes, of course I do. Although I have a hard time thinking of anything but the way he looked the day he died. You should be glad you didn't have to see him. What about you, do you think about him?'

'Sure, all the time. But it feels like I'm watching a film, if you know what I mean. I remember how he was always happy and the way he used to joke around and dance and swing me up in the air. But I see everything from a distance, just like in a film.'

'I know what you mean.'

They lay side by side staring up at the ceiling while the rain hammered on the sheet-metal above them.

Stefan said quietly, 'He loved us, didn't he, Robert?'

Robert replied just as quietly, 'He certainly did, Stefan, he certainly did.'

* * *

Erica heard Patrik shaking out his umbrella on the front steps and heaved herself up from the sofa to meet him at the door.

'Hello?' he said in surprise as he looked around. Apparently he wasn't expecting everything to be calm and quiet. Actually she should have been a bit annoyed with him because he hadn't called her all day, but she was too glad to see him at home to be annoyed. She also knew that he was never more than a mobile phone call away, and she had no doubt that he thought about her a thousand times a day. She felt a great sense of security when she thought about their relationship. It was very comforting.

'Where are Conny and the bandits?' he whispered, still not sure whether they had left or not.

'I dumped a bowl of macaroni and Falun sausage on Britta's head, so they didn't want to stay around any longer. Such ungrateful guests.'

Erica was amused at Patrik's shocked expression.

'I simply blew up. You have to draw the line somewhere. It doesn't look like we'll be getting any invitations from that side of the family for the next century, but it's not anything I regret. Do you?'

'Good Lord, no.' He rolled his eyes. 'Did you really do that? Dump a whole plate of food on her head?'

'Swear to God. All my good upbringing went straight out the window. Now I'll probably never get to Heaven.'

'Mmm, you're a little bit of heaven yourself, so you don't have to . . .'

He nibbled at her neck, right where he knew she was ticklish. She shoved him away with a laugh.

'I'll fix myself some hot chocolate, and then you have to tell me all about the Big Row.' Patrik took her hand and led her into the kitchen, where he helped her lower herself onto a chair.

'You look tired,' she said. 'How are things going?'

He sighed as he whipped some O'Boy into a pan of milk.

'Well, the case was going okay, but not any more. It was lucky that the techs finished going over the crime scene before this weather arrived. If we'd found the bodies today rather than day before yesterday, there wouldn't have been a thing left to search for. Thanks for that information you looked up for me, by the way. It turned out to be really useful.'

He sat down facing her while he waited for the chocolate to heat up.

'And what about you, how are you doing? Everything all right with the baby?'

'Everything's fine with us. Our future little football star has been running riot as usual, but I had a lovely day after Conny and Britta left. That was just what I needed. I was finally able to relax and read for a while. All it took was a visit from a bunch of crazy relatives.'

'That's great. So I don't have to worry about you two?'

'No, not a bit.'

'Do you want me to try and stay home tomorrow? Maybe I could do a little work from here – at least I'd be nearby.'

'That's sweet of you, but I'm doing fine, really. I think it's more important that you concentrate on finding the murderer before the trail goes cold. I'll be demanding your presence soon enough.' She smiled and patted him on the hand. Then she went on, 'Besides, a general sense of hysteria seems to be brewing. I've received a number of calls today from people trying to pump me about how much the police know. Naturally I wouldn't say a word, even if I did know anything, which I don't.' She paused to catch her breath. 'And the tourist bureau isn't the only place getting a lot of cancellations from people who don't dare come here. A lot of the sailboat traffic has headed for other harbours. So if you haven't yet heard from the local tourism industry, you might as well prepare yourself.'

Patrik nodded. He'd been afraid that this would happen.

The hysteria was going to spread and get worse until they had someone to put behind bars. For a town like Fjällbacka that lived off the tourist trade, the homicides spelled disaster. He recalled a summer a couple of years ago when a rapist had committed four rapes during the month of July before he was finally apprehended. The town's businesses had taken a beating, because tourists had gone elsewhere, to nearby communities such as Grebbestad and Strömstad. A murder would create an even worse situation. Fortunately it was the chief's job to handle such matters. He was glad to let Mellberg deal with those types of issues.

Patrik rubbed the bridge of his nose. He could feel a bad headache coming on. He was about to take a pain tablet when he suddenly realized that he hadn't had a thing to eat all day. Food was normally one of the indulgences he permitted himself in life, and an incipient bulge around his waist bore witness to that fact. He couldn't remember when he'd last missed a couple of meals, or even one. He was too tired to cook. Instead he made a couple of open-faced sandwiches with cheese and caviar, which he dipped in his hot chocolate. As usual Erica gave him a slightly disgusted look at the sight of this gastronomically repulsive combination, but for Patrik it was sheer ambrosia. Three sandwiches later, his headache was only a memory, and he felt a new spurt of energy.

'Sweetheart, why don't we invite Dan and his girlfriend over this weekend?' he said to Erica. 'We could do a little barbecuing.'

Erica frowned and did not look overly enchanted.

'Listen, you haven't really given Maria a chance. How many times have you met her? Twice?'

'All right, all right, I know. But she's just so . . .' she searched for the right word. 'Such a twenty-one-year-old.'

'Well, she can't help that. I agree that she does seem a little clueless, but who knows, maybe she's just shy? And it's worth it to make an effort for Dan's sake, at least. I mean, he did choose her, after all. And after the divorce from Pernilla it's nice that he's met someone new.'

'It's astounding how tolerant you've become lately,' said Erica sullenly, though she had to admit that he had a point. 'Why are you being so magnanimous?'

'I'm always magnanimous when it comes to twenty-one-year-olds. They have such fine qualities.'

'Oh yeah, like what?' Erica snapped before she realized that Patrik was teasing her. 'Oh, never mind. You're probably right. Of course we should invite Dan and his little cutie.'

'Listen to you.'

'All right, all right, Dan and *Maria*. I'm sure it'll be fun. I could get out Emma's old doll house so she'll have something to do while we grown-ups have dinner.'

'Erica . . .'

'Okay, I'll stop. It's just so hard to resist. It's like some sort of tic.'

'You wicked girl. Come here and get a hug instead of hatching your dastardly plans.'

She took him at his word and they curled up on the sofa together. For Patrik this was what made it possible for him to face the darker sides of humanity that he encountered in his work. Erica, and the thought that perhaps he could make a small contribution to ensuring the world would be a safer place for the baby now pressing the soles of its feet against his palm inside the skin stretched across Erica's belly. Outside their windows the wind died down as twilight fell, and the colour of the sky turned from grey to flaming pink. He predicted that tomorrow it would be sunny again.

Patrik's premonitions about sunshine turned out to be true. The next day it seemed as though the rain had never come. By noon the asphalt was steaming again. Although he was dressed in shorts and a T-shirt, Martin was sweating but that

112

was starting to feel like a normal state. Yesterday's cool temperature was only a dream.

Martin felt a bit bewildered about how to proceed with his assignment. Patrik was in Mellberg's office, so Martin hadn't had a chance to confer with him yet. One problem he had was the information from Germany. The German police might get back to him at any time, and he was afraid of missing anything they might say, because of his poor knowledge of German. So the best thing would be to find someone who could help him interpret, in a three-way phone hook-up. But who would he ask for help? The interpreters Martin had worked with before had mostly been people who spoke the Baltic languages, along with Russian and Polish, because of problems with stolen vehicles that kept vanishing to those countries. He'd never needed help with German before. He took out the phone book and paged through it more or less at random, not sure what he was looking for. One heading gave him a bright idea. Considering the number of German tourists that streamed through Fjällbacka each year, the Fjällbacka tourist bureau must have someone on staff who was fluent in the language. He eagerly dialled their number.

A bright, cheerful female voice answered the phone. 'Fjällbacka Tourist Bureau, good morning, this is Pia.'

'Hello, this is Martin Molin at the Tanumshede police station. I wonder whether you have anyone there who's fluent in German?'

'Well, I suppose that would be me. What's this about?'

Her voice sounded more and more attractive with each second, and Martin had a brilliant idea.

'Could I come down there and discuss it with you? Do you have time?'

'Of course. I'm going to lunch in half an hour. If you could be here by then, maybe we could meet for lunch at Café Bryggan.'

'That sounds perfect. I'll see you there in half an hour.'

Exhilarated, Martin hung up the phone. He wasn't really sure what sort of foolishness had come over him, but she had such a pleasant voice.

He parked his car half an hour later outside the ironmonger's shop and walked across Ingrid Bergman's Square making his way through all the summer visitors. He was starting to get cold feet. This isn't a date, this is police business, he reminded himself. But he couldn't deny that he would be cruelly disappointed if Pia at the tourist bureau turned out to have buck teeth and weigh 450 pounds.

He headed along the wharf to the café tables and looked around. At one of the tables by the railing a young woman in a blue blouse and a colourful scarf with the tourist bureau's logo on it was waving to him. He heaved a sigh of relief, immediately followed by a sense of triumph that he had guessed right. Pia was as sweet as a piece of chocolate. Big brown eyes and dark, curly hair. A big smile with gleaming teeth and charming dimples. This was going to be a much more pleasant lunch than shovelling down a cold pasta salad with Hedström in the lunchroom at the station. Not that he didn't like Hedström, but his colleague was certainly no match for this peach!

'Hello, I'm Martin Molin.'

'I'm Pia Löfstedt.'

After the introductions were made, they each ordered fish soup from the tall, blonde waitress.

'We're in luck,' said Pia. '"The Herring" is here this week.' She could see that Martin had no idea what she was talking about.

'Christian Hellberg. Chef of the Year in 2001. He's from Fjällbacka. You'll see once you taste the fish soup. It's divine.'

She gestured eagerly the whole time she was talking, and Martin found himself staring at her in fascination. Pia was totally unlike the girls he usually met, and that was probably why it felt so great to be sitting across from her. He had to remind himself again that this wasn't a date; it was a working lunch, and he actually did have business to discuss.

'I have to admit that it's not every day the police ring us up. I assume this has to do with the body you found in the King's Cleft, right?'

The question was posed as a statement of fact, not as an attempt to sensationalize, and Martin nodded affirmatively.

'Yes, that's correct. As you've probably heard, the victim was a German tourist, and we may need some help with interpreting. Do you think you could handle it?'

'I studied in Germany for two years, so it shouldn't be any problem.'

Their soup arrived, and after one spoonful Martin was inclined to agree with Pia's evaluation of 'divine'. He tried hard not to slurp it up, but couldn't help himself. He hoped that she had read *Emil in Lönneberga* by Astrid Lindgren. 'You have to slurp it up or you won't know it's soup . . .'

'That's funny . . .' said Pia, pausing to eat another spoonful of soup. A light breeze swept over the tables now and then, providing a few seconds of cool air. Both of them watched an old-fashioned cutter as it struggled forward with its sails barely luffing. There wasn't enough wind for a good day of sailing, so most of the boats were running their engines. Pia went on, 'That German girl . . . Tanja was her name, wasn't it? She came into the bureau about a week ago, wanting help translating some articles.'

Martin's interest was instantly aroused. 'What sort of articles?'

'About those girls that were found with her. Articles about their disappearance. Old articles she'd photocopied, apparently from the library, I would guess.'

His spoon clattered when he dropped it into his bowl out of sheer astonishment. 'Why did she want help reading them?'

115

'I really don't know. And I didn't ask her, either. We're actually not supposed to do stuff like that during working hours, but it was the middle of the day and all the tourists were out on the skerries swimming, so it was quiet. And besides, she seemed so anxious that I felt sorry for her.' Pia hesitated. 'Do you think it has anything to do with the murder? Maybe I should have called and told you about it earlier . . .'

She sounded worried, and Martin hastened to reassure her. For some reason he didn't want to risk prompting any sort of unpleasant feelings in Pia.

'There's no way you could know that it might be important,' he said. 'But it's good that you told me about it.'

They ate their lunch and talked about more pleasant subjects. Her lunch hour was over way too soon. Pia had to rush off to the little information kiosk in the middle of the square before her colleague got annoyed at having her own lunch delayed. Before Martin knew it she was gone, after a too-hasty goodbye. It was on the tip of his tongue to ask whether they could meet again, but he couldn't quite get the words out. Muttering and swearing, he walked to his car. On the way back to Tanumshede his thoughts reluctantly turned to what Pia had told him about Tanja asking for help. Why was she interested in those girls? Who was she? What was the connection between Tanja, Siv and Mona? What was he not seeing?

Life was good. Life was very good. He couldn't recall when the air had seemed so clean, the aromas so strong or the colours so bright. Life was truly good.

Mellberg looked at Hedström, who was sitting in the chair opposite him. A handsome fellow, and a talented cop. He may not have expressed it in just those terms before, but he was going to make the most of the opportunity right now. It was important for his colleagues to feel appreciated.

He had read somewhere that a good leader should offer criticism and praise with the same firm hand. Previously he might have been a bit too free with the criticism. His newfound clarity allowed him to see that, and he intended to rectify the situation.

'How's it going with the investigation?' he asked.

Hedström ran down the main points of the work they had done so far.

'Excellent, excellent,' said Mellberg, nodding jovially. 'I've had a number of unpleasant calls today. People are very anxious for this case to be solved quickly so that it won't have long-lasting effects on the tourism industry, as someone expressed it so aptly. But that's not anything you need to worry about, Hedström. I've personally assured everyone that the Department's finest are working night and day to put the perpetrator behind bars. So just keep working at your usual high level and I'll take care of the town's bigwigs.'

Hedström gave his boss an odd look.

Mellberg kept his eyes fixed on his colleague and fired off a broad smile. If Hedström only knew . . .

The debriefing with Mellberg had taken over an hour. Patrik looked for Martin on the way back to his office, but he didn't seem to be around. So Patrik went to Hedemyr's and bought a plastic-wrapped sandwich, which he wolfed down with a cup of coffee in the lunchroom. Just as he finished eating he heard Martin coming down the hall. He signalled to him to come into his office.

Patrik started off by saying, 'Have you noticed anything funny about Mellberg recently?'

'Besides the fact that he doesn't complain or criticize, laughs all the time, has lost a lot of weight and is wearing clothes that actually look as if they were in fashion as recently as the Nineties? No.' Martin smiled.

'There's something fishy going on. Not that I'm complaining.

He's not interfering in the investigation, and today he praised me so much that I blushed. But there's something . . .' Patrik shook his head. But their speculations about the new Bertil Mellberg would have to wait; there were more pressing matters to discuss. Some things should just be enjoyed without questioning.

Martin told him about making a fruitless visit to the campground and how they hadn't got anything else useful out of Liese. Then he reported on what Pia had said about Tanja, that she had come in to get some articles about Mona and Siv translated. That was when Patrik's interest perked up.

'I knew there had to be a connection there! But what the heck could it be?' he said, scratching his head.

'What did the parents tell you yesterday?'

The two photographs Patrik had been given by Albert and Gun lay on the desk. He picked them up and handed them to Martin. He described the meeting with Mona's father and Siv's mother, unable to hide his distaste for the latter.

'Still, it must be a relief for them to hear that the girls have finally been found. It must have been torture to go through year after year without knowing where they were. People say that the uncertainty is the worst.'

'Yes, although now I hope that Pedersen confirms that the second skeleton is Siv Lantin, or else we'll really be in hot water.'

'That's true, but the odds are that it's her skeleton. Is there still nothing on the analysis of the dirt found on the bones?'

'No, unfortunately. And I don't know how much that will tell us anyway. They could have been buried anywhere. Even if we identify the type of soil, it's like searching for a needle in a haystack.'

'The DNA is what I'm counting on most. As soon as we have a suspect, we'll know if it's the right person by analysing his DNA and comparing it with what we have.'

'Sure, all we have to do now is find the right person.'

They thought about the case for a while in silence, until Martin broke the dismal mood and stood up.

'Well, we're not going to get anything done just sitting here. I'd better be off to the salt mines again.'

He left a meditative Patrik sitting at his desk.

The mood at dinner was very tense. That was nothing unusual, ever since Linda had moved in, but just now the air was so thick they could cut it with a knife. Her brother had just told them as briefly as possible about Solveig's visit to their father, but he wasn't particularly keen on discussing the subject.

Linda didn't intend to let that stop her. 'So it wasn't Uncle Johannes who murdered those girls after all. Pappa must feel really awful. He fingers his own brother who later turns out to be innocent.'

'Shut your mouth – you shouldn't talk about things you know nothing about.'

Everyone at the table gave a start. Jacob seldom if ever raised his voice. Even Linda felt a bit scared for a moment, but she swallowed hard and went on. 'So why did Pappa think that it was Uncle Johannes anyway? Nobody has ever told me.'

Jacob hesitated a moment but realized that it wouldn't do to tell her to stop asking questions, so he decided to oblige her. At least partly.

'Pappa saw one of the girls in Johannes's car the night she disappeared.'

'Why was Pappa out driving in the middle of the night?'

'He'd been to visit me at the hospital and decided to drive home instead of staying overnight.'

'So that's all it was? That was the reason he reported Johannes to the police? I mean, there must be plenty of other explanations for something like that. Maybe he was giving her a ride part-way home.'

'Could be. Although Johannes denied that he even saw

the girl that night. He claimed that he'd been at home in bed at that hour.'

'But what did Grandpa say? Wasn't he furious when Gabriel called the police about Johannes?'

Linda was totally fascinated. She'd been born after the girls had disappeared and had never heard more than fragments of the story. Nobody ever wanted to talk about what had happened, so most of what Jacob was now saying was completely new to her.

Jacob snorted. 'Was Grandpa angry? You'd better believe it. Besides, he was in hospital at the time, fully engaged with saving my life, so he was furious at Pappa that he could do something like that.'

The children had been sent out of the room. Otherwise their eyes would have sparkled at the mention of how their old grandfather had saved the life of their Pappa. They had heard the story many, many times and never tired of it.

Jacob went on, 'He was so angry that he even considered changing his will and naming Johannes as sole heir, but there was no time for that before Johannes died. If he hadn't died, we might have been the ones living in the forester's cottage, instead of Solveig and the boys.'

'But why did Pappa think so badly of Johannes?'

'Well, I don't really know. Pappa has never been very talkative on the subject, but Grandpa told us a great deal that might explain it. Mamma's father died when Johannes was born, and after that they travelled about with Grandpa when he drove up and down the west coast giving sermons and worship services. Grandpa told me that he understood early on that both Johannes and Gabriel had the power to heal, so each worship service concluded with them healing people with handicaps and illnesses who were in the audience.'

'Pappa did that? Healed people, I mean? Can he still do it?'

Linda's mouth fell open in astonishment. The door to a

whole new room in her family history had been opened wide. She hardly dared breathe for fear that Jacob would clam up and refuse to share what else he knew. She'd heard that he and Grandpa had always had a special bond, especially after it turned out that Grandpa's bone marrow was a perfect match as a donor for Jacob, who was suffering from leukaemia. But Linda hadn't known that Grandpa had told him so much. Naturally, she'd heard that Grandpa was called 'the Preacher' in popular parlance. She'd also heard mutterings that he somehow had swindled his way to his fortune, but she'd never viewed the stories about Ephraim as anything other than exaggerated tales. Linda was so young when he died that he seemed merely a stern older man in the family photographs.

'No, I hardly believe he can.' Jacob smiled a little at the thought of his correct father as a healer of the sick and lame. 'As far as Pappa is concerned, probably nothing ever happened. And according to Grandpa it's not unusual for a person to lose the ability when he enters puberty. It may be possible to regain the ability later, but it's not easy. I believe that both Gabriel and Johannes lost it after they reached adulthood. I think Pappa detested Johannes because they were so different. Johannes was very handsome and could charm the trousers off anyone, but he was hopelessly irresponsible with everything in his life. Both he and Gabriel received a large portion of the money when Grandpa was still alive, but it took only a year before Johannes had run through his share. That made Grandpa furious, and he changed his will making Gabriel his primary heir instead of dividing the inheritance equally between them. But as I mentioned, if he had lived longer he might have changed his mind again.'

'But there must have been something else,' Linda said. 'Pappa couldn't have hated Johannes so much just because he was nicer-looking and more charming. That's no reason to report your brother to the police, is it?'

121

'No, my guess is that the last straw was when Johannes stole Pappa's fiancée.'

'What? Pappa was going to marry Solveig? That fat cow?'

'Haven't you seen pictures of Solveig from the old days? She was a real looker, I have to tell you, and she and Pappa were engaged. But one day she told him that she was in love with Uncle Johannes and that she was going to marry him instead. I think that really devastated Pappa. You know how he hates any kind of disarray or drama in his life.'

'Yes, that must have made him flip out completely.'

Jacob got up from the table as if to signal that the conversation was over. 'Well, that should be enough family secrets for now. But it should make you understand why things are a bit tense between Pappa and Solveig.'

Linda giggled. 'I would have given anything to be a fly on the wall when she showed up to chew Pappa out. What a circus that must have been.'

Even Jacob showed a hint of a smile. 'Yes, circus is probably the right word for it. But try to restrain your mirth when you see Pappa, all right? I don't think he'll see anything funny about it.'

'Okay, okay, I'll be a good girl.'

She set her plate in the dishwasher, thanked Marita for the meal, and went up to her room. It was the first time in ages that she and Jacob had laughed at anything together. He could be really pleasant if he only tried, thought Linda, adroitly ignoring the fact that she hadn't exactly been a bundle of laughs in recent years.

She picked up the phone and tried to get hold of Stefan. To her astonishment she realized that she actually cared about how he was doing.

Laine was afraid of the dark. Terribly afraid. Despite all the evenings she had spent at the farm without Gabriel, she had never got used to it. Before, at least, she'd had Linda at home, and before that Jacob, but now she was all alone. She knew that Gabriel had to travel a good deal, yet she couldn't help feeling bitter. This wasn't the life she had dreamt of when she married into wealth. Not that the money was so important in and of itself; a sense of security was what had enticed her. The security she found in Gabriel's predictable nature and the security of knowing there was money in the bank. She wanted to lead a life completely different from her mother's.

As a girl she had lived in terror of her father's drunken rages. He had tyrannized the whole family and turned his children into people who felt insecure and thirsted for love and tenderness. Of the three siblings, she was the only one left. Both her brother and her sister had succumbed to the darkness within them, one by turning the darkness inwards, the other by turning it outwards. Laine was the middle child who had done neither. She was merely insecure and weak. Not strong enough to act out her insecurity either internally or externally; she just left it to fester, year after year.

This was most evident when she wandered alone through the silent rooms in the evenings. That was when she clearly recalled the stinking breath, the beatings and the clandestine caresses at night.

She had truly believed that she had finally found the key to unlock the dark place inside her heart when she married Gabriel. But she wasn't stupid. She knew that she was a consolation prize. He had settled for her because he couldn't have the one he really wanted. But that made no difference. In a way it was easier this way. There were no feelings that might ruffle the calm surface. Only boring predictability in the endless chain of days. She thought it was all she wanted.

Thirty-five years later she knew how wrong she had been. Nothing was worse than being alone while married. That was what she got when she said 'I do' in Fjällbacka Church.

They had lived parallel lives. Tended the farm, brought up their children, and talked about the wind and weather in the absence of other topics of conversation.

She alone knew that there was another man inside Gabriel than the one he showed to the world every day. Over the years she had observed him, studying him in secret, and gradually she came to know the man he could have been. It astonished her what longing that had awakened inside her. Behind that boring, reserved exterior was a passionate man, but he was buried so deep that she didn't think he even realized it himself. She saw a lot of anger gathering, but believed there was an equal amount of love, if only she'd had the ability to coax it forth.

Even when Jacob lay sick they hadn't been able to approach each other. Side by side they had sat with their son, assuming that Jacob was on his deathbed, and yet they could offer each other no consolation. She'd often had the feeling that Gabriel didn't really want her there.

Gabriel's uncommunicativeness could be blamed in large part on his father. Ephraim Hult had been an imposing man who made everyone with whom he came in contact join one of two camps: friend or foe. No one was unimportant to the Preacher, but Laine understood how difficult it must have been to grow up in the shadow of such a man. His sons couldn't have been more different. Johannes was like a big baby his entire life, brief though it was. He was a hedonist who took what he wanted and never paused long enough to notice the chaos he left in his wake. Gabriel had chosen the opposite course. Laine had seen how ashamed he was of his father and Johannes, of their sweeping gestures, their ability to shine like a beacon in any setting. Gabriel wanted to disappear behind an anonymity that would show the world that he had nothing in common with his father. Gabriel strove for respectability, order and justice more than anything else. He never talked about his childhood and the years he spent travelling with Ephraim and Johannes. Laine knew a little about it, though, and she understood how important it was for her husband to hide that part of his past, which was so discordant with the image he wanted to project to the outside world. The fact that it was Ephraim who had brought Jacob back to life had aroused mixed feelings in Gabriel. His joy at finding a way to vanquish Jacob's illness had been clouded by the fact that it was his father, and not himself, who was the knight in shining armour who came to the rescue. He would have given anything for the chance to be his son's hero.

Laine's meditations were interrupted by a sound from outside. Out of the corner of her eye she saw a shadow, then two, rapidly passing through the garden. Terror seized her once again. She went searching for the cordless phone and managed to work herself into a panic before she finally found it in its place in the charger. With trembling fingers she dialled the number of Gabriel's mobile. Something struck the window and she screamed. The window was shattered by a rock, which now lay among shards of glass on the floor. Another rock came through the window next to it. With a sob she dashed out of the room and upstairs, where she locked herself in the bathroom while she desperately waited to hear Gabriel's voice. Instead she got the monotone of a mobile phone voicemail, and she heard the terror in her own voice when she left an incoherent message for him.

Shaking, she sat down on the floor with her arms tightly wrapped round her knees and listened for sounds outside the door. Nothing more was heard, but she didn't dare budge from the spot.

When morning came she was still sitting there.

The ring of the telephone woke Erica. She glanced at the clock. Ten thirty in the morning. She must have dozed off after tossing and turning half the night, sweating and uncomfortable.

'Hello.' Her voice was heavy with sleep.

'Hi, Erica. Sorry, did I wake you?'

'Yes, but it doesn't matter, Anna. I shouldn't be lying down to sleep in the middle of the morning like this anyway.'

'Sure you should – sleep as much as you can. Soon sleep will be a luxury. How are you feeling, anyway?'

Erica took a moment to grumble about all the hardships of pregnancy to her sister, who knew exactly what Erica was talking about having two kids of her own.

'You poor thing . . . the only consolation is that you know it will pass, sooner or later. How's it going having Patrik around the house? Aren't you getting on each other's nerves? I remember that I just wanted to be left in peace the last few weeks.'

'I know what you mean. I was almost climbing the walls, I have to admit. So I didn't object too loudly when he got a homicide case and he had to go in and work.'

'A murder case? What happened?'

Erica told her about the young German woman who'd been murdered and the two missing women that were now found.

'Jesus, that's terrible.' The connection crackled.

'Where are you, anyway? Are you having a good time on the boat?'

'Yeah, we're having a great time. Emma and Adrian love it, and they're going to be full-fledged sailors soon if Gustav has anything to say about it.'

'Ah, Gustav. How's it going between the two of you? Will he be ready to present to the family soon?'

'That's actually why I'm calling. We're in Strömstad now and thought we'd sail down to your neck of the woods. Be sure to tell me if you're not up for it – otherwise we planned to stop in Fjällbacka tomorrow and come by to say hello. We're sleeping on the boat, so we won't be any trouble. Just say the word if you think it's too much. It would just be so great to see you.'

'Of course you can come by. We're having Dan and his girlfriend over for a barbecue tomorrow, so it's no trouble to sling a couple of extra burgers on the grill.'

'Oh, that's cool, then I can finally meet the lambchop.'

'Listen, Anna. Patrik has already been after *me* to be nice, so don't you start in too . . .'

'Okay, but it does require a little extra preparation. We have to check on what sort of music is in with the kids today and which styles are hot and whether flavoured lip gloss is still popular. Here's the plan: if you check out MTV, I'll pick up that teen magazine *Weekly Review* and do a little research. Is *Starlet* still publishing, do you think? If it is, that would probably be a good idea too.'

Erica was holding her stomach, she was laughing so hard. 'Stop it, I'm dying. Now be nice . . . You shouldn't throw stones in glass houses, you know. We haven't met Gustav, so as far as we know, he might be a real geek. You remember the pastor from that film, don't you? The one who starts working with real lowlifes?'

'Well, I don't know if "geek" is quite the right word I would associate with Gustav.'

Erica could hear that her joking comment had made Anna turn grumpy. To think that her sister could be so thin-skinned.

'I consider myself lucky that someone like Gustav, with his social standing, even looks in my direction, single mother and all. He could have his pick of the girls on the debutante list, yet he chose me, and I think that says a good deal about him.'

Erica also thought that said a great deal about him, but unfortunately not in the way her sister had intended. Anna had never been a very good judge of men, and the way she was talking about Gustav sounded a bit worrisome. But Erica decided not to judge him in advance. Hopefully her misgivings would come to naught as soon as she had a chance to meet him.

She said cheerfully, 'When will you be here?'

'Around four. Is that all right?'

'That's perfect.'

'I'll see you then. Hugs. Bye.'

After Erica hung up she felt a bit concerned. There was something in Anna's forced tone of voice that made her wonder how good her relationship with the fantastic, upper-class Gustav af Klint really was for Anna.

She'd been glad when Anna divorced Lucas Maxwell, the children's father. Anna had then gone back to her dream of studying art and antiquities, and she'd had the great good fortune to find a part-time job at the Stockholm Auction Association. That's where she had met Gustav. He came from one of Sweden's most blue-blooded families. He spent his time administering the family estate in Hälsingland, which back in the sixteenth century had been conferred upon one of his ancestors by King Gustav Vasa. His family mixed socially with the royal family, and if his father was busy, Gustav instead would sometimes be sent the invitation to the King's annual hunt. Awestruck, Anna had related all this to her sister. Erica felt a bit uneasy, having seen a bit too much of the upper-class louts who frequented the clubs around Stureplan. She had never met Gustav, so perhaps he was different from the rich heirs who, safe behind their wealth and titles, chose to behave like swine in places such as the Riche and the Spy Bar. She would find out tomorrow. She crossed her fingers that she was wrong and that Gustav would be of a completely different calibre. There was nobody who deserved happiness and stability more than Anna.

Erica turned on the fan and thought about how she was

going to spend her day. Her midwife had explained that the hormone oxytocin, more of which is secreted as a woman approaches the time of delivery, creates strong nesting instincts in pregnant women. That explained why Erica in recent weeks had been almost manically sorting, numbering and cataloguing everything in their home as if her life depended on it. She was obsessed with the idea that every- thing had to be ready and in order before the baby arrived. But now she had reached a stage where there wasn't much more to organize in the house. The wardrobes were cleaned, the nursery was ready, and the silverware drawers had been tidied. The only thing left to put in order was the cellar, which was filled with junk. No sooner said than done. She got up, puffing, and resolutely stuck the table fan under her arm. She'd better hurry before Patrik discovered what she was doing.

He'd taken a five-minute break to sit outside the police station and have a choc-ice, when Gösta stuck his head out of one of the open windows and shouted to him.

'Patrik, there's a call for you. I think you should take it.'

Patrik quickly finished his Magnum and went inside. He picked up the receiver on Gösta's desk and was a little surprised to hear who it was. After a brief conversation while he jotted down some notes, he hung up. To Gösta, who had been watching him from his office chair, he said, 'As you heard, somebody has broken the windows at Gabriel Hult's house. Do you want to come along and take a look?'

Gösta seemed surprised that Patrik asked him instead of Martin, but he nodded.

As they came up the front drive a few minutes later, they couldn't help emitting envious sighs. The manor house where Gabriel Hult resided was truly magnificent. It shimmered like a white pearl in the middle of all the greenery, and the alders lining the road to the house bent deferentially in the wind. Patrik thought that Ephraim Hult must have been a real genius of a preacher to be given such splendour.

Even the crunching of the gravel beneath their feet as they walked up the path to the front steps sounded luxurious. He was very curious to see the inside of the house.

It was Gabriel himself who opened the door. Both Patrik and Gösta wiped their feet carefully on the doormat before they entered the foyer.

'Thanks for coming so quickly. My wife is very upset about all this. I was out of town on business last night, so she was at home alone when it happened.'

As he spoke he led the way to a large, lovely room, with high windows that let in as much sunshine as possible. On a white sofa sat a woman with a worried expression on her face. She rose to greet them as they entered the room.

'Laine Hult. I'm grateful you could come so promptly.'

She sat down again, and Gabriel motioned Patrik and Gösta to take a seat on the opposite sofa. Both of them felt slightly out of place. Neither of them dressed up to go to work so they were wearing shorts. Patrik at least had on a nice T-shirt, while Gösta was wearing a very old short-sleeved shirt made of some synthetic material with a mint-green pattern. The contrast was even greater since Laine was wearing a light dress in natural-coloured linen while Gabriel was dressed in a business suit. Must be hot, thought Patrik, hoping that Gabriel didn't always have to wear clothes like that in the summer heat. But it was pretty hard to imagine him in anything less formal, and he didn't even seem to be sweating in his dark-blue suit. Patrik, on the other hand, was getting wet under the arms just thinking about wearing that sort of outfit this time of year.

'Your husband told me briefly on the phone what happened, but perhaps you could tell me in more detail?'

Patrik gave Laine a reassuring smile as he took out his little notebook and a pen. He waited.

'Well, I was at home by myself yesterday. Gabriel is often out travelling, so there are quite a few solitary nights for me.'

Patrik heard the sadness in her voice when she said that, and wondered whether Gabriel did too.

'I know it's foolish,' she went on, 'but I'm very afraid of the dark, so I usually stay in two rooms when I'm by myself, my bedroom and the TV room, which is right next door.'

Patrik noticed that she said 'my' bedroom and couldn't help reflecting on how deplorable it was that married couples didn't even sleep in the same bed. That would never happen to him and Erica.

'I was just about to ring Gabriel when I saw something moving outside. The next instant something came flying through one of the windows at the end of the house, to the left of where I was standing. I managed to see that it was a big rock before another one broke the window next to it. Then I heard only the sound of running feet outside, and I saw two shadows disappear at the edge of the forest.'

Patrik took notes using brief keywords. Gösta hadn't said a thing since they arrived, other than his name when he was introduced to Gabriel and Laine. Patrik gave him an enquiring look to see whether he wanted to have anything clarified regarding the incident, but he sat in silence, carefully studying his cuticles. I could just as well have brought along a doorstop, Patrik thought.

'Do you have any idea of a possible motive?'

The reply came quickly from Gabriel, almost as if he wanted to ward off something that Laine might say.

'No, nothing other than good old envy. It has always been a thorn in the side that my family lives here at the manor, and we've experienced a number of drunken attacks over

131

the years. Just innocent pranks. And that's how this would have ended too, if my wife hadn't insisted on calling in the police.'

He cast an ill-humoured glance at Laine, who for the first time during the conversation showed a little energy and angrily glared back. The defiance of her action seemed to ignite a smouldering spark in her. To Patrik she said calmly, without even a glance at her husband, 'I think you should have a talk with Robert and Stefan Hult, my husband's nephews, and ask them where they were yesterday.'

'Laine, that is quite unnecessary!'

'You weren't here, so you don't know how horrid it is to have rocks come flying through your window just a few feet away. They could have hit me. And you know as well as I do that it was those two idiots who did it.'

Gabriel spoke through clenched teeth, his jaw muscles visibly tensed. 'Laine, we agreed – '

'*You* agreed!' She ignored him and turned to Patrik, fortified by her own unusual show of defiance.

'As I said, I didn't see them, but I could swear that it was Stefan and Robert. Their mother, Solveig, was here earlier in the day, and she behaved very unpleasantly. Those two are real bad eggs, as you already know. You've undoubtedly dealt with them before.'

She gestured towards Patrik and Gösta, who could do nothing but nod in agreement. Of course they'd had dealings with the notorious Hult brothers, and at an alarming rate, ever since they were no more than pimply teenagers.

Laine gave Gabriel another withering look as if to see whether he dared contradict her, but he merely shrugged his shoulders in resignation. It was a gesture that indicated he was washing his hands of the matter.

'What caused the row with their mother?' asked Patrik.

'Not that someone like her needs much of an excuse. She has always hated us, but what really made her lose it yesterday

132

was the news about the bodies you found in the King's Cleft. With her limited intelligence Solveig made it sound like it proved that her husband Johannes had been innocently accused, and she blamed Gabriel for it.'

Her voice rose with agitation and she pointed at her husband, who now looked as if he'd mentally retreated from the whole conversation.

'I've gone through the old papers from when the girls went missing,' said Patrik. 'I saw that you reported your brother to the police as a suspect. Could you tell us a little about that?'

Gabriel flinched almost imperceptibly, a little tell-tale sign that the question bothered him, but his voice sounded calm when he replied.

'It was many, many years ago. But if you're asking whether I still maintain that I saw my brother with Siv Lantin, then the answer is yes. I'd been at the hospital in Uddevalla, visiting my son who was then sick with leukaemia, and I was driving home. On the way up to Bräcke I saw my brother's car. I thought it was a bit odd for him to be out driving in the middle of the night, so I looked more closely. That's when I saw the girl sitting in the passenger seat with her head leaning on my brother's shoulder. It looked like she was asleep.'

'How did you know it was Siv?'

'I didn't. But I recognized her again the moment I saw her picture in the paper. I'd like to point out that I never said my brother murdered those girls, the way people here in town would have you believe. All I did was report that I saw him with the girl named Siv, because I considered it my civic duty. It had nothing to do with any conflict between the two of us, or revenge, as some have claimed. I told the police what I saw. As for what it meant, I left that up to the authorities to find out. And obviously they never found any evidence against Johannes, so I think this whole discussion is beside the point.'

'But what did *you* think?' said Patrik with a curious glance at Gabriel. He was having a hard time understanding how anyone could be so conscientious that he would finger his own brother.

'I don't speculate; I stick to the facts.'

'But you knew your brother well. Do you think he would have been capable of murder?'

'My brother and I didn't have much in common. Sometimes I was amazed that we shared the same genes, we were so unlike each other. You ask whether I think he was capable of taking someone's life?' Gabriel threw out his hands. 'I don't really know. I didn't know my brother well enough to be able to answer that question. And it seems to be superfluous now anyway, considering the latest developments, don't you think?'

With that he considered the discussion over and he got up from the armchair. Patrik and Gösta took the hint, thanked him for his time and left.

'What do you say, shall we go have a chat with the boys about their activities last night?'

The question was rhetorical, and Patrik had already started driving towards Stefan and Robert's house without waiting for Gösta to reply. The older man's lack of participation during the interview annoyed him. What would it take to shake some life into the old fogey? It's true he didn't have much time left until he retired, but until then, damn it, he was on duty and was expected to do his job.

'Well, what's your take on all this?' The irritation in Patrik's voice was clear.

'Well, I don't know which alternative is worse. That we have a murderer who's killed at least three girls in the past twenty years, and we have no idea who he is. Or that it really was Johannes Hult who tortured and murdered Siv and Mona and that we now have a copycat. To follow up on the first alternative, we should probably check with the prison register. Is there anyone who was incarcerated after Siv and Mona disappeared and then released before the murder of the German girl? That would explain the break between the killings.' Gösta's tone was thoughtful, and Patrik looked at him in amazement. The old guy wasn't as lost in the fog as he'd thought.

'That should be pretty easy to check out. We don't have many prisoners in Sweden that have served a twenty-year sentence. Will you check on it when we get back to the station?'

Gösta nodded and then sat in silence, looking out the side window.

The track leading to the old forester's cabin grew worse and worse. As the crow flies, it was only a short distance between Gabriel and Laine's residence and the little cabin where Solveig and her sons lived. But it was a considerably longer distance in social standing. The place looked like a junkyard: three ramshackle cars in varying states of disrepair looked as if they'd been flung there and there was a lot of refuse of indeterminate character. The family were obviously packrats. Patrik suspected that if he rummaged about he might also find a good deal of stolen goods that had been reported missing from summer-cabin break-ins in the area. But that's not why they were here today. It was a matter of choosing one's battles.

Robert came towards them from a shed where he'd been tinkering with one of the old wrecked cars. He was dressed in dirty work coveralls of a washed-out denim. Oil covered his hands, and he had apparently rubbed his face, leaving behind streaks and flecks of oil. He wiped his hands on a rag as he came to meet them.

'What the hell do you want now? If you're looking for something here I'm going to have to see the proper documents before you can touch anything.' His tone was familiar.

And justifiably so, since they had met on many occasions over the years.

Patrik held up his hands. 'Take it easy. We're not looking for anything. We just want to have a little talk.'

Robert gave them a suspicious look but then nodded.

'And we want to talk to your brother too. Is he here?'

Reluctantly Robert nodded again and yelled towards the house, 'Stefan, the cops are here. They want to talk to us!'

'How about if we go inside and sit down?'

Without waiting for a reply, Patrik headed towards the door with Gösta following close behind. Robert had no other choice but to follow. He didn't bother taking off his work overalls or washing his hands. After staging previous raids, Patrik knew that there was no reason to do so. Filth clung to everything in the house. Many years before, the cabin had no doubt been very cosy, if small. But years of neglect had taken their toll, and now the place was a disaster zone. The wallpaper was a dismal brown, with loose patches and plenty of spots. Besides the dirt, everything seemed to be covered with a thin film of grease.

The two detectives nodded to Solveig, who was sitting at the rickety kitchen table, busy with her photo albums. Her dark hair hung in limp strands along her face, and when she nervously brushed the fringe out of her eyes, her fingers shone with grease. Unconsciously, Patrik wiped his hands on his shorts and then sat down cautiously on the very edge of a straight-backed chair. Stefan came out from one of the adjoining little rooms and sullenly sat down next to his brother and mother on the kitchen bench. When they sat in a row Patrik could see the family resemblance. Solveig's former beauty was preserved like an echo in the faces of her sons. According to what Patrik had heard, Johannes had been a handsome fellow, and if his sons would straighten their backs they would look fairly decent. But there was a volatility about them that hinted at a slightly slippery temperament.

'Dishonesty' was probably the word that Patrik was searching for. If someone's appearance could be dishonest, then that description would certainly apply to Robert. Patrik still held out a little hope for Stefan. On the occasions when they had run into each other officially, the younger boy had always presented a less hardened veneer than his brother. Sometimes Patrik could sense an ambivalence in him about the path in life he had chosen, following in Robert's wake. It was a shame that Robert exerted such an influence on him, otherwise Stefan might have had a completely different life. But it was probably too late for that.

'What the hell do you want now?' Stefan asked the same surly question as his brother.

'We'd just like to hear what you were doing last night. Were the two of you out visiting your aunt and uncle and amusing yourselves with a little rock-throwing?'

A conspiratorial glance passed between the brothers before they put on a mask of utter ignorance.

'No, why would we do that? We were at home all evening yesterday, weren't we, Mamma?'

They both turned to Solveig, who nodded. She had closed the album temporarily and now sat listening attentively to the conversation between her sons and the police.

'Yes, both of them were here last night. We were watching TV together. We had a nice family evening.' She didn't even bother concealing her sarcasm.

'And Stefan and Robert didn't go out for a little while? Say, around ten o'clock?'

'No, they weren't gone even a minute. Didn't even go to the loo, as far as I remember.' Still the same sarcastic tone of voice, and her sons couldn't help sniggering. 'So somebody broke a couple of windows at their house last night. That must have scared the shit out of them.'

The sniggering now turned into a chorus that made Patrik think of Beavis and Butthead.

137

'No, just your aunt, actually. Gabriel was out of town yesterday, so she was alone in the house.'

Disappointment was written across their faces. They had probably hoped to scare both of them, and they hadn't reckoned with Gabriel not being at home.

'I heard that you also paid them a little visit at the manor house yesterday, Solveig. And some threats were made. Do you have anything to say about that?' It was Gösta who asked the question. Patrik as well as the Hult brothers stared at him in astonishment.

Solveig gave a vulgar laugh. 'So, they said I threatened them, did they? Well, I didn't say anything that they didn't deserve. It was Gabriel who fingered my husband as a murderer. He was the one who took my husband's life, just as if he had tied the noose himself.'

A muscle twitched in Robert's face at the mention of the way his father had died. Patrik recalled at once what he'd read: that it was Robert who had found his father after he hanged himself.

Solveig continued her harangue. 'Gabriel always hated Johannes. He'd been jealous of him ever since they were little. Johannes was everything that his brother was not, and Gabriel knew it. Ephraim always favoured Johannes, and in a way I understand. Naturally you should never favour one child over another,' she said, nodding at the boys seated next to her on the bench. 'But Gabriel was a cold fish, while Johannes was full of life. I should know; I was engaged first to one and then the other. It was impossible to get Gabriel excited about anything. He was always so damned proper. He said we had to wait until we were married. It got on my nerves. Then his brother came along and began hovering about, and that was something completely different. Those hands of his could be all over you at once. He made me burn with lust just by looking at me.' She chuckled and stared into space, as if she were reliving her hot nights of youth.

'Damn it, will you shut up, Mamma?'

Disgust was visible on her sons' faces. They obviously wanted to be spared the details of their mother's amorous past. Patrik pictured a naked Solveig, her greasy body writhing in passion, and he had to blink to get rid of the image.

'As soon as I heard about the girl who was murdered, and they'd found Siv and Mona too, I went over there to give them a real piece of my mind. Out of sheer envy and nastiness, Gabriel destroyed Johannes. He destroyed our lives too, me and the boys, but now the truth is finally staring people in the face. Now they'll be ashamed and realize that they listened to the wrong brother. And I hope Gabriel burns in hell for his sins!'

She had begun to work herself up to the same rage she had displayed the day before. Stefan placed a soothing and admonitory hand on her arm.

'Well, no matter what the reason, you can't go around threatening people. And you shouldn't throw rocks through people's windows, either!' Patrik pointed at Robert and Stefan. He didn't for an instant believe their mother's story that they'd been at home in front of the TV. They knew that he knew, and now he was warning them that he'd be keeping an eye on them. They just mumbled in reply.

But Solveig seemed to ignore the warning. Her cheeks were still red with fury.

'For that matter, Gabriel isn't the only one who should be ashamed! When are we going to get an apology from the police? The way you ran around at Västergården turning everything upside down. And you took Johannes away in a police car for questioning. You did your part in sending him to his death. Isn't it about time to beg my forgiveness?'

For the second time Gösta spoke up. 'Until we figure out

exactly what happened to those three girls, there won't be any begging forgiveness for anything. And until we get to the bottom of this, I want you to behave like decent folks, Solveig.'

The firmness in Gösta's voice seemed to come from some unexpected place.

Back out in the car, Patrik asked in surprise, 'Do you and Solveig know each other?'

Gösta grunted. 'Depends what you mean by "know". She's the same age as my youngest brother and was over at our house a good deal when we were boys. By the time she reached her teens, everybody knew about Solveig. She was the prettiest girl in the district, I must tell you, even though it's hard to believe, the way she looks now. Yep, it's a darned shame. To think that things could turn out so badly for her and the boys.' He shook his head with regret. 'And I can't even say that she's right about Johannes dying an innocent man. We really don't know a damn thing!'

In frustration he pounded his thigh with his fist. Patrik thought it was like seeing a bear wake up from a long hibernation.

'Are you going to check the prisons when we get back?'

'Yeah, yeah, I already told you! I'm not so old that I can't understand an order the first time I hear it. Here I am, taking orders from a whippersnapper who's barely dry behind the ears . . .' Gösta stared dismally out the windscreen.

They still had a long way to go, Patrik thought wearily.

By Saturday Erica realized she was looking forward to having Patrik at home again. He'd promised to take the weekend off, and now they were putting out in their 13-foot wooden boat towards the skerries. They'd been fortunate to find a boat that was almost exactly like the *snipa* that Erica's father Tore had owned. It was the only type of boat she could imagine having. She'd never really been big on sailing, despite a couple of outings in sailing school, and a fibreglass motor-boat went faster, of course, but who was in a hurry?

The sound of the *snipa*'s motor was for her the sound of her childhood. As a little girl she had often slept on the warm wooden floor, with the lulling throb of the motor in her ears. These days she preferred to climb up and sit on the raised prow in front of the windscreen, but in her present, less-than-graceful condition she didn't dare. Instead she sat on one of the thwarts behind the protective panes. Patrik stood at the tiller, with the wind in his brown hair and a smile on his face. They had set out early to get there before the tourists, and the air was fresh and clear. A fine spray showered the boat from time to time, and Erica could taste the salt in the air she was inhaling. It was hard to imagine that inside her she was carrying a tiny person who, within a couple of years, would be sitting beside Patrik in the stern, dressed in a baggy orange life-jacket with a big collar, just as she had done so many times with her father.

Erica's eyes began to smart at the thought that her father would never get to meet his grandchild. Nor would her mother, but since she had never really cared about Erica or Anna it seemed unlikely that another grandchild would have aroused much feeling in her. Especially since her mother had always acted unnaturally stiff when she met Anna's children. She would give them an awkward hug if the situation and the company seemed to require it. Bitterness welled up inside Erica again, but she swallowed hard to repress it. In her darker moments she was afraid that motherhood would prove to be just as burdensome for her as it had been for Elsy – that with one fell stroke she would turn into her cold and inaccessible mother. The logical part of her brain said that it was ridiculous even to have such thoughts, but fear was not logical. On the other hand, Anna was a warm and loving mother to Emma and Adrian, so why shouldn't Erica be one too? That was how she tried to reassure herself. At least she had chosen the right father for the child, she thought as she gazed at Patrik. His steadfast calm and confidence offset her own restlessness in a way that nobody had done before. He was going to be a splendid father.

They went ashore in a little protected cove and spread out their towels on the bare, flat rock. This is what she had missed when she lived in Stockholm. The archipelago there was so different, with all its woods and underbrush. In some way it had always felt jumbled and intrusive. A flooded garden, as West Coasters contemptuously called it. The islands were so pure in their bare simplicity. The pink and grey granite reflected the crystalline water against the heartrending loveliness of a cloudless sky. Tiny flowers growing in the rock crevices were the only vegetation, and in this barren setting their beauty could be fully appreciated. Erica closed her eyes and felt herself slip away into pleasant slumber to the sound of the lapping water and the boat lightly tapping against its mooring.

When Patrik gently woke her she didn't quite know at first where she was. The sharp sunlight blinded her for a few seconds when she opened her eyes, and Patrik was just a dark shadow looming over her. When she got her bearings she realized that she had slept for almost two hours. Now she was ravenous to eat the snack they had brought along.

They poured coffee from the thermos into big mugs and ate the cinnamon buns. Nowhere did food taste so good as out on an island, and they enjoyed it to the fullest. But Erica couldn't help taking up the forbidden topic of discussion again.

'How's it going for you guys, anyway?'

'So-so. One step forwards and two steps back.' Patrik's reply was curt. It was obvious that he didn't want the evil that regularly insinuated its way into his work to invade this sun-drenched peacefulness.

But Erica's curiosity was too great, and she couldn't help trying to find out a little more. 'Were those articles I found of any use? Do you think the whole thing is about the Hult family? Or was Johannes just unlucky to be drawn into it?'

Patrik sighed as he sat with the coffee mug in his hands. 'If only I knew. The whole Hult family feels like a darned hornets' nest, and I would really prefer not to root around in their affairs. But there's something that doesn't seem quite right. Whether it has to do with the murders or not, I don't know. Maybe it's the thought that the police may have contributed to an innocent person committing suicide that makes me hope there was some basis for our suspicions. After all, Gabriel's testimony was the only sensible lead the police had when the girls went missing. But we can't focus on that alone; we have to do a broad search.' He paused for a few seconds and then went on. 'I'd really prefer not to talk about this. Right now it feels as though I need to disconnect from everything that has to do with murder and think about something else.'

She nodded. 'I promise not to ask any more questions. Another bun?'

He didn't say no, and after a couple of hours of reading and sunning themselves on the island, they saw by the clock that they should be getting home to prepare for the arrival of their guests. At the last minute they had decided to invite Patrik's father and his wife as well, so besides the children there were eight adults who would have to be fed from the grill.

Gabriel always grew restless on the weekend when he was expected to relax and not work. The problem was that he didn't know what to do when he wasn't working. Work was his life. He had no free-time interests, no desire to spend time with his wife, and by now the children had moved out, even though Linda's situation might be open to discussion. The result was that he usually locked himself in his office with his nose buried in the account books. Numbers were the one thing that he understood in life. Unlike people with their troublesome emotions and irrationality, numbers obeyed strict rules. He could always rely on them. He felt comfortable in their world. It didn't take a genius to understand where this craving for order and clarity came from. Gabriel himself had long ascribed it to his chaotic childhood, but it was nothing that he ever dwelled on. His need for order had served him well; the origin of the craving had consequently little or no significance.

His time on the road with the Preacher was something he tried not to think about. But when he did recall his childhood, the image of his father as the Preacher always popped up. A faceless, terror-inducing figure who filled their days with shrieking, jabbering, and hysterical people. Men and women who tried to grab him and Johannes. Who seized them with their clawlike hands, trying to get them to alleviate whatever physical or mental pain plagued them. Who believed that he and his brother had the answer to their prayers. A direct channel to God.

Johannes had loved those years. He had basked in the attention and gladly put himself in the spotlight. Sometimes Gabriel had come upon him gazing at his hands in fascination at night when they went to bed, as if to try and see the source of all the wondrous miracles.

Gabriel had felt an enormous gratitude when the gift vanished, but Johannes had been disconsolate. He couldn't deal with the fact that now he was merely an ordinary boy with no special gift; he was just like everybody else. He had wept and beseeched the Preacher to help him regain the gift. But that life was over, said their father curtly, and

144

another would be starting. Inscrutable were the ways of the Lord.

When they moved into the manor house outside Fjällbacka, the Preacher became Ephraim, not Father, in Gabriel's eyes, and he loved that new life from the first moment. Not because he grew closer to his father – Johannes had always been the favourite and that's what he continued to be – but because he had finally found a home. A place where he could stay, a setting around which he could order his life, with strokes of the clock to follow and times to respect. A school to attend. He also loved the farm and dreamed about being able to run it someday the way he wished. He knew that he would be a better manager than either Ephraim or Johannes, and in the evenings he prayed that his father would not make the mistake of letting his favourite son take over the farm when they grew up. It didn't matter to him if Johannes got all the love and attention, as long as he, Gabriel, got the farm.

And that was what happened. But not in the way he had imagined. In his imaginary world Johannes had always been there too. Not until he died did Gabriel understand the need he had for his carefree brother; he needed to worry about Johannes and he needed to rage at him. And yet Gabriel could not have acted otherwise.

He had asked Laine to keep quiet about the fact that they assumed it was Stefan and Robert who had thrown the rocks through the windows. That had surprised him. Had he begun to lose his feeling for law and order, or did he subconsciously have guilty feelings about the family's fate? He didn't know, but afterwards he was grateful that Laine chose to defy him and tell the police everything. But that too had astonished him. In his eyes, his wife was more of a shrill, loose-jointed nodding doll rather than a human being with her own will. He had been shocked by the acrimony in her tone of voice and the spite that he saw in her eyes. It had disturbed him

145

greatly. With all that had happened in the past week, he felt as though his entire world order was about to be altered. For a man who detested change, it was a frightening vision of the future. Gabriel retreated even farther into the world of numbers.

The first guests arrived punctually. Patrik's father Lars and his wife Bittan came on the dot at four, bringing flowers and a bottle of wine for their hosts. Patrik's father was a big, tall man with a large paunch. His wife of twenty years was petite and short and round as a little ball. But it suited her, and the laugh lines around her eyes showed an ever-present readiness to smile. Erica knew that Patrik in many ways found it was easier to get along with Bittan than with his own mother, Kristina, who was a much more abrupt and strict sort of person. The divorce had been bitter, but over time a peace accord had been established between Lars and Kristina, though they would never be friends. They could even get along in social situations occasionally. But it was still simpler to invite each of them separately. Since Kristina was in Göteborg at the moment visiting Patrik's younger sister, there was no reason to worry that they had only invited Lars and Bittan to the barbecue.

Fifteen minutes later, Dan and Maria arrived. They had scarcely taken their seats out in the garden and politely greeted Lars and Bittan, before Erica heard her niece Emma calling from the slope leading up towards the house. She went to meet them, and after hugging the kids she was introduced to the new man in Anna's life.

'Hello, how nice to meet you at last!'

She held out her hand to greet Gustav af Klint. The first impression confirmed her prejudices. He looked exactly like the other young, upper-class Östermalm men who hung out at the clubs around Stureplan in Stockholm. Dark hair slicked

146

back. Shirt and trousers in a deceptively casual style, but Erica had some idea of their price, as well as the obligatory jumper draped over his shoulders. She had to remind herself not to judge him in advance. He had barely opened his mouth when she was already heaping scorn on him in her mind. For a second, she wondered worriedly whether it was sheer envy that made her bristle whenever she had to deal with someone who'd been born with a silver spoon in his mouth. She hoped that wasn't true.

'So how's Auntie's baby? Are you being nice to your mamma?'

Her sister put her ear to Erica's belly to listen for an answer to her question. Then she laughed and gave her sister a big hug. After Patrik had been given one too, they were steered out to the rest of the guests in the garden and introduced. The children were let loose in the garden, while the grown-ups drank wine, or cola in Erica's case, and the meat was put on the grill. As usual, the males gathered round the barbecue, feeling like he-men while the women sat and talked. Erica had never understood the thing about men and barbecuing. Men who would normally claim to have no idea how to cook a piece of meat in a frying pan regarded them-selves as complete virtuosos when it came to getting the meat exactly right on an outdoor grill. Women might be entrusted to provide the side dishes, and they also functioned as excel-lent beer-fetchers.

'God, what a lovely place you have here!' Maria was already into her second glass of wine, while the others had scarcely begun to sip their first.

'Thank you. Yes, we like it.'

Erica had a hard time displaying any warmth towards Dan's girlfriend. She couldn't understand what he saw in her, especially compared to his ex-wife Pernilla. She suspected that it was another one of those mysteries about men that women couldn't comprehend. The only thing she knew for sure was that he hadn't chosen Maria for her conversational ability. Apparently, though, Maria aroused maternal instincts in Bittan, who was paying some extra attention to her. That left Anna and Erica to talk to each other.

'He's so cute,' said Anna, looking at Gustav in admiration. 'Imagine that a guy like that is interested in me!'

Erica looked at her beautiful younger sister and wondered how a person like Anna could lose her self-confidence so completely. Once she had been a strong, independent, free soul, but the years with Lucas and all his abuse had broken her spirit. Erica had to restrain a desire to shake her. She looked at Emma and Adrian chasing wildly round them and wondered how her sister could help feeling pride and self-esteem when she saw what fine children she had raised. Despite everything they had been through in their short lives, they were happy and strong, and they loved their family and friends. And that was all thanks to Anna.

'I haven't had much chance to talk to him yet,' said Erica, 'but he seems nice. I'll have to get back to you with a more detailed evaluation after I've got to know him better. But it sounds as though things went well when you were cooped up in a little sailboat together. That bodes well, I should think.' Her smile felt stiff and pasted on.

'I wouldn't exactly call it a little sailboat,' said Anna with a laugh. 'He borrowed a friend's Najad 400. There was enough room for a small army.'

Their talk was interrupted when the meat was brought to the table, and the male half of the party sat down with them, pleased at having performed the modern equivalent of slaughtering a sabre-toothed tiger.

'And what are you girls sitting here babbling about?'

Dan put his arm round Maria, who cuddled up to him. The cuddle developed into a regular clinch. Even though it had been years since Erica and Dan had been together, she didn't

148

appreciate the sight of those two in a lip-lock. Gustav also looked disapproving but, Erica couldn't help noticing, out of the corner of his eye he was careful to scope out Maria's deep décolletage.

'Lars, don't pour so much sauce on your meat. You know you have to watch your weight because of your heart.'

'What do you mean, I'm as strong as a horse! All this is pure muscle,' Patrik's father announced loudly, slapping his paunch. 'And Erica said that there's olive oil in the sauce, so it's good for me. Olive oil is good for the heart. Anyone will tell you that.'

Erica controlled her desire to point out that the amount he'd poured on his meat couldn't be considered a recommended serving. They'd had the same discussion many times before, and Lars was an expert at taking only the nutritional advice that suited him. Food was his great passion in life, and he viewed all attempts to circumscribe his eating habits as a personal assault. Bittan had long since resigned herself to his ways, but she still tried now and again to give him little tips. All attempts to get him on a diet had failed, since he sneaked food whenever she turned her back. Then he would open his eyes wide in astonishment that he hadn't lost weight even though, by his own testimony, he ate no more than your average rabbit.

'Do you know E-Type?' Maria had stopped plumbing the depths of Dan's mouth and was now gazing in fascination at Gustav. 'I mean, he hangs with the Princess and her pals, and Dan said that you know the royal family, so I thought maybe you knew him. He's so cool!'

Gustav seemed totally amazed that anyone would think it was cooler to know E-Type than the King, but he replied guardedly to Maria's question. 'I'm a bit older than the Crown Princess, but my little brother knows her and Martin Eriksson too.'

Maria looked confused. 'Who's Martin Eriksson?'

Gustav sighed heavily and said reluctantly after a short pause, 'E-Type.'

'Oh, I get it. Cool.' She laughed and looked very impressed.

Good Lord, is she even twenty-one as Dan claimed? thought Erica. She would have guessed more like seventeen. But she was cute, even Erica had to admit that. She cast a glance down at her own heavy breasts, confirming that the days when her nipples pointed up to the sky like Maria's were long gone.

The party was probably not the most successful one they'd given. Erica and Patrik did their best to keep the conversation going, but Dan and Gustav could have come from different planets, and Maria had drunk far too much wine and far too fast. She had to throw up in the toilet. The only one having a good time was Lars, who was steadily nibbling away at all the leftovers on the platter, happily ignoring Bittan's withering looks.

By eight o'clock everyone had left, and Patrik and Erica were alone with the dirty dishes.

They decided to ignore them for a while and sat down with their glasses in their hands.

'Oh, how I'd like a glass of wine right now.' Erica gazed glumly at her glass of cola.

'Well, after this dinner I can understand why you'd need a glass. Dear Jesus, how did we manage to put such a motley crew together? And what the heck were we thinking?' He laughed and shook his head. '"Do you know E-Type?"' Patrik switched to a falsetto to imitate Maria, and Erica couldn't help giggling.

'"God, how cool!"' He kept up the falsetto and Erica's giggle turned into unrestrained laughter.

'"My mamma says it doesn't matter if you're a little dumb, as long as you're cuuute!"'

Now he had tilted his head in an endearing fashion at the

same time, and Erica was holding her stomach and gasping with laughter, 'Stop, I can't take any more. Weren't you the one who told me that *I* had to be nice?'

'Okay, all right, I know. It's just so hard to resist.' Patrik turned serious. 'Erica, what do you think about that Gustav? Doesn't seem like the warmest person in the world. Do you really think he's right for Anna?'

Erica's laughter died out abruptly and she frowned. 'No, I'm a bit worried. Anyone would be better than a wife-beater, I should think, but I would have . . .' She hesitated, searching for the right word, 'I would have wished for something better for Anna. Did you see how disapproving he looked when the kids were making noise and running around? I'll bet he's the type that thinks children should be seen and not heard. And that would be so wrong for Anna. She needs somebody who's nice and warm and loving. Somebody who makes her feel good. Whatever she says now, I can see that she isn't feeling good. But she doesn't think she deserves better.'

They sat and watched the sun setting in the sea like a fiery red ball, but for once the evening's beauty was wasted. Worry about her sister was weighing on Erica. Sometimes the responsibility felt so huge that she had a hard time breathing. If she felt such responsibility for her sister, how was she going to handle the responsibility for another small life?

She leaned her head on Patrik's shoulder and let the twilight sink over them.

Monday began with good news. Annika was back from her holiday. Suntanned and healthy, relaxed after plenty of lovemaking and wine-drinking, she sat at her desk in the reception area and beamed at Patrik when he came trudging in. Usually he hated Monday mornings, but the sight of Annika suddenly made the day seem brighter. In some way she was the hub around which the rest of the station revolved.

She organized, argued, chided and dispensed praise, as the situation required. No matter what the problem, they could always count on a wise and consoling word. Even Mellberg had begun to have a certain respect for her. He no longer dared give her clandestine pinches and leering looks, which had been all too frequent when he first came to the station.

It only took an hour after Patrik came into the station before Annika knocked on his door with a serious look on her face.

'Patrik, I have a couple who want to report their daughter missing.'

They looked at each other, well aware of what the other was thinking.

Annika showed in the worried couple, who with drooping shoulders sat down in front of Patrik's desk. They introduced themselves as Bo and Kerstin Möller.

'Our daughter never came home last night.' It was the father who spoke. He was a short, stocky man in his forties. As he talked he nervously picked at his loud-patterned shorts and stared down at the desk. The reality of sitting in the police station to report their daughter missing seemed to make the panic finally erupt from them. His voice broke, and his wife, also short and chubby, continued.

'We're staying at the campground in Grebbestad. Jenny was going to go into Fjällbacka around seven with some young people she had met. They were going clubbing, I think, but she promised to be back by one o'clock. They had arranged to get a ride back, and they were taking the bus into town.'

Her voice, too, became hoarse, and she had to pause before she went on. 'When she didn't come home, we began to worry. We stopped by the tent of one of the other girls she was supposed to be with and woke both her and her parents. She said that Jenny never showed up at the bus stop where they'd agreed to meet. They thought she'd just decided not to go along. That's when we knew that something serious had happened. Jenny would never do something like that to us. She's our only child, and she's very conscientious about telling us if she's going to be late. What could have happened to her? We heard about the girl they found at the King's Cleft. Do you think . . .'

Here her voice failed her, and she broke into sobs of despair. Her husband put his arms around her, but tears had also welled up in his eyes.

Patrik was uneasy. Very uneasy. But he tried not to show it.

'I don't think there's any reason to draw such conclusions at this point.'

Jesus, how correct I sound, thought Patrik, but he always had a hard time handling situations like this. The anxiety these people were feeling brought a lump to his throat in sympathy, but he couldn't permit himself to give in to it. His defence was an almost bureaucratic correctness.

'Let's start with some information about your daughter. Her name is Jenny, you say. How old is she?'

'Seventeen, almost eighteen.'

Kerstin was still crying with her face pressed against her husband's shirt, so it was Bo who had to give Patrik the necessary details. As an answer to the question of whether they had a recent picture of her, Jenny's mother dried her eyes with a tissue and took out a colour school photo from her handbag.

Patrik took the photo and studied it. The girl was a typical seventeen-year-old, with a little too much make-up and a slightly defiant look in her eyes. He smiled at her parents and tried to present an air of confidence.

'Sweet girl. I'm sure you're very proud of her.'

They both nodded eagerly, and Kerstin even managed a little smile.

'She's a good girl. Even though teenagers have their issues. She didn't want to go on a camping holiday with us this year, even though we'd been doing it every summer since she was little, but we pleaded with her. We told her that it was probably the last summer we could do something together, so she gave in.'

When Kerstin heard what she had said about their last summer, she burst into tears again and Bo stroked her hair.

'You'll take this seriously, I hope?' the man said. 'We've heard that twenty-four hours have to pass before a search is begun, but you have to believe us when we say that something must have happened. Otherwise she would have called us. She's not the type of girl who would just take off and let us sit and worry.'

Once again Patrik tried to look as calm as possible, but inside his thoughts were already flying wildly. The image of Tanja's naked body in the King's Cleft appeared in his mind, and he blinked to get rid of it.

'We won't wait twenty-four hours, that's only in American films. But you do have to try not to worry. Even if I take you at your word that Jenny is an extremely conscientious girl, I've seen this happen before. A young person meets somebody, forgets the time, forgets that Mamma and Pappa are worrying at home. It's nothing unusual. But we'll start asking around at once. Leave us a number where we can reach you with Annika on your way out, and I'll let you know as soon as we know anything. And do inform us if you hear from her, or if she shows up back at the campground, if you would. It will all work out, you'll see.'

After they left, Patrik wondered whether he'd promised too much. He had a churning sensation in his stomach that didn't bode well. He looked at the photo of Jenny that they'd left. He hoped she was just out partying.

Patrik got up and went to see Martin. It would be best if

they started looking immediately. If the worst had happened, there wasn't a minute to lose. According to the medical examiner's report, Tanja had lived for about a week as a prisoner before she died. The clock was ticking.

6

The pain and the darkness made time slip away in a dreamless mist. Day or night, life or death, it didn't matter. Not even the footsteps over her head, the certainty of approaching evil, could induce reality to penetrate into her dark abode. Or the sound of bones being broken mixed with someone's painful screams. Maybe they were hers. She didn't really know.

The isolation was the worst. The total absence of sound, movement, or any feeling of contact on her skin. She never could have imagined how excruciating the lack of human contact could be. It defied all pain. It cut through her soul like a knife and gave her shivering fits that shook her whole body.

The smell of the stranger was entirely familiar by this time. Not nasty. Not the way she would have imagined evil would smell. Instead it was fresh and full of promises of summer and warmth. It felt almost palpable in contrast to the dark, humid air that she constantly drew in through her nostrils. The air that surrounded her like a soft blanket and bit by bit devoured the last remnants of who she was before she ended up here. That's why she greedily drank in the smell of warmth when the stranger came near. It was worth enduring the evil to be allowed for a moment to drink in the smell of life that must be proceeding as usual somewhere up above. At the same time it conjured up an aching feeling of loss. She was no longer the same person she had once been; she missed the person she would never be again. It was a painful farewell to take, but to survive she had to do it.

But what plagued her most down here was the thought of the child. Ever since her daughter's birth she had blamed her for being alive, but now in the eleventh hour she understood that her daughter had actually been a gift. The memory of her soft arms around her neck, or the big eyes that hungrily watched her, looking for some- thing that she was unable to give, haunted her in colourful dreams. She could see before her every single detail of her daughter. Every little freckle, every strand of hair, even the little swirl at the back of her head that was just like her own. She promised herself and God over and over again that if she ever escaped this prison she would make amends to the little one for each second she had been denied her mother's love. If . . .

'You're not going out like that!'

'I'll go out any way I like, and you've got nothing to say about it.'

Melanie glowered at her father, who glowered back. The source of their quarrel was familiar by now: how much, or rather how little, she was wearing.

Melanie had to admit that there wasn't much fabric in the clothes she chose, but she thought they were nice and her friends dressed exactly the same way. And she was seventeen, after all. She wasn't a child, so what she wore was actually up to her. Contemptuously she studied her father, whose anger had made his face and neck take on a reddish tinge. Fuck if she was going to get old and flabby. His shiny Adidas shorts went out of style fifteen years ago, and his speckled short-sleeve shirt clashed with the shorts. The paunch he'd acquired from eating too many bags of chips on the TV sofa threatened to pop some of his buttons. To top it all off, he wore disgusting plastic flip-flops on his feet. She was ashamed to be seen with him, and she hated having to sit around this fucking camp-ground all summer.

When she was little she had loved taking camping holidays in their caravan. There had always been plenty of kids to play with, and they could go swimming and run about freely amongst the parked caravans. But now her friends were back in Jönköping, and worst of all was the fact that she'd been forced to leave Tobbe. Now that she wasn't there to protect her interests, she was sure he'd hook up with that fucking Madde, who kept hanging on him like a sticking plaster. If that happened, she'd made a solemn vow to hate her parents for the rest of her life.

Sitting in a campground in Grebbestad really sucked, and on top of that they treated her like she was five years old, not seventeen. She couldn't even choose what she was going to wear. She tossed her head defiantly and straightened her top, which was not much bigger than a bikini top. Her minimal denim shorts did cut rather uncomfortably into her buttocks, but the looks she got from the boys made it worth all the discomfort. The best part of her outfit was the pair of sky-high platform shoes that added at least four inches to her five foot three frame.

'As long as we're paying for your food and a roof over your head, we get to decide, and now you're so – '

Her father was interrupted by a loud knock at the door of their caravan. Grateful for the reprieve, Melanie hurried to open it. Outside stood a dark-haired man about thirty-five, and she automatically straightened up and pushed out her chest. A little too old for her taste perhaps, but he looked nice, and besides she enjoyed irritating Pappa.

'My name is Patrik Hedström and I'm with the police. May I come in for a moment? It's about Jenny.'

Melanie stepped aside to let him in, but only enough so that he was forced to squeeze past her lightly-clad figure.

After Patrik and her father shook hands they sat down at the tiny table.

'Should I get my wife too? She's down at the swimming hole.'

'No, that won't be necessary. It's Melanie I'd like to have

a few words with. As you probably know, Bo and Kerstin Möller have reported their daughter Jenny missing. They said that you and Jenny were supposed to go into Fjällbacka yesterday, is that right?'

Melanie imperceptibly tugged at her top to show a little more cleavage and moistened her lips before she answered. A cop. That was really sexy.

'Uh-huh, we were supposed to meet at the bus stop at seven to catch the number ten into town. Some boys we met were going to hop on at Tanum Strand. We were going to go in and see if anything was happening. We didn't have any special plans.'

'But Jenny never showed up?'

'No, it was weird. We don't know each other that well, but she seemed pretty reliable. I was really surprised when she, like, didn't show up. I can't say I was all that disappointed. She was kind of hanging on me, and I didn't mind having Micke and Fredde to myself. The guys from Tanum Strand, I mean.'

'Melanie!' said her father, giving her an angry look. She glared back.

'What? I can't help it if I thought she was a little dorky. It's not my fault that she disappeared. She probably just went back home to Karlstad. She talked about some boy she'd met there. If she had any sense she'd shit on this fucking caravan holiday and go back to him.'

'Don't you even think of doing something like that! That Tobbe . . .'

Patrik found himself forced to break up the quarrel between father and daughter. He waved his hand cautiously to attract their attention. They calmed down, fortunately.

'So you have no idea why she didn't show up?'

'No, not a clue.'

'Do you know if she hung out with any other kids here at the campground? Anyone that she may have confided in?'

161

As if by accident Melanie brushed her bare leg against the policeman's and enjoyed seeing him jump. Guys were so damned easy. It didn't matter how old they were, they only had one thing on their minds. If a girl knew that, she could get them to do anything she wanted. She brushed against his leg again. He was starting to look a little sweaty on his upper lip. Although it was pretty stuffy inside the caravan too.

She paused for a moment before answering.

'There was a guy, some bloody nerd she must have been seeing here in the summertime ever since she was little. Totally pathetic, but as I said she wasn't super-cool herself, so they were a good match.'

'Do you know his name, or maybe where I can find him?'

'His parents have a caravan parked two rows over. It's the one with the brown-and-white-striped awning and all the bloody geraniums in pots in front.'

Patrik thanked the girl for her help and with flushed cheeks squeezed past Melanie on his way out.

She tried to strike as seductive a pose as she could in the doorway when she waved goodbye to the policeman. Pappa had started in on his harangue again, but she turned a deaf ear. He never said anything worth listening to anyway.

Sweaty for more reasons than the oppressive heat, Patrik quickly walked away. It was a relief to escape from the cramped little caravan into the crowded grounds outside. He'd felt like a paedophile when that little teenager had thrust her small breasts at his face, and when she started pressing against his leg he hadn't known what to do. He thought it was so unpleasant. And she wasn't wearing much, either. About as much fabric as a handkerchief was distributed in total over her body. In a flash, he realized that in seventeen years, his own daughter might be dressing that way and making passes at older men. He shuddered at the thought and hoped all at

162

once that Erica was carrying a son. At least he knew how teenage boys functioned. This girl had felt like a creature from another planet, with all her make-up and big, dangly jewellery. Nor could he avoid noticing the ring she had in her navel. Maybe he was getting old, but it didn't seem the least bit sexy to him. Instead he thought about the risk of infection and scarring. But no doubt it had to do with his age. The memory was still fresh in his mind how his mother had chewed him out when he came home with a ring in one ear, and he'd been nineteen at the time. The ring came off at once, and that was as daring as he'd ever been.

He lost himself among the caravans, which were set so close to each other that they almost looked as if they'd been stacked up. Personally he couldn't understand why people would voluntarily spend their holidays packed together like sardines with a crowd of other people. But purely intellectually he understood that for many it had become a lifestyle, and what appealed to them was the company of other campers who returned to the same spot every year. Some of the caravans could hardly be called caravans any longer, the way they were built out with tents in every direction. They looked more like small permanent houses, set up in the same spot, year after year.

After asking for directions, Patrik finally found his way to the caravan that Melanie had described. He saw a tall, gangly and extremely pimply young man sitting outside. Patrik felt sorry for him when he saw the red and white pustules. The boy couldn't seem to keep from squeezing them a bit, despite the fact that he would certainly end up with scars that would last long after the acne was gone.

The sun shone in Patrik's eyes as he stopped in front of the young man, and he had to shade his eyes with his hand. He'd left his sunglasses back at the station.

'Hello, I'm with the police. I spoke with Melanie down the way, who said that you know Jenny Möller, is that right?'

163

The boy nodded mutely. Patrik sat down on the grass beside him and saw that, unlike the teenage Lolita a few caravans away, he looked genuinely worried.

'My name's Patrik, what's yours?'

'Per.'

Patrik raised his eyebrows to indicate he expected something more.

'Per Thorsson.' He was impatiently pulling tufts of grass out of the ground and staring hard at what he was doing. Without looking at Patrik he said, 'It's my fault that something happened to her.'

'What do you mean?' said Patrik, startled.

'It was because of me she missed the bus. We've been meeting here every summer since we were little, and we always had a great time together. But after she met that little monkey Melanie, she got so damn boring. All she talked about was Melanie this and Melanie that and Melanie says this and on and on. Before, I could talk to Jenny about important things, things that meant something, but now it was just make-up and clothes and shit like that. She didn't even dare tell Melanie if she was going to meet me, because Melanie obviously thought I was nerdy or something.'

He was pulling up grass at a faster pace now, and a little bald spot was forming in front of him, growing bigger with each tuft he pulled up. The strong smell of food on the grill hovered over their heads, insinuating itself into their nostrils. It made Patrik's stomach growl.

'That's how teenage girls are. It'll pass, I promise. Then they'll be regular people again.' Patrik smiled, but then turned serious. 'But how do you mean, it was your fault? Do you know where she is? Because if you do, you should know that her parents are terribly worried . . .'

Per waved his hand dismissively.

'I have no idea where she is, I just know that something

bad must have happened to her. She would never run away like this. And since she was going to hitchhike – '

'Hitchhike? Where to? When did she hitchhike?'

'That's why it's all my fault.' Per was speaking with exaggerated patience to Patrik, as if he were a little child. He went on, 'I started quarrelling with her just as she was going to go and meet Melanie at the bus stop. I got so pissed off because Jenny seemed to think that I was only good enough to hang out with as long as that damn Melanie didn't know about it. I grabbed Jenny when she walked by and started yelling at her. She looked unhappy but didn't argue. She just stood there and took it. After a while she said that now she'd missed the bus and she'd have to hitchhike into Fjällbacka. Then she left.'

Per raised his eyes from the bald spot on the lawn and looked at Patrik. His lower lip was quivering, and Patrik could see that he was feverishly fighting to avoid the humiliation of crying in the midst of all the other campers.

'So that's why it's my fault. If I hadn't started arguing with her about something that now seems totally fucking meaningless, then she would have caught that bus and all this never would have happened. She got picked up hitchhiking by some fucking psycho and it's all my fault.'

His voice rose an octave and broke into falsetto. Patrik kept shaking his head.

'It's not your fault. And we don't even know that anything's happened to her. That's what we're trying to find out. Who knows, she could show up here anytime. Maybe she was just out getting into some mischief.'

His tone was soothing, but Patrik himself could hear how false it sounded. He knew that the worry he saw in the boy's eyes was also in his own. Only a couple of hundred metres away the Möllers were sitting in their caravan, waiting for their daughter. Patrik had an icy feeling in his stomach that

165

Per was right, and that they might be waiting in vain. Somebody had picked up Jenny. Somebody who did not have good intentions.

While Jacob and Marita were at work and the children were at day care, Linda waited for Stefan. It was the first time they were going to meet inside the house at Västergården, instead of in the hayloft in the barn, and Linda thought it was exciting. The knowledge that they were illegally meeting under her brother's roof added a little extra spice to the rendezvous. Not until she saw the expression on Stefan's face when he came in the door did she realize that for him it aroused quite different emotions to be back in this house.

He hadn't been back since they had to leave Västergården right after Johannes died. With hesitant steps Stefan walked about, first in the living room, then in the kitchen, and even to the bathroom. He seemed to want to take in every detail. Much was changed. Jacob had done woodwork and painted the walls. The house no longer looked the way Stefan remembered. Linda followed close behind him.

'It's been a long time since you were here.'

Stefan nodded and ran his hand along the mantelpiece in the living room.

'Twenty-four years. I was only five when we moved away from here. He's done a lot with the house.'

'Yes, everything has to be so damned fine for Jacob. He's always doing carpentry work and fixing things up. It all has to be so perfect.'

Stefan didn't answer. He seemed to be in another world. Linda began to regret inviting him home. All she was thinking of was a carefree romp in the bed, not a trip through Stefan's sad childhood memories. She would rather not think about that side of him, the part with feelings and experiences that didn't include her. He'd been so enchanted with her, almost worshipful. It was affirmation that she wanted from him, not the sight of this pensive, worried grown man who was now walking about the house.

She pulled at his sleeve and he started as if waking from a trance.

'Why don't we go upstairs? My room is in the attic.'

Stefan followed her passively up the steep stairway. They passed through the second floor, but when Linda began climbing up the stairs to the attic, Stefan followed more reluctantly. He and Robert had had their room up here, and their parents' bedroom was up here too.

'Wait a minute, I'll be right there. I just have to check on something.'

He didn't pay attention to Linda's protests, but opened with a trembling hand the first door in the hall. Inside was his boyhood room. It was still a room for a little boy, but now it belonged to William, with his toys and clothes strewn all over. He sat down on the little bed and saw in his mind's eye the way the room had looked when he had lived in it. After a while he got up and went into the room next door, the one that had been Robert's. It was changed even more than his old room. Now it was clearly a girl's room, painted pink with tulle and spangles as the dominant decoration. He left almost instantly. Instead he was drawn like a magnet to the room at the end of the hall. Many nights he had padded down the carpet his mother had laid in the hall, towards the white door, which he carefully pushed open, and then crawled into his parents' bed. There he could sleep securely, free of nightmares and monsters under the bed. He most liked to curl up next to his father to sleep. He saw that Jacob and Marita had kept the grand old bedstead; this room had been changed the least.

He could feel tears burning beneath his eyelids and blinked to prevent them from spilling out before he turned round to face Linda. He didn't want to appear so weak in front of her.

'Are you done looking around yet? There's nothing here to steal if that's what you're thinking.'

Her tone of voice had a nasty ring to it that he'd never heard before. Anger was ignited in him like a spark. And the spark was further kindled by the thought of everything that might have been. Stefan grabbed Linda hard by the arm.

'What the hell are you talking about? You think I'm checking to see if there's anything I could steal? You must be crazy. I lived here long before your brother moved in, and if it weren't for your fucking father, we would still own this house. So shut your damn trap.'

For a second Linda was speechless with shock at the change in Stefan, who was always so gentle. Then she tore her arm away and snarled, 'You know, it's not my Pappa's fault that your father gambled and frittered away all his money. And no matter what Pappa did, he couldn't help that your father was such a coward that he committed suicide. He was the one who chose to abandon you, and you can't blame Pappa for that.'

Rage made white spots form in Stefan's field of vision. He clenched his fists. Linda looked so small and fragile that he wondered if he could snap her in two, but he forced himself to take deep breaths and calm down. In an odd, wheezing voice he said, 'There's plenty that I can and will blame Gabriel for. Your father destroyed our lives out of sheer envy. Mamma has told me how it was. She said that everyone loved my father, and they thought Gabriel was nothing but a dried-up sourpuss, and he couldn't tolerate that. But Mamma was up at the farm yesterday and told him a thing or two. It's just a shame that she didn't give him a good thrashing too, but I suppose she doesn't dare lay a hand on him.'

Linda laughed scornfully. 'Once upon a time she didn't seem to mind touching him. It's disgusting to think of my Pappa together with your filthy mamma, but that's how it was, at least until she worked out that it was probably easier to milk money out of your father than out of mine. Then she really got friendly with him. You know what they call somebody like that, don't you? A whore!'

A fine spray of saliva landed on Stefan's face when Linda, who was almost the same height, threw these words in his face.

Afraid that he wouldn't be able to control himself, Stefan backed slowly towards the stairs. He would have liked to put his hands around her thin neck and squeeze, just to shut her up, but instead he fled.

Confused over how the situation had suddenly degenerated and angry that she didn't have the hold over him that she'd imagined, Linda leaned over the banister and screamed venomously after him, 'Go ahead and run away, you fucking loser. You were only good for one thing anyway. And you weren't even very good at that.'

She flipped him the finger, but he was already on the way out the front door and didn't see it.

Linda slumped forwards. Subject to the rapid mood swings of a teenager, she was already sorry about what she'd said. She had just been so damned furious.

When the fax from Germany arrived, Martin had just hung up the phone after speaking with Patrik. The news that Jenny had probably been picked up by a stranger in a car didn't make the situation any better. Anyone could have picked up the girl; the best they could do now was rely on the all-seeing eye of the public. The press had been ringing Mellberg like madmen. With the news coverage that they now expected, Martin hoped that anyone who had seen Jenny getting into a car outside the campground would call in. He hoped they'd be able to sort out the real information from the onslaught of nuisance calls – those that came from mentally disturbed people or those who took the opportunity to make trouble for someone they didn't like.

It was Annika who brought in the fax, which was brief and concise. He stumbled through the few sentences, able to make out that they were looking for Tanja's ex-husband as next of kin. It surprised Martin that a woman so young was already divorced, but the fact was there in black and white. After a moment's hesitation and a quick consultation with Patrik on his mobile, he dialled the number of the Fjällbacka tourist bureau. He couldn't help but smile when he heard Pia's voice on the line.

'Hello, it's Martin Molin.' There was silence for a second too long. 'With the police in Tanumshede.' It irked him that he had to explain who he was. He could have told anyone her shoe size if they asked him.

'Oh yes, hi, forgive me. I'm completely hopeless with names, but I'm better with faces. A good thing, with this job.' She laughed. 'What can I help you with today?'

Where should I begin? Martin thought, but then reminded himself why he was calling and pulled himself together.

'I have to make an important call to Germany and I don't dare try it with my poor grades in high-school German. Could you listen in on a third line and interpret for me?'

'Absolutely,' she replied instantly. 'I just have to ask my colleague to mind the shop while I'm gone.'

He heard her talking to someone in the background, and then her voice was back on the line.

'All right, I'm ready. How does this work? Will you ring me, or what?'

'Yes, I'll patch you in, then just wait by the phone until I call back in a few minutes.'

Exactly four minutes later, he had both Tanja's ex-husband Peter Schmidt and Pia on the line at the same time. He started cautiously by offering his condolences and saying he was sorry to be calling under such unfortunate circumstances. The German police had already informed Peter of his ex-wife's death, so Martin didn't have to break the news to him, but it

170

felt very uncomfortable to be ringing so soon after the man was informed. This was one of the most difficult aspects of Martin's job. Thank goodness it was a rather rare occurrence in his daily police work.

'How much do you know about Tanja's trip to Sweden?'

Pia translated the question fluently into German, and then translated Peter's reply back to Swedish.

'Not a thing. Unfortunately we did not part as friends, so after the divorce we hardly spoke to each other. When we were married she never mentioned that she wanted to travel to Sweden. She was more fond of taking sunny holidays in the south, to Spain or Greece. I should think she would have regarded Sweden as a country too cold to visit.'

Cold, Martin thought ironically, looking out the window at the water vapour steaming off the pavement. Okay, and there are polar bears walking the streets . . . He continued his questioning.

'So she never mentioned that she had some business to take care of in Sweden, or any other connection here? Nothing about a place called Fjällbacka?'

Peter once again answered in the negative, and Martin couldn't think of anything else to ask. He still didn't know what Tanja had told her travelling companion was the purpose of her trip. One last question occurred to him just as he was about to thank Peter and say goodbye.

'Is there anyone else we could ask? The only relative the German police told us about was you, but perhaps she had a woman friend?'

'You really ought to ring her father. He lives in Austria. That's probably why the police don't have him in their records. Wait a minute, I'll get his phone number.'

Martin heard Peter walk away and the sound of things being moved about. After a moment he returned. Pia continued translating, speaking extra clearly when she said the numbers he read off to her.

'I'm not sure whether he can tell you anything either. Two years ago, right after we got divorced, he and Tanja had a real falling-out. She didn't want to tell me why, but I don't think they'd spoken in a long time. But you never know. Say hello to him from me.'

The conversation hadn't produced much, but Martin thanked him for his help and asked if he might ring again if more questions came up.

Pia stayed on the line and anticipated his request by asking whether he wanted to ring Tanja's father now so that she could help with interpreting.

The phone rang and rang, but there was no answer. But Tanja's ex-husband's remark about a quarrel between Tanja and her father had aroused Martin's curiosity. What would a father and daughter quarrel about that was serious enough to make them completely cut off contact with each other? And did it have any connection with Tanja's trip to Fjällbacka and her interest in the disappearance of the two girls?

Deep in thought, Martin almost forgot that Pia was still on the line. He hurried to thank her profusely for her help. They agreed that she would help him ring Tanja's father again the next day.

Martin stared long and hard at the photo of Tanja from the morgue. What was Tanja looking for in Fjällbacka, and what did she find?

Waddling cautiously, Erica made her way along the pontoon wharf in the marina. It was very unusual to see vacant spaces among the boat docks at this time of the year. Usually the sailboats were tied up in rows two and even three deep. But Tanja's murder had thinned out the crowds and made quite a few sailors look for other harbours. Erica really hoped that Patrik and his colleagues would solve the case soon, otherwise it would be a hard winter for many of those who made their living from the tourists in the summertime.

Anna and Gustav had chosen to go against the flow and stay a couple of extra days in Fjällbacka. When Erica saw the boat, she understood why she couldn't convince them to stay in the house with her and Patrik. It was magnificent. Dazzling white with a wooden deck, and big enough to house at least two other families, it loomed at the end of the wharf.

Anna waved happily when she saw Erica approaching and then helped her into the boat. Erica was fairly winded when she sat down, and Anna hurried to bring her a big glass of cold cola.

'I suppose you must be getting sick and tired of this by now, towards the end?'

Erica rolled her eyes. 'As if. But it's probably nature's way of getting us to look forward to the delivery. If only it wasn't so bloody hot.' She wiped her brow with a paper napkin, but instantly felt more drops of sweat running down her temples.

'Poor baby.' Anna gave her a sympathetic smile.

Gustav came up from the cabin and politely greeted Erica. He was as impeccably dressed as last time, and his teeth gleamed white in his suntanned face. In a disapproving tone of voice he said to Anna, 'The breakfast dishes are still on the table below decks. I told you I wanted you to keep a little order on the boat. It won't work otherwise.'

'Oh, sorry. I'll take care of it right away.'

The smile vanished from Anna's face and with a lowered gaze she hurried down below. Gustav sat down next to Erica with a cold beer in his hand.

'It's impossible to live on a boat if you don't keep things orderly and neat. Especially with children, otherwise everything gets so messy.'

Erica wondered to herself why he couldn't have cleared the breakfast dishes himself, if it was such a big deal. He didn't look crippled.

The mood was a little oppressive between them. Erica felt the chasm created by differences in background and

173

upbringing begin to widen. She felt that she had to break the silence.

'She's a very lovely boat.'

'Yes, she's a real beauty.' He swelled with pride. 'I borrowed her from a good friend, but now I'm anxious to take the plunge and buy one myself.'

Silence again. Erica was grateful when Anna came back up the companionway and sat down next to Gustav. She set her drink on the other side. An annoyed frown appeared on Gustav's face.

'Could you please not put your glass there. It'll leave a ring on the wood.'

'Sorry,' said Anna. Her voice was small and apologetic. She quickly picked up the glass.

'Emma.' Gustav switched his attention from mother to daughter. 'You may not play with the sail, I already told you that. Get away from there at once.' Anna's four-year-old daughter played deaf and ignored him. Gustav was about to get up when Anna jumped to her feet.

'I'll get her. She didn't hear you.'

The little girl wailed in fury at being lifted up and she put on her sulkiest face as Anna carried her over to the grown-ups.

'You're dumb.' Emma aimed a kick at Gustav's shin and Erica smiled to herself.

Gustav took hold of Emma's arm to scold her, and for the first time Erica saw a spark ignite in Anna's eyes. She tore Gustav's hand away and pulled Emma close.

'Don't you touch her!'

He held his hands in the air. 'Excuse me, but your kids are always misbehaving. Somebody has to teach them some manners.'

'My children are very well brought up, thank you, and I can manage their manners myself. Come on now, let's go to Acke's and buy some ice cream.'

She motioned to Erica, who was more than happy to have her sister and kids to herself for a while, without Mister Stuck-Up. They pulled Adrian in the wagon and Emma ran on ahead.

'Erica, do you think I'm being oversensitive? He just touched her arm. I mean, I know that Lucas made me a little overprotective of the kids . . .'

Erica linked arms with her sister. 'I don't think you're a bit overprotective. Personally I think that your daughter is an excellent judge of character, and you should have let her give him a real kick in the shins.'

Anna's face clouded over. 'Now I think you're the one who's exaggerating. It wasn't that bad, now that I think about it. If you're not used to kids, it's no wonder you get stressed out.'

Erica sighed. For a moment she'd thought that her sister would show a little backbone and demand the treatment she and the children deserved, but Lucas had done his work well.

'How's it going with the custody battle?'

At first Anna looked like she wanted to ignore the question once again, but then she replied in a low voice, 'It's going nowhere. Lucas has decided to use all the dirty tricks he can, and the fact that I've met Gustav has made him even more furious.'

'But he doesn't have anything up his sleeve, does he? I mean, how could he possibly say that you're a bad mother? If anyone has good reason to deny someone custody, it's you.'

'Sure, but Lucas seems to think that if he makes up enough stuff, something is bound to stick.'

'But what about your police report on him, for child abuse? Shouldn't that count for more than anything he could ever make up?'

Anna didn't reply, and a nasty thought popped into Erica's brain.

'You never reported him, did you? You lied to my face and said you reported him, but you never did it.'

175

Her sister refused to look her in the eye.

'Well, answer me. Is it true? Am I right?'

Anna's reply sounded peevish. 'Yes, you're right, dear big sister. But please don't judge me. You haven't walked in my shoes, so you don't know a thing about the way things are. Constantly living in fear of what he might do. If I'd reported him he would have hunted me as far as I could run. I hoped that he'd leave us alone if I didn't go to the police. And it seemed to work at first, don't you think?'

'Okay, but now it's not working. Damn it, Anna, you have to learn to think farther than the end of your nose.'

'That's easy for you to say! You sit here with all the security anyone could ask for, with a man who worships you and would never harm you. And now you even have money in the bank after that book about Alex. It's fucking easy for you to say! You don't know what it's like to be alone with two kids and slave to put food on the table and clothes on their backs. Everything always goes so well for you. And don't think I haven't seen the way you look at Gustav with your nose in the air. You think you know so fucking much, but you don't know shit!'

Anna refused to give Erica a chance to reply to her outburst. She hurried off towards the square with Adrian in the wagon and Emma firmly in hand. Erica was left standing on the pavement with tears rising in her throat. She wondered how things could have gone so wrong. She hadn't meant any harm. All she wanted was for Anna to have the life she deserved.

Jacob kissed his mother on the cheek and shook hands formally with his father. Their relationship had always been this way. Distant and correct rather than warm and hearty. It was odd to view his father as a stranger, but that was the most apt description. Certainly he'd heard the stories about how his father had watched over him day and night at the

176

hospital along with his mother, but he had only a foggy memory of that time. It had not brought them closer together. Instead he had been close to Ephraim, whom he often regarded as more of a father than a grandfather. Ever since Ephraim saved his life by donating his own bone marrow, he had worn a hero's halo in Jacob's eyes.

'Aren't you going to work today?'

His mother sounded as anxious as usual as she sat next to him on the sofa. Jacob wondered what sort of perils she thought lurked round the corner. She had spent her whole life as if balancing on the edge of the abyss.

'I thought I'd go in a little later today. And work some this evening instead. I had an urge to drop by and see how things were with both of you. I heard about the broken windows. Mamma, why didn't you call me instead of Pappa? I could have been here in no time.'

Laine smiled lovingly. 'I didn't want to bother you. It's not good for you to get upset.'

He didn't answer, but gave her a gentle smile.

She put her hand on his. 'I know, I know, but let me have my way. It's hard to teach an old dog new tricks, you know.'

'You're not old, Mamma, you're still just a girl.'

She blushed in delight. This exchange was an old game of theirs. He knew that she loved to hear such comments, and he gladly offered them. She hadn't had an easy time of it with his father over the years, and compliments were hardly Gabriel's strong suit.

Gabriel snorted impatiently from his armchair. He got up.

'Well, now the police have spoken with your good-for-nothing cousins, so let's hope they'll shut up for a while.' He started towards his office. 'Do you have a minute to look at the figures?'

Jacob kissed his mother's hand, nodded, and followed his father. Gabriel had begun involving his son in the affairs of the farm several years ago, and his training was still ongoing. His

177

father wanted to assure himself that one day Jacob would be fully capable of taking over from him. As luck would have it, Jacob had a natural talent for running a farm, and he handled the accounts as well as the more manual tasks splendidly.

After sitting with their heads together over the books for a while, Jacob stretched and said, 'I thought I'd go upstairs and visit Grandpa. It's been a long time since I've been up there.'

'Hmm, what? Oh fine, go ahead.' Gabriel was deep in the world of numbers.

Jacob went upstairs and walked slowly towards the door leading to the left wing of the manor house. That was where Grandpa had lived out his days until his death, and Jacob had spent many hours of his childhood up there.

He stepped inside. Everything was untouched. It was Jacob who had asked his parents not to move or change anything in the wing, and they had respected his wish, well aware of the unique bond that tied him to Ephraim.

The room bore testimony to strength. The decor was masculine and muted. It differed sharply from the rest of the manor's bright decor, and Jacob always felt like he was stepping into a whole other world.

He sat down in the leather armchair by the window and put his feet up on the ottoman. As a boy he had curled up on the floor at his grandfather's feet like a puppy and reverently listened to his stories from the old days.

The stories about the revival meetings had excited him. Ephraim had described in great detail the ecstasy visible in people's eyes and how they focused completely on the Preacher and his sons. Ephraim had a voice like thunder, and Jacob never doubted that it could hold people spellbound. The parts of the stories he loved best were when Grandpa told him about the miracles that Gabriel and Johannes had performed. Each day had brought a new miracle, and for Jacob this seemed quite amazing. He never understood why his father refused to talk about this period in his life; instead, Gabriel seemed ashamed of it. Imagine having the gift of healing: to be able to cure the sick and heal the lame. What sorrow the brothers must have felt when the gift vanished. According to Ephraim, it disappeared overnight. Gabriel had shrugged his shoulders, but Johannes had been in despair. He prayed to God at night to give him back the gift, and whenever he saw an injured animal he ran over and tried to conjure up the power he had once possessed.

Jacob never understood why Ephraim laughed so heartily when he talked about those days. It must have been a great sadness for Johannes, and a man who stood so close to God as the Preacher did should have understood that. But Jacob loved his grandfather and never questioned anything he said, or the way he said it. In his eyes his grandfather was infallible. After all, he had saved Jacob's life. Not through laying on of hands perhaps, but by donating his marrow to Jacob and in that way infusing life into him again. Because of that, Jacob worshipped him.

But best of all was the way Ephraim always ended his stories. He would pause dramatically, look his grandson deep in the eye, and say, 'And you, Jacob, you also have the gift within you. Somewhere, deep inside, it's waiting to be lured out.'

Jacob loved those words.

He had never succeeded in finding the power, but it was enough for him to know that Grandpa had said it was there. When Jacob lay ill he had tried to close his eyes and call it up, to heal himself, but he had only seen darkness, the same darkness that now held him in an iron grip.

Maybe he could have found the way if Grandpa had only lived longer. He had taught Gabriel and Johannes, after all, so why couldn't he have taught his grandson too?

The loud screeching of a bird outside woke Jacob from his brooding. The darkness inside him again formed a tight band round his heart, and he wondered if it might grow so strong that it could make his heart stop. Lately, the darkness had come more often and felt tighter than ever before.

He pulled up his legs and wrapped his arms round his knees. If only Ephraim were here. His grandfather could have helped him find the healing light.

'At this stage we'll assume that Jenny Möller is not staying away of her own accord. We would also like to have the assistance of the public, and we ask anyone who has seen her to call us, especially anyone who saw her in or near a car. According to the information we have, she was trying to hitchhike to Fjällbacka, and any sightings connected with that are of the greatest interest.'

Patrik looked each and every one of the assembled reporters in the eye. At the same time Annika passed around the photograph of Jenny Möller. She would also see to it that all the newspapers were given a copy for publication. This wasn't always common procedure, but at this stage they felt they could use the press.

To Patrik's great surprise, it was Mellberg who suggested that he hold the hastily called press conference. Mellberg himself sat in the back of the little conference room at the station and watched Patrik, who stood up front.

Several hands were raised.

'Does Jenny's disappearance have any connection with the murder of Tanja Schmidt? And have you found any evidence to link the most recent murder with the deaths of Mona Thernblad and Siv Lantin?'

Patrik cleared his throat. 'First of all, we haven't obtained a positive ID on Siv yet, so I would appreciate it if you didn't write about that. Otherwise I don't want to comment on what we may or may not have concluded, so as not to hamper the ongoing investigation.'

The reporters sighed at being stymied once again by

'investigative concerns', but they still waved their hands in the air to ask questions.

'The tourists have started to leave Fjällbacka. Are they right to be uneasy about their safety?'

'There is no reason for concern. We're working very hard to solve this case, but right now we have to focus on finding Jenny Möller. That's all I have to say. Thank you.'

Patrik left the room despite protests from the reporters, but out of the corner of his eye he saw that Mellberg had stayed behind. He just hoped his boss wouldn't say anything stupid.

He went into Martin's office and sat down on the edge of his desk.

'Jesus, it's like sticking your hand in a hornets' nest.'

'Sure, but this time they might be of some use.'

'Yes, someone might have seen Jenny get into a car, if she was hitchhiking as the boy claimed. With all the traffic on Grebbestadsvägen it would be a wonder if nobody saw anything.'

'Stranger things have happened,' said Martin with a sigh.

'You still haven't got hold of Tanja's father?'

'I tried again. Thought I'd wait till this evening. He might be at work.'

'You're probably right. Do you know if Gösta checked with the prisons?'

'Yes, incredibly enough he did. Not a thing. There are no prisoners who've been locked up that whole time until now. I don't suppose you thought there would be, either. I mean, you'd have to shoot the King or something, and even then you'd still get out after a couple of years for good behaviour. In fact you'd probably get probation after a few weeks.' He tossed his pen onto the desk in irritation.

'Look, don't be so cynical. You're way too young for that. After ten years on the job you're allowed to start feeling

181

bitter, but until then you have to stay naïve and put your faith in the system.'

'Yes, old man.' Martin gave him a limp pretend salute and Patrik got up, laughing.

'By the way,' Patrik went on, 'we can't presume that Jenny's disappearance has any connection with the murders in Fjällbacka. So for safety's sake ask Gösta to check whether there are any known rapists or other sex offenders who were recently released from prison. Ask him to cross-check everyone who's done time for rape, aggravated assault on women and so on, anyone who might be operating in the district.'

'Good thought, but it could just as easily be someone from outside who's here as a tourist.'

'True, but we have to start somewhere, and this is as good as any.'

Annika stuck her head in the door. 'Excuse me for disturbing you gentlemen, but Forensics is on the line for you, Patrik. Should I patch it over here, or will you take it in your office?'

'I'll take it my office. Give me half a minute.'

He sat down in his office and waited for the telephone to ring. His heart was pounding a little faster. Hearing from Forensics was a little like waiting for Father Christmas. You never knew what surprises were going to be in the package.

Ten minutes later, he was back in Martin's office, but he remained standing in the doorway.

'It's been confirmed that Siv Lantin is the second skeleton, just as we thought. And the soil analysis is ready. We may have something useful there.'

Martin leaned forward in his chair with interest and folded his hands.

'Okay, don't keep me on tenterhooks. What did they find?'

'First of all, the same kind of soil found on Tanja's body was on the blanket she was lying on as well as on the skeletons. It means that at one time they were located in the same place. Then the Swedish Crime Lab found a fertilizer in the soil that's

182

only used in agriculture. They also managed to work out what type it was and the name of the manufacturer. But best of all – it's not sold retail, but purchased directly from the manufacturer. It's also not one of the more common types on the market. So if you could bounce a reply back to them and ask them to compile a list of the customers who've purchased this chemical, we might finally get somewhere. Here's a note with the name of the fertilizer and the manufacturer. Their number is probably in the Yellow Pages.'

Martin waved his hand dismissively. 'I'll take care of it. I'll let you know as soon as I get the lists.'

'Great.' Patrik gave him a thumbs up and drummed lightly on the door jamb.

'By the way . . .'

Patrik was already on his way down the corridor and spun round at the sound of Martin's voice.

'Yes?'

'Did they say anything about the DNA they found?'

'They're still working on that. SCL is running the analyses, and they apparently have a hell of a back-up. Lots of rapes this time of year, you know.'

Martin nodded dismally. He knew all too well. It was one of the big advantages of the winter half of the year. Lots of rapists thought it was too cold outside to pull down their trousers, but in the summertime it didn't bother them.

Patrik hummed as he walked back to his office. Finally they had a lead. Even though it wasn't much, at least they had something concrete.

Ernst treated himself to a hot dog with mashed potatoes on the square in Fjällbacka. He sat down on one of the benches facing the sea and kept an eye on the seagulls circling him. If they had the chance they'd snatch his hot dog from him, so he didn't take his eyes off them for a second. Fucking dumb birds. When he was a kid he used to amuse himself by tying

183

a fish to a line and holding the other end. When the unsuspecting gull gobbled up the fish, he would have his own living kite, flapping helplessly in the air in panic. Another favourite trick had been to sneak some of his father's home-made moonshine and dip pieces of bread in it. Then he would fling the bread to the gulls. The sight of them reeling in the sky always made him laugh so hard that he had to lie down on the ground and hold his stomach. He didn't dare pull any boyish pranks like that any longer, but he wished he could. Fucking rats of the sea is what they were.

Out of the corner of his eye he spied a familiar face. Gabriel Hult pulled up to the kerb in front of the Central Kiosk in his BMW. Ernst straightened up on the bench. He had kept himself up-to-date with the investigation into the murder of the German girl, in sheer fury at being left out of it, so he knew all about Gabriel's testimony against his brother. Maybe, just maybe, Ernst thought, there was more to be squeezed out of that toffee-nosed fuck. The mere thought of the farm and the fields that Gabriel owned made his mouth water with envy, so it would feel fantastic to squeeze him a little. And if there was the tiniest chance that he could find out something new for the investigation to show up that fucking Hedström, then that would be a real bonus.

He tossed the rest of his hot dog and mashed potatoes in the nearest rubbish bin and sauntered over to Gabriel's car. The silver BMW gleamed in the sunshine, and he couldn't resist running his hand longingly over the roof. Damn, this was the car to have. He snatched his hand back when Gabriel came out of the kiosk with a newspaper, giving Ernst a suspicious glance as he stood listlessly by the passenger door.

'Excuse me, but that's my car you're leaning on.'

'Yes, it is.' Ernst's tone was as insolent as he dared. It was best to establish respect at once. 'Ernst Lundgren, Tanumshede police station.'

Gabriel sighed. 'What is it now? Have Stefan and Robert been up to something again?'

Ernst laughed. 'I'm sure they have, if I know those two rotters, but nothing we've heard about at the moment. No, I have a couple of questions regarding the women who were found in the King's Cleft.' He nodded in the direction of the wooden stairs that wound up the side of the hill to the location that he'd mentioned.

Gabriel crossed his arms with his newspaper anchored under one arm.

'What in the world would I know about that? I hope it's not the old story about my brother again. Some of your colleagues have already asked me about that. First of all, it was a hell of a long time ago, and considering the events of the past few days, it should be obvious that Johannes had nothing to do with it. Look at this!'

He unfolded the newspaper and held it up in front of Ernst. The front page was dominated by a photograph of Jenny Möller, next to a blurry passport photo of Tanja Schmidt. The headline, not surprisingly, was pure sensationalism.

'Do you think my brother rose up from the grave and did this?' Gabriel's voice shook with emotion. 'How much time are you going to waste on interrogating my family while the real killer runs free? The only thing you have against us is testimony I gave over twenty years ago. Back then, I was positive about what I saw, but what the hell. It wasn't really light outside, I'd been sitting by my ailing son's sickbed, and maybe I simply made a mistake!'

Furious, Gabriel walked round the car to the driver's side and pressed the remote control to trip the central lock. Before he got into the car he directed one last agitated harangue at Ernst.

'If this keeps up, I'll have to bring in our lawyers. I'm sick of having people staring at me so that their eyes are about to fall out ever since you found those bodies. And I don't intend to let you keep sparking rumours about my family just because you can't come up with anything better.'

Gabriel slammed the door and roared off. He drove up Galärbacken at a speed that made pedestrians dive for cover.

Ernst chuckled to himself. Gabriel Hult might have money, but as a policeman Ernst had the power to stir up trouble in his little pampered world. All at once life felt much better.

'We're facing a crisis that will affect the entire community.' Stig Thulin, the most influential citizen in the community, narrowed his eyes at Mellberg, who did not look noticeably impressed.

'Yes, as I've told you and everyone else who has called, we're working at full speed on this investigation.'

'I get dozens of calls every day from worried business-people, and I understand their concern. Have you seen how the campgrounds and marinas look around here? This is affecting not only business in Fjällbacka, which would have been bad enough. After the latest disappearance, tourists are fleeing from nearby towns as well. Grebbestad, Hamburgsund, Kämpersvik, even all the way up to Strömstad it's beginning to be felt. I want to know what concrete measures you're going to take to resolve this situation!'

Stig Thulin, normally sporting a toothy grin, now had a worried frown furrowing his noble brow. He had been the town's foremost representative for more than a decade, and he even had a reputation as something of a stud in the district. Mellberg had to admit that he could understand why local women were receptive to his charms. Not that Mellberg leaned that way, he was quick to point out to himself, but not even a man could avoid seeing that Stig was in particularly good shape for a gent of fifty, with attractive greying temples combined with boyish blue eyes.

Mellberg smiled soothingly. 'You know as well as I do,

Stig, that I can't go into detail on how we're working this investigation. You'll have to take my word for it when I say that we're putting all our efforts into finding the Möller girl and the person who has committed this crime.'

'Do you really have the resources for such a complex investigation? Shouldn't you call in support from, I don't know, Göteborg, maybe?'

Stig's grey temples were glistening with sweat. His political status was dependent on how satisfied the businesspeople in the community were with his efforts. They had been so upset in the past few days that it didn't bode well for the next election. He thrived in the corridors of power. He also guessed that his political prominence was largely the reason for his successes in bed.

Now an annoyed furrow also appeared on Mellberg's equally noble brow.

'We don't need any help with this case, I can assure you. And I must say that I don't appreciate your lack of faith in our expertise when you ask such a question. We haven't ever had any complaints about our work methods, and I see no reason for any unwarranted criticism in this particular situation.'

Thanks to his excellent people skills, which had served him well in politics, Stig understood when it was time to retreat. He took a deep breath and reminded himself that it didn't serve his purposes to tangle with the local police department.

'All right, perhaps it was a bit premature to start questioning your methods. Naturally you enjoy our fullest confidence. But I really must stress the gravity of resolving this matter as soon as possible.'

Mellberg merely nodded in reply. After the usual polite formalities of farewell, the community's most influential citizen swept out of the police station.

* * *

187

Melanie examined herself critically in the full-length mirror that she had pestered her father to put up in the caravan. Not bad. Although losing a few more pounds wouldn't hurt. She smoothed the skin on her stomach and sucked it in. There, now it looked better. She didn't want even an ounce of fat to be visible. She decided that for the next few weeks she would eat only an apple for lunch. Her mamma could say whatever she liked, but Melanie would give anything not to be as fat and disgusting as her mother.

After adjusting her string bikini one last time, Melanie took her beach bag and towel and was just about to set off for the swimming area. A knock on the door interrupted her. She thought it was some of her pals on their way out for a swim. They probably wanted to ask her to come along. She opened the door. The next instant she was flung back into the caravan and the small of her back slammed against the little table. The pain made her vision go black. The blow knocked the wind out of her lungs and made it impossible for her to utter a sound. A man forced his way in, and she searched her memory for where she had seen him before. He was vaguely familiar, but the shock and the pain made it hard for her to focus. But one thought popped up immediately: Jenny's disappearance. Panic now stripped her of all resistance, and she sank defenceless to the floor.

She didn't protest when he yanked her up by one arm and forced her over to the bed. But when he started to pull on the bikini strings tied at her back, terror gave her strength, and she aimed a kick back at his crotch. She missed and hit his thigh instead, and the reply came at once. A fist landed on the small of her back exactly where she had struck the table, and the wind was knocked out of her again. She sank onto the bed and gave up. The force of the man's blow made her feel small and helpless, and survival was the only thought in her head. She prepared herself to die. Just as she was now sure that Jenny had died.

A sound made the man turn round just as he'd pulled Melanie's bikini bottoms to her knees. Before he could react, something hit the man in the head, and with a guttural moan he sank to his knees. Behind him Melanie saw Per – the nerd – with a baseball bat in his hand. The heavy bat. That was all she managed to notice before everything went black.

'Damn, I should have recognized him!'

Martin was stamping his feet out of sheer frustration and gesticulating at the man now being shoved into the back seat of a police car with handcuffs on.

'How the hell could you have done that? He beefed up at least forty pounds in the joint and bleached his hair blond. Not even his mother would have recognized him. Besides, all you've ever seen is a photo.'

Patrik tried to console Martin as best he could, but suspected that he was speaking to deaf ears. They were standing in Grebbestad campground, next to the caravan belonging to Melanie's parents. All around them a big crowd of gawkers had gathered to see what was going on. Melanie had already been taken away by ambulance to Uddevalla Hospital. Her parents had been at Svinesund shopping centre when Patrik got hold of them on their mobile, and in shock they had driven straight to the hospital.

'I looked straight at him, Patrik. I think I even nodded to him. He must have laughed himself silly when we drove off. Besides, his tent was right next to Tanja and Liese's. Shit, how fucking stupid could I be?'

He hit his forehead with his fist to emphasize his words, feeling anxiety beginning to swell in his chest. The 'what-if game' had already begun its devilish play with him. If only he had recognized Mårten Frist, Jenny would have been home with her parents now. If, if, if.

Patrik was well aware what was going on in Martin's mind, but he didn't know what words he could offer to soothe his colleague's torment. He probably would have gone through the same thing in his position, even though the self-criticism was completely groundless. It had been next to impossible to identify the rapist who'd been arrested for four rapes five summers ago. Mårten Frisk was then only seventeen years old, a skinny, dark-haired youth who used a knife to force his victims into submission. Now he was a blond mountain of muscle who obviously thought he only needed to rely on strength to be the master of the situation. Patrik also suspected that steroids, which were easy to get hold of in the country's penal institutions, had played a role in Mårten's physical transformation. And the man's newfound strength had done nothing to alleviate his inherent aggressiveness; instead it had converted a smouldering glow into a raging inferno.

Martin pointed at the young man standing a little awkwardly off to the side, nervously biting his nails. The bat had already been confiscated by the police, and nervousness was clearly apparent on his face. He was probably unsure whether he would be called a hero or a criminal by the long arm of the law. Patrik nodded to Martin to come with him, and they went over to the boy where he stood shifting his weight from one foot to another.

'It's Per Thorsson, isn't it?'

He nodded.

Patrik explained to Martin. 'He's Jenny Möller's friend. He's the one who told me she was going to hitchhike into Fjällbacka.'

Patrik turned back to Per. 'That was a great thing you did. How did you know that Melanie was about to be raped?'

Per looked down at the ground. 'I like to sit and watch the people who come by. I noticed the guy right away when he pitched his tent here the other day. There was something about the way he went around showing off to all the young girls. He thought he looked so cool with his fucking gorilla arms. I saw the way he looked at the girls too. Especially if they weren't wearing much.'

190

'And what happened today?' Martin impatiently steered him onto the right track.

Still staring at the ground, Per continued. 'I noticed that he was sitting and watching when Melanie's parents drove off, and then he just sat and waited for a while.'

'How long?' said Patrik.

Per thought about it. 'Five minutes, maybe. Then he walked over to Melanie's caravan, looking determined, and I thought maybe he was going to make a pass at her or something. But when she opened the door he just lunged in, and I thought, shit, he must be the one who took Jenny. So I went and got one of the baseball bats that the kids have and then I ran inside and hit him on the head with it.'

Per had to stop and catch his breath, and for the first time he raised his eyes and looked straight at Patrik and Martin. They could see his lower lip quivering.

'Am I going to get in trouble for this? Because I hit him on the head, I mean?'

Patrik put a comforting hand on his shoulder.

'I can promise you there won't be any repercussions because of what happened. Not that we encourage civilians to take action on their own, don't get me wrong – but the truth is that if you hadn't stepped in, he probably would have raped Melanie.'

Per literally collapsed with relief, but he soon straightened up again and said, 'Could he have been the one who . . . with Jenny, I mean?'

He couldn't even say the words, and here Patrik's comforting assurances ceased. Because Per's question went right to the heart of what he was thinking himself.

'I don't know. Did you notice whether he ever looked at Jenny that way?'

Per thought feverishly, but at last shook his head. 'I don't know. I mean, I'm sure he did, he looked at all the girls who went by, but I can't say that he looked at her in particular.'

They thanked Per and turned him over to his worried parents. Then they drove off towards the station. There, already in custody, was perhaps the person they had been looking for so intently. Martin and Patrik were both crossing their fingers that he was the perp.

In the interrogation room the mood was tense. The thought of Jenny Möller was putting on the pressure and they were all eager to get the truth out of Mårten Frisk, but they also knew that certain things could not be forced. Patrik was leading the interrogation, and it hadn't surprised anyone that he asked Martin to assist him. After going through the obligatory procedures, stating names, date and time for the benefit of the tape recorder, they set to work.

'You're under arrest for the attempted rape of Melanie Johansson. Do you have anything to say about that?'

'Yeah, you'd better believe it!'

Mårten was lazily leaning back in his chair, with one of his enormous biceps draped over the chair back. He was wearing summer clothes: a tank shirt and short shorts with minimal fabric to expose as much muscle as possible. His bleached hair was a little too long and a lock kept falling into his eyes.

'I didn't do anything she didn't agree to, and if she says otherwise she's lying! We'd made a date when her parents would be away, and we'd just started to get a little cosy when that fucking idiot comes rushing in with his bat. And by the way, I want to press charges for assault. So you can write that down in your notes.' He pointed at the notebooks that both Patrik and Martin had in front of them, and laughed.

'We can talk about that later. Right now we're talking about the accusations directed at you.'

Patrik's curt tone contained all the contempt that this man brought out in him. Big guys who attacked small girls belonged to the lowest of the low in his world.

Mårten shrugged his shoulders as if it made no difference to him. His years in prison had schooled him well. The last time he'd sat before Patrik he'd been a skinny, insecure seventeen-year-old who reeled off a confession to the four rapes almost as soon as they sat down. Now he'd learned from the big boys, and his physical transformation matched the mental development that he'd undergone. What remained the same was his hatred and aggression towards women. As far as the police knew, this had previously led him to commit brutal rapes, but not murder. Patrik worried that the years in prison had caused more damage than they could imagine. Had Mårten Frisk advanced from rapist to murderer? If so, where was Jenny Möller and how was her disappearance connected to the deaths of Mona and Siv? When the two girls were killed, Mårten had not even been born!

Patrik sighed and continued his questioning. 'Let's pretend that we believe you. We still have a big coincidence that bothers us, namely that you were staying at Grebbestad campground when a girl named Jenny Möller disappeared. You were also staying at Sälvik campground in Fjällbacka when a German tourist disappeared and was later found murdered. And your tent was right next to the tent belonging to Tanja Schmidt and her friend. A little strange, we think.'

Mårten turned noticeably pale. 'Hey, what the fuck? I didn't have anything to do with all that.'

'But you know which girl we mean?'

Reluctantly he said, 'Yeah, I saw those lesbos in the tent next to mine, but I've never been much for that type, and besides, they were a little too old for my taste. They both looked like hags to me.'

Patrik thought of Tanja's somewhat plain but friendly face in her passport photo. He repressed an impulse to throw his notebook in Mårten's face. His eyes were ice-cold when he looked at the man in front of him.

'What about Jenny Möller? Seventeen, a pretty blonde. She'd be just your type, right?'

Little beads of sweat began to appear on Mårten's forehead. He had small eyes that blinked rapidly when he got nervous, and now he was blinking frantically.

'I didn't have a fucking thing to do with that. I never touched her, I swear!'

He threw up his hands to signal that he was innocent. Against his will, Patrik thought he heard a note of truth in the man's protests. His behaviour when Tanja and Jenny were mentioned was quite different from when they were questioning him about Melanie. Out of the corner of his eye, Patrik could see that Martin looked pensive as well.

'Okay, I'll admit that this chick today maybe wasn't going along with everything, but you have to believe me, I have no idea what you're talking about when it comes to the other two. I swear!'

The panic in Mårten's voice was obvious. In a wordless exchange of glances, Martin and Patrik agreed to break off the interrogation. Unfortunately, they believed the man. That meant that somewhere, somebody else was holding Jenny Möller captive, unless she was already dead. All at once it seemed very unlikely that they would fulfil their promise to Albert Thernblad to find his daughter's killer.

Gösta was nervous. It was as though he'd suddenly regained life in a part of his body that had been numb for a long time. Police work had filled him with indifference for so long that it was strange to feel something again that almost resembled commitment. He knocked cautiously on Patrik's door and said, 'May I come in?'

'What? Oh, sure.' Patrik looked up absentmindedly from his desk.

Gösta slouched in and sat down in the visitor's chair. He said

194

nothing, and after a moment Patrik had to give him a nudge. 'Yes? Was there something you had on your mind?'

Gösta cleared his throat and studied his hands in his lap. 'I got the list yesterday.'

'What list?' Patrik frowned quizzically.

'The one with the rapists from the district who were released from prison. There were only two names on it, and one of them was Mårten Frisk.'

'And why the long face because of this?'

Gösta looked up. The anxiety felt like a big hard ball in his stomach.

'I didn't do my job. I thought I'd check out the names, where they were, what they were doing, have a talk with them. But I just didn't have the energy. That's the honest truth, Hedström. I couldn't be bothered with it. And now . . .'

Patrik didn't reply. He just waited for the rest.

'Now I realize that if I'd done my job, maybe that kid wouldn't have been attacked, almost raped today, and we would have also had a chance to question him about Jenny a whole day earlier. Who knows, it might have made the difference between life and death for her. Yesterday she might have been alive, and today she might be dead. And all because I'm so damned lazy and didn't do my job!' He pounded his fist on his thigh for emphasis.

Patrik sat quietly for a moment but then leaned across the desk and folded his hands. The tone in his voice was encouraging, not reproachful as Gösta had expected. He looked up at his colleague in amazement.

'It's true, your work does leave something to be desired at times, Gösta. Both you and I know that. But it's not my job to have this discussion; that's something for our chief to handle. With regard to Mårten Frisk and the fact that you didn't check him out yesterday, you can forget about it. First of all, you could never have tracked him to the campground that fast; it would have taken at least a couple of days. Second, I'm afraid he wasn't the one who abducted Jenny Möller.'

Gösta gave Patrik a surprised look. 'But I thought it was as good as solved?'

'I did too. And I'm still not completely convinced, but during the interrogation neither Martin nor I got the impression that he was the abductor.'

'Shit.' Gösta thought about this in silence. But his anxiety had still not abated. 'Is there anything I can do?'

'As I said, we're not completely certain, but we took a blood sample from Frisk, which will definitely determine whether he's the right man. It's already been sent off to the lab, and we told them it was a rush. I'd appreciate it if you could lean on them a little. If Frisk is the one after all, every hour could be crucial for the Möller girl.'

'Sure, I'll take care of it. I'll be on them like a pit bull.'

Patrik smiled at the reference. If he were to compare Gösta with a breed of dog, it would probably be a tired old beagle.

Now eager to please, Gösta leapt out of his chair and with a speed never seen before, he dashed out of the room. His relief over not being to blame for a big mistake made him feel like he was flying. He promised himself that he would work harder than ever, maybe even put in a little overtime tonight. No, he almost forgot, he had a tee time booked at the golf course for five o'clock. Oh well, he could work late another day.

Laine detested having to go in among all the filth and junk. It was like stepping into another world. She cautiously picked her way around old newspapers, trash bags, and God knows what.

'Solveig?' No answer. She pressed her handbag against her body and went farther down the hall. There she saw her. The repugnance she felt was a physical sensation in her whole body. She hated this woman more than she'd ever hated anyone,

196

including her father. At the same time she was dependent on her. That thought always turned her stomach.

Solveig broke out in a smile when she saw Laine.

'Well, would you look at that. Punctual as ever. You're certainly dependable, Laine.' She closed the album she was fussing with and motioned to Laine to have a seat.

'I'd rather just drop it off. I'm in a bit of a rush . . .'

'Look, Laine, you know the rules of the game. First, a cup of coffee in peace and quiet and then the payment. It would be awfully rude of me not to offer some refreshment when I have such a high-class visitor.'

Scorn dripped from her voice. Laine knew better than to object. This was a dance they had danced many times over the years. She carefully brushed a few crumbs off the kitchen bench, unable to help grimacing with distaste when she sat down. Every time she came here, she felt dirty for several hours afterwards.

Solveig slowly got up from her straightbacked chair and carefully put away her albums. She set out two chipped coffee cups, and Laine had to resist the urge to wipe hers off. Then a basket of crumbled Finnish rolls appeared, and Solveig urged Laine to serve herself. She took a small piece of pastry, silently praying that the visit would soon be over.

'How pleasant this is, don't you think?'

Solveig dipped a pastry in her coffee and peered at Laine, who said nothing.

Solveig went on, 'It's hard to believe that one of us lives in a manor house and the other in a crappy shack. Yet here we sit like two old friends. Am I right, Laine?'

Laine closed her eyes and hoped that the humiliation would soon be over. Until next time. She knotted her hands under the table and reminded herself why she subjected herself to this torment, time after time.

'Do you know what bothers me, Laine?' Solveig spoke with her mouth full of pastry. Little crumbs spilled out of her mouth onto the table. 'The fact that you sent the police after my boys. You know, Laine, I thought we had an agreement, you and I. But the police came here and claimed something absurd. They said you told them that my boys smashed some windows at your place. So it's no surprise I start to wonder.'

All Laine could do was nod.

'I think I deserve an apology, don't you? Because as I explained to the police, the boys were here all night. So they couldn't have been throwing rocks at the manor.' Solveig took a swallow of coffee and motioned towards Laine with her cup. 'Well? I'm waiting.'

'I apologize,' Laine muttered down at her lap, humiliated.

'Pardon me, I didn't quite hear what you said.' Solveig demonstratively cupped her hand behind her ear.

'I apologize. I must have made a mistake.' Her eyes were spiteful when she met Solveig's gaze, but her sister-in-law seemed satisfied.

'So, now that's out in the open. That wasn't so hard now, was it? Should we see about getting that other little matter out in the open too?'

She leaned across the table and licked her lips. Laine reluctantly lifted her handbag from her lap and took out an envelope. Solveig reached for it greedily and expertly counted the contents with her greasy fingers.

'Right on the nose. As usual. Yes, as I always said, you certainly have all your ducks in a row, Laine. You and Gabriel, you're both so conscientious.'

With a feeling of being trapped like a hamster inside a wheel, Laine stood up and headed for the exit. Once she was outside, she took a deep breath of the fresh summer air. Behind her she could hear Solveig yelling before the door slammed, 'Always pleasant to see you, Laine. We'll have to do this again next month!'

Laine closed her eyes and forced herself to breathe calmly. Sometimes she wondered whether it was all really worth it.

Then she remembered the stench of her father's breath in her ear and why the life she had made for herself had to be preserved at any cost. It simply had to be worth it.

As soon as Patrik came in the door he saw that something was wrong. Erica was sitting on the veranda with her back to him, but her whole posture told him that something wasn't right. Anxiety overpowered him for a second, before he realized that she would have rung on his mobile if there was anything amiss with the baby.

'Erica?'

She turned to him and he saw that her eyes were red from weeping. In a couple of strides he reached her and sat down next to her on the wicker sofa.

'What is it, my dear?'

'I had a fight with Anna.'

'What is it this time?'

He knew about all the twists and turns in their complicated relationship, and all the reasons why they kept ending up on a collision course. But ever since Anna had broken loose from Lucas, the two sisters had seemed to enter some sort of temporary ceasefire. Patrik wondered what had gone wrong this time.

'She never reported Lucas to the police for what he did to Emma.'

'What the hell?'

'Right, and now that Lucas has initiated a custody battle for the children, I thought that would be her trump card. But now there's nothing in the police records on him, while he's going to dream up as many lies as he can about why Anna is not a suitable mother.'

'Okay, but he doesn't have any proof.'

'No, we know that. But imagine if he throws so much shit her way that some of it sticks. You know how cunning he is. I wouldn't be the least bit surprised if he managed to charm

199

the court and get the judge on his side.' Erica leaned her face on Patrik's shoulder. 'Imagine if Anna loses the children. That would be the end of her.'

Patrik put his arm round her and pulled her tight. 'Now let's not let our imagination run wild. It was stupid of Anna not to file a report, but I can understand why she didn't. Lucas has always shown that he won't be trifled with, so it's not so strange that she'd be afraid of him.'

'You're probably right. But what made me saddest was the fact that she's been lying to me this whole time. Now I feel deceived too. Every time I asked her about that police report, she would just give a vague answer about how the police in Stockholm are so busy that it takes them a long time to work through all the reports they receive. But it was all a lie. And somehow she always manages to make me out to be the villain.' Erica burst into tears.

'Come on, dear. Just calm down. We don't want the baby to get the impression that he's coming into a vale of tears.'

Erica couldn't help laughing after that, and she dried her eyes on her sleeve.

'Now listen to me,' said Patrik. 'Sometimes you and Anna act more like mother and daughter than like sisters. You took care of Anna when your mother wouldn't. And that made Anna need you to take care of her, at the same time that she needs to liberate herself from you. Do you understand what I mean?'

Erica nodded. 'Sure, I know. But it feels so damned unfair that I have to be punished because I took care of her.' She started sobbing again.

'You're probably just feeling a little sorry for yourself, aren't you?' He stroked back a curl from Erica's forehead. 'You and Anna will work this out just as you've always worked things out sooner or later. Besides, I think you could be the generous one this time. Anna seems to be having a rough time right now. Lucas is a tough opponent, and I can honestly understand that she'd be worried. So cut her some slack and stop feeling sorry for yourself.'

Erica freed herself from Patrik's embrace and gave him a dirty look. 'Aren't you going to back me up?'

'That's what I'm doing, dear, that's what I'm doing.' He stroked her hair but looked as if he were miles away in his thoughts.

'Forgive me,' said Erica. 'Here I sit bawling about my personal problems. How's it going for you guys?'

'Jeez, don't even mention it. Today was really the shits . . .'

'But you can't give me any details,' Erica finished his sentence.

'No, I can't. But it was a really crappy day.' He sighed then straightened up. 'So, why don't we have a cosy evening together? It sounds like we both need a little cheering up. I'll run down to the fish market and buy something good while you set the table. How does that sound?'

Erica nodded and turned up her face for a kiss. Patrik was basically an optimist, her baby's father.

'Get some chips and dip too, if you would. No need to watch my weight when I'm already so fat!'

He laughed. 'Will do, boss.'

Martin was tapping his pen on the desk. He was annoyed with himself. Yesterday's events had made him completely forget to ring Tanja Schmidt's father. He could have kicked himself. His only excuse was that he hadn't thought it was important any longer, after they had Mårten Frisk in custody. Now he probably wouldn't be able to get hold of the father before this evening, but at least he could try. He looked at the clock. Nine. He decided to see whether Herr Schmidt was at home first, before he rang Pia and asked her to interpret.

It rang four times, and he was just about to hang up. But on the fifth ring, a groggy voice picked up. Embarrassed at having woken him, Martin managed to explain in his broken German who he was and that he would call right back. He was in luck. Pia answered the phone at the tourist information bureau. She promised to help him out one more time, and a few minutes later Martin had both parties on the line.

'I want to start by expressing my condolences.'

The man on the other end thanked him quietly for his thoughtfulness, but Martin could feel his grief spreading over the conversation like a heavy pall. He was unsure how to continue. Pia's soft voice translated everything he said, but while he was pondering what to say, nothing was heard but their breathing.

'Do you know who did this to my daughter?' The father's voice quavered a little, and Pia didn't really have to translate. Martin understood.

'Not yet. But we're going to find out.'

Just like Patrik when he met Albert Thernblad, Martin wondered if he was promising too much, but he wanted to assuage the man's grief in the only way he could.

'We spoke with Tanja's travelling companion, and she said that Tanja had a reason for coming to Fjällbacka here in Sweden. But when we asked Tanja's ex-husband, he had no idea why she wanted to come here. Do you know anything about it?'

Martin held his breath. An excruciating silence followed. Then Tanja's father began to speak.

When Martin finally ended the conversation with Herr Schmidt, he wondered if he had really heard right. The story seemed way too fantastic. But it did have an unmistakable ring of truth to it, and he believed Tanja's father. Just as he was about to put down the phone, he realized that Pia was still on the line.

Hesitantly she asked, 'Did you get everything you needed? I think I translated it all correctly.'

'I'm sure it was fine. And yes, I found out what I needed to know. I know I don't have to point this out, but . . .'

'I know, I can't tell anyone. I promise not to disclose a word.'

'That's great. By the way . . .'

'Yes?'

Did he hear right? Was her tone hopeful? But his courage failed him, and he also felt that this wasn't the time.

'No, nothing. Some other time.'

'Okay.'

Now she almost sounded disappointed, but his self-confidence was still much too low after his latest failure on the love front. He must be imagining things.

After he thanked Pia and hung up, his thoughts turned elsewhere. He quickly typed up his notes from the conversation and took the transcript over to Patrik's office. Finally, they had a breakthrough in the case.

They were both on their guard when they met. It was the first time since the disastrous meeting at Västergården, and both expected the other to take the first step towards reconciliation. Stefan was the one who rang, but Linda was actually feeling guilty for her part in the fight, so she spoke first.

'You know, I said some stupid things the other day. I didn't mean it. I was just so damn mad.'

They were sitting in their usual meeting place up in the hayloft of the barn at Västergården. Stefan's profile looked like it was carved from stone. Then Linda saw his features relax.

'Oh, let's just forget about it. I probably reacted a little strongly too. It was just – ' He hesitated and turned away, searching for the right words. 'It was so bloody difficult to go there with all the memories and everything. It really had nothing to do with you.'

Still a bit cautious, Linda crept up behind Stefan and put

her arms round him. Their quarrel had prompted an unexpected result. She had gained a certain measure of respect for Stefan. She had always viewed him as a little boy, someone who hung on his mother's apron-strings and clung to his big brother, but on that day she had seen a real man. That made him more attractive. Incredibly attractive. She had also seen a dangerous side to him, and that too had increased his attraction in her eyes. He had actually been close to striking her, she had seen it in his eyes. Now as she sat with her cheek pressed against his back, the memory made her tingle inside. It was like flying near a candle flame, close enough to feel the heat, but controlled enough not to get burned. If there was anyone who had mastered that sort of balancing act, it was her.

She let her hands wander forwards. Hungry and demanding. She could still feel some resistance from him, but she felt secure that she was still the one who had the power. In spite of everything, their relationship had been defined from a purely physical perspective, and in that respect she felt that women in general, and she in particular, had an advantage. An advantage that she was now using. With satisfaction she noticed how his breathing got deeper and how the resistance inside him melted away.

Linda moved to his lap, and when their tongues met she knew that she had won this battle. She held on to that illusion until she felt Stefan's hand take a firm grip on her hair and bend her backwards until he could look into her eyes from above. If his intention was to make her feel small and helpless, it worked. For a moment she saw the same gleam in his eyes as during the fight at Västergården. She found herself wondering whether her cry for help would be heard all the way to the main building. Probably not.

'You know, you better be nice to me,' Stefan said. 'Otherwise a little bird might whisper to the police what I saw here at the farm.'

Linda's eyes grew wide. Her voice came in a whisper. 'You wouldn't! You promised, Stefan.'

'According to what people are saying, a promise from anyone in the Hult family doesn't mean much. Just so you know.'

'Don't do it, Stefan. Please, I'll do anything you want.'

'So, it turns out that blood really is thicker than water, after all.'

'You said yourself that you can't understand what Pappa did to Uncle Johannes. Are you going to act the same way?' Her voice trembled. The situation had completely slipped out of her control. In bewilderment she wondered how she could have ended up in such a weak position. She had always been the one who was in control.

'Why shouldn't I? In a way you could say it's karma. Everything would come full circle.' He gave her a nasty smile. 'But maybe you have a point. I'll keep my mouth shut. But don't forget that I can change my mind at any time, so it's best if you're nice to me – darling.'

He caressed her face but still kept a painful grip on her hair. Then he forced her head lower down. She didn't protest. The balance of power had definitely turned.

7

She awoke to the sound of someone crying in the dark. It was hard to tell where the sound was coming from, but she scooted slowly across the floor until she felt fabric and something moving under her fingers. The heap on the floor began to scream in terror, but she calmed the girl down by shushing her and stroking her hair. Of all people, she knew how fear could rip at your heart until it was replaced by a dull hopelessness.

She was aware that it was a selfish feeling, but she couldn't help being happy that she was no longer alone. It felt like an eternity since she'd had the company of another person, but she didn't believe it would last more than a couple of days. It was so hard to keep track of time down here in the dark. Time was something that only existed up above. In the light. Down here, time was an enemy. It made her aware that there was another life which by now might have passed her by.

When the girl's sobbing ebbed away, a flood of questions began. She had no answers to give her. Instead she tried to explain the importance of submitting, not fighting against the evil. But the girl didn't want to understand. She cried and asked questions, pleaded and prayed to a God in whom she had never for an instant believed, other than maybe long ago in her childhood. Because for the first time she found herself hoping that she was wrong, that there really was a God. Otherwise how would life seem to the baby, without either a mother or God to turn to? It was for her daughter's sake that she had given in to the fear, immersed herself in it. The other girl's urge to fight it began to arouse her anger. Over and over again she tried to explain that it wouldn't do any good, but the girl wouldn't listen. Soon the girl would infect her with her fighting spirit, and then it wouldn't be long before hope also returned and made her vulnerable.

She heard the hatch being opened and the steps approaching. She quickly shoved the girl away, who'd been lying with her head on her lap. Maybe she would be lucky. Maybe he would hurt the other girl instead of her this time.

The silence was deafening. Jenny's chatter usually filled the entire small space of the caravan, but now there was only silence. They sat across from each other at the little table, enclosed in their separate bubbles. Each of them lost in a world of memories.

Seventeen years flickered quickly past like in some sort of internal film. Kerstin felt the weight of Jenny's little newborn body in her arms. Unconsciously she formed her arms into a cradle. The baby grew and after a while everything seemed to go so fast. Much too fast. Why had they spent so much of their precious time bickering and squabbling? If only she had known what was going to happen, she wouldn't have said a single mean word to Jenny. Sitting at the table with a hole in her heart, she swore that if everything ended well, she would never raise her voice to her daughter again.

Bo looked like a mirror image of his wife's own internal chaos. In only a couple of days he had aged ten years, and his face was furrowed and dejected. Now was the time when they ought to be reaching out to each other, leaning on each other, but terror had paralysed both of them.

His hands on the table were shaking. Bo clasped them in an attempt to quiet the trembling, but unfolded them quickly because it looked like he was praying. So far he had refused to call on any higher powers. That would force him to admit what he had not yet dared confront. He clung to a vain hope that his daughter was off on some innocent adventure. But deep inside he knew that too much time had passed for that to be plausible. Jenny was altogether too considerate and too loving to inflict such worry on her parents deliberately. They had certainly had their quarrels, especially the past two years, but he had always been secure in the knowledge of the strong bond that existed between them. He knew that Jenny loved them. The only answer to why she hadn't come home had to be something dreadful. Something had happened. Someone had done something to their beloved Jenny. He tried to break the silence. But his voice failed him and he had to clear his throat before he could go on.

'Shall we ring the police again and hear if they've made any progress?'

Kerstin shook her head. 'We've already called them twice today. We'll hear from them if they find out anything.'

'But we can't just sit here, damn it.' He jumped up, striking his head on the cabinet above. 'It's so effing cramped here! Why did we have to force her to come on a bloody caravan holiday again? She didn't want to come. If only we'd stayed home instead. Let her hang out with her friends instead of forcing her to sit cooped up here with us in this bloody hole!'

He started pounding on the cabinet. Kerstin let him be. When his rage turned to tears she got up without a word and put her arms around him. They stood there in silence for a long time, united in their terror and a rising sense of grief which they couldn't ward off, despite all their efforts to cling to hope.

Kerstin could still feel the weight of the baby in her arms.

This time the sun was shining when Patrik walked down Norra Hamngatan. He hesitated a second before he knocked on the door. But then his sense of duty took over and he knocked firmly several times. No one came to the door. He tried again, now even more determined. Still no response. Typical. He should have rung them before he came over. But when Martin arrived and told him what Tanja's father had said, Patrik reacted on impulse. Now he looked all around. A woman was tending to her plants outside the house next door.

'Excuse me, do you happen to know where the Struwers are? Their car is here, so I assumed they were at home.'

She broke off what she was doing and nodded. 'They're in the boat-house.' She pointed with a little garden trowel to one of the little red buildings facing the sea.

Patrik thanked her and walked down a short stone staircase leading to the front of the boat-house. A sun chair was set up on the pier, and he could see that Gun was sunbathing in a skimpy bikini. He noticed that her whole body was as ginger-snap brown as her face, and just as wrinkled. Some people apparently didn't care about the risk of skin cancer. He cleared his throat to get her attention.

'Hello, please forgive me for bothering you like this in the morning, but I wonder whether I could have a few words with you.' Patrik had put on his formal tone, as always when he was the bearer of bad news. Assume the role of policeman, not fellow human being – that was the only way to be able to go home and get a good night's sleep.

'Not at all. Just a moment, I just have to put something on.' She vanished inside the boat-house.

Patrik sat down at a table to wait, permitting himself for a second to enjoy the view. The harbour was emptier than usual, but the sea was glittering and the gulls were still flying over the piers in search of food. It took a few minutes, but when Gun finally emerged she was wearing shorts and a top, and she had Lars in tow. He said a solemn hello to Patrik and sat down at the table with his wife.

211

'What's happened? Did you catch the person who killed Siv?' Gun's voice was eager.

'No, that's not why I'm here.' Patrik paused and weighed his next words. 'This morning we happened to talk to the father of the young German woman whose body we found with Siv's.' Another pause.

Gun raised her eyebrows quizzically. 'Yes?'

Patrik told her the name of Tanja's father and was not disappointed by Gun's reaction. She jumped and gasped for air. Lars gave her a puzzled look, unaware of what the connection could be.

'But that's Malin's father. What are you telling me? Malin is dead, isn't she?'

It was difficult to express himself diplomatically. But to be crass, it wasn't his job to be a diplomat. He decided to give her the unvarnished truth.

'She didn't die. It was just as he said. According to him, he clearly viewed your demand for compensation as a bit – how should I say it? – troublesome? So he made up a story that your granddaughter had died.'

'But the girl who died here was named Tanja, wasn't she, not Malin?' Gun looked confused.

'Obviously he changed her name, to one that sounded more German. But there's no doubt that Tanja was actually your granddaughter Malin.'

For once Gun Struwer was speechless. Then Patrik saw that rage was beginning to boil inside her. Lars tried to put a comforting hand on her shoulder, but she shook it off.

'Who the hell does he think he is? Have you ever heard anything so shameless, Lars? To lie right to my face and tell me that my granddaughter, my own flesh and blood, is dead! All these years she's been living in the best of health while I went around thinking that my poor darling died a terrible death! And to have the nerve to claim that he did it because I was too troublesome – have you ever heard the

212

like, Lars? Just because I demanded what was rightfully mine, now I'm troublesome!'

Lars again tried to calm her down, but she shook him off. She was so upset that little bubbles of saliva were forming in the corners of her mouth.

'Well, I'm certainly going to give him a piece of my mind. The police must have his telephone number. I'd like to have it, please. That German devil is going to hear what I think about this whole matter.'

Patrik sighed to himself. He could understand that she had a right to be upset, but in his view she was missing the whole point of what he'd told her. He let her rage on for a few moments and then said calmly, 'I know this must be difficult to hear, but it's your granddaughter that we found murdered a week ago. Along with Siv and Mona. So I have to ask you: Have you ever had any contact with a young woman who called herself Tanja Schmidt? She didn't get in touch with you in some way?'

Gun shook her head vigorously, but Lars looked thoughtful. Hesitantly he said, 'There was someone who rang a couple of times without saying anything. Don't you remember that, Gun? It must have been two or three weeks ago, and we thought it was a prank call. Do you think it could have been her?'

Patrik nodded. 'Very likely. Her father had told the whole story to her two years ago, and she may have thought it would be difficult after that to get in touch with you. She also went to the library and made copies of articles about her mother's disappearance, so she probably came here to find out what really happened to her mother.'

'My poor little heart.' Gun had finally realized what was expected of her and turned on the crocodile tears. 'To think that my little darling was still alive, and that she was so close. If only we could have met before . . . What sort of person would do something like this to me? First Siv and then my little Malin.' A thought occurred to her. 'Do you think I'm in danger? Is there someone who wants to get me? Do I need police protection?' Gun's eyes flicked nervously between Patrik and Lars.

'I don't think that will be necessary. We don't believe that the murders are connected to you in any way, so I shouldn't worry.' Then he couldn't resist the temptation: 'Besides, the murderer only targets *young* women.'

He regretted saying it at once, and got up to show that the conversation was over. 'I'm really sorry to be the bearer of such terrible news. But I'd be grateful if you'd ring me if you think of anything else. We'll start by checking up on that telephone call.'

Before Patrik left he cast one last envious glance at the view of the sea. Gun Struwer was the ultimate proof that good things didn't always come to those who deserved them.

'What did she say?'

Martin was sitting in the lunchroom with Patrik. As usual, the coffee-maker had been on for far too long, but they were used to it and drank the coffee greedily.

'I shouldn't say this, but damn, what a ghastly person she is. What she was most worried about wasn't that she'd missed so many years of her granddaughter's life, or that the girl had just been murdered. It bothered her more that the father discovered such an effective way of squelching her demand for financial compensation.'

'That's terrible.'

Their mood was dismal as they sat pondering the pettiness of human beings. It was unusually quiet in the station. Mellberg hadn't shown up; he seemed to have awarded himself a sleep-in. Gösta and Ernst were out 'chasing road pirates', as they called it. Actually they were probably having a snack at some roadside rest stop, hoping that the pirates would walk up and introduce themselves and ask to be taken to jail. 'Preventive police work,' they called it. And they were probably right. That rest stop was safe, at least as long as they were sitting there.

'What do you think Tanja planned to gain by coming here? Surely she wasn't thinking of playing private eye and finding out what happened to her mother.'

Patrik shook his head. 'No, I don't think so. But I can understand that she'd be curious about what happened. She probably wanted to see the place with her own eyes. I'm sure that sooner or later she would have got in contact with her grandmother. But I should think that what she'd heard from her father wouldn't have been all that flattering, so I can see why she postponed the visit. I wouldn't be the least bit surprised if, when we get the phone records from Telia, it turns out that the calls to Lars and Gun Struwer came from one of the public telephones in Fjällbacka, probably the one at the campground.'

'But how did Tanja end up in the King's Cleft together with the skeletons of her mother and Mona Thernblad?'

'Your guess is as good as mine. The only thing I can imagine is that she must have stumbled on something, or rather someone, who was involved in the disappearance of her mother and Mona.'

'If so, that automatically excludes Johannes. He's lying safe in his grave in Fjällbacka churchyard.'

Patrik looked up. 'Do we know that? Do we know beyond all doubt that he's really dead?'

Martin laughed. 'Are you joking? He hanged himself in 1979. You can't get much deader than that!'

A certain agitation had slipped into Patrik's voice. 'I know this sounds incredible, but listen to this: imagine if the police began to get too close to the truth and he could feel the law breathing down his neck. He was a Hult and could scrape up plenty of money, if not by himself then through his father.

215

A bribe here, another one there, and bingo – you have a false death certificate and an empty coffin.'

Martin laughed so hard he had to hold his stomach. 'You're out of your mind! This is Fjällbacka we're talking about – not Chicago in the Twenties. Are you sure you weren't out in the sun too long? It sounds like you have sunstroke. Take the fact that it was his son who found him. How do you get a six-year-old to tell a story like that if it isn't true?'

'I don't know, but I intend to find out. Are you coming?'

'Where to?'

Patrik rolled his eyes and enunciated every syllable. 'To talk to Robert, of course.'

Martin sighed but got to his feet. He muttered, 'As if we don't have enough to do.' On the way out he remembered something. 'What about the fertilizer? I thought I'd look into that before lunch.'

'Ask Annika to do it,' Patrik called back over his shoulder.

Martin stopped at the reception desk and left Annika the information she would need. She was having a slow day and was grateful for something specific to do.

Martin couldn't help wondering if they were wasting valuable time. Patrik's theory seemed much too far-fetched, much too imaginative to have any relation to reality. But he was the boss on this case . . .

Annika threw herself into the task. The past few days had been hectic, since she was the one who'd sat like a spider in the centre of the web and organized the search parties for Jenny. But now they'd been called off after three days of fruitless searching. Because the lion's share of the tourists had left the area as a direct result of the events of the past week, the switchboard at the station was eerily quiet. Even the reporters had begun to lose interest in favour of the next sensational new stories.

Annika stared at the information Martin had given her

216

and looked up a phone number in the book. After being shunted round to various parts of the company, she finally got the name of the sales manager. She was placed in a telephone queue, and with canned music fizzing in her ear she spent the time on hold in dreamy recollections of her week in Greece, which now seemed an eternity away. When she'd returned from her holiday she had felt rested, strong and beautiful. After being thrown into the maelstrom at the station, the effects of the break were long gone. She yearned for the white beaches, the turquoise water and big bowls of tzatziki. Both she and her husband had put on about five pounds eating the wonderful Mediterranean food, but it didn't worry them. Neither of them had ever been thin, and they had accepted this as a fact of life. They were happily unfazed by the slimming tips offered in the newspapers. When they lay close to each other their curves fit together perfectly, and they became one big, warm wave of billowing flesh. And there had been plenty of that during their holiday . . .

Annika's holiday memories were abruptly interrupted by a melodious male voice speaking with the unmistakable accent of Lysekil to the south.

Annika told him what she needed to know.

'Oh, how exciting. A murder investigation. Despite thirty years in the fertilizer business, this is the first time I've ever been asked for help with a homicide.'

Happy to be able to gild your day, thought Annika sourly, but she kept her caustic comment to herself, so as not to stifle his eagerness to assist her. Sometimes the public's appetite for sensation bordered on the morbid.

'We'd like some help compiling a customer list for your fertilizer FZ-302,' Annika told the man.

'Well, that's not going to be easy. We stopped selling that type in 1985. Fantastic product, but new environmental regulations forced us to stop manufacturing it.' The sales manager sighed heavily at the injustice of environmental protection laws circumscribing the sales of a successful product.

'But I assume you have some form of documentation?' Annika coaxed him.

'Well, I'd have to check it with the administrative department, but it's possible there's information on it in the old archives. In fact, up until 1987 we had manual storage of all such data; after that everything was computerized. But I don't think we threw anything out.'

'You don't recall anyone who purchased . . . ,' she checked her notes again, 'the product FZ-302 in this area?'

'No, my dear. That was so many years ago that I can't just pick the information out of thin air.' He laughed. 'There's been a lot of water under the bridge since then.'

'Okay, I didn't really think it would be that easy. How long would it take for you to gather the information?'

He thought for a moment. 'Let's see, if I take some pastries over to the girls in admin with a few kind words, I should say you might be able to get an answer late today or early tomorrow morning. Will that do?'

That was faster than Annika had dared hope when he started talking about the old archives, so she thanked him profusely. She wrote a note to Martin about the result of her conversation and put it on his desk.

'Say, Gösta?'
   'Yes, Ernst?'
'Does life get any better than this?'

They were sitting at a rest stop outside Tanumshede, having laid claim to one of the picnic tables. They were no amateurs at this, so they had been foresighted enough to bring along a thermos of coffee from Ernst's house. Then they bought a big bag of buns at the bakery in Tanumshede. Ernst had unbuttoned his shirt to expose his sunken white chest to the sun. Out of the corner of his eye he discreetly watched a bunch of young women in their early twenties who were laughing and chattering, taking a pause in their driving trip.

'Hey, put your tongue back in your mouth. And button up your shirt, for that matter. What if one of our colleagues drove past? We're supposed to look like we're working.'

'Oh, relax, will you? They're all busy searching for that teenage chick. Nobody cares what we're doing.'

Gösta's face clouded over. 'Her name is Jenny Möller. Not "that teenage chick". And shouldn't we be helping out too, instead of sitting here like a couple of bloody dirty old men?' He nodded towards the scantily clad girls a couple of tables away. Ernst could hardly tear his eyes away from them.

'You're a fine one to talk. I've never heard you complain before when I've rescued you from the daily grind. Don't tell me that the devil has gone and got religion in his old age.'

Ernst turned to look at him, and his eyes had narrowed in an alarming way. Gösta got cold feet. Maybe it was stupid to have said anything. He'd always been a little afraid of Ernst. He reminded him too much of the boys at school who had stood waiting for him outside the schoolyard. Boys who could smell weakness and then ruthlessly exploited their superiority. Gösta had seen for himself what happened to people who contradicted Ernst, and he regretted his words. He mumbled a reply.

'Oh, I didn't mean anything by it. I just feel sorry for her parents. The girl's only seventeen.'

'They don't want our help anyway. Mellberg has started kissing that fucking Hedström's arse for some reason, so there's no way I'm going to bust my rear end for nothing.' His voice was so loud and hostile that the girls turned to look at them.

Gösta didn't dare tell Ernst to quiet down, but he lowered his own voice and hoped that Ernst would follow his example. He wasn't about to mention whose fault it was that Ernst wasn't included on the investigative team. Ernst himself had conveniently repressed his failure to report Tanja missing.

'I think Hedström's doing a damn good job. Molin has been working hard too. And to be honest, I haven't contributed as much as I could have done,' said Gösta.

Ernst looked as if he couldn't believe his ears. 'What the hell are you saying, Flygare? Are you sitting here claiming that two striplings who don't have a fraction of our combined experience can do a better job than we can? Is that what you're saying, you stupid shit?'

If Gösta had thought before he opened his mouth he would have foreseen the effect his comment would have on Ernst's wounded ego. Now he had to back-pedal as fast as he could.

'No, that's not quite what I meant. I just said that . . . no, of course they don't have the experience we have. And they haven't exactly come up with any results yet, so – '

'No, they certainly haven't,' Ernst agreed, slightly mollified. 'They haven't been able to show shit yet.'

Gösta exhaled in relief. His desire to try to display a little backbone had rapidly faded.

'So, what do you say, Flygare? Should we have another drop of coffee and another bun?'

Gösta simply nodded. He had lived so long by the law of least resistance that by now it was the only thing that came natural to him.

Martin looked around with interest when they turned in by the little cabin. He'd never been to visit Solveig and her boys before, and he gazed at the chaos in fascination.

'How the hell can anyone live like this?'

They got out of the car and Patrik threw his arms out. 'It's beyond me. My fingers are itching to clean up this mess. Some of these wrecked cars were here back in Johannes's time, I think.'

They heard shuffling footsteps when they knocked on the

door. Solveig had probably been sitting in her usual spot at the kitchen table, and she was in no hurry to open the door.

'Now what? Can't honest folks be left in peace?'

Martin and Patrik exchanged a glance. Her assertion was contradicted by the extensive rap sheet of her sons.

'We'd like to talk with you a bit. And to Stefan and Robert too, if they're home.'

'They're asleep.'

Sullenly Solveig stepped aside and let them come in. Martin couldn't conceal a disgusted expression, and Patrik elbowed him in the side as a warning. Martin quickly put on his best poker-face and followed Patrik and Solveig into the kitchen. She left them there while she went to wake up her sons, who were sleeping in the room they shared, just as she'd said. 'Up and at 'em, boys, the cops are here snooping around again. Get moving so we can get rid of these jailers quick.'

She didn't seem concerned about whether Patrik and Martin might hear what she said. She came waddling back to the kitchen and calmly sat down in her place.

Groggy with sleep, Stefan and Robert came out dressed only in their underpants.

'These guys don't ever quit, do they? It's starting to look like harassment to me,' said Robert. He was as cool as ever.

Stefan peered at them from under the shock of hair hanging in his eyes. He reached for a packet of cigarettes on the table and lit one, dribbling the ash nervously until Robert hissed at him to stop.

Martin wondered how his colleague would deal with this sensitive matter. He was still pretty sure that Patrik was out tilting at windmills.

'We have a few questions regarding your husband's death.'

Solveig and her sons stared at Patrik in astonishment.

'Johannes's death? Why? He hanged himself, and there

221

isn't much more to say about it. Except that it was people like you who drove him to it!'

Robert angrily hushed his mother. He glowered at Patrik. 'What is it you're after, anyway? Mamma's right. He hanged himself, and that's all there is to say.'

'We just want to get everything clarified. You were the one who found him?'

Robert nodded. 'Yes, and I'll have to live with that image for the rest of my life.'

'Could you tell us exactly what happened that day?'

'I don't see what good that would do,' said Robert sourly.

'I'd still appreciate it if you'd tell us,' Patrik cajoled him, and after waiting a moment he received an indifferent shrug in reply.

'Well, if it'll give you something to work on, then . . .' Like his brother he lit a cigarette. The smoke now hovered in a thick cloud over a corner of the kitchen.

'I came home after school and went out in the yard to play for a while. I saw that the door to the barn was open and I got curious. I went over to check. It was dark in there, as usual. The only light was whatever seeped through the slats. It smelled like hay.' Robert looked as though he'd disappeared into his own private world. He went on, 'Something wasn't right.' He paused. 'I can't really describe it, but it felt different.'

Stefan was watching his brother in fascination. Martin got the impression that it was the first time he'd ever heard in detail about the day his father hanged himself.

Robert continued. 'I crept farther inside, pretending that I was sneaking up on Indians. Ever so quietly I tiptoed over to the hayloft, and when I got a few steps into the barn I saw that something was lying on the ground. I went up to it. When I saw that it was Pappa I was happy. I thought he was playing a joke on me. I thought that I was supposed to go over to him and then he would jump up and start tickling

222

me or something.' Robert swallowed hard. 'But he didn't move. I poked at him with my foot, but he was completely still. Then I saw that he had a rope round his neck. When I looked up I saw that a piece of rope was hanging from the roof-beam too.'

His hand holding the cigarette was trembling. Martin cast a glance at Patrik to see how he reacted to the story. It was quite obvious to him that Robert was not making this up. Robert's pain was so palpable that Martin felt that he could reach out his hand and touch it. He saw that his colleague was thinking the same thing.

Downhearted, Patrik continued. 'Then what did you do?'

Robert blew a smoke ring and watched as it disintegrated and vanished.

'I went to get Mamma, of course. She came out to the barn and started shrieking so loud I thought my eardrums were going to burst. Then she rang Grandpa.'

Patrik was taken aback. 'Not the police?'

Solveig scratched nervously on the tablecloth and said, 'No, I called Ephraim. That was the first thing that occurred to me.'

'So the police never came here?'

'No, Ephraim took care of everything. He rang Dr Hammarström, who was the district doctor in those days, and he came over and examined Johannes. Then the doctor wrote up one of those certificates about the cause of death, or whatever it's called, and saw to it that the undertaker came and took him away.'

'But no police?' Patrik persisted.

'No, I told you that. Ephraim took care of everything. Dr Hammarström certainly talked to the police, but they never came out here. Why should they? It was suicide!'

Patrik chose not to explain that the police always have to be called to the scene of a suicide. Obviously Ephraim Hult and this Dr Hammarström had decided on their own authority not to contact the police before the body was removed from the scene. The question was: why? In any case, it was clear that they weren't going to get any farther right now. But Martin had an idea.

'You haven't seen a young woman here in this area? Twenty-five, brown hair, normal build.'

Robert laughed. The serious nature of his story had not left any traces in his voice. 'Considering how many chicks run around here, you'll have to be a bit more specific.'

Stefan was watching them intently. He said to Robert, 'You saw a picture of her. She's the one on the newspaper placards. The German tourist they found with the other girls.'

Solveig reacted explosively. 'What the hell are you talking about? Why would she have been here? Are you going to drag us through the mud all over again? First, you accuse Johannes of abducting some girls and now you come here and ask my boys incriminating questions. Get out! I don't ever want to see you here again! Go to hell!'

She stood up and hustled them out with the sheer force of her huge body. Robert laughed, but Stefan looked pensive.

When Solveig returned, snorting after slamming the door behind Martin and Patrik, Stefan went back into the bedroom again without a word. He pulled the covers over his head and pretended to sleep. There was something he needed to think about.

Anna felt miserable as she sat on the luxurious sailboat. Gustav had agreed without question to set sail immediately and leave her in peace in the bow, where she was sitting with her arms wrapped around her knees. With a magnanimous air he had accepted her excuses and promised to take her and the children to Strömstad. From there they could take the train home.

Her whole life had been nothing but a constant bloody chaos. The injustice of Erica's words made her eyes sting with tears of anger, but her rage was mixed with sorrow that they kept ending up on a collision course. Everything was so complicated with Erica. She was never content to be the big sister – to offer advice and encouraging remarks. Instead she'd taken it upon herself to play the role of mother without understanding that it only increased the vacuum left behind by the maternal support they should have had.

Unlike Erica, Anna had never blamed Elsy for the indifference she had displayed towards her daughters. Or at least Anna had believed that she'd accepted it as one of the hard facts of life. But when both their parents had suddenly died, Anna realized that she had always hoped that Elsy would soften with the years and step into the maternal role. It would have given Erica more space to simply be the sister. But when their mother died the two sisters became stuck in roles that neither of them knew how to change. Periods of tacit peace were inevitably replaced by trench warfare, and every time that happened, a part of Anna's soul was torn from her body.

At the same time Erica and the children were all she had now. Even though Anna hadn't wanted to admit it to Erica, she did see Gustav for what he was – a superficial, spoiled little boy. And yet she couldn't withstand the temptation; it was a boost to her self-esteem to show up with a man like Gustav. On his arm she became visible. People whispered and wondered who she was. Women gave approving looks to the lovely designer clothes that Gustav showered on her. Even out on the water, people would turn and point at the magnificent sailboat, and she felt a foolish pride as she lay on the bow like a bathing beauty.

But at other times she was ashamed to realize that it was the children who had to pay the price for her need for re-assurance. They had already put up with too much during the years with their father, and Anna couldn't in good conscience claim that Gustav was a decent substitute for a father. He was stern and impatient with the children, and she was reluctant to leave them alone with him.

Sometimes she felt so envious of Erica that she could throw up. While Anna was in the middle of a fierce custody battle with Lucas, having difficulties making ends meet, and involved in what was (to be quite honest) an empty relationship, Erica sailed forth like a pregnant madonna. The man Erica had chosen to be the father of her child was precisely the sort of man that Anna herself needed to be happy. But she kept going for the wrong types out of sheer self-destruction. Erica was now living a financially trouble-free life and even enjoying a certain celebrity status. And that made the envious little demons of sibling rivalry reappear. Anna didn't want to be petty, but it was hard to resist feeling bitter when her own life was painted only in dull grey hues.

The excited shrieks of the children followed by Gustav's frustrated wailing snapped her out of her self-pity and brought her back to reality. She pulled her sailing jacket tighter and walked carefully along the railing back to the stern. After getting the children to calm down, she forced herself to smile at Gustav. Even when you had a lousy hand you had to play the cards you were dealt.

Like so many times before, Laine wandered about in the big house. Gabriel was gone on another of his business trips, and she was alone. The meeting with Solveig had left a nasty taste in her mouth, and again she felt the hopelessness of the situation. She would never be free. Solveig's filthy, distorted world clung to her like a bad smell.

She stopped in front of the stairs leading to the top floor in the left wing of the manor house. Ephraim's floor. Laine hadn't been up there since he died, or many times before that either. It had always been Jacob's domain, and occasionally Gabriel's as well. Ephraim had sat up there and held audiences for the men, like a feudal lord. Women in his world had been mere shadow figures, assigned to please and look after the ground-floor service facilities.

Hesitantly she climbed the stairs. She stopped in front of the door. Then she resolutely pushed it open. The flat looked exactly as she remembered it. An air of masculinity still hovered over the silent rooms. It was here that her son had spent so many hours of his childhood. She had been so jealous. In comparison with grandfather Ephraim, both she and Gabriel had come up short. To Jacob they had seemed ordinary, sad, and deadly dull, while he viewed Ephraim as practically divine in status. When he died so suddenly, shock had been Jacob's first reaction. How could Ephraim simply disappear like that? Here one day, gone the next. He had seemed like an impregnable fortress, an ineradicable fact.

Laine was ashamed to admit it, but when she heard that Ephraim was dead, relief was the first emotion she felt. But also a kind of triumphant joy that not even he could control the laws of nature. Sometimes she had even doubted his mortality. He had seemed so sure that he could manipulate and influence even God.

Ephraim's armchair stood by the window, with a view of the forest outside. Just like Jacob, she couldn't resist the temptation to sit in his chair, and for a moment she thought she felt his spirit in the room. Her fingers pensively traced the seams of the upholstery.

The story about Johannes and Gabriel's ability to heal had affected Jacob. She had not approved. Sometimes he would come downstairs with a trance-like look on his face. It always frightened her. Then she would give her son a big hug and press his face to her body until she felt him relax. When she released him everything would return to normal. Until the next time.

But now the old man was long dead and buried. Thank God.

*   *   *

227

'Do you really think there's anything to your theory? That Johannes might not be dead?'

'I don't know, Martin,' said Patrik as he drove. 'But right now I'm prepared to grasp at any straw I can find. You have to admit it's a bit strange that the police were not allowed to see his body at the scene of the suicide.'

'I know, but that presumes that both the doctor and the undertaker were in on it,' said Martin.

'It's not as far-fetched as it sounds. Don't forget that Ephraim was very well-to-do. Money has bought far greater services. And I wouldn't be surprised if they knew each other well. All of them prominent men in the community, certainly active in fraternal associations, the Lions, the chamber of commerce, you name it.'

'But helping a murder suspect to flee?'

'Not a murder suspect, a kidnapping suspect. From what I understand, Ephraim Hult was also a man with great persuasive powers. Maybe he talked them into believing that Johannes was innocent, but that the police were out to put him away, and this was the only way to save him.'

'But still. Would Johannes leave his family adrift like that? With two young sons?'

'Don't forget how Johannes has been described. A player, a man who always followed the path of least resistance. Someone who took a dim view of rules and commitments. If there's anyone who would be ready to save his own skin at the cost of his family, it's Johannes. The scenario fits him perfectly.'

Martin was still sceptical. 'Then where has he been all these years, if that's the case?'

Patrik looked carefully in both directions before he turned left towards Tanumshede. He said, 'Abroad perhaps. With plenty of his Pappa's money in his pocket.' He looked at Martin. 'You don't seem very convinced of the brilliance of my theory.'

Martin laughed. 'No, you can say that again. I think it sounds totally off the wall, but on the other hand nothing has been particularly logical about this case so far, so why not?'

Patrik turned serious. 'I keep seeing Jenny Möller in my mind. Held captive somewhere, by someone who's torturing her. It's because of her that I'm trying to think outside the box. We can't afford to be as conventional as we normally are. There's not enough time for that. We have to consider what's even highly implausible. It's possible that this is only a crazy idea on my part, but I haven't found anything yet to convince me otherwise. I owe it to the Möller girl to investigate all avenues, even if I'm declared an idiot as a result.'

Martin now understood Patrik's reasoning much better. He was even inclined to admit that his colleague might be right. 'But how can you get an exhumation order on such flimsy grounds, and so quickly?'

The expression on Patrik's face was grim when he explained, 'Stubbornness, Martin, sheer stubbornness.'

They were interrupted by the ring of Patrik's mobile phone. He answered, speaking only in curt syllables, while Martin nervously looked on and tried to work out what the conversation was about. After only a minute or so Patrik put down the phone.

'Who was that?'

'It was Annika. The lab called back about the DNA sample we took from Mårten Frisk.'

'And?' He sincerely hoped that he and Patrik were wrong. That Tanja's murderer was now sitting in jail.

'The samples don't match. The semen we found on Tanja did not come from Mårten Frisk.'

Martin hadn't realized that he was holding his breath until the air was slowly released in one long gasp.

'Damn. Still, that's hardly a surprise, is it?'

'No, but we were hoping.'

They sat in dismal silence for a while. Then Patrik heaved

a deep sigh, as if marshalling his powers for the task that still loomed as large as Mount Everest before them.

'No, all we have to do now is get permission for an exhumation in record time.'

Patrik picked up his mobile and set to work. He would have to be more persuasive than he'd ever been before in his professional life. And not even he was convinced he could do it.

Erica's mood was rapidly approaching rock bottom. The enforced idleness made her wander through the house, pottering about first here, then there. Memory of the row she'd had with Anna was festering in the back of her mind like a hangover, dragging her mood down even further. She was also feeling a little sorry for herself. She had actually been a bit relieved when Patrik went back to work, but she hadn't reckoned with the fact that he would become so swallowed up by this case. Even when he was home she could see that his mind was still occupied with the homicide. She recognized the gravity of what he was doing and understood it, but there was still a pitiful little voice inside her that selfishly wished he would focus more of his attention on her.

She rang up Dan. Maybe he was home and had time to come over for a cup of coffee. His eldest daughter answered and said that Pappa was out with Maria in the boat. Typical. Everyone was busy with their own lives while here she sat with her big belly twiddling her thumbs.

When the telephone rang she threw herself on it so eagerly that she almost knocked it off the bench.

'Hello, Erica Falck.'

'Yes, hello. I'm looking for Patrik Hedström.'

'He's at work. May I help you with something, or would you like his mobile number?'

The man on the other end hesitated.

'Well, it's like this. I got his number from his mother. Our families have known each other for a long time, and the last time I talked to Kristina she thought I should give Patrik a buzz if our paths crossed. So now my wife and I have just arrived in Fjällbacka, and . . .'

Erica had a brilliant idea. Here was the solution to her boredom.

'Would you like to come over? Patrik will be home at five, so you can surprise him. And we'll have time to get to know each other. You were childhood friends, you said?'

'Yes, that would be fantastic. We did hang out a lot when we were kids. We haven't seen much of each other as adults, but we do manage it once in a while. Time flies.' He gave a small chuckle.

'Well then, we definitely need to remedy that situation. How soon could you be here?'

He conferred with someone in the background and was soon back on the line.

'We don't have anything special planned, so we could come over right away, if that's all right.'

'Super!'

Erica felt her enthusiasm return at the prospect of a break in the routine. She gave them directions and hurried to put on a pot of coffee. When the doorbell rang, she realized she'd forgotten to ask their names. Well, they could start with introductions . . .

Three hours later, Erica was bored close to tears. She blinked her eyes and summoned the last of her strength in an attempt to look interested.

'One of the most interesting aspects of my work is following the flow of the CDRs. As I explained earlier, CDR stands for "Call Data Record", or the values that contain the information about how long someone talks on the telephone, where one is calling, et cetera. When we compile all the CDRs, we get a quite fantastic source of information regarding our customers' behaviour patterns . . .'

It seemed as if he had been talking for an eternity. Would the guy ever shut up? Jörgen Berntsson was so dull that he made Erica's eyes water, and his wife wasn't far behind. Not because she spouted the same sort of long, totally uninteresting expositions as her husband, but because she hadn't said a word other than her name.

When Erica heard Patrik's footsteps on the front porch she jumped up gratefully from the sofa and went to meet him.

'We have visitors,' she hissed.

'Who?' he whispered back.

'One of your childhood friends. Jörgen Berntsson. And his wife.'

'Oh no, tell me you're joking.' He uttered a groan.

'Sorry, I'm not.'

'How the hell did they end up here?'

Erica guiltily cast down her eyes. 'I invited them. As a surprise for you.'

'You did *what*?' His voice was a little louder than he intended and he whispered, 'Why did you invite them here?'

Erica threw out her hands. 'I was so damn bored, and he said he was an old friend, so I thought you'd be pleased.'

'Do you have any idea how many times he was foisted on me when we were kids? And he wasn't a bit more fun back then.'

They realized that they'd been standing for a suspiciously long time in the hall. They both took a deep breath to gather their strength.

'Well, hello there! What a surprise!'

Erica was impressed by Patrik's histrionics. She simply gave a pale smile as they sat down with Jörgen and Madeleine.

An hour later, she was ready to commit hara-kiri. Patrik had a couple of hours to go yet and was still managing to look relatively interested.

'So, are you just passing through?'

'Yes, we thought we'd drive up the coast. We stopped to

visit an old classmate of Madde's in Smögen and a guy in Lysekil I once took a course with. The best of both worlds. Go on holiday and rekindle old acquaintances at the same time!'

Jörgen brushed off an imaginary speck of dust from his trousers and exchanged a glance with his wife before he turned back to Patrik and Erica. Actually, he didn't even have to open his mouth. They knew what was coming.

'Well, now that we see what a nice house you have here – and so spacious too – ' he took in the living room in a glance like a tax assessor, 'we thought we'd ask whether it might be possible to stay over a night or two? Most of the hotels are jammed full.'

Jörgen and Madeleine gazed at Patrik and Erica expectantly. And Erica didn't need to be telepathic to feel the vindictive thoughts that Patrik was sending in her direction. But hospitality was like a natural law to the two of them. There was no way to escape it.

'Of course you can stay over if you like. We have a guest room you can use.'

'Super! My God, this is going to be fun! Where was I, anyway? Oh yes, when we've gathered enough CDR material to be able to run statistical analyses, then . . .'

The evening vanished as if in a mist. But they did learn more than they could ever hope to forget about the technology behind telecommunications.

The telephone rang and rang at the other end. No answer. The voicemail picked up: 'Hi, this is Linda. Leave a message after the beep and I'll call back as soon as I can.' In annoyance, Stefan punched off. He had already left four messages, and she hadn't called back yet. Hesitantly he entered the number to Västergården. He hoped Jacob was at work. He was in luck. Marita answered.

'Hello, is Linda there?'

'Yes, she's in her room. Who may I say is calling?'

He hesitated again. But presumably Marita wouldn't recognize his voice even if he said his name.

'Tell her it's Stefan.'

He heard her put down the receiver and go upstairs. In his mind's eye he visualized the interior of the manor house at Västergården, now much clearer in his mind after seeing it for the first time in so many years.

After a while Marita returned. Now her voice sounded wary.

'She says she doesn't want to talk to you. May I ask which Stefan you are?'

'Thanks for the help, but I have to be going.' He hurried to hang up.

Conflicting emotions tore at him. He had never loved anyone the way he loved Linda. If he closed his eyes he could still imagine the touch of her bare skin. At the same time he hated her. The chain reaction had already started when they met like two combatants at Västergården. The feeling of hatred and the desire to hurt her had been so strong that he almost couldn't control himself. How could two such different feelings exist side by side?

Maybe he'd been stupid to believe that they actually had something good together. That it was more than a game for her. Sitting by the phone he now felt like an idiot, and that feeling added more fuel to the fury burning inside him. But there was something he could do to make her share his feeling of humiliation. She would rue the day that she believed she could do as she liked with him.

He was going to tell what he had seen.

Patrik had never thought he would view an exhumation as a welcome break in the monotony of his day. But after the long and excruciating evening with Jörgen and Madeleine, even this looked like a pleasant activity.

Mellberg, Martin and Patrik stood silently in Fjällbacka churchyard and observed the macabre scene that was playing out before them. It was seven o'clock in the morning and the temperature was pleasant, even though the sun had already been up for hours. Few cars drove past the churchyard, and except for the twittering of birds the only sound was the scraping of shovels being thrust into the earth.

It was a new experience for all three of them. A disinterment was a rare occasion in a policeman's daily routine, and none of them had actually had any idea how it was done, from a purely practical standpoint. Did they bring in a little backhoe and plough down through the layers of soil to the coffin? Or did a team of professional gravediggers come in to perform the gruesome task manually? The latter alternative turned out to be closer to the truth. The same men who dug the graves for burials were now attempting to lift out someone who had already been buried. Doggedly they shoved their spades into the earth, without a word. What was there to say? Chat about the match on TV last night? Talk about the barbecue last weekend? No, the gravity of the moment laid a heavy veil of silence over their work and it would remain until the coffin could finally be lifted out of its resting place.

'Are you sure you know what you're doing, Hedström?'

Mellberg looked worried, and Patrik shared his apprehension. He had employed all his persuasive powers yesterday – pleaded, threatened and begged – to get the wheels of justice to grind faster than ever before, so that they would get permission to open Johannes Hult's grave. But the suspicion was still only a hunch, and nothing more.

Patrik was not a religious person, but the thought of disturbing the peace of the grave bothered him nevertheless. There was something sacred about the stillness in the churchyard, and he hoped that he would find that the dead had been disturbed with good reason.

'Stig Thulin rang me yesterday from the town hall, and he was not happy, I have to tell you. Apparently one of the people you rang and pestered yesterday got hold of him and told him that you were raving about some conspiracy between Ephraim Hult and two of the most respected men in Fjällbacka. You had mentioned bribes and God knows what else. He was extremely upset. Ephraim might be dead, but Dr Hammarström is alive and kicking, along with the undertaker from those days. If it comes out that we're promoting baseless accusations, then . . .'

Mellberg threw out his hands. He didn't have to finish his sentence. Patrik knew what the consequences would be. First he would get the tongue-lashing of his life, and then he would be the eternal laughing-stock of the station.

Mellberg seemed to read his mind. 'So you'd damn well better be right, Hedström!'

He pointed a stubby finger at Johannes's grave and shifted from one foot to the other impatiently. The pile of dirt had grown to more than a metre in height, and sweat glistened on the brows of the gravediggers. It wouldn't be much longer now.

Mellberg's previous good humour had been a bit diminished this morning. And it didn't seem only to do with the early hour and the unpleasant task. It was something more. The peevishness that had formerly been a constant aspect of his personality had returned after a couple of remarkable weeks of changed temperament. As yet his foul mood hadn't reached full force, but it was well on the way. He had done nothing but complain, swear and grumble the whole time they were waiting. In a strange way, it felt more comfortable than his brief period of geniality. Or at least more familiar. Mellberg left them, still swearing, to go and suck up to the team from Uddevalla that had just arrived to assist.

Martin whispered out of the corner of his mouth, 'Whatever it was, it seems to be over.'

'What do you think it was?' asked Patrik.

'Temporary insanity?'

'Annika heard a funny rumour yesterday.'

'What's that? Tell me.'

'He left work early yesterday . . .' Patrik began.

'Nothing revolutionary about that.'

'No, you're probably right. But Annika heard him ring Arlanda Airport in Stockholm. And he seemed to be in a terrible hurry.'

'Arlanda? Was he supposed to collect someone there? He's here, so he couldn't have been flying anywhere himself.' Martin looked just as astonished as Patrik felt. And curious.

'I don't know any more than you do about what he was doing there. But the plot thickens . . .'

One of the men by the grave waved to them. They warily went over to the big pile of dirt and looked down in the hole. A brown coffin had been exposed.

'There's your boy. Should we bring him up?'

Patrik nodded. 'Just be careful. I'll tell the team, then they'll take over as soon as you get the coffin raised.'

He went over to the three technicians from Uddevalla. They were looking serious and talking with Mellberg. A hearse from the funeral home had been driven up the gravel path and stood with its back door open, ready to transport the coffin, with or without a body.

'They're almost ready. Are we going to open the coffin here, or will you do it in Uddevalla?'

The head of the technical unit, Torbjörn Ruud, didn't answer Patrik but instead instructed the only woman on the team to go over and take some photos. Only when that was done did he turn to Patrik.

'We'll probably open the lid here. If you're right and we don't find a body in the coffin, then our part is done. If the more likely scenario occurs and there's a corpse in that coffin, then we'll take it to Uddevalla for identification. Because I assume that's what you want done, right?'

His walrus moustache bobbed up and down as he gave Patrik a quizzical look.

Patrik nodded. 'Yes, if there's a body in the coffin, I'd very much like it to be confirmed with one hundred per cent certainty that it is Johannes Hult.'

'We'll be able to do that. I already requisitioned his dental records yesterday, so you won't have long to wait. I realize it's urgent, after all . . .'

Ruud lowered his eyes. He had a seventeen-year-old daughter and didn't need to have the urgency of the situation spelled out for him. It was enough to imagine for a fraction of a second the horror that Jenny Möller's parents must be feeling.

In silence they watched the coffin slowly approach the edge of the grave. Finally they saw the lid appear, and Patrik's hands began to itch with nervousness. Soon they would know. Out of the corner of his eye he saw something moving at the edge of the churchyard. He turned to look. Damn it all! Through the gate to the Fjällbacka fire station he saw Solveig come steaming, full speed ahead. It was impossible for her to run, so she waddled along like a ship in heavy seas, with her eyes fixed on the grave where the coffin was now visible in its entirety.

'What the hell do you think you're doing, you fucking cocksuckers?'

The techs from Uddevalla, who had never encountered Solveig Hult before, winced at the raw language. In hindsight Patrik realized that they should have anticipated this and arranged for some sort of cordon. He'd thought that the early hour would be enough to keep people away from the exhumation. Although Solveig was not just anyone, of course. He went to meet her.

'Solveig, you shouldn't be here.'

Patrik took her lightly by the arm. She tore herself away and steamed past him.

'Don't you ever give up? Now you're going to disturb

238

Johannes in his grave? Are you trying to destroy our lives at any cost?'

Before anyone could react, Solveig was at the coffin and cast herself over it. She wailed like an Italian widow at a funeral, pounding her fists on the lid. Everyone stood as if frozen. Nobody knew what to do. Then Patrik caught sight of two figures running from the same direction where Solveig had appeared. Stefan and Robert gave the police officers a hateful glance as they ran up to their mother.

'Don't do this, Mamma. Come on, let's go home.'

No one moved. Only Solveig's keening and her sons' imploring voices were heard in the churchyard. Stefan spun round.

'She's been up all night. Ever since you rang and told her what you were going to do. We tried to stop her, but she slipped out. You devils, will this never end?'

His words were like an echo of his mother's. For a moment they all felt a collective shame over the nasty deed they'd been forced to do, but forced was the right word. They had to finish what they'd started.

Torbjörn Ruud nodded to Patrik and they went over and helped Stefan and Robert lift Solveig away from the coffin. It seemed as though her last strength had been spent, and she collapsed against Robert's chest.

'Do what you have to do, but then leave us in peace,' said Stefan without looking at them.

The sons supported their mother between them, heading towards the gate leading out of the churchyard. Nobody moved until they had vanished from view. Nobody commented on what had happened.

The coffin stood next to the open grave, still harbouring its secrets.

'Does it feel like there's a body inside?' Patrik asked the men who had lifted it up.

'Hard to say. The coffin itself is so heavy. And sometimes

239

dirt can seep in through a hole. The only way to know is to open it.'

The moment could no longer be put off. The photographer had taken all the pictures they needed. Ruud and his colleagues put on gloves and set to work.

Slowly the lid of the coffin was opened. Everyone held their breath.

Annika rang at eight o'clock on the dot. They'd had all of yesterday afternoon to search the archives, and they must have found something by now. She was right.

'What timing you have. We just found the folder with the client list for FZ-302. Although I'm sorry to tell you I don't have good news. Or maybe it is good news after all. We had only one customer in your vicinity. Rolf Persson, still a client by the way, but not for that product, of course. Here's the address.'

Annika jotted down the information the man gave her on a Post-it note. It was actually a disappointment not to get more names. It felt a bit meagre with only one customer to check out, but the sales manager might be right. Maybe it was good news. A single name was really all they needed.

'Gösta?' She rolled her office chair over to the door and stuck her head into the corridor to call his name.

No answer. She called again, louder this time, and was glad to see Gösta poke his head into the corridor too.

'I've got a job for you. We got the name of a farmer in the area who used the fertilizer that was found on the girls' bodies.'

'Shouldn't we ask Patrik first?'

Gösta was reluctant to move. He was still half-asleep and had spent the past fifteen minutes in front of his keyboard, yawning and rubbing his eyes.

'Patrik, Mellberg and Martin are at the disinterment. We can't bother them right now. You know why it's a rush. We can't go by the book this time, Gösta.'

240

Even under normal circumstances it was difficult to say no to Annika when she insisted on something, and right now Gösta was inclined to agree that her reasons for wanting his help were particularly urgent. He sighed.

'Don't go alone,' Annika said. 'It's not some ordinary lousy bootlegger that we're after, don't forget. Take Ernst with you.'

Then she mumbled something so low that Gösta had to strain to hear it.

'We have to use that shithead for something.' Then she spoke normally again. 'And be sure to look the place over carefully. If you see the slightest sign of anything suspicious, don't let on, but come back here and report it to Patrik. Then he can decide what we should do.'

'I had no idea you'd been promoted from secretary to chief of police, Annika. Did that happen during your holiday?' Gösta muttered sourly. But he didn't dare say it loud enough for Annika to hear. That would really be asking for trouble, and he wasn't that crazy.

Seated behind her window, Annika smiled. Her computer glasses were perched on the very tip of her nose as usual. She knew exactly what sort of rebellious thoughts were ricocheting between the ears of Gösta, but she didn't much care. She'd stopped respecting his opinion long ago. If only he would just do his job and not screw up this assignment. He and Ernst could be a dangerous combination to send out together. But in this case she had to quote Kajsa Warg, the famous eighteenth-century Swedish cookbook author: 'You have to use what you have on hand.'

Ernst didn't appreciate being rousted out of bed. Knowing that the chief was somewhere else this morning had made him reckon on a little extra snooze before his presence was required at the station. The shrill ring of the doorbell definitely disturbed his plans.

'What the hell is it?'

Outside the door stood Gösta with his finger pressed stubbornly to the bell.

'We've got work to do.'

'Can't it wait an hour?' Ernst said peevishly.

'No, we have to go out and interview a farmer who bought that fertilizer that the techs found on the bodies.'

'Did that damned Hedström order this? Did he say that I have to go along? I thought I was banned from his fucking investigation?'

Gösta debated with himself whether to lie or tell the truth. He decided on the latter.

'No, Hedström is in Fjällbacka with Molin and Mellberg. It was Annika who asked us to go.'

'Annika?' Ernst gave a rough laugh. 'Since when do you and I take orders from a fucking secretary? No, I'm going back to bed for a while.'

Still chuckling, he started to close the door in Gösta's face, but a foot stuck in the door stopped him.

'Look, I really think we have to go check this out.' Gösta paused and then used the only argument he knew Ernst would listen to. 'Imagine the look on Hedström's face if we're the ones who crack this case. Who knows, maybe this bloody farmer has the girl out there at his place. Wouldn't it be nice to present Mellberg with that news?'

A light passed over Ernst's face, confirming that the argument had hit the mark. He could already hear the words of praise from the chief.

'Okay, hold on, I just have to throw on some clothes. See you out at the car.'

Ten minutes later they were on their way towards Fjällbacka. Rolf Persson's farm lay just south of the Hult family's property, and Gösta couldn't help wondering whether it was a coincidence. After taking one wrong turn they found the right road and parked in the yard. Not a sign of life was visible. They climbed out of the car and looked all around as they walked up to the farmhouse.

The farm looked like every other farm in the area. A barn with red wooden walls stood a stone's throw from the house, which was white with blue trim around the windows. Despite all the press reports that sales to the EU had rained manna over Sweden's farmers, Gösta knew that the reality was more gloomy. An inescapable impression of decay lay over the farm. The owners seemed to be doing their best to maintain the farm, but the paint had begun to peel on both the farmhouse and the barn, and a diffuse feeling of hopelessness clung to the walls. Gösta and Ernst climbed the steps to the veranda, where the glorious carpentry work showed that the house had been built before modern times had turned speed and efficiency into holy concepts.

'Come in.'

An old woman's creaky voice called to them, and they carefully wiped their feet on the mat by the front door before they stepped inside. The low ceiling made Ernst bend his head, but Gösta, who had never belonged to the stately tribe of tall people, walked straight in without worrying about hitting his head.

'Good morning, we're with the police. We're looking for Rolf Persson.'

The old woman, who had been preparing breakfast, wiped her hands on a dish towel.

'Just a moment, I'll fetch him. He's taking a nap on the sofa, see. That's what happens when you get old.' She chuckled and disappeared into the house's inner domains.

Gösta and Ernst looked around irresolutely and then sat down at the kitchen table. The kitchen reminded Gösta of his childhood home, even though the Perssons were only ten years older than himself. The old woman had looked older at first, but on closer inspection he noticed that her eyes were younger than her body seemed. Hard work could do that to a person.

They were still using an old wood-stove to cook on. The floor was covered with linoleum, probably concealing a wonderful hardwood floor. It was popular amongst the younger generation to uncover such floors, but for his and the Perssons' generation, it was still much too strong a reminder of childhood poverty. When linoleum was first introduced, it became a blatant symbol of a life no longer mired in the poverty of the previous generation.

The worn panelling on the walls also rekindled sentimental memories. Gösta couldn't resist running his finger along the gap between two panels. The feeling was the same as when he'd done that as a boy in his parents' kitchen.

The faint ticking of a kitchen clock was the only sound to be heard, but after waiting for a while they heard murmuring from the next room. They could hear enough to tell that one voice sounded excited, the other pleading. After a couple of minutes, the old woman came back with her husband in tow. He also looked older than his estimated seventy years. Being woken from his nap had not been to his advantage. His hair stood on end and weary furrows limned deep tracks on his cheeks. The old woman went back to the stove. She kept her eyes lowered and focused on the pot of porridge she was stirring.

'What sort of business brings the police here?'

Persson's voice was authoritative, and Gösta couldn't help noticing that the old woman flinched. He began to have an idea why she looked so much older than her years. She made a clatter with the pot and Persson yelled, 'Can you stop doing that? You can finish making breakfast later. Leave us in peace now.'

She bent her head and quickly took the pot off the stove. Without a word, she left them in the kitchen. Gösta had a desire to go after her and say a friendly, conciliatory word, but he refrained.

Persson poured himself a shot and sat down. He didn't ask Ernst and Gösta if they wanted one, and they wouldn't have dared say yes. When he downed the shot in one gulp he wiped his mouth with the back of his hand and gave them a defiant look.

'Well? What is it you want?'

Ernst looked longingly at the empty glass. Gösta was the one who spoke.

'Did you ever use a fertilizer called . . .' he consulted his notebook, 'FZ-302?'

Farmer Persson gave a hearty laugh. 'Is that why you woke me from my beauty sleep? To ask me what fertilizer I use? Jesus, the police must not have much to do these days.'

Gösta's expression didn't change. 'We have our reasons for asking. And we'd like to get an answer.' His dislike of the man was growing with every second.

'All right, all right, there's no reason to get excited. I have nothing to hide.' He laughed again and poured himself another shot.

Ernst licked his lips and fixed his eyes on the glass. Judging by Persson's breath, these were not the first drinks he'd had that morning. With cows that needed milking, he'd already been up a couple of hours, so it was probably about lunchtime for him. Although it might still be a little early for booze, thought Gösta. Ernst didn't seem to agree.

'I used that type of fertilizer up until sometime in '84 or '85, I think. Then there was some bloody environmental agency that decided it could have a "negative effect on the eco-balance".' He spoke in a shrill voice and made quotation marks in the air with his fingers. 'So then we had to switch to a fertilizer that was ten times worse and ten times more expensive. Fucking idiots.'

'How long did you use that fertilizer?'

'Oh, probably about ten years. I have the exact figures in my books, but I think it was sometime in the mid-Seventies that I started. Why are you so interested in it?' He peered suspiciously at Ernst and Gösta.

'It has to do with an investigation we're working on.'

Gösta said no more, but he could see a light slowly go on for the farmer.

'It's about those girls, isn't it? The girls in the King's Cleft? And the one who disappeared? Do you think I had something to do with that? Is that what you've got into your heads? Jesus Christ.'

Persson got up unsteadily from the table. He was a big man. He didn't show any of the normal signs of physical decline that come with age. His upper arms were sinewy and strong under his shirt. Ernst raised his hands and stood up too. He was always useful in these sorts of situations, Gösta thought gratefully. He lived for moments like this.

'Now let's all calm down. We have a lead that we're following up, and we have several people to visit. There's no reason to feel yourself singled out. But we would like to have a look around, just so we can cross you off the list.'

The farmer looked suspicious but then nodded. Gösta was careful to interject, 'Would you mind if I use the toilet?'

His bladder had seen better days, and his need to relieve himself had been building up and was now acute. Persson nodded and pointed towards a door with the letters 'WC' on it.

'Yes, damn it, people steal like ravens,' Ernst was saying. 'What are honest folks like you and I – ' He broke off guiltily when Gösta returned. An empty glass in front of Ernst revealed that he'd had the drink he'd been yearning for, and he and the farmer looked like two old friends.

Half an hour later, Gösta screwed up his courage to admonish his colleague.

'Jeez, you stink of booze. How do you think you're going to get past Annika with that breath of yours?'

'Oh, come on, Flygare. Don't be such a bloody schoolmarm. I only had a little nip, there's nothing wrong with that. Besides, it's impolite to refuse when someone offers you a drink.'

Gösta just snorted but made no comment. He felt depressed. Half an hour of wandering about the farmer's property hadn't produced a damn thing. There was no trace of any girl or any recently dug-up grave for that matter, and the morning felt wasted. But Ernst and the farmer had found common ground while Gösta was in the toilet emptying his bladder and had chatted the whole time they walked around the property. Personally Gösta felt that it would have been more appropriate to keep their distance from a possible suspect in a murder investigation, but Ernst followed his own counsel, as always.

'Did Persson say anything useful?'

Ernst exhaled into his cupped hand and then sniffed. He ignored Gösta's question at first. 'Say, Flygare, could you stop here so I can get some throat lozenges?'

Sullen and silent, Gösta turned in at the OK Q8 petrol station and waited in the car while Ernst ran in to buy something to remedy his breath problem. When he got back in the car, Ernst answered the question.

'No, we were really wasting our time out there. Hell of a nice guy, though, and I could swear he didn't have anything to do with it. No, we can cross off that theory right now. The thing with the fertilizer is a blind alley too. Those fucking forensic techs sit on their arses all day in a lab analysing themselves to death, while we working stiffs out in the real world see how ridiculous their theories are. DNA and hairs and fertilizer and tyre tracks and all that shit they potter about with. No, a good thrashing in the right spot, that's what really makes a case open up like a book, Flygare.' He clenched his fist to illustrate his views. Satisfied that he'd demonstrated how real police work was supposed to be conducted, he leaned his head back against the headrest and closed his eyes.

Gösta drove on in silence towards Tanumshede. He wasn't so sure.

*   *   *

247

The news had also reached Gabriel and his family. All three of them sat silently at the breakfast table, each lost in thought. To their great surprise, Linda had arrived home with her overnight things the night before and without a word went to bed in her room, which stood ready for her.

Hesitantly Laine broke the silence. 'How nice that you came home, Linda.'

Linda muttered something in reply, with her eyes fixed on the piece of bread she was buttering.

'Talk louder, Linda, it's not polite to mumble like that.'

Gabriel got a withering look from Laine, but he didn't much care. This was his house and he had no intention of making a fuss over the girl simply for the dubious pleasure of having her at home for a while.

'I told you I'll only be here for a night or two, then I'm going back to Västergården. Just needed a change of scene. All that hallelujah crap was getting to me. And it's damned depressing to see the way they treat the kids. I think it's really creepy too, the way the kids go around talking about Jesus . . .'

'Yes, I've told Jacob that I think they're a little too strict with the children. But they mean well. And faith is important for Jacob and Marita, we have to respect that. I know for instance that Jacob gets very upset when he hears you swearing. It's actually not language that's becoming for a young lady.'

Linda rolled her eyes in annoyance. She'd simply wanted to get away from Stefan for a while, and she knew he wouldn't dare ring her here. But the harping was already starting to get on her nerves. She'd probably have to go back to her brother's place tonight anyway. She couldn't live like this.

'Yes, I assume you heard at Jacob's house about the exhumation,' said Laine. 'Pappa rang there yesterday when the police contacted him. What an idiotic theory they've come up with! They're talking about some plan that Ephraim supposedly cooked up to make it look like Johannes was dead. That's the dumbest thing I've ever heard.'

Red patches appeared on the white skin of Laine's chest, and she kept fidgeting with her pearl necklace. Linda had to stifle an urge to reach over and tear off the necklace and shove all those fucking pearls down her throat.

Gabriel cleared his throat and joined the discussion with an authoritative voice. The whole business with the exhumation bothered him. It disturbed his routines and stirred up dust in his well-ordered world. He was strongly against the whole idea. He didn't think for a minute that the police had any reason for their assertions, but that wasn't the problem. Nor was it the thought that the peace of his brother's final resting place would be disturbed, even though that was definitely not pleasant. No, it was the disruption that the whole procedure involved. Coffins were supposed to be buried, not dug up. Once graves were dug they should be left untouched, and coffins that were once closed should remain closed. That's how things should be. Debit and credit. Everything in its proper order.

'Well, I think it's a little strange that the police are allowed to take arbitrary action like this,' said Gabriel. 'I don't know what arms they had to twist to get permission, but I intend to get to the bottom of it, believe me. This isn't a police state we live in, after all.'

Once again Linda muttered something into her plate.

'Pardon me, what did you say, dear?' said Laine, turning to her daughter.

'I said shouldn't you at least give a thought to how this must be for Solveig, Robert and Stefan? Do you have any idea how it must feel for them to have Johannes dug up like this? But no, the only thing you can do is complain about what a shame it is for you. Why don't you think a little about someone else for a change?'

249

She threw her napkin on the plate and left the table. Laine's hands flew to her necklace again and she seemed to be wondering whether to follow after her daughter or not. A look from Gabriel made her stay where she was.

'Well, we know where she got that high-strung temperament.'

His tone was accusatory. Laine didn't say a word.

'She has the nerve to claim that we don't care about how Solveig and the boys are taking all this. Of course we care, but time after time they've shown that they don't want our sympathy. As you make your bed, so must you lie in it . . .'

Sometimes Laine hated her husband. He sat there so smug, eating his eggs with a good appetite. In her mind she pictured herself going over to him, picking up his plate and slowly rubbing it against his chest. Instead she set about clearing the table.

8

They were sharing the pain now. Like two Siamese twins they were squeezed together into a symbiotic relationship that was held together by equal parts love and hate. On the one hand there was a security in not having to be alone down there in the dark. On the other, an antagonistic relationship was created from the desire to be spared, the wish that the other girl would have to endure the pain the next time he appeared.

They didn't speak much. Their voices echoed in a much too ghastly way in the blindness underground. When the footsteps approached they flew apart from each other, relinquishing the skin to skin contact that was their only defence against the cold and the dark. Now only the flight from pain was relevant, and they threw themselves at each other in a struggle to make the other girl the first to land in the hands of the evil one.

This time she won, and she heard the screams begin. In a way it was almost as bad to be the one who escaped. The sound of bones being broken was well imprinted on her auditory memory, and she felt every scream in her own mangled body. She also knew what would come after the screams. Then the hands that prised and twisted, cut and wounded would be transformed, now warm and tender,

251

placed on the spot where the pain was worst. Those hands she now knew as well as her own. They were big and strong, but at the same time smooth, without roughness or irregularities. The fingers were long and sensitive like a pianist's. And even though she had never actually seen them she could picture them quite clearly in her mind's eye.

Now the screams intensified, and she wished that she could lift her arms to put her hands to her ears. But her arms hung limp and useless by her side and refused to obey her instructions.

When the screams died out and the little hatch above their heads was opened and then closed again, she crawled across the cold, damp surface to the source of the screams.

Now it was time for solace.

When the lid of the coffin was lifted, there was total silence. Patrik caught himself half turning to stare nervously at the church. He didn't know what he expected. Maybe a bolt of lightning from the church tower that would strike them down in the midst of their blasphemous activity. But nothing of the sort occurred.

When Patrik saw the skeleton in the coffin his heart sank. He was wrong.

'Well, Hedström. This is a hell of a mess you've landed us in here.'

Mellberg shook his head in regret. With that one sentence he made Patrik feel as if his head had been placed on the chopping block. But his boss was right. It was a hell of a mess.

'We're going to take the body with us then, so we can confirm that it's the right guy. But there probably won't be any surprises on that point. You don't have any theories about switched bodies or the like, do you?'

Patrik just shook his head. He assumed that he'd got what he deserved. The techs did their job, and a while later when the skeleton was on its way to Göteborg, Patrik and Martin got into their car to drive back to the station.

'You could have been right. It wasn't that far-fetched.'

Martin's voice was consoling, but Patrik merely shook his head again.

'No, you were right. The conspiracy theories were a little too grandiose to be plausible. I suppose I'm going to have to live with this mistake for a long time to come.'

'Yes, you can probably count on that,' said Martin sympathetically. 'But ask yourself this: could you have lived with yourself if you hadn't done it? What if later on you found out you were right and it cost Jenny Möller her life? At least you tried. We just have to keep working with all the ideas that pop into our heads, crazy or not. That's our only chance to find her in time.'

'If it's not already too late,' said Patrik dismally.

'See, that's exactly the way we shouldn't be thinking. We haven't found her dead yet, so she must be alive. There isn't any other alternative.'

'You're right. But I simply don't know which way to turn. Where should we look? We keep coming back to that damned Hult family, but there's never enough to give us anything concrete to go on.'

'We have the connection between the murders of Siv, Mona and Tanja.'

'But nothing that connects them to Jenny's disappearance.'

'No,' Martin admitted. 'But it doesn't really matter, does it? The main thing is that we do everything we can to search for Tanja's killer and for whoever kidnapped Jenny. Whether it's the same person, or two different perps, time will tell. But we're doing everything we can.'

Martin stressed every word in that last sentence, hoping that the significance of what he was saying sank in. He understood why Patrik was kicking himself after the disinterment that failed to support his theory, but right now they couldn't afford an investigative leader with no self-confidence. Patrik had to believe in what they were doing.

When they arrived back at the station, Annika stopped

254

them at the reception desk. She was holding the phone in one hand and covering the mouthpiece with her other so the person on the other end wouldn't hear what she said to Patrik and Martin.

'Patrik, it's Stefan Hult. He's very anxious to get hold of you. Can you take it in your office?'

Patrik nodded and strode off. A second later the phone on his desk rang.

'Hello, Patrik Hedström.'

He listened eagerly, interrupted with a couple of questions, and then dashed into Martin's office with renewed energy.

'Let's go, Molin, we're off to Fjällbacka.'

'But we just came from there. Where are we going?'

'We have to have a little talk with Linda Hult. I think something interesting is developing, something really interesting.'

Erica had hoped that her guests, like the Flood family, would want to go boating during the day, so that she would be rid of them for a while. She was wrong on that score.

'We're not much for the sea, Madde and I. We'd rather keep you company here in the garden. It's such a beautiful view.'

Jörgen happily gazed towards the islands and prepared himself for a day in the sun. Erica suppressed a laugh. He looked idiotic. He was as pale as an albino and apparently intended to remain that way. He had smeared himself head to toe with sunblock, which made him even whiter, if that was possible. His nose was also covered with some kind of neon-coloured cream that provided extra protection. A big sun hat completed the look, and after half an hour of pottering about he settled with a contented sigh into a garden chair next to his wife. Erica had felt called upon to fetch chairs for them.

'Ah, this is paradise, don't you think, Madde?'

He closed his eyes, so Erica reckoned that she could sneak inside for a while.

Then he opened one eye and said, 'Would it be too much trouble to ask you to bring us something to drink? A big glass of juice would be wonderful. Madde would probably like one too.'

His wife just nodded without looking up. She had been engrossed in a book about tax law since she first came outside, and she too seemed to have a panicky terror of getting any kind of suntan. Ankle-length slacks and a long-sleeved shirt took care of that risk. She also had a sun hat on and a neon-coloured nose. Evidently one could never be safe enough. Side by side they looked like two aliens who had landed on Erica and Patrik's lawn.

Erica waddled inside and mixed some juice. As long as she didn't have to talk to them. They were the most amazingly tedious pair she'd ever encountered. If anyone had asked her last night to choose between talking with them or watching paint dry, there was no doubt which she would have chosen. When the time came, she would give Patrik's mother a piece of her mind for so generously giving them their phone number.

Patrik could at least escape for a while by going to work. Although she could tell that he was exhausted. She'd never seen him so haunted, so determined to produce results. But there had never been so much at stake before.

She wished she could have been more help to him. During the investigation of her friend Alex's death, she was able to help the police in several instances, but then she'd had a personal involvement with the case. Now she was also hindered by her gigantic body. Her belly and the heat had conspired to force her into involuntary idleness for the first time in her life. In some sense it felt as though her brain was also in neutral. All her thoughts were directed at the baby in her belly and the Herculean effort that would be required very soon. Her mind stubbornly refused to focus on other matters for long. She was amazed by the mothers who worked right up until the day before delivery. Perhaps she was simply different, because as the pregnancy progressed she had become more and more reduced – or elevated, depending on how you wanted to look at it – to a brooding, pulsating, nourishing organism of propagation. Every fibre in her body was concentrated on giving birth to the baby, and that's why interlopers were even more of a bother. They disturbed her concentration. She couldn't believe that she'd felt so restless being at home by herself. Right now the prospect seemed like paradise.

With a sigh, she mixed up a big pitcher of juice with crushed ice and carried it outside along with two glasses to the people from Mars on her lawn.

A quick check of Västergården revealed that Linda was not there. Marita looked puzzled when the two policemen showed up, but she didn't ask any questions. Instead she directed them to the manor house. For the second time in as many days, Patrik drove down the long avenue. Once again he was struck by how beautiful the place was. He could see Martin sitting next to him with his mouth hanging open.

'Damn, some people sure know how to live.'

'Yes, some have it good,' said Patrik.

'So only two people are living in that huge house?'

'Three if you count Linda.'

'Jesus, it's no wonder there's a housing shortage in Sweden.'

This time it was Laine who answered the door when they rang the bell.

'How can I help you?'

Did Patrik sense a hint of nervousness in her voice?

'We're looking for Linda,' Martin said. 'We were just at Västergården, but your daughter-in-law told us she was here.' Martin nodded vaguely in the opposite direction.

'What do you want from her?' Gabriel came up behind

Laine, who still hadn't opened the door enough to allow them in.

'We have some questions for her.'

'Nobody asks questions of my daughter unless we know what it's about.' Gabriel puffed out his chest, preparing to defend his offspring.

As Patrik was about to launch into his argument, Linda came walking round the corner of the manor house. She was dressed in riding clothes and appeared to be on her way to the stable.

'Are you looking for me?'

Patrik nodded, relieved at not having to enter into a direct confrontation with her father. 'Yes, we have a few questions for you. Would you like to go inside or stay out here?'

Gabriel interrupted. 'What's this all about, Linda? Have you been up to something we should know about? We have no intention of letting the police question you unless we're present, just so you know.'

Linda, who all at once looked like a frightened little girl, nodded weakly.

'Let's go inside,' she said.

Listlessly, she followed Martin and Patrik through the front door and into the living room. She didn't seem to worry about the furniture as she flopped down on the sofa in clothes that stank of horse. Laine couldn't help wrinkling her nose and casting a worried glance at the white upholstery. Linda gave her mother a defiant look.

'Is it all right if we ask you some questions with your parents present? If this were an official interview we wouldn't be able to forbid them from taking part since you're underage, but right now we just want to ask a few questions, so . . .'

Gabriel looked as though he were about to cast himself into a new argument about this point, but Linda shrugged her shoulders. For a moment, Patrik also thought he glimpsed a certain amount of expectant satisfaction mixed with her nervousness. But it vanished instantly.

'We recently received a call from Stefan Hult, your cousin. Do you know what it might have been about?'

Linda shrugged again and began absently picking at her cuticles.

'The two of you have been seeing each other a good deal, right?'

Patrik was advancing cautiously, one step at a time. Stefan had explained a little about their relationship, and Patrik understood that the news would not be well received by Gabriel and Laine.

'Yes, that's right, we've been seeing each other a good deal.'

'What the hell are you saying?'

Both Laine and Linda jumped. Like his son, Gabriel never used strong language. They couldn't remember ever hearing him utter such words before.

'What do you care? I'll see whoever I want to see. It's none of your business.'

Patrik intervened before the situation had a chance to deteriorate. 'We don't care whether you've been seeing each other or how often, and as far as we're concerned, you can keep that to yourself. But there is one occasion we are extremely interested in. Stefan said that you met one evening about two weeks ago, in the hayloft of the barn at Västergården.'

Gabriel's face turned beet-red with fury, but he said nothing as he waited for Linda's reply.

'That's possible. We've met there several times, but I'm not sure exactly when.'

She was still picking at her fingernails with great concentration and not looking at any of the grown-ups around her.

Martin took up where Patrik had left off. 'On this particular evening you saw something special, according to Stefan. You still don't know what I mean?'

'Since you seem to know, why don't you tell me instead?'

'Linda! Don't make matters worse by talking back! Now please answer the officer's questions. If you know what he's talking about, then tell us. But if it's something that that . . . hoodlum got you into, then I'm going to – '

'You? You don't know shit about Stefan. You're so fucking sanctimonious, but – '

'Linda . . .' Laine's voice warned her off. 'Don't make matters worse for yourself. Do as Pappa says and answer the policeman's questions. Then we'll talk about the rest later.'

After pondering for a moment, Linda seemed to accept her mother's reprimand and continued sulkily, 'I assume that Stefan told you that we'd seen that girl?'

'What girl?' The question mark was evident on Gabriel's face.

'That German girl, the one who was murdered.'

'Yes, that's what Stefan told us,' said Patrik. He waited Linda out in silence.

'I'm not as sure as Stefan was that it was her. We saw the photo on the flyers and it looked something like her, but there must be plenty of girls that look something like that. And what would she be doing at Västergården anyway? It's not exactly on the tourist route.'

Martin and Patrik ignored the question. They knew precisely what sort of business she had at Västergården. She was following the only clue she had that was linked to her mother's disappearance – Johannes Hult.

'Where were Marita and the children that night? Stefan said that they weren't at home, but he didn't know where they went.'

'They were staying for a few days with Marita's parents in Dals-Ed.'

'Jacob and Marita do that occasionally,' Laine explained. 'When Jacob wants a little peace and quiet to do some carpentry on the house, she and the kids spend a few days with the children's maternal grandparents. It gives them a chance to see each other a little more often. We live so close by that we see the children almost every day.'

'Let's forget whether it was Tanja Schmidt or not that you saw. But can you describe what the girl looked like?'

Linda hesitated. 'Dark hair, normal build. Shoulder-length hair. Like almost anybody. Not very pretty,' she added with the superiority of someone who knows she was born good-looking.

'And how was she dressed?' Martin leaned forward to try and catch the teenager's eye. He failed.

'Well, I don't really remember. It was about two weeks ago and it was getting dark outside . . .'

'Try,' Martin urged her.

'Jeans, I think. Some sort of tight T-shirt and a jacket. Blue jacket and white T-shirt, I think, or was it the other way round? Oh, and a red shoulder bag.'

Patrik and Martin exchanged glances. She had described exactly what Tanja was wearing the day she disappeared. The T-shirt was white and the jacket blue, not the other way round.

'What time did the two of you see her?'

'Fairly early in the evening, I think. About six, maybe.'

'Did you see whether Jacob let her in the house?'

'Nobody came to the door. Not when she knocked, at least. Then she went round the house and we couldn't see her any longer.'

'Did you see whether she left?' said Patrik.

'No, you can't see the road from the barn either. And as I said, I'm not as sure as Stefan that the girl we saw was Tanja Schmidt.'

'Do you have any idea who else it could have been? I mean, there aren't very many strangers who come and knock on the door out here at Västergården, are there?'

Another indifferent shrug. After a moment Linda said, 'I have

261

no idea who it might have been. For all I know, it could have been someone selling something.'

'But Jacob didn't mention a visitor later?'

'No.'

She didn't embellish her answer, and both Patrik and Martin understood that she was considerably more worried about what she'd seen than she wanted to let on. Either to them or to her parents.

'May I ask what it is you're looking for?' said Gabriel. 'As I said before, I think this is beginning to look like harassment of my family. As if it's not bad enough that you dug up my brother! How did that go, anyway? Was the coffin empty?'

Gabriel's tone was scornful, and Patrik couldn't help taking the bite of his criticism personally.

'We did find a body in the coffin. Probably your brother Johannes.'

'Probably,' Gabriel snorted, crossing his arms over his chest. 'Are you going to start pestering poor Jacob too?'

Laine shot her husband a dismayed look. Only now did she seem to understand the implications of the officers' questions.

'You don't think that Jacob . . .' Laine's hands wandered up to her throat.

'We don't think anything just yet. But we're extremely interested in finding out where Tanja went before she disappeared. So Jacob may be an important witness.'

'Witness! You're certainly trying to wrap things up nice and neat, I have to give you that. But don't think for a moment that we're going to fall for it. You're trying to clear up what your clumsy-ass colleagues started in '79, and it doesn't matter who you throw in jail, as long as it's a Hult, am I right? First you make it look like Johannes is still alive and started murdering girls here after twenty-four years. Then when he turns up dead as a doornail in his coffin, you start in on Jacob.'

Gabriel stood up and pointed to the door. 'Get out! I don't want to see you here again unless you have the proper warrant and I've had a chance to ring my lawyer. Until then you can go to hell!'

The curse words had begun to roll off his lips with ease, and a foam of spit had formed in the corners of his mouth. Patrik and Martin knew when their presence was no longer welcome, so they packed up and headed for the door. As the front door closed with a dull thud behind them, the last thing they heard was Gabriel's voice yelling at his daughter, 'Now what the hell have you been up to, young lady?'

'Even in the calmest waters . . .'

'Yes, I wouldn't have believed that there was such a volcano smouldering beneath that surface,' said Martin.

'Although I can't say that I blame him. Seen from his perspective . . .' Patrik's thoughts slipped away again to the morning's monumental fiasco.

'I told you not to think about that any more. You did the best you could. You can't keep wallowing in self-pity forever,' Martin said curtly.

Patrik looked at him in astonishment. Martin saw the look and shrugged his shoulders in apology. 'I'm sorry. The stress is starting to get to me too, I think.'

'No, no. You're quite right. This is no time to be feeling sorry for myself.' He took his eyes off the road for a second and looked at his colleague. 'And don't ever apologize for being honest.'

'Okay.'

They rode in embarrassed silence for a moment. When they passed the Fjällbacka golf course Patrik lightened the mood by saying, 'Aren't you going to get that green club card soon, so we can go out and shoot a round?'

Martin smiled impishly. 'Are you sure you dare? I might turn out to be a born golfer and mop the floor with you.'

'I doubt it. I'm a bit of a talent with a golf ball.'

'Well, we'll have to hurry, because there won't be much time later for games.'

'What do you mean?' Patrik looked truly baffled.

'Maybe you forgot, but you've got a kid on the way in a couple of weeks. Then there won't be much time left over for amusing yourself, you know.'

'Oh, it'll all work out. They sleep so much, those little babies, so we could probably squeeze in a round of golf. And Erica understands that I have to get out and do something on my own once in a while. We agreed on that when we decided to have a baby. We agreed to give each other space to do our own thing and not just be parents all the time.'

By the time Patrik finished his sentence, Martin's eyes were filled with tears of laughter. He chuckled and shook his head at the same time.

'Oh sure, there'll be plenty of time for you to do your own thing. They sleep so much, those little babies,' Martin mimicked him. That made him laugh even more.

Patrik, who knew that Martin's sister had five kids, began to look a little worried. He wondered whether Martin knew something that he didn't. But before he could ask, the mobile phone rang.

'Hedström.'

'Hello, it's Pedersen. Is this a good time to talk?'

'Actually, no. Hold on a second, I have to find someplace to park.'

They were just approaching the Grebbestad campground, which made a dark cloud pass across Patrik's face. He drove another couple of hundred metres until he came to the car park at Grebbestad Wharf. There he turned in and stopped so he could talk on the mobile.

'Now I'm parked. Have you found anything?'

He couldn't hide the eagerness in his voice, and Martin watched him tensely. Outside, the car tourists were streaming past, going in and out of the shops and restaurants. Patrik looked with envy at their happy and unsuspecting faces.

'Yes and no. We're going in for a closer look now, but considering the circumstances I thought you might be glad to hear that something good has come of your exhumation order, which was somewhat hastily performed, as I understand it.'

'Yes, I can't deny that. I feel a bit of an idiot, so anything you've got would be of interest.' Patrik held his breath.

'First of all, we've checked the dental records, and the guy in the coffin is without a doubt Johannes Hult, so on that point I can't give you anything interesting. On the other hand,' and the pathologist couldn't resist the temptation to pause for effect, 'it's pure nonsense that he was supposed to have died by hanging. His premature demise was more likely caused by something hard striking the back of his head.'

'What the hell are you saying?' Patrik yelled, making Martin jump. 'What kind of hard object? Was he clubbed in the head, or what are you telling me?'

'Something along those lines. But he's lying on the post-mortem table right now, so as soon as I know more I'll ring you again. Until I have a chance to do a more detailed examination, that's all I can tell you.'

'Thank you for ringing so soon. Let me know as soon as you know more.'

Triumphantly Patrik flipped shut the lid on his phone.

'What did he say, what did he say?' Martin was practically dying of curiosity.

'That I'm not a total idiot.'

'Well, it would take a psychiatrist to confirm something like that, but what else did he say?' replied Martin dryly since he didn't appreciate being kept on tenterhooks.

'He said that Johannes Hult was murdered.'

Martin bent his head forward and rubbed his face with both hands in mock despair. 'I'm resigning from this sodding investigation. This is crazy. You're telling me that the prime suspect for Siv and Mona's disappearance, or death as it turns out, was himself murdered?'

'That's exactly what I'm saying. And if Gabriel Hult thinks he can yell loud enough to make us stop rooting about in the family's dirty laundry, he's got another think coming. If there's anything that proves they've got a skeleton in the closet, then this is it. One of them knows how and why Johannes was murdered, and how his death is connected to the murders of the girls, I'll bet you that!' He pounded his fist into his palm, indicating that the morning's dismal events had now been replaced by renewed energy.

'I just hope we can work it out quickly enough. For Jenny Möller's sake,' Martin said.

His comment acted like a bucket of cold water over Patrik's head. He mustn't let his competitive instinct take over. He mustn't forget why they were doing this job. They sat for a moment and watched the people passing by. Then Patrik started the car and drove off towards the station.

Kennedy Karlsson believed that it had all started with his name. There wasn't really much else to blame it on. Many of the other guys had good excuses; their parents drank and beat them. But he had only his name to blame, it seemed.

His mother had spent a few years in the USA after she graduated. Back then it was still a big deal if somebody in the community went to the States. But in the mid-Thirties, when his mother made the trip, a ticket to the USA was no longer one-way. There were many people who had grown children who went off to the big cities of Sweden or abroad. The only thing that was different was that if someone left the security of the little town, tongues would wag, predicting that things were bound to turn out badly. And in his mother's case, they had more or less been right. After a couple of years in the promised land, she came back with a baby in her belly.

Kennedy Karlsson had never heard a word about his father.

But even that wasn't a good excuse. Just before he was born, his mother married Christer, and he'd been as good as a real father. No, it was all about the name. He assumed that she wanted to call attention to herself and show that she had been out in the big world, even though she came home with her tail between her legs. He would always be a reminder of that. So she never missed a chance to tell someone that her eldest son was named after John F. Kennedy, 'because during her years in the USA she had admired that man so much'. He wondered why she couldn't have simply named him John, in that case.

His mother and Christer had given his siblings a better fate. For them it sufficed to be called Emelie, Mikael and Thomas. Ordinary, honest Swedish names, which made him stick out even more. The fact that his father had been black didn't make matters any better, but Kennedy didn't believe that was what made him so odd. He was convinced it was the fucking name.

As a child he had actually looked forward to starting school. He remembered it well. The excitement, the joy, the eagerness to begin something new, to see a whole new world open up. It took only a day or two before they had pounded that enthusiasm out of him. Because of the bloody name. He soon learned what a sin it was to stick out from the crowd. A funny name, strange haircut, old-fashioned clothes, were all things that showed someone wasn't like the others. In his case it was also regarded as an aggravating circumstance that he, according to the others, thought he was superior because he had such an odd name. As if he were the one who picked it. If he'd been able to choose, he would have wanted a typical Swedish name like Stefan or Oskar or Fredrik. Something that gave him automatic entry to the group.

His hellish first days at school went from bad to worse. The taunts, the beatings, his outsider status all made him build a wall as strong as granite around himself. Soon his actions

267

were affected by his thoughts. All the anger he had built up inside the wall began to escape like steam from little holes that got bigger and bigger until everyone could see his anger. By then it was too late. School was lost to him, as was his family's confidence in him. And his friends were not the sort of friends he should have had.

Kennedy himself had resigned himself to the fate that his name had bestowed upon him. 'Problem' was tattooed on his brow, and all he needed to do was live down to expectations. An easy but paradoxically difficult way to live.

All that changed when he reluctantly came to the farm in Bullaren. It was a condition of his probation after he was caught in the unfortunate theft of a car. At first his attitude was to offer the least possible resistance so he could get out of the place as soon as possible. Then he met Jacob. And through Jacob he met God.

But in his eyes the two were nearly the same.

It hadn't happened through any miracle. He hadn't heard a thundering voice from above, or seen a bolt of lightning strike at his feet to prove that God existed. Instead it happened through the hours he spent with Jacob and their conversations. Little by little, he saw the image of Jacob's God appear. Like a puzzle that slowly takes the shape of the image shown on the outside of the box.

At first Kennedy had resisted. He ran off and carried on with his mates. He got roaring drunk and was ignominiously dragged back. The next day with an aching head he encountered Jacob's kind gaze which always, strangely enough, seemed to lack reproach.

He had complained to Jacob about his name, explaining that his name was to blame for all the mistakes he'd made. Jacob had countered by explaining to him that his name was something positive and that was actually an indicator of how his life would go. His name was a gift, Jacob had explained. To receive from the first moment of his life such a unique identity could only mean that God had chosen him above all others. The name made him special, not odd.

With the same enthusiasm that a starving man displays at the dinner table, Kennedy had clung to Jacob's words. Slowly it dawned on him that Jacob was right. The name was a gift. It made him special and showed that God had a specific plan for him, Kennedy Karlsson. And he had Jacob Hult to thank for finding this out before it was too late.

It bothered him that Jacob had been looking so worried lately. Kennedy hadn't been able to avoid hearing the gossip about how the family was connected with the dead girls, and he thought he understood the reason for Jacob's concern. He himself had felt the ill-will from a community out for blood. Now it was obviously the Hult family's turn to be the target.

Cautiously Kennedy knocked on Jacob's door. He thought he'd heard agitated voices coming from inside. When he opened the door Jacob was just hanging up the phone with a harried expression on his face.

'What is it?'

'Just a small family problem. Nothing that need concern you.'

'Your problems are my problems, Jacob. You know that. Can't you tell me what it is? Trust me the way I've trusted you.'

Jacob wearily rubbed his eyes and seemed to collapse.

'It's so stupid, all of it. Because of a mistake that my father made twenty-four years ago, the police have got the idea that we have something to do with the murder of that German tourist that was in all the papers.'

'That's terrible.'

'Yes, and the latest news is that they dug up my uncle Johannes's grave this morning.'

'What? They violated the peace of the grave?'

Jacob gave him a crooked smile. A year ago Kennedy wouldn't have understood what that meant.

'Unfortunately, yes. The whole family is suffering. But there's nothing we can do.'

Kennedy felt the familiar anger rising in his chest. Although it felt better now. Nowadays it was the wrath of God.

'But can't you report them? For harassment or something?'

Once again Jacob's crooked, sad smile. 'So you're saying that your experience with the police shows that something like that would work?'

No, that was clear. His respect for cops was low, almost non-existent. He of all people could understand Jacob's frustration.

Kennedy felt a tremendous gratitude that Jacob had chosen to share his worries with him. It was another gift that he would remember to thank God for in his evening prayers. He was just about to open his mouth to tell Jacob this when the ring of the telephone interrupted them.

'Excuse me.' Jacob picked up the receiver.

When he hung up several minutes later he looked even paler. From listening to half of the conversation Kennedy had gathered that it was Jacob's father who rang. He made an effort not to look as if he'd been eagerly eavesdropping.

'Did something happen?'

Jacob slowly put down his eyeglasses.

'Tell me, what did he say?' Kennedy couldn't hide the fact that his heart was aching with anxiety and concern.

'That was my father. The police were there asking my sister questions. My cousin Stefan rang the police and claimed that he and my sister saw the murdered girl at my farm. Just before she disappeared. God help me.'

'God help you,' Kennedy whispered like an echo.

They had gathered in Patrik's office. It was crowded, but with a little effort they had all managed to squeeze in. Mellberg had offered his office, which was three times the size of the other offices, but Patrik didn't want to move everything he had put up on the bulletin board behind his desk.

The board was full of notes and scraps of paper, and in the middle were the photos of Siv, Mona, Tanja and Jenny. Patrik was sitting on the edge of his desk, partially turned away from the others. For the first time in ages, they were all gathered in the same place: Patrik, Martin, Mellberg, Gösta, Ernst and Annika. The entire brain trust of the Tanumshede police station. All with their eyes focused on Patrik. Suddenly he felt the weight of responsibility drop onto his shoulders, and tiny beads of sweat began to form at the small of his back. He had always hated being the centre of attention, and the thought that everyone was waiting for what he had to say made his skin crawl. He cleared his throat.

'Half an hour ago I got a call from Tord Pedersen at Forensic Medicine, who told me that the exhumation this morning was not wasted effort.' Here he paused and permitted himself a moment of satisfaction over what he'd just said. He had not been looking forward to being the butt of jokes from his colleagues for a considerable time to come.

'The post-mortem on Johannes Hult's body shows that he did not hang himself. Instead it looks as though he received some sort of hard blow to the back of the head.'

A gasp went through the room. Patrik went on, aware that now he had everyone's undivided attention. 'So we have yet another murder, even though it's not fresh. I thought it was time we had a meeting to go over what we know. Any questions so far?' Silence. 'All right. Then let's get started.'

Patrik began by going over all the old material they had about Siv and Mona, including Gabriel's testimony. He continued with Tanja's death and the medical evidence showing that she had the exact same type of injuries as Siv and Mona. He also mentioned another connection that Tanja turned out to be Siv's daughter, and then went on to discuss Stefan's account of having seen Tanja at Västergården.

Gösta weighed in. 'But what about Jenny Möller? I, at least, am not convinced that there's any connection between her disappearance and the murders.'

Everyone's eyes sought out the photo of the blonde seventeen-year-old smiling at them from the bulletin board. Patrik looked at it too. He said, 'I agree with you there, Gösta. It's only one theory among many right now. But the search parties didn't turn up anything, and our scrutiny of known violent offenders in the area gave us only the blind alley of Mårten Frisk. So our only hope is that the public will come to our assistance and that somebody saw something. At the same time we need to keep working on the possibility that the same person who murdered Tanja also abducted Jenny. Does that answer your question?'

Gösta nodded. Basically it meant that they didn't know a thing, and it pretty much confirmed what he was thinking.

'By the way, Gösta, I heard from Annika that you and Ernst went to check up on that fertilizer lead. Did it produce anything?'

Ernst replied instead of Gösta. 'Not a damn thing. The farmer we talked to has nothing to do with all this.'

'But you took a look around, for safety's sake?' Patrik was not convinced by Ernst's assurances.

'Yes, of course we did. And as I said, not a thing,' Ernst replied sourly.

Patrik shot Gösta a questioning glance, and he nodded in agreement.

'All right then. We'll have to do some thinking about whether anything useful will result if we proceed along that track. Meanwhile, as I mentioned, we've received a report from someone who saw Tanja just before she vanished. Johannes's son, Stefan, rang this morning and reported that he saw a girl he swears was Tanja at Västergården. His cousin Linda, Gabriel's daughter, was with him. Martin and I drove out there and spoke with her today. She confirmed that they had seen a girl, but she wasn't as convinced as Stefan that it was Tanja.'

'Can we trust this witness, though? Stefan's police record and the rivalry within the family seem to make it extremely doubtful how much credence we can give to what he says, don't you think?' said Mellberg.

'Yes, that worries me too. We'll probably have to wait and see what Jacob Hult says. But I think it's interesting that we keep coming back to that family, one way or another. Wherever we turn, we run into the Hult family.'

The temperature was rising fast in the cramped office. Patrik had opened a window, but it didn't help much since there wasn't any cool air outside either. Annika tried fanning herself with her notebook. Mellberg wiped the sweat from his brow with his hand, and Gösta's face had turned an alarming grey beneath his suntan. Martin had unbuttoned the top buttons of his shirt, which made Patrik enviously note that at least some people managed to put in time at the gym.

Only Ernst looked completely unaffected. He said, 'Yep, in that case I'd put my money on one of those bloody bastards. They're the only ones who've been in trouble with the police before.'

'Except for their father,' Patrik reminded him.

'Exactly, except for their father. It only goes to show that there's something rotten in that branch of the family.'

'And what about the information that Tanja was last seen at Västergården? According to the sister, Jacob was at home at that time. Doesn't that seem to point to him?'

Ernst snorted. 'And who is it that says the girl was there? Stefan Hult. No, I wouldn't believe a word that guy says.'

'When do you think we ought to talk to Jacob?' asked Martin.

'I was thinking that you and I should go over to Bullaren right after the meeting here. I rang to check, and he's working today.'

'Don't you think Gabriel might have called to warn him?'

'Sure, but there's nothing we can do about that. We'll have to see what he says.'

'What are we going to do with the information that Johannes was murdered?' Martin went on stubbornly.

Patrik didn't want to admit that he didn't really know. There were too many things to keep track of right now, and he was afraid that if he took a step back and looked at the big picture, the overwhelming nature of the task would make him powerless to act. He sighed. 'We'll have to take one thing at a time. We won't mention anything about it to Jacob when we talk to him. I don't want Solveig and the boys to be tipped off.'

'So the next step is to talk to them?'

'Yes, I think that would be best. Unless someone else has a better suggestion?'

Silence. Nobody seemed to have any other ideas.

'What should the rest of us do?' Gösta was breathing heavily, and Patrik suddenly worried that he might be having a heart attack in this heat.

'Annika said that information from the public has been trickling in since we posted the pictures of Jenny on the flyers. She arranged them according to what seemed the most interesting, so you and Ernst can start browsing through the list.'

Patrik hoped that he wasn't making a mistake by allowing Ernst back into the investigation. He would give his colleague one more chance. That was what he'd decided after Ernst seemed to have toed the line when he and Gösta followed up the lead about the fertilizer.

'Annika, I'd like you to contact the company again that sold the fertilizer and ask them to widen the area in their search for customers. I have a hard time believing that the bodies were transported very far, but it would still be a good idea to check.'

'No problem.' Annika fanned herself even harder with the notebook. Beads of sweat had formed on her upper lip.

Mellberg was given no assignment. Patrik knew that he had a hard time giving orders to the chief, and so he preferred not to have him involved in the daily work of the investigation. Although he had to admit that Mellberg had done astonishingly good work by keeping the politicians out of his hair.

There was still something unusual about him. Normally Mellberg's voice was the loudest of all, but right now he was sitting quietly, looking like he was in a foreign country. The cheerfulness that had bewildered them all for the past couple of weeks had been replaced by an even more worrisome silence.

Patrik asked, 'Bertil, do you have anything you'd like to add?'

Mellberg gave a start. 'What? Pardon me, what did you say?'

'Do you have anything to add?'

'Oh, I see,' said Mellberg, clearing his throat when he noticed that all eyes were directed at him. 'No, I don't think so. You seem to have the situation under control.'

Annika and Patrik exchanged glances. Normally he was as sharp as an eagle about everything that went on at the station, but now he simply shrugged and raised his eyebrows to show that he had no better ideas to offer, either.

'Any questions? No? All right. Let's get back to work.'

Gratefully they all exited the hot office to try and find somewhere cooler. Only Martin remained behind.

'When do we leave?'

'I thought we should have lunch first and then leave right afterwards.'

'Okay. Should I run out and buy something for us? Then we can eat in the lunchroom.'

'Sure, that would be great. Then I'll have time to ring Erica first.'

'Say hi from me.' Martin was already on his way out.

Patrik dialled the number at home. He hoped that Jörgen and Madde weren't boring her to death . . .

* * *

'This is certainly a rather isolated spot.' Martin looked around but saw only trees. They had driven for fifteen minutes on narrow forest roads, and he was starting to wonder if they were lost.

'Don't worry, I've got it covered. I was out here once before when one of the boys got a bit out of hand, so I can find the place.'

Patrik was right. A couple of minutes later, they turned in towards the farm.

'Looks like a nice location,' Martin said.

'Yes indeed, and they have quite a good reputation. Or at least they've managed to keep up a good façade to the outside world. I myself get a little sceptical as soon as there's too much hallelujah, but that's just me. Even if the initial purpose of these free-religious societies is good, sooner or later they always seem to attract a lot of strange people. They offer a strong sense of community and family which appeals to people who don't feel that they belong anywhere.'

'It sounds like you know what you're talking about.'

'Well, my sister was once enticed into a rather strange situation. You know, during that searching period in her teens. But she came out of it with her skin intact, so it wasn't all bad. But I learned enough about how things worked to develop a healthy scepticism. But as I said, I've never heard anything negative about this specific group, so there's probably no reason to suspect otherwise.'

'Yes, well, it doesn't really have anything to do with our investigation,' said Martin.

It sounded like a warning, and that's partially what he intended. Patrik was usually so together, but there had been a tone of contempt in his voice that made Martin a bit concerned about how his personal feelings might affect their interview with Jacob.

Patrik seemed to read his mind. He smiled. 'Don't worry.

It's just one of my pet peeves, but it has nothing to do with the case.'

They parked and got out of the car. The farm was seething with activity. Boys and girls seemed to be working everywhere, both inside and out. A group was swimming down at the lake, and the noise level was high. It looked so idyllic. Martin and Patrik knocked on the door. A boy in his late teens opened it. They both gave a start. If it hadn't been for his glum expression they wouldn't have recognized him.

'Hello, Kennedy.'

'What do you want?' His tone was aggressive.

Neither Patrik nor Martin could help staring. Gone was the long hair that he always had hanging in his face. Gone, too, were the black clothes and the unhealthy complexion. The boy standing before them now was so clean and well-groomed that he fairly shone. But the aggressive look was something they remembered from the many times they had booked him for car theft, drug possession and more.

'Looks like you're doing well, Kennedy,' Patrik said in a friendly tone. He had always felt sorry for the boy.

Kennedy didn't deign to reply. Instead he repeated, 'What do you want?'

'We'd like to speak with Jacob. Is he in?'

Kennedy blocked their path. 'What do you want with him?'

Still friendly, Patrik said, 'It's nothing to do with you. So I'll ask again, is he in?'

'I'll be damned if you're going to come here and harass him. Or his family. I've heard what you're trying to do, and you should know that I think it's fucked. But you'll get your just deserts. God sees everything, and He can see into your hearts.'

Martin and Patrik exchanged a look. 'Okay, that's fine, Kennedy, but now it's best that you move aside and let us in.'

Patrik's tone was threatening now, and after a moment

of this test of wills, Kennedy backed off and reluctantly let them in.

'Thanks,' said Martin curtly and followed Patrik down the hall. Patrik seemed to know where he was going.

'His office is at the end of the corridor, as I recall.'

Kennedy followed a couple of paces behind them, like a silent shadow. Martin shivered in spite of the heat.

They knocked on the door. Jacob was sitting behind his desk when they entered. He didn't look surprised to see them.

'Well, look who we have here. The long arm of the law. Don't you have any real crooks to catch?'

Behind them, Kennedy stood in the doorway with his fists clenched.

'Thank you, Kennedy, you can go now. And close the door.'

Silently but reluctantly, he obeyed the order.

'So you know why we're here, I presume,' Patrik said.

Jacob took off his computer glasses and leaned forward. He looked harried.

'Yes, I had a call from my father about an hour ago. He told me a crazy story that my dear cousin claimed he'd seen the murdered girl at my house.'

'Is the story true?' Patrik scrutinized Jacob.

'Of course not.' He was tapping his glasses on the desk. 'Why would she have come to Västergården? From what I understand she was a tourist, and the farm is hardly on the tourist route. And as far as Stefan's so-called testimony is concerned . . . well, you know by this time what our family situation is like. Unfortunately Solveig and her sons take every opportunity to paint our family black. It's very annoying, but some people do not have God in their hearts. What they have is something entirely different . . .'

'Be that as it may,' said Patrik, smiling courteously, 'we actually have an idea why she might have had business at Västergården.' Did he see a worried glint in Jacob's eyes? He went on, 'She wasn't in Fjällbacka as a tourist, but to look

278

for her roots. And perhaps to find out more about her mother's disappearance.'

'Her mother?' said Jacob, bewildered.

'Yes, she was Siv Lantin's daughter.'

Jacob's glasses clattered onto the desk. Was the surprise feigned or genuine? Martin wondered, leaving Patrik to carry on the interview. In the meantime, he devoted himself to watching Jacob's reactions as they talked.

'Well, that's big news, I must say. But I still don't understand what sort of business she would have at Västergården.'

'As I said, she seemed to be trying to find out more information about what happened to her mother. And considering the fact that your uncle was the prime suspect in the case . . .' He didn't finish the sentence.

'I must say that this all sounds like wild speculation to my ears. My uncle was innocent, and yet you drove him to his death with your insinuations. With him gone, you apparently want to try and put another one of us in prison. Tell me, what sort of splinter is in your heart that gnaws at you and makes you feel such a need to tear down what someone else has created? Is it our faith and the joy we find in it, that sticks in your craw?'

Jacob had switched to sermonizing, and Martin understood why he was such an esteemed preacher. There was something spellbinding about the rising and falling cadence of his gentle voice.

'We're just doing our job.'

Patrik's tone was curt and he had to stop himself from showing his distaste for all that he regarded as religious drivel. But he too had to admit that Jacob had a certain power when he spoke. Weaker people than himself might easily give in to that voice and be tempted by its message. He went on, 'So you're saying that Tanja Schmidt never came to Västergården?'

Jacob threw out his hands. 'I swear that I never saw the girl. Is there anything else?'

Martin thought about what they had learned from Pedersen, the pathologist. The fact that Johannes did not commit suicide. That information would probably shake up Jacob quite a bit. But he knew that Patrik was right. They would hardly be out of the room before the phones would probably start ringing at the homes of the rest of the Hult family.

'No, I think that's all. But it's possible that we'll return later on.'

'I wouldn't be surprised.'

Jacob's voice had lost its preaching tone and was again mild and calm. Martin was just about to reach for the door handle when the door quietly swung open. Kennedy had been standing silently outside, and he opened it at precisely the right moment. There was no doubt that he'd been eavesdropping. A black fire was blazing in his eyes. Martin shrank from the hatred he saw there. Jacob must have been teaching him more about 'an eye for an eye' than 'love thy neighbour'.

The mood was oppressive around the little table. Not that it had ever been cheerful. Not since Johannes died.

'When is this going to end?' said Solveig, pressing her hand to her breast. 'Why do we always have to land in the shit? Everyone seems to believe that we're just sitting here waiting for someone to kick us!' she wailed. 'What are people going to say now, when they hear that the police dug up Johannes! I thought the gossip would finally come to an end when they found that last girl, but now it's all starting up again.'

'Let people talk, damn it! What do we care what they gossip about in their homes?' Robert stubbed out a cigarette so hard that the ashtray tipped over.

Solveig snatched away her albums. 'Robert! Be careful! You could get burn marks on the albums.'

'I'm so sick of your fucking albums! Day in, day out you

sit there fiddling with those damned old photos. Don't you get it? Those days are gone. It's like a hundred years ago, but you keep sighing and messing about with your sodding pictures. Pappa is gone and you're no beauty queen any more. Just look at yourself.'

Robert grabbed the albums and flung them across the floor. Solveig threw herself after them with a shriek and began gathering up the pictures that were scattered all over the floor. That just made Robert even more furious. He ignored Solveig's pleading look, bent down, picked up a handful of photos and began tearing them into tiny bits.

'No, Robert, no, not my pictures! Please, Robert!' Her mouth was like an open wound.

'You're a fat old woman, haven't you realized that? And Pappa killed himself. It's time you dealt with that.'

Stefan had sat as if frozen during this scene. Now he got up and took a firm grip on Robert's hand. He prised loose the rest of the photos that Robert was clutching and forced his brother to listen.

'Now, you calm down. This is exactly what they want, don't you see that? They want to turn us against each other so that our family will be torn apart. But we won't give them that satisfaction, do you hear me? We're going to stick together. Now help Mamma pick up the albums.'

Robert's anger fizzled out like the air from a balloon. He rubbed his hand over his eyes and looked in horror at the mess he had made. Solveig lay on the floor like a big, soft heap of despair, sniffling, with pieces of photos sliding through her fingers. Her sobs were heartrending. Robert sank to his knees and put his arms round her. Tenderly he stroked a greasy strand of hair from her forehead and then helped her up.

'Forgive me, Mamma, I'm so sorry, so sorry. I'll help you fix up the albums again. I can't mend the pictures I tore up, but there weren't very many. See, the best ones are still here. Look at you in this one, how beautiful you were.'

He held up a picture in front of her. Solveig posing in a modestly cut bathing suit with a banner across her breast that said 'May Queen 1967'. And she really was beautiful. Her sobs changed to a hacking cough. She took the pictures from him and smiled. 'I really was beautiful, wasn't I, Robert?'

'Yes, Mamma, you were. The most beautiful girl I ever saw!'

'Do you really think so?'

She gave him a coquettish smile and stroked his hair. He helped her over to the kitchen chair.

'Yes, I do. Cross my heart.'

A moment later, everything was gathered up and she was once again fiddling happily with her albums. Stefan signalled to Robert that they should go outside. They sat on the steps outside the cabin and each lit a cigarette.

'Damn, Robert, you can't flip out now.'

Robert scraped his foot in the gravel. He said nothing. What should he say?

Stefan took a deep drag and enjoyed the feeling of the smoke seeping out between his lips. 'We can't play into their hands. I meant what I said in there. We have to stick together.'

Robert still sat in silence. He was ashamed. A big hole in the gravel had formed where he was dragging his foot back and forth. He tossed the fag-end in the hole and covered it with dirt, though that was quite unnecessary. The ground around them was littered with old cigarette butts. After a while he turned to look at Stefan.

'Stefan, you said you saw that girl at Västergården.' He hesitated. 'Was it true?'

Stefan took one last drag on his cigarette and tossed the butt to the ground as well. He stood up without looking at his brother.

'Damn straight it's true.' Then he went back inside the cabin.

Robert sat there and for the first time in his life he felt that a chasm had opened up between him and his brother. It scared the shit out of him.

The afternoon passed in deceptive calm. Until they heard more details about the post-mortem on Johannes, Patrik didn't want to do anything hasty, so he more or less sat and waited for the telephone to ring. He felt restless and went in to see Annika to have a chat.

'How's it going for you?' As usual she peered at him over the rim of her glasses.

'This heat doesn't make it any easier.' As he said that he noticed a pleasant breeze in Annika's office. A big fan was whirring on her desk, and Patrik closed his eyes with pleasure.

'Why didn't I think of that? I bought a fan for Erica to have at home, so why didn't I get one for the office as well? That's the first thing I'm going to do in the morning, that's for sure.'

'So, how's it going with Erica's pregnancy? It must be miserable for that poor girl in this heat.'

'Yes, before I bought her the fan, she was about to climb the walls. She's not sleeping well, she has cramps in her calves, and she can't lie on her stomach at all. You know how it is.'

'No, I can't say as I do,' said Annika.

Patrik realized with a shock what he'd said. Annika and her husband had no children, and he'd never dared ask why. Perhaps they couldn't have children. If so, he'd really put his foot in it with his rash comment. She saw his embarrassment.

'Don't worry about it. It's a conscious decision on our part. We've never felt any great desire to have children. For us it's enough to lavish our affection on the dogs.'

Patrik could feel the colour returning to his cheeks. 'I was afraid I'd put my foot in it there. In any case, it's hard for both of us right now, even though it's obviously harder for Erica. We just want to get it over with somehow. And our house has been sort of invaded lately.'

283

'Invaded?' Annika raised an eyebrow.

'Relatives and acquaintances who think that Fjällbacka in July sounds like a fantastic idea.'

'And they really enjoy bossing you around, right?' Annika said. 'Yes, we know all about that. We had the same problem with our summer house at first, until we'd had enough and told all the freeloaders to get lost. We haven't heard from them since, but we noticed that we didn't miss them at all. Real friends show up in November too. The others you can afford to lose.'

'True, so true,' said Patrik, 'but easier said than done. Erica basically threw out the first bunch that came, but now we're stuck with the next round of guests, trying to be hospitable. And poor Erica, who's at home all day, has to keep waiting on them.' He sighed.

'Then maybe you need to be a man about it and resolve the situation.'

'Me?' Patrik gave Annika an offended look.

'Sure, if Erica is stressed out while you manage to escape all day long, maybe you should put your foot down and see to it that she gets a little peace and quiet. It can't be easy for her. She's used to having her own career and all, and suddenly she has to sit at home and stare at her navel while your life rolls along as usual.'

'I never thought of it that way,' Patrik said sheepishly.

'No, I figured you hadn't. So this evening you need to throw out the guests, no matter what Martin Luther is whispering in your ear. And then you have to make a proper fuss over the expectant mother. Have you talked to her and asked how she's doing, alone at home all day? I assume she can't go out, either, in this heat, so she's pretty much a prisoner in the house.'

'Right.' Patrik was whispering by now. It was like being run over by a steamroller. His throat felt thick with worry. It didn't take a genius to see that Annika was right. A mixture of short-sighted selfishness and his habit of letting himself get swallowed up by his work had made him neglect Erica. He had assumed that it must be great for her to take a holiday and devote herself to the pregnancy. What made him so embarrassed was that he knew Erica better than that. He knew how important it was for her to be doing something meaningful. It wasn't like her to be idle. No doubt it had suited his purposes to fool himself.

'So, don't you think you should go home a little early and take care of your wife?'

'But I'm waiting for a call,' was his automatic response. The look Annika gave him told him that was the wrong answer.

'Your mobile phone only works within the walls of the station, you mean? Kind of a limited range, don't you think?'

'Right,' Patrik whimpered. He jumped up from his chair. 'I'm going home right now. Will you patch any calls through to my mobile . . . ?'

Annika looked at him as if he were developmentally challenged, and he backed out the door. If he'd had a cap, he would have been clutching it in his hands, bowing his way out the door . . .

But unforeseen events intervened, and it was more than an hour before he left the station.

Ernst was trying to choose amongst the coffee cakes at Hedemyr's. He'd intended to try the bakery, but the queue there made him change his mind.

In the middle of deciding between cinnamon buns and Delicato balls, his attention was caught by a dreadful commotion upstairs. He put down the cakes and went to check on things. The shop was divided into three floors. On the ground floor was the restaurant, kiosk and bookshop, on the next floor groceries, and the top floor had clothing, shoes and gifts. Two women were standing by the cash register tugging at a handbag.

One woman was wearing a badge on her chest that identified her as one of the staff, while the other woman looked like someone in a low-budget Russian film. A short miniskirt, net stockings, a top that would have fit a twelve-year-old, and enough make-up to colour a road map from Beckers.

'No, no, my bag!' shrieked the woman in broken English.

'I saw you took something,' replied the shop assistant, also in English but with a distinct Swedish intonation. She looked relieved when she spied Ernst.

'Thank goodness, please arrest this woman. I saw her walking about and stuffing things in her handbag, and then she brazenly tried to walk out of here with them.'

Ernst didn't hesitate. In two long strides he reached the woman and took the suspected shoplifter by the arm. Since he knew no English, he didn't bother to ask any questions. Instead he tore the capacious handbag brusquely from her grasp and simply dumped the contents on the floor. A hair dryer, a shaver, an electric toothbrush and, for some unknown reason, a ceramic pig with a midsummer wreath on its head, all poured out of the bag.

'What do you say to this, eh?' Ernst said in Swedish. The assistant translated.

The woman just shook her head and tried to look as though she was stunned. She said, 'I know nothing. Speak to my boyfriend, he will fix this. He is boss of police!'

'What's the dame saying?' Ernst hissed. It irritated him to have to rely on a woman to translate for him.

'She says that she doesn't know anything. And that you should talk to her boyfriend. She says he's the Chief of Police?'

The assistant looked back and forth in astonishment between Ernst and the woman, who now stood with a superior smile on her face.

'Oh yes, she'll get a chance to talk to the police, all right. Then we'll see if she keeps up with her bullshit story about a "boyfriend who's chief of police". That number might work in Russia or wherever the hell you come from, lady, but it won't work around here,' he yelled, his face only a couple of centimetres from the woman's. She didn't understand a word, but for the first time she looked a little uncertain.

Ernst roughly escorted her out of Hedemyr's and across the street to the police station. The woman was practically dragged behind him in her high heels, and people slowed down in their cars to watch the spectacle. Annika opened her eyes wide as he stormed past the reception desk.

'Mellberg!' Ernst called so it echoed down the corridor. Patrik, Martin and Gösta all stuck their heads out to see what was going on. Ernst yelled once again towards Mellberg's office. 'Mellberg, come here, I have your girlfriend here!' He chuckled to himself. Now she'd get her comeuppance. It was alarmingly quiet in Bertil's office, and Ernst began to wonder whether the chief had slipped out while he was shopping. 'Mellberg?' he called a third time, now a bit less enthusiastic about his plan to make the woman eat her words. Ernst stood in the corridor with the woman in a firm grip and everyone stared at him. Finally Mellberg emerged from his office with his gaze fixed on the floor. Ernst felt a lump forming in his stomach as he realized that things were probably not going to work out as splendidly as he had imagined.

'Be-e-ertil!' The woman tore herself loose and ran over to Mellberg, who froze in his tracks like a deer in the headlights. Since she was twenty centimetres taller than he was, it looked funny when she pressed him close in an embrace. Ernst's jaw dropped open. Feeling like sinking through the floor, he decided to start writing his letter of resignation at once. Before he got the boot. In horror he realized that several years of steady kissing-up to the chief had been ruined by one unfortunate act.

The woman released her hold on Mellberg and turned to point at Ernst, who stood sheepishly holding her handbag.

'This brutal man put hands on me! He say I steal! Oh, Bertil, you must help your poor Irina!'

Mellberg awkwardly patted her on the shoulder, which meant that he had to lift his hand about to the level of his own nose. 'You go home, Irina, okay? To house. I come later. Okay?'

His English could be termed halting at best, but she understood what he said and did not appreciate it.

'No, Bertil. I stay here. You talk to that man, and I stay here and see you work, okay?'

He shook his head firmly and began shooing her out ahead of him. She turned anxiously and said, 'But Bertil, honey, Irina not steal, okay?'

Then she strutted out on her high heels after casting one last spiteful look of triumph at Ernst. For his part he was still staring down at the carpet and didn't dare meet Mellberg's gaze.

'Lundgren! In my office now!'

In Ernst's ears this sounded like doomsday. He slouched obediently after Mellberg. In the corridor heads were still sticking out, with mouths agape. Now at least they knew the cause of all the mood swings.

'Now would you please tell me what happened?' said Mellberg.

Ernst nodded feebly. Sweat broke out on his brow. This time it wasn't because of the heat.

He told his boss about the commotion at Hedemyr's and how he saw the woman involved in a tug-of-war with the shop assistant. With a quavering voice he also recounted how he had dumped out the contents of the handbag, and how a number of items had not been paid for. Then he fell silent and waited for the judgement. To his surprise Mellberg leaned back in his chair with a deep sigh.

'It's a hell of a mess I've landed in.' He paused for a moment, then leaned down and pulled out a drawer. He took out something that he tossed on the desk towards Ernst.

'This is what I expected. Page three.'

Curious, Ernst picked up what looked like a class catalogue and turned to page three. The pages were full of photos of women, with brief descriptions of height, weight, eye colour and interests. He suddenly realized what Irina was: a 'mail-order bride'. Although, there was not much similarity between the actual Irina and the portrait of her in the catalogue. In the description she had deducted at least ten years, ten kilos and a kilo of make-up. In the pictures she was beautiful and innocent, staring into the camera with a broad smile. Ernst looked at the portrait and then at Mellberg, who threw his arms wide.

'You see, *that* was what I expected. We exchanged letters for a year, and I could hardly wait to get her here.' He nodded at the catalogue in Ernst's lap. 'And then she arrived.' He sighed. 'It was a hell of a cold shower, I have to tell you. And it started immediately: "Bertil, darling, buy this and buy that." I even caught her going through my wallet when she thought I wasn't looking. I swear, it's a hell of a mess.'

He patted the nest of hair on top of his head, and Ernst noticed that the Mellberg who was so careful about his appearance was gone. Now his shirt was once again stained, and the sweat rings under his arms were as big as salad plates. It felt reassuring somehow. Things were back to their natural order.

'I'm counting on you not to go babbling about this.' Mellberg wagged his finger at Ernst, who shook his head vigorously. He wouldn't say a word. Relief washed over him; he wasn't going to get the sack after all.

'Could we forget about this little incident, then? I'll see to it that it's taken care of. The first plane home is what it's going to be.'

Ernst got up and backed out of the office with a bow.

'And you can tell everyone out there to stop whispering and start doing an honest day's work instead.'

Ernst broke out in a wide grin when he heard Mellberg's gruff voice. The chief was back in the saddle.

If Patrik had any doubt about the correctness of Annika's advice, it disappeared as soon as he walked through the door. Erica flung herself into his arms, and he saw the exhaustion like a veil covering her face. His guilty conscience immediately started gnawing at him. He should have been more sensitive, more attentive to Erica's state of mind. Instead, he had buried himself in work even more than he did normally and let her wander about the house with nothing interesting to occupy her time.

'Where are they?' he whispered.

'Out in the garden,' Erica whispered back. 'Oh, Patrik, I can't stand it if I have to put up with them another day. They've been sitting on their bums all day and expecting me to wait on them. I can't take any more.'

She collapsed in his arms and he stroked her hair. 'Don't worry, I'll take care of this. I'm sorry, I shouldn't have worked so much the past week.'

'You asked me whether it was all right and I said okay. And you didn't really have a choice,' Erica murmured against his shirt front.

Despite his guilty conscience, Patrik was inclined to agree. How could he do otherwise when a girl was missing, perhaps held captive somewhere? At the same time, he needed to put Erica and the baby and their health first.

'I'm not the only one at the station. I can delegate a good deal. But first we have a more urgent problem to solve.'

He detached himself from Erica, took a deep breath and went out in the garden.

'Hello, all. Have you been having a good time?'

Jörgen and Madde turned their neon-coloured noses towards him and nodded happily. I bet you've had a good time, he thought – with full service all day long, thinking that this is some fucking hotel.

'Listen, I've solved your dilemma. I called round and checked it out. There are vacancies at the Grand Hotel, because so many people have left Fjällbacka, but since you seem to be travelling on such a tight budget perhaps that wouldn't be appropriate?'

Jörgen and Madde, who at first looked nervous, eagerly agreed. No, it was not appropriate.

'But don't worry,' said Patrik, seeing to his gratification the furrows on their brows appear once again. 'I also rang the youth hostel on Valö, and would you believe it? They have a vacancy! Great, isn't it? Cheap and clean. Couldn't be better!'

He clapped his hands in exaggerated delight, anticipating the objections he saw forming on his guests' lips. 'So it's probably best if you start packing right away. The boat leaves in an hour from Ingrid Bergman's Square.'

Jörgen started to say something, but Patrik held up his hands. 'No, no, there's no need to thank me. It was really no trouble. All it took was a couple of phone calls.'

With a grin he went back to the kitchen, where Erica was eavesdropping from the window. They high-fived each other and had to restrain themselves to keep from giggling.

'Nice,' Erica whispered with admiration. 'I didn't know I was living with a master of such Machiavellian calibre!'

'There's a lot you don't know about me, darling. I'm a very complex person, you see . . .'

'Indeed, you are. And here I always thought you seemed rather one-track,' she teased him with a smile.

'Well, if you didn't have that big belly in the way, you'd see exactly how one-track I am,' Patrik flirted back. He felt the tensions begin to melt away with their affectionate banter.

He turned serious. 'Have you heard any more from Anna?'

Erica's smile vanished. 'No, not a peep. I went down to the pier to check but the boat wasn't moored there.'

'Do you think she went home?'

'I don't know. Either that or they're sailing farther up the coast somewhere. But you know what? I just don't have the energy to worry about it. I'm so damned sick of her touchiness and the way she turns sour as soon as I say anything wrong.'

She sighed and started to say something else, but they were interrupted by Jörgen and Madde sweeping past them to go pack up their things.

A while later, after Patrik had given the reluctant holiday-makers a lift down to the boat for Valö, they settled down on the veranda to enjoy the silence. Eager to please and still with a feeling of having a good deal to make up for, Patrik massaged Erica's swollen feet and calves as she sighed with pleasure. He pushed away any thoughts of the murdered girls, and the missing Jenny Möller. Sometimes his soul had to get a little rest.

The call came in the morning. As a part of his decision to take care of his wife a little better, Patrik had decided to take the morning off. They were sitting eating breakfast in the peace and quiet of the garden when Pedersen rang. With an apologetic look at Erica he got up from the table, but she just waved him away with a smile. She already looked much more content.

'Have you come up with something interesting?' said Patrik.

'You might say that. If we start with the cause of death for Johannes Hult, my first observation was correct. Johannes did not hang himself. If you tell me that he was found on the floor with a noose round his neck, then the noose was placed there after death had occurred. The cause of death was actually a powerful blow to the back of the head with a hard object, but not a blunt one. Something with a sharp edge. He also has a crushing injury to his jaw, which could indicate a blow from the front.'

'So there's no doubt that we're talking about murder?' Patrik had a tight grip on the phone.

'No, it would have been impossible for the wounds to be self-inflicted.'

'How long has he been dead?'

'It's hard to say. But he's been in the ground a long time. My guess is that the time of death corresponds quite well with the time he was assumed to have hanged himself. So he wasn't buried at some later date, if that's what you're after,' said Pedersen in an amused tone.

A moment of silence followed as Patrik pondered what Pedersen had told him. Then a thought occurred to him. 'You indicated that you found something more when you examined Johannes. What was it?'

'Oh yes, you're going to like this. We have a summer intern here who's a real go-getter, and she got the idea of taking a DNA sample from Johannes, since he'd been dug up anyway, and compare it with the semen sample that was found on Tanja Schmidt.'

'Yes?' Patrik could hear himself breathing hard, tense with anticipation.

'The devil take me if there isn't a close similarity! The person who murdered Tanja Schmidt is definitely related to Johannes Hult.'

Patrik had never heard the very proper Pedersen swear before, but now he was inclined to echo his sentiments. Well, I'll be damned, he thought. He paused to collect his wits and then said, 'Can you tell how they're related?' His pulse was pounding in his chest.

'Yes, and we're looking at it now. But we need more reference material, so your task now will be to gather blood samples from all known members of the Hult family.'

'All of them?' said Patrik. It made him tired just thinking about how the clan would react to that incursion into their privacy.

He thanked Pedersen for the information and went back to the breakfast table, where Erica sat like a madonna, with her white nightgown billowing and her blonde hair flowing. She still took his breath away.

'Go on,' she said, waving him away, and he kissed her gratefully on the cheek.

'Do you have anything to do today?' he asked.

'One advantage of having demanding guests is that I look forward to spending a day relaxing. In other words, I've decided not to do a thing today. Just lie outside and read, and eat a little good food.'

'That sounds like a plan. So I'll see to it that I get home early today. I'll be here by four at the latest, I promise.'

'Do the best you can. I'll see you when I see you. Run along now, I can tell that your shoe soles are burning.'

She didn't have to say it twice. He hurried off to the station.

When he came in twenty minutes later. the others were sitting in the lunchroom drinking their morning coffee. Guiltily, he saw that it was later than he thought.

'Hi, Hedström, did you forget to set your alarm clock today or what?'

Ernst, whose self-confidence had now been fully restored, sounded as overbearing as usual.

'Just taking a few hours off to make up for all that overtime. My wife needed some TLC too,' said Patrik, winking at Annika, who'd just popped in from her place at the reception desk.

'Well, that's probably one of the perks of being chief investigator, to sleep in a few extra hours when he pleases,' Ernst couldn't help retorting.

'I am in charge of this investigation, of course, but I'm not the chief,' Patrik pointed out mildly. The look Annika gave Ernst was not as friendly.

Patrik went on, 'And as the head of the investigation I have some news – and a new assignment.'

He told them what Pedersen had said, and for a moment the mood felt triumphant in the lunchroom of the Tanumshede police station.

'So, now we've rapidly narrowed the field to four possible suspects,' said Gösta. 'Stefan, Robert, Jacob and Gabriel.'

'Yes, and don't forget where Tanja was seen last,' said Martin.

'According to Stefan, that is,' Ernst reminded them. 'Don't forget that it's Stefan who *claims* to have seen her. Personally, I'd like to find a witness who's a bit more reliable.'

'But Linda also says that they saw someone when they were there that evening, so – '

Patrik interrupted Ernst and Martin. 'It may be a moot point. As soon as we've brought in everyone in the Hult family and done a DNA test on them, we won't need to speculate any longer. We'll know. On the way over here, I rang to request the permissions we'll need. Everyone knows why this is urgent, so I'm expecting a go-ahead from the prosecutor's office any time now.'

He poured himself a cup of coffee and sat down with the others. He placed his mobile in the centre of the table, and nobody could help glancing at it.

'So what did you all think about that scene yesterday?' Ernst chuckled. He had quickly forgotten his promise not to gossip about what Mellberg had told him in confidence. By this time they had all heard about Mellberg's mail-order bride, and they hadn't had such a good laugh in a year and a day. It was something that would be discussed out of the chief's earshot for a long time to come.

'The poor devil,' laughed Gösta. 'If you're so desperate for a woman that you have to order one from a catalogue, then you only have yourself to blame.'

'What a face he must have made when he went to collect her at the airport and he realized that his expectations had been crushed, to put it mildly.' Annika had a good laugh at the chief's expense. Laughing at others' misfortune didn't feel quite as bad when it was Mellberg who was the target.

'Well, I must say that she didn't rest on her laurels. She went straight to the shop to fill up her bag. And it didn't seem to matter much what she stole, either, as long as it had a price tag on it,' laughed Ernst. 'Although speaking of stealing, listen to this. Old man Persson, the one Gösta and I went out to visit yesterday, told us that some idiot used to steal that damned fertilizer from him. He'd lose a couple of big sacks every time he ordered a new supply. Can you believe that someone would be so damned stingy that he'd pinch sacks of shit? Of course the shit is obviously expensive, but still . . .' He slapped his knees. 'Oh, Jesus,' he said, wiping a tear from the corner of his eye. Then he realized that it was dead silent all round him.

'What did you just say?' asked Patrik in an ominous voice. Ernst had heard that voice only a couple of days before, and he knew that he'd screwed up again.

'Yeah, well, he said that somebody used to steal sacks of fertilizer from him.'

'And considering that Västergården is the closest farm, it didn't occur to you that this might be valuable information?'

His colleague's voice was so cold that Ernst felt frostbite on his skin. Patrik turned to Gösta. 'Did you hear this, Gösta?'

'No, the farmer must have told him that when I was in the toilet for a couple of minutes.' He glowered at Ernst.

'I didn't think anything of it,' said Ernst with a whine. 'Damn it, I can't remember everything.'

'That's exactly what you're supposed to do. But we'll talk more about this later. The question is, what does it mean for us?'

Martin held up his hand, as if he were still in school. 'Am I the only one who thinks we should start to zero in on Jacob?' No one answered so he explained. 'First of all, we have testimony, albeit from a dubious source, saying that Tanja was at Västergården right before she vanished. Second, the DNA that was found on Tanja's body is from someone related to Johannes. And third, sacks of fertilizer were stolen from a farm literally next door to Västergården. That's at least enough reason to make me think we should bring him in for a little chat. And during that time we can take a look round his property.'

Still no comment, so Martin went on with his argument. 'As you said yourself, Patrik, it's urgent. We have nothing to lose by looking round a bit and tightening the thumb-screws on Jacob. The only way we lose is if we do nothing. Sure, we'll find out something after we've tested all the Hults and compared the DNA, but we can't sit here in the meantime twiddling our thumbs. We have to do something!'

Finally Patrik took the floor. 'Martin is right. There's good reason to believe it would be worthwhile to have a talk with him, and it couldn't hurt to take a look at Västergården as well. So this is what we're going to do: Gösta and I will bring in Jacob. Martin, you contact Uddevalla and ask them for reinforcements to do a search of the whole farm. Ask Mellberg for help getting the warrants, but make sure that they apply not only to the residence but to all the other buildings on the grounds too. We'll all report in to Annika as needed. Okay? Any questions?'

'Yes, what should we do about the blood samples?' asked Martin.

'Damn, I forgot about that. We need to clone ourselves.' Patrik thought for a moment. 'Martin, can you take care of that too, if you get help from Uddevalla?' Martin nodded. 'Good, then contact the clinic in Fjällbacka and take along someone who knows how to take blood samples. And be damned sure that the samples are labelled correctly. Then drive them down to Pedersen's lab as fast as you can. All right, let's move. And don't forget why we're in a hurry!'

'So what should I do?' Ernst saw his chance to regain favour.

'You stay here,' said Patrik, and wasted no words on further discussion.

Ernst muttered but knew it was time to lie low. But he should really have a talk with Mellberg when this was all over. He hadn't screwed up that badly. He was only human, after all.

Marita's heart swelled in her breast. The outdoor worship service was wonderful as usual, and in the centre of it stood her Jacob. Straight-backed and strong and sure of voice he proclaimed God's word. Many people had gathered. Besides most of those on the farm – some of them had not yet seen the light and refused to participate – another hundred faithful followers had come. They sat on the grass with their eyes fixed on Jacob, who stood in his usual place on the rock with his back to the lake. Around them stood a towering grove of birches, providing shade when the heat was most oppressive and rustling in accompaniment to Jacob's melodious voice. Sometimes she could hardly believe her good fortune. That the man whom all regarded with such admiration in their eyes had chosen her.

When she first met Jacob she was only seventeen. Jacob was twenty-three and already had won a reputation as a powerful man in the congregation. This was partly thanks to his grandfather, whose fame had rubbed off on him, but most of it was thanks to his own charisma. The unusual combination of kindness and strength gave him a radiance that no one could avoid noticing. Marita and her parents had been members of the congregation for a long time and never missed a worship service. Even before they attended the first service that Jacob Hult was going to lead, Marita felt a tingle inside her like a premonition that something great was about to happen. And it did. She hadn't been able to tear her eyes away from him. She had stared at his mouth, from which God's word had spilled as easily as flowing water. When Jacob's eyes began to meet hers she had started sending prayers to God. Feverish, imploring, entreating prayers. She, who had been taught that one must never pray for anything for oneself, was praying for something as worldly as a man. But she couldn't stop. Despite the fact that she felt the fires of purgatory beginning to scorch her in their hunt for the sinner, she kept up her fervent prayers and didn't stop until she saw that Jacob was looking at her with desire in his eyes.

Actually, she didn't really understand why Jacob had chosen her as his wife. She knew that she'd always had a rather plain appearance, and her personality was quiet and introverted. But he had wanted her, and the day they got married she promised herself never to worry about or question God's will. The Lord had obviously seen both of them in the crowd and decided that their marriage would be good, and with that she had to let herself be content. Maybe a strong person like Jacob needed a weak partner so as not to be worn down by resistance. What did she know?

The children were fidgeting restlessly as they sat on the ground beside her. Marita hushed them sternly. She knew that their legs were itching to run about and play, but there would be time for that later. Right now they had to listen to their father as he preached God's word.

'Faith is tested when we are confronted by difficulties. But that's also when our faith grows stronger. Without resistance faith grows weak and makes us become sated and lazy. We begin to forget why we should turn to God for guidance. And soon we end up going astray. I myself have had to endure tests lately, as you know. And my family has been tested too. Evil forces are working to test our faith. But they are doomed to failure. Our faith has grown so strong that the powers of evil have no opportunity to reach me. Praise the Lord, who grants me such strength!'

He raised his hands to Heaven and the congregation burst out in a 'Hallelujah', their faces shining with joy and conviction. Marita raised her hands to Heaven and thanked God. Jacob's words make her forget the difficulties of the past week. She relied on him and she trusted in the Lord, and if both of them were together, nothing could budge them.

When Jacob finished the service a while later, crowds of people gathered round him. Everyone wanted to shake his hand, thank him and offer support. Everyone seemed to have a need to touch him and in that way take some of his calm and conviction home with them. They all wanted a piece of him. Marita stayed in the background, triumphantly aware that Jacob was hers. Sometimes she wondered guiltily whether it was a sin to feel such a desire to own her husband, to want to have every fibre of him to herself, but she always rejected those thoughts. It was obviously God's will for them to be together, so it could never be considered wrong.

When the crowd began to disperse around Jacob, she took the children by the hand and went up to him. She knew him so well. She saw that what had filled him during the service had now begun to fade away, and instead the weariness filled his eyes.

'Come, let's go home, Jacob.'

'Not yet, Marita. I have something I have to do first.'

'There's nothing that can't wait until tomorrow. I'm taking you home now so you can rest. I can see you're tired.'

He smiled and took her hand. 'As usual you're right, my wise wife. I just have to fetch my things from the office, then we can go.'

They had started heading up to the house when two men came walking towards them. At first, with the sun in their eyes, they couldn't see who they were, but when they came closer Jacob let out an irritated groan.

'What do you want now?'

Marita looked in bewilderment from Jacob to the men,

until she realized that, judging from Jacob's tone of voice, they must be police. She gave them a fierce look. They were the ones who had been causing Jacob and the family so much trouble recently.

'We need to have a little chat with you, Jacob.'

'What more could there be to say that I didn't tell you yesterday?' he said with a sigh. 'All right, we might as well get it over with. Let's go to my office.'

The police officers didn't move. They cast an embarrassed glance at the children, and Marita began to smell a rat. Instinctively she drew the children closer.

'Not here. We'd like to talk to you down at the station.'

It was the younger officer who spoke. The older one stood a bit to the side and watched Jacob with a solemn expression. Fear sank its claws into Marita's heart. It was, in truth, the forces of evil that were approaching, just as Jacob had said in his sermon.

9

She knew that the other girl was gone. From her corner in the dark she heard her utter her last breath, and with clasped hands she prayed frantically to God to accept her comrade in suffering. In a way she was envious of the girl. Envious that now her suffering was over.

The girl had been there before her when she landed in hell. The fear had paralysed her at first, but the girl's arms around her and her warm body had offered an odd security. At the same time she hadn't always been nice. The struggle to survive had forced them together but also apart. She herself had retained hope. The other girl had not. She knew that sometimes she was hated for having hope. But how could she abandon hope? Her whole life she had been taught that every impossible situation had its solution, and why should this one be any different? She could see her father and mother's faces in her mind's eye and she was convinced that they would find her soon.

That poor other girl, who'd had nothing. She realized who she was as soon as she felt her warm body in the dark, even though they had never spoken to each other in their lives up there. And by a tacit agreement they did not call each other by name, which would have seemed too normal. Neither of them would have been able to

303

bear that burden. But the other girl had talked about her daughter. It was the only time there was any life in her voice.

To fold her hands and pray for the one who now was gone had demanded an almost superhuman effort. Her limbs would not obey her, but by marshalling all the strength she had left she had willed her unruly hands into a pose that resembled an attitude of prayer.

She waited patiently in the dark with her pain. Now it was only a matter of time before they found her. Mamma and Pappa. Soon ...

Irritated, Jacob said, 'Yes, I'll come to the station. But that'll be an end to it, do you hear me!'

Out of the corner of her eye Marita saw Kennedy approaching. She had never liked him. There was something nasty in his eyes that was mixed with adoration whenever he looked at Jacob. But Jacob had admonished her when she told him how she felt. Kennedy was an unhappy child who had finally begun to find some sense of inner peace. What he needed now was love and consideration, not suspicion. But the anxiety never really left her. A dismissive signal from Jacob made Kennedy reluctantly turn and go back to the house. He was like a watchdog who wanted to defend his master, Marita thought.

Jacob turned to her and took her face in his hands. 'Go home with the children. There's no danger. The police just want to throw a little extra wood on the fire that will eventually consume them.'

He smiled to take the sting out of his words, but she held on to the children even tighter. They looked back and forth between her and Jacob with worried expressions. In their own way they could feel that something was upsetting the balance of their world.

The younger policeman spoke again. This time he looked a bit embarrassed when he said, 'I would recommend that you not take the children home before this evening. We . . .' he hesitated, 'we're doing a search of your house this afternoon.'

'What do you think you're playing at?' Jacob was so upset that the words stuck in his throat.

Marita could feel the children fidgeting anxiously. They weren't used to hearing their father raise his voice.

'We'll explain everything to you at the station. Shall we go?'

Unwilling to upset the children even more, Jacob nodded in resignation. He patted the children on their heads, kissed Marita on the cheek and walked off between the two policemen towards their car.

When the police drove off with Jacob, she stood as if frozen to the spot and watched them go. Over by the house Kennedy also stood and watched. His eyes were as dark as night.

Emotions were running high at the manor house as well.

'I'm calling my lawyer! This is utterly absurd! Taking blood samples and treating us like common criminals!'

Gabriel was so enraged that his hand trembled on the door handle. Martin stood on the front steps and calmly met Gabriel's gaze. Behind him stood Fjällbacka's district doctor, Dr Jacobsson, sweating copiously. His huge body was not suited to the prevailing heat, but the main reason the sweat was running down his forehead was that he found the situation extremely unpleasant.

'You are free to do so, but be sure to tell him the type of document we have, so he can confirm that we are within our rights as stipulated by law. If he cannot be here within fifteen minutes, we have the right to implement the warrant in his absence, in view of the urgent nature of the situation.'

Martin was consciously speaking in as bureaucratic a manner

as he could. He guessed that this was the sort of language that would best reach Gabriel. And it worked. Reluctantly Gabriel let them in. He took the document that Martin showed him and went straight to the phone to ring his lawyer. Martin motioned inside the two policemen who had been sent as reinforcements from Uddevalla and prepared to wait. Gabriel was talking agitatedly on the phone and gesticulating. A few minutes later he returned to where they were standing in the hall.

'He'll be here in ten minutes,' said Gabriel sullenly.

'Good. Where are your wife and daughter? We have to take samples from them as well.'

'In the stable.'

'Would you fetch them, please?' said Martin to one of the officers from Uddevalla.

'Certainly. Where is the stable?'

'There's a little path past the left wing of the house,' said Gabriel. 'Follow that. The stable is a couple of hundred metres from here.' With body language that clearly showed how distasteful he considered the situation, Gabriel still tried to keep a stiff upper lip. He said guardedly, 'I take it that the rest of you may come in while we wait.'

They were sitting in silence on the edge of the sofa, all feeling uncomfortable, when Linda and Laine came in.

'What's going on here, Gabriel? The officer says that Dr Jacobsson is here to take blood samples from us. This has got to be a joke!'

Linda, who had a hard time taking her eyes off the young man in uniform who'd fetched them from the stable, had another view of the matter. 'Cool,' she said.

'Unfortunately they seem to be quite serious, Laine. But I've called our lawyer Lövgren, and he'll be here any second. There will be no blood samples taken before then.'

'But I don't understand. Why do you want to do this?' Laine looked composed but puzzled.

'I'm afraid we can't divulge that for technical reasons

307

pertaining to the investigation. But everything will be explained in time.'

Gabriel sat studying the warrant in front of him. 'It says here that you also have permission to take blood samples from Jacob and Solveig and the boys, is that right?'

Was it Martin's imagination, or did he see a shadow pass across Laine's face? A second later there was a light knock on the door and Gabriel's lawyer entered.

When the formalities were completed and the lawyer had explained to Gabriel and his family that the police had all the proper documents, the blood samples were taken from them one by one. First Gabriel, then Laine, who to Martin's surprise still seemed to be the most composed of them all. He noticed that Gabriel was also regarding his wife with surprised approval. Finally they took a sample from Linda, who had established such eye contact with the young policeman that Martin had to give him a stern look.

'So, that's that.' Dr Jacobsson got up from his chair and gathered up the tubes of blood. They were carefully labelled with the name of each of the Hults and placed in a cooler.

'Are you going to Solveig's place now?' Gabriel asked. He suddenly laughed. 'Make sure you have your helmets on and your truncheons out, because she probably won't let you take any blood without a fight.'

'We can handle the situation,' said Martin dryly. He didn't like the malicious gleam in Gabriel's eyes.

'Well, don't say I didn't warn you . . .' He chuckled.

Laine snapped at him, 'Gabriel, act like an adult.'

Astounded at being scolded like a child by his wife, Gabriel shut up and sat down. He looked at her as if he were seeing her for the first time.

Martin led his colleagues and the doctor outside, and there they split up into two cars. On the way to Solveig's, Patrik rang on the mobile.

'Hi, how's it going out there?'

'As expected,' said Martin. 'Gabriel flew off the handle and called his lawyer. But we got what we came for, so now we're on the way over to Solveig's place. I don't reckon it will go as smoothly there.'

'No, probably not. Just make sure the situation doesn't get out of hand.'

'Definitely not, I'll be very diplomatic. Don't worry. How's it going with you?'

'Fine. We've got Jacob in the car and we'll be in Tanumshede soon.'

'Good luck, then.'

'You too.'

Martin flipped his phone shut just as they turned in at Solveig's wretched little cabin. This time Martin wasn't as shocked by its state of disrepair. But he still wondered how people could bring themselves to live like this. Being poor was one thing, but that didn't mean they couldn't keep the place neat and clean.

With some trepidation, he knocked on the door but not even in his wildest fantasies could he have imagined the reception he would get.

Smack! A hard slap landed on his right cheek, making it sting. The shock took his breath away. He felt rather than saw the officers behind him tense up to enter the fray, but he held up a hand to stop them.

'Calm down, calm down. There's no need to use force here. Is there, Solveig?' he said in a soothing voice to the woman standing in front of him. She was breathing hard but seemed reassured by his tone of voice.

'How dare you show yourself here after you dug up Johannes!' She propped her hands on her hips and blocked the way into the house.

'I understand that this is difficult, Solveig, but we were just doing our job. And we have to do our job now as well. I'd appreciate it if you'd co-operate.'

309

'What do you want now?' she spat.

'Could I come in for a moment and talk? Then I'll explain.'

He turned to the three men behind him and said, 'Wait here a minute, I'm going to go in and have a little chat with Solveig.'

He followed up his words by simply walking inside and closing the door behind him. Startled, Solveig backed up and let him in. Martin mobilized all his diplomatic skills and carefully explained the situation to her. After a while her protests died down, and a few minutes later he opened the door and let in the others.

'We have to fetch the boys too. Where are they?'

She laughed. 'They're probably outside behind the house, lying low until they know why you're here. I'm sure they're as sick of looking at your ugly mugs as I am.' She laughed and opened a grimy window.

'Stefan, Robert, come on inside. That cop is here again!'

There was a rustling in the bushes and then Stefan and Robert came slouching in. They cast a wary glance at the group that was squeezed into the kitchen.

'What's this all about?'

'Now they want to take our blood too,' said Solveig, a cold statement of fact.

'What the hell, are you nuts? The fuck if I'm giving you any of my blood!'

'Robert, now don't make a fuss,' Solveig said wearily. 'The police and I have talked it over, and I said we wouldn't try to interfere. So sit down and shut up. The sooner we get rid of them the better.'

To Martin's relief they decided to obey her. Sullenly they both let Dr Jacobsson draw a blood sample. When he'd also taken a sample from Solveig, the doctor put the marked tubes away and announced that his part of the job was done.

'What are you going to do with the blood?' asked Stefan, more curious than anything else.

Martin gave him the same answer he'd given Gabriel. Then he turned to the younger officer from Uddevalla. 'Go pick up the samples from Tanumshede, and see to it that they're taken to Göteborg ASAP.'

The young man who'd been flirting too much with Linda at the manor house nodded. 'Okay, I'll take care of it. Two more officers are on the way from Uddevalla to assist you . . .' – he lowered his voice and cast a wary glance at Solveig and her sons, who were listening intently to the conversation – 'regarding the *other* matter. They'll meet you . . .' again an awkward pause, 'at the *other* location.'

'Good,' said Martin. He turned to Solveig. 'Then I'll thank you for your co-operation.'

For a moment he considered telling them about Johannes, but didn't dare go against Patrik's direct order. Patrik didn't want anyone to know yet, and so he refrained from saying anything.

Outside the cabin Martin paused for a moment. Ignoring the dilapidated little house and the wrecked cars and other junk lying about outside, they actually lived in an incredibly beautiful spot. He hoped that they occasionally managed to raise their eyes from their own misery to see the beauty all around them. But he doubted it.

'All right, now to Västergården,' said Martin, striding off towards the cars. One task was completed, another waited. He wondered how it was going for Patrik and Gösta.

'Why do *you* think you're here?' said Patrik. He and Gösta sat next to each other facing Jacob in the little interrogation room.

Jacob regarded them calmly, his hands folded on the table. 'How should I know? There hasn't been any logic to the way you've been harassing my family, so I suppose all I can do is lean back and try to keep my head above water.'

'Are you saying in all seriousness that the police think their primary task is to persecute your family? What motive would we have for doing that?' Patrik leaned forward with interest.

Again the same calm tone from Jacob. 'Evil and ill-will require no motive. But what do I know? Maybe you feel that you screwed up with Johannes and now you're trying somehow to justify it to yourselves.'

'What do you mean?' said Patrik.

'I mean that maybe you feel that if you can put us away for something now, then you must have been right about Johannes.'

'Don't you think that sounds a bit far-fetched?'

'What should I believe? All I know is that you've latched on to us like ticks and refuse to let go. My only consolation is that God sees the truth.'

'You talk a lot about God, my boy,' said Gösta. 'Is your father this devout?'

The question seemed to bother Jacob, precisely as Gösta intended. 'My father's faith is somewhere deep inside him. But his . . .' he seemed to ponder which word to choose, '*complicated* relationship with his own father affected his faith in God. But it's still there.'

'Ah, *his* father. Ephraim Hult. The Preacher. You and he had a close relationship,' said Gösta. It was more a statement than a question.

'I don't understand why this interests you, but yes, Grand-father and I were very close.' Jacob pressed his lips together.

'He saved your life, didn't he?' asked Patrik.

'Yes, he did.'

'How did your father feel about the fact that the father with whom he had a . . . "complicated relationship" – your own choice of words – was able to save your life, while *he* couldn't?' Patrik went on.

'Every father wants to be his son's hero, but I don't think Pappa saw it that way. Anyway, Grandpa saved my life and Pappa was eternally grateful to him.'

'And Johannes? How was his relationship with Ephraim – and your father?'

'Honestly, I don't see what importance this could possibly have. It was over twenty years ago!'

'We're aware of that, but we'd still appreciate it if you answered our questions,' said Gösta.

Jacob's calm façade had begun to crumble at the edges, and he ran his hand through his hair.

'Johannes . . . well, he and Pappa no doubt had their problems, but Ephraim loved him. Not that they had any sort of outwardly close relationship, but that generation was like that. You weren't supposed to wear your emotions on your sleeve.'

'Did your father and Johannes quarrel a lot?' said Patrik.

'I don't know whether I'd call it quarrelling. They had their disagreements, but siblings always do bicker.'

'According to what people have said, they were more than disagreements. Some have even said that Gabriel hated his brother.' Patrik pressed on.

'Hate is a strong word that you shouldn't bandy about. No, Pappa certainly had no tender feelings to spare for Johannes, but if they'd had the time I'm sure that God would have intervened. A brother should not stand against his brother.'

'I presume you're referring to Cain and Abel. Interesting that you should think of that particular Bible story. Were things that acrimonious between them?' Patrik asked.

'No, not really. And of course Pappa didn't end up killing his brother!' Jacob seemed to be regaining some of the calm he'd started to lose, and he folded his hands again as if in prayer.

'Are you sure about that?' Gösta's voice was full of undertones.

Bewildered, Jacob stared at the two men in front of him.

'What are you talking about? Johannes hanged himself, everybody knows that.'

'Well, the problem is that we examined Johannes's remains, and they show something different. Johannes didn't commit suicide. He was murdered.'

Jacob's hands that lay folded on the table began to shake uncontrollably. He seemed to be trying to form words with his mouth, but none emerged. Patrik and Gösta leaned back in unison, as if choreographed, and observed Jacob in silence. It seemed that this was news to him.

'How did your father react to the news of Johannes's death?'

'I, I . . . I don't really know,' Jacob stammered. 'I was still in hospital then.' A thought struck him like a bolt of lightning. 'Are you trying to make it look like Pappa killed Johannes?' The thought made him start to snigger. 'You're out of your minds. My father, murder his brother? No, that's impossible!' The snigger changed to a laugh. Neither Gösta nor Patrik looked amused.

'Do you think this is something to laugh at? The fact that your uncle Johannes was murdered? Is that something you think is amusing?' said Patrik, carefully enunciating each word.

Jacob abruptly fell silent and looked down. 'No, of course not. It's just such a shock . . .' He raised his eyes again. 'But now I understand even less why you want to talk to me. I was just ten years old and in hospital at the time, so I presume you're not going to try to claim I had anything to do with it.' He emphasized 'I' to show how absurd it was. 'It seems quite obvious what happened. Whoever murdered Siv and Mona must have thought it was perfect when you picked Johannes to be the scapegoat. And because the real killer could never be completely absolved, he killed Johannes and made it look like a suicide. The murderer knew how people here would react. They would regard it as proof of his guilt; it was as good as a written confession. And the same person must have murdered that German tourist. That makes sense, doesn't it?' he said eagerly. His eyes were shining.

314

'A very good theory,' said Patrik. 'Not bad at all, if you ignore the fact that we compared the DNA that we took from Johannes yesterday with a DNA sample that we took from the semen on Tanja's corpse. It turned out that Johannes is related to the person who murdered Tanja.' He waited for Jacob's reaction. There was none. He seemed turned to stone.

Patrik went on. 'So today we took blood samples from everyone in your family. We're going to send them to Göteborg for analysis, along with the sample we took from you when you arrived here. We're quite sure that we'll soon have proof in black and white of who the murderer is. So don't you think it would be a good idea if you told us what you know, Jacob? Tanja was seen at your house, the murderer is related to Johannes – it's quite a coincidence, don't you think?'

The colour in Jacob's face had changed. It alternated from pale to blazing crimson, and Patrik could see his jaws grinding.

'That testimony is bullshit, and you know it. Stefan only wanted to get me arrested because he detests our family. And as far as blood tests and DNA and all that is concerned, you can take all the samples you want, but you'll beg my forgiveness when you've got the results!'

'In that event I promise to beg your forgiveness personally,' Patrik replied calmly. 'But until then I intend to get the answers I need.'

He wished that Martin and his group could have finished searching the house before they interrogated Jacob, but with the clock ticking they had to make the best of things. The question they most wanted answered was whether analyses of the soil at Västergården showed traces of FZ-302. Patrik hoped that Martin would report on any physical traces of Tanja or Jenny soon, but they couldn't do the soil analyses on the spot – those would take time. He was actually sceptical about whether they would succeed in finding anything at the farm. Was it possible to conceal someone and murder the person without Marita or the children seeing anything?

Instinctively Patrik felt that Jacob fit the role of prime suspect, but that very fact troubled him. How could Jacob have hidden his victims at the farm where he lived, without the family suspecting anything?

As if Jacob could read his thoughts, he said, 'I certainly hope that you haven't turned everything upside down at home. Marita will be beside herself if she comes home and the house is one huge mess.'

'I believe the men are very careful,' said Gösta.

Patrik looked at his telephone. He hoped Martin would call soon.

Stefan had retreated to the silence of the shed. Solveig's reaction first to the exhumation and then the blood tests had made his skin crawl. He couldn't stand all the emotions and needed to sit by himself for a while and think over everything that had happened. The concrete floor he was sitting on was hard, but wonderfully cool. He wrapped his arms round his legs and rested his cheek on one knee. Right now he missed Linda more than ever, but his longing was still mixed with anger. Maybe it would never be any different. At least he had lost some of his naïveté and taken back control. He never should have let it go. But she had been like poison in his soul. Her firm young body had turned him into a babbling idiot. He was furious with himself for letting a girl get under his skin like that.

He knew that he was a dreamer. That's why he had felt so infatuated with Linda. Even though she was way too young, too self-assured, too selfish. He was convinced that she would never stay in Fjällbacka and that they didn't have a ghost of a chance of a future together. But the dreamer in him had still had a hard time accepting that. Now he knew better.

Stefan promised himself that he would improve. He would try to become more like Robert. Tough, hard, invincible. Robert always landed on his feet. Nothing seemed to touch him. Stefan envied him that.

A sound behind him made him turn round, thinking that Robert had come in. Hands gripped his throat and he could hardly breathe.

'Don't move or I'll break your neck.'

Stefan vaguely recognized the voice but couldn't place it. When the grip round his neck was released he was tossed hard against the wall. The air was knocked out of him.

'What the hell are you doing?' Stefan tried to turn round, but someone had seized hold of him and was pressing his face against the cold concrete wall.

'Shut up.' The voice was implacable. Stefan wondered whether he should call for help but didn't think anyone would hear him up at the house.

'What the hell do you want?' The words were difficult to form with half his face pressed hard against the wall.

'What I want? Well, you're going to find out.'

When the attacker made his demands, at first Stefan didn't understand any of it. But when he was turned round so that he stood eye to eye with the person who had attacked him, all the bits fell into place. A punch in the face told him that the assailant was serious. But defiance welled up inside him.

'Fuck you,' mumbled Stefan. His mouth was slowly filling with some fluid that could only be blood. His thoughts had begun to grow hazy, but he refused to give in.

'You're going to do as I say.'

'No,' Stefan mumbled.

Then the punches started raining down on him. They struck him rhythmically until a vast darkness swept in.

The farm was marvellous. Martin couldn't help making that observation as they started their work of encroaching on the private lives of Jacob and his family. The colours in the house were pastel, the rooms radiated warmth and calm and had

317

a country feel to them, with white linen tablecloths and light, fluttering curtains. He would have loved to have a home like this. And now they had to disturb this peace. Methodically they went through the house, bit by bit. No one said a word; they worked in utter silence. Martin concentrated on the living room. The frustrating thing was that they didn't know what they were looking for. Martin wasn't sure that they would recognize traces of the girls even if they found any.

For the first time since he had so strongly advocated that Jacob was the one they were searching for, he began to have his doubts. It was impossible to imagine that someone who lived like this in such peaceful surroundings would be able to kill someone.

'How's it going?' he called to the officers upstairs.

'Nothing yet,' one of them called back. Martin sighed and continued opening bureau drawers and turning over everything that wasn't nailed down.

'I'll go out and start checking the barn,' he said to the officer from Uddevalla who was taking part in the search of the ground floor.

The barn was mercifully cool. He understood why Linda and Stefan had made this their trysting place. The smell of hay tickled his nostrils and brought back memories from his childhood summers. He climbed up the ladder to the loft and peered out through the cracks between the boards. Yes, there was a good view of Västergården from here, just as Stefan had said. It would be no problem to recognize someone from this distance.

Martin climbed back down. The barn was empty except for some old agricultural implements that were rusting away. He didn't think they would find anything here, but he would still ask some of the others to take another look. He left the barn and scanned the area. Besides the manor house and the barn there was only a little garden shed and a playhouse that they hadn't yet searched. He held no hope of finding anything in either place. Both were too small to hold a person, but for safety's sake they should still check them.

The sun was broiling his scalp and making beads of sweat form on his forehead. He went back to the manor house to help with the search, but his enthusiasm from earlier in the day had begun to wane. His heart sank. Jenny Möller was somewhere. But not here.

Even Patrik had begun to despair. After a couple of hours of interrogation they had got nowhere with Jacob. He seemed to be genuinely shocked at the news that Johannes was murdered, and he stubbornly refused to say anything but that they were harassing his family and he was innocent. Time after time Patrik caught himself glancing at the mobile phone, mocking him with its silence as it lay on the table in front of him. He was in desperate need of some good news. They wouldn't have any answers about the blood samples until at least early tomorrow morning, he knew that, so he had fixed his hopes on Martin and the team going through Västergården. But no call came. It wasn't until just after four in the afternoon that Martin rang and dejectedly reported that they had found nothing and were giving up. Patrik motioned to Gösta to come out of the interrogation room.

'That was Martin. They didn't find anything.'

The hope in Gösta's eyes died out. 'Nothing?'

'No, not a damn thing. So we don't seem to have any other choice but to release him. Shit.' Patrik slapped his hand on the wall but then collected himself quickly again. 'Oh well, it's only temporary. Tomorrow I expect to get a report on the blood samples, and then maybe we can pick him up for good.'

'Sure, but think what he might do before then. He knows what we've got on him now, and if we release him he could go straight back and kill the girl.'

'So what the hell do you think we should do?' Patrik's frustration turned to anger, but he saw the injustice of lashing out at Gösta and immediately apologized.

'I want to make one more attempt to get some answers about the blood samples before we let him go. They might have been able to find something we can use right now. They know why we're in a hurry, and they've put us first in line.'

Patrik went into his office and dialled the number for Pathology on his landline. By this time he knew the number by heart. Outside the window the traffic was roaring past as usual in the summer sunshine. For a moment he was envious of all the clueless holiday-makers driving past with their cars stuffed full. He wished that he too could be so oblivious.

'Hello, Pedersen, it's Patrik Hedström. Thought I'd check to see if you'd found anything before we release our suspect.'

'Didn't I tell you we wouldn't be done until early tomorrow morning? And we're going to have to put in a bunch of overtime tonight, you should know.' Pedersen sounded stressed and irritated.

'I know, but I just wondered if you'd found anything.'

A long silence indicated that Pedersen was fighting an internal battle about something, and Patrik sat up straighter in his chair.

'You did find something, didn't you?'

'It's only preliminary. We have to check and double-check before we can release any information, otherwise the consequences could be disastrous. Besides, the tests then have to be repeated by the Swedish Crime Lab. Our equipment isn't anywhere near as sophisticated as theirs, and – '

'Yeah, yeah,' Patrik interrupted, 'I know that, but a seventeen-year-old girl's life is at stake here, so if there's any time when you should relax the rules, it's now.' He held his breath and waited.

'All right, but use the information cautiously. You have no

320

idea how much shit I could get if . . .' Pedersen didn't finish his sentence.

'Word of honour, now tell me what you've got.' He was holding the receiver so tight that it felt sweaty.

'Naturally we began by analysing Jacob Hult's blood sample. And we found some interesting things – preliminary of course,' Pedersen warned him again.

'Yes?'

'According to our first test, Jacob Hult's DNA does *not* match the semen sample taken from the victim's body.'

Patrik slowly exhaled. He hadn't even realized he'd been holding his breath.

'How certain is it?'

'As I said, we have to run the test several times to be completely certain, but that's actually only a formality to protect the legal rights of the individual. You can probably count on it being correct.'

'Damn it all. That does throw a different light on the case.' Patrik couldn't keep the disappointment out of his voice. He saw now that he'd been completely positive that Jacob was the one they were looking for. This as good as took them back to square one.

'And you didn't find a match when you examined the other samples?'

'We haven't got that far yet. We assumed that you wanted us to concentrate on Jacob Hult, and that's what we did. So besides him we've only finished with one other person. But sometime in the morning I'll be able to inform you about the rest.'

'Well, by then I'll have to let the guy go from the interrogation room. And offer him an apology,' Patrik sighed.

'Oh, there's one more thing.'

'Yes?'

Pedersen hesitated. 'The second sample we got started analysing is Gabriel Hult's. And . . .'

'Yes?' said Patrik even more insistently.

'Well, according to our analysis of their respective DNA structure, it's impossible for Gabriel to be Jacob's father.'

Patrik sat dead still in his chair, dumbstruck.

'Are you still there?'

'Yes, I'm here. That was just not anything I'd expected. Are you sure?' Then he realized what the answer would be and anticipated what Pedersen was going to say: 'It's only preliminary and you have to do more tests et cetera et cetera, I know, you don't have to tell me again.'

'Is it something that might be important for the investigation?'

'Right now everything is important, so it's certainly something we could use. Thanks for everything.'

Patrik sat bewildered for a moment, thinking hard with his hands clasped behind his head and his feet on the desk. Jacob's negative test would force them to rethink the case completely. The fact still remained that Tanja's killer was related to Johannes, and with Jacob out of the game only Gabriel, Stefan and Robert remained. One down, three to go. But even though Jacob wasn't their perp, Patrik could bet that he knew something. During the entire interrogation he had noticed something evasive about Jacob, something the man fought hard to keep below the surface. The information that Patrik had received from Pedersen might give the police the advantage they needed to shake Jacob up enough to make him talk. Patrik took his feet down from the desk and got up. He briefly summarized for Gösta what he'd found out, and then they went back to the interrogation room, where Jacob, bored to death, sat picking at his fingernails. They had hastily agreed on the tactic they would use.

'How long do I have to sit here?'

'We have the right to hold you for six hours. But as we mentioned, you also have the right to have a lawyer present whenever you want. Do you want to call a lawyer?'

'No, it's not necessary,' replied Jacob. 'An innocent man needs no other defender than his faith that God will set everything right.'

'Okay, then you must be well equipped. You and God seem to be like this,' said Patrik, holding up his hand with the first two fingers together.

'We know where we stand with each other,' said Jacob guardedly. 'And I feel sorry for anyone who goes through life without God.'

'So you feel sorry for us poor wretches, is that what you're saying?' said Gösta with amusement in his voice.

'It's a waste of time talking to you two. You've closed your hearts.'

Patrik leaned towards Jacob. 'Interesting, all this talk about God and the Devil and sin and that whole song and dance. How do your parents fit into the picture? Are they living in accordance with God's commandments?'

'Father may have taken a step back from the congregation, but his faith remains strong. Both he and Mother are God-fearing people.'

'Are you sure about that? I mean, what do you actually know about how they live?'

'What do you mean? I know my own parents. Have you cooked up something else to drag their names through the mud?'

Jacob's hands were trembling, and Patrik felt a certain satisfaction at being able to upset his stoic calm.

'I only mean that there's no way for you actually to know what goes on in someone else's life. Your parents may have sins on their conscience that you have no idea about, isn't that right?'

Jacob got up and headed for the door. 'No, now that's enough. Arrest me or let me go, because I'm not going to sit here any longer listening to your lies!'

'Did you know, for example, that Gabriel is not your father?'

Jacob stopped short, with his hand halfway to the door handle. He turned round slowly. 'What did you say?'

'I asked if you knew that Gabriel is not your father. I just spoke with the lab doing the tests on the blood samples you all provided, and there is definitely no doubt about it. Gabriel is not your father.'

All colour had drained from Jacob's face. The news had certainly caught him by surprise. 'They tested my blood?' he said with a quavering voice.

'Yes, and I did promise to apologize if I was wrong.'

Jacob just stared at him.

'I apologize,' said Patrik. 'Your blood does not match the DNA we found on the victim.'

Jacob collapsed like a punctured balloon. He sat down heavily on the chair. 'So, what happens now?'

'You are no longer a suspect in the murder of Tanja Schmidt. But I still think you're hiding something from us. Now you have a chance to tell us what you know. I think you should take it, Jacob.'

He merely shook his head. 'I don't know anything. I don't know anything any more. Please, can't I go now?'.

'Not yet. We want to talk to your mother first, before you leave. Because I assume you may have a few things you want to ask her about.'

Jacob nodded mutely. 'But why do you want to talk to her? Surely it can't have anything to do with your investigation.'

Patrik found himself repeating what he'd said to Pedersen. 'Right now everything has to do with the investigation. You're all hiding something. I would bet a month's salary on it. And we intend to find out what it is, by any means necessary.'

All the fight seemed to have gone out of Jacob, and all he could do was nod in resignation. The news seemed to have put him in a state of shock.

'Gösta, could you drive out and pick up Laine?'

'We don't have a warrant to bring her in, do we?' Gösta said morosely.

'She has no doubt heard that we have Jacob under interrogation, so it probably won't be hard to convince her to come along voluntarily.'

Patrik turned to Jacob. 'We'll bring you something to eat and drink, and then you'll have to wait here until we've talked with your mother. After that you'll have a chance to talk to her yourself. Okay?'

Jacob nodded apathetically. He seemed deep in his own thoughts.

It was with mixed feelings that Anna put the key in the lock back home in Stockholm. Getting away for a while had been wonderful, both for her and the children, but it had also cooled her enthusiasm for Gustav. To be honest, it had been rather trying to be cooped up on a sailboat with him and all his nit-picking. And there was also something in Lucas's tone of voice the last time they talked that had worried her. Despite all the abuse he had subjected her to, he had always given the impression of being in full control over himself and the situation. Now for the first time she had heard a note of panic in his voice, a hint that things might be happening that were not under his control. From a mutual acquaintance she'd heard the rumour that things were starting to fall apart for him at work. He had flown off the handle during an in-house meeting and insulted a client on another occasion. Cracks had begun to appear in his façade. And that scared her. It scared her enormously.

Something was wrong with the lock. The key wouldn't turn in the proper direction. After trying for a while, she realized that it was because the door wasn't actually locked. She was sure that she'd locked it when she left home a week ago. Anna told the children to stay where they were and carefully opened the door. She let out a gasp. Her first flat of her own, in which she had taken so much pride, was destroyed. There wasn't a single piece of furniture left undamaged. Everything was smashed to bits, and all over the walls somebody had sprayed black paint like graffiti. 'WHORE' was on the living-room wall in huge letters, and she clapped her hand to her mouth as the tears came to her eyes. She didn't need to wonder who had done this to her. What had been gnawing in the back of her mind ever since she'd talked to Lucas had now become a certainty. He had clearly begun to fall apart. The hatred and anger that had always simmered just beneath the surface was breaking through his mask.

Anna retreated to the landing. She took both her children and hugged them tight. Her first instinct had been to ring Erica. Then she decided that she would have to take care of this herself.

She'd been so happy with her new life and had felt so strong. For the first time she had felt like her own woman. Not Erica's little sister. Not Lucas's wife. Her own. Now it was all in tatters.

She knew what she had to do. The cat had won. The mouse had only one place to take refuge. Anything not to lose the children.

But there was one thing. She was willing to give up herself; he could do whatever he liked with her. But if he ever touched one of the children again, she would kill him. Without hesitation.

It had not been a good day. Gabriel had been so upset over what he termed the assault by the police that he locked himself in his office and refused to come out. Linda had gone back out to the horses, and Laine sat alone on the sofa in the living room, staring at the walls. The thought of Jacob being interrogated at the police station brought tears of humiliation to her eyes. It was her instinct as a mother to protect him from anything bad, whether he was a child or an adult. Even though she knew that the situation was out of her control, it felt as if she'd failed. A clock ticked in the silence and the monotonous sound had almost put her in a trance. When someone knocked on the front door, she nearly jumped out of her seat. She opened the door with trepidation. Nowadays every knock seemed to bring unpleasant news. So she wasn't greatly surprised to see Gösta standing there.

'What do you want now?'

Gösta flinched with embarrassment. 'We need your help with a few questions. At the station.' He seemed to be waiting for a torrent of protests. But Laine merely nodded and followed him down the stairs.

'Aren't you going to tell your husband where you're going?' Gösta asked in surprise.

'No,' she said curtly, and he gave her a searching look. For a brief second he wondered if they had pressed the Hult family too far. Then he remembered that somewhere in their complicated relationships there was a murderer and a missing girl. The heavy oak door fell shut behind them, and like a Japanese housewife Laine followed a few paces behind Gösta to the car. They drove all the way to the station in a tense silence that was broken only by a question from Laine, who wanted to know if the police were still holding her son. Gösta merely nodded, and Laine spent the rest of the trip to Tanumshede staring out of the window at the passing countryside. It was already early evening, and the sun had begun to colour the fields red. But the beauty of their surroundings was not something either of them noticed.

Patrik looked relieved when they came through the doors of the station. In the time it had taken Gösta to drive out there and back, Patrik had restlessly paced in the corridor outside the interrogation room, fervently wishing that he could have read Jacob's mind.

'Hello,' he said, nodding curtly to Laine when she arrived.

327

It was starting to feel superfluous to keep introducing himself, and under the circumstances shaking hands seemed an altogether too ingratiating gesture. They weren't here to exchange pleasantries. Patrik had been a little worried about how Laine would handle their questioning. She had seemed so fragile, so vulnerable, with her nerves terribly exposed. He quickly saw that he needn't have worried. As she walked behind Gösta she looked resigned, but calm and collected.

Since Tanumshede police station had only one interrogation room, they went into the lunchroom and sat down. Laine said no thanks to a cup of coffee, but both Patrik and Gösta felt the need for a caffeine infusion. The coffee tasted bitter but they drank it anyway, although not without a grimace. Neither of them knew how to begin, and to their amazement Laine was the first to speak.

'Your colleague here' – she nodded towards Gösta – 'said you had a few questions.'

'Ye-e-es,' said Patrik hesitantly. 'We've obtained some information and we're a bit unsure how to handle it. We don't know how it fits into the investigation. Perhaps not at all, but right now time is too short to handle anything with kid gloves. So I'll get right to the point.' Patrik took a deep breath. Laine continued to meet his gaze unmoved, but when he looked down at her clasped hands resting on the table, he saw that her knuckles were white.

'We have received a preliminary result of the analysis of the blood samples we took from your family.' Now he also saw her hands start to tremble. He wondered how long she would be able to retain her apparent composure. 'And first of all I can tell you that Jacob's DNA does not match the DNA that we found on the victim.'

Right before his eyes, Laine started going to pieces. Her hands were now shaking uncontrollably, and he realized that she had come to the station prepared for the news that her son had been arrested for murder. Relief shone in her face, and she had to swallow several times to check the sobs rising in her throat. She said nothing, so he went on.

'However, we did discover something odd when comparing Jacob's and Gabriel's blood. It clearly shows that Jacob cannot possibly be Gabriel's son . . . ?' With his tone of voice he made the assertion into a question and then waited for Laine's reaction.

But the relief that Jacob had been cleared of murder charges seemed to have lifted a stone from her breast. She hesitated only a second before saying, 'Yes, that's correct. Gabriel is not Jacob's father.'

'In that case, who is?'

'I don't understand what this has to do with the murders. Especially now that Jacob is apparently not guilty.'

'As I said before, right now we don't have time to sit and decide what's important and what isn't, so I'd appreciate it if you would please answer my question.'

'Of course we can't force you,' said Gösta, 'but a young girl is missing and we need all the information we can get our hands on, even if it seems irrelevant.'

'Will my husband be told about this?'

Patrik hesitated. 'I can't promise anything, but I see no reason why we should run and tell him. But,' he hesitated, 'Jacob does know about it.'

She gave a start. Her hands began shaking again. 'What did he say?' Her voice was now no more than a whisper.

'I won't lie to you. He was upset. And of course he wonders who his real father is.'

A heavy silence settled over the table, but Gösta and Patrik waited her out calmly. After a while she answered, still in a whisper. 'It's Johannes.' Her voice took on strength. 'Johannes is Jacob's father.'

It seemed to surprise her that she could say that sentence aloud without a bolt of lightning crashing through the roof and killing her on the spot. The secret must have grown heavier and harder to bear with each passing year, and now it seemed almost a relief for her to let the words spill from her lips. She kept talking, fast.

'We had a brief affair. I couldn't resist him. He was like a force of nature that just came and took whatever he wanted. And Gabriel was so . . . different.' Laine hesitated over her choice of words, but Patrik and Gösta could easily fill in what she meant.

'Gabriel and I had already been trying to have a child for some time, and when it became evident that I was pregnant he was overjoyed. I knew that the baby could be either his or Johannes's, but despite all the complications it would involve, I fervently wished that it would be Johannes's. A son by him would be . . . magnificent! He was so alive, so beautiful, so . . . vibrant.'

A shimmer came into her eyes which brightened her features and in one blow made her look ten years younger. There was no doubt that she had been in love with Johannes. The thought of their affair, even after so many years, still made her blush.

'How did you know that it was Johannes's child and not Gabriel's?'

'I knew it as soon as I saw him, at the very second he was placed at my breast.'

'And Johannes, did he know that Jacob was his son and not Gabriel's?' Patrik asked.

'Oh yes. And he loved him. I always knew that I was only a passing amusement for Johannes, no matter how much I wanted something more, but with Jacob it was different. When Gabriel was out of town, Johannes would often come over to look at the boy and play with him. Until Jacob got old enough that he might say something, and then Johannes had to stop,' Laine said sadly. 'He hated to see his brother raising his firstborn, but he was not prepared to give up the life he was living. And he wasn't prepared to give up Solveig, either,' Laine admitted reluctantly.

'And how was life for you?' Patrik asked with sympathy.

She shrugged her shoulders. 'At first it was hell. Living so close to Johannes and Solveig, seeing them with their boys, brothers to Jacob. But I did have my son, and later, many years later, I had Linda. And this may sound improbable, but over the years I actually came to love Gabriel. Not the same way I loved Johannes, but perhaps in a more realistic way. Johannes was not a person anyone could love at close range without being destroyed. My love for Gabriel is not as exciting, but it's easier to live with.'

'Weren't you afraid that the truth would come out when Jacob got sick?' asked Patrik.

'No, there were other things I was much more afraid of,' Laine said sharply. 'If Jacob died, nothing would have any meaning, least of all who his father was.' Then her voice softened. 'But Johannes was so worried. He was in despair that Jacob was sick and there was nothing he could do. He couldn't even show his fear openly, couldn't sit by his son's side at the hospital. It was hard for him.' She lost herself in a distant time, but snapped out of it, forcing herself back to the present.

Gösta got up to refill his coffee cup and raised the pot enquiringly to Patrik, who nodded. When he sat down again he asked, 'Was there really no one who suspected anything, no one who knew? Have you never confided in anyone?'

A frown passed over Laine's face. 'Yes, in a moment of weakness Johannes told Solveig about Jacob. As long as he was alive she never dared do anything about it, but after Johannes died she began insinuating things that turned into bigger and bigger demands as her money began to run out.'

'So she practised extortion?' said Gösta.

Laine nodded. 'Yes, for twenty-four years I've been paying her.'

331

'How could you do that without Gabriel noticing? Because I presume large sums were involved?'

Another nod. 'It wasn't easy. But even though Gabriel is finicky about the bookkeeping for the farm, he's never been stingy with me. I've always been given money when I asked for it, for shopping and personal items, and the household in general. To pay Solveig I had to economize. I gave her most of what I got.' Her voice was bitter, with an undertone of something even stronger. 'But I assume that now I have no choice but to tell Gabriel everything. So from now on, I won't have that problem with Solveig any longer.'

She gave a wry smile but soon her expression turned serious again. She looked Patrik straight in the eye. 'If there is anything good to come out of all this, it's the fact that I no longer care what Gabriel will think, even though it's something that has haunted me for thirty-five years. The most important thing for me is my children, Jacob and Linda. That's why nothing else matters except that Jacob has now been exonerated – because I assume that is the case?' she said defiantly, narrowing her eyes at both of them.

'Yes, it does seem so, yes.'

'Then why are you still holding him? Can I go now and take Jacob with me?'

'Yes, you can,' Patrik said calmly. 'But we would like to ask you one favour. Jacob knows something about all this, and for his own sake it's important that he talk with us. Spend some time with him here and talk through everything. Try to convince him that he mustn't hold back anything he knows.'

Laine snorted. 'I do understand him, actually. Why should he help you after all you've done to him and our family?'

'Because the faster we work everything out, the sooner you can all get on with your lives.'

It was difficult for Patrik to sound convincing. He didn't want to tell her about the results of the analysis that showed that the perp may not have been Jacob, but it was still *someone* related to Johannes. That was their trump card, and he didn't intend to play it until it was absolutely necessary. Until then he hoped that Laine would believe what he said and accept his reasoning. After waiting a moment he got what he wanted. Laine nodded.

'I'll do what I can. But I'm not sure that you're right. I don't believe that Jacob knows any more about this than anyone else.'

'That remains to be seen,' was his curt reply. 'Are you coming?'

With hesitant steps she walked towards the interrogation room.

Gösta turned to Patrik with a frown. 'Why didn't you tell her that Johannes had been murdered?'

Patrik shrugged his shoulders. 'I don't know. But I have a feeling that the more I can stir things up between the two of them in there, the better. Jacob will tell Laine, and hopefully that will knock her off-balance too. And maybe, just maybe, we can get one of them to open up.'

'Do you think Laine is hiding something too?' said Gösta.

'I don't know, but didn't you see the expression on her face when we said that Jacob had been taken off the list of suspects? It was surprise.'

'I hope you're right,' said Gösta, stroking his face wearily. It had been a long day.

'We'll wait until they've had a chance to talk to each other in there. Then we'll go home and have a little food and get some sleep. We won't be any use if we're completely worn out,' said Patrik.

They sat down to wait.

Solveig thought she heard something outside. But then it was quiet again. She shrugged and shifted her concentration back to her albums. After all the emotional upheavals of the past few days, it was lovely to sink into the security of the well-thumbed photographs. They never changed, although they may have become a bit faded and yellowed over the years.

She looked at the kitchen clock. The boys came and went as they pleased, but this evening they had promised to be home for supper. Robert was going to bring pizzas from Captain Falck's, and she could feel hunger pangs beginning to grind in her stomach. All at once she heard footsteps on the gravel outside and got up to take out glasses and silverware. Plates were not needed. They always ate straight out of the box.

'Where's Stefan?' Robert said, setting the pizzas on the bench and looking around.

'I thought you would know. I haven't seen him in hours,' said Solveig.

'He's probably in the shed. I'll go see if he's there.'

'Tell him to hurry up, I don't intend to wait,' Solveig called after him, greedily lifting the lid of the box to find her pizza.

'Stefan?' called Robert before he reached the shed, but he got no answer. Oh well, it didn't have to mean anything; sometimes Stefan seemed practically deaf and blind when he sat in there.

'Stefan?' He raised his voice another notch, but heard only his own voice in the stillness.

Feeling annoyed he opened the door of the shed, ready to scold his little brother because he sat there daydreaming. But the thought instantly vanished from his mind.

'Stefan! What the fuck!'

His brother was lying on the floor with a big red halo round his head. It took a second before Robert realized that it was blood. Stefan didn't move.

'Stefan!' Robert's voice turned plaintive and a sob began to form in his chest. He sank to his knees next to Stefan with his hands hovering irresolutely over his battered body. He wanted to help but didn't know how, and he was afraid of making the injuries worse if he touched him. A moan from his brother made him take action. He got up from the floor with blood-soaked knees and ran to the house.

'Mamma, Mamma!'

Solveig opened the door and squinted at him. Her mouth and fingers were greasy since she had already started eating. Now she was annoyed at being disturbed.

'What the hell is all the commotion about?' Then she saw the spots on Robert's clothes. She knew that it wasn't paint. 'What's happened? Is it Stefan?'

She ran towards the shed as fast as her shapeless body could manage, but Robert caught up with her before she got there.

'Don't go in. He's alive, but somebody beat the shit out of him. He's in bad shape. We have to call an ambulance!'

'Who . . . ?' sobbed Solveig and collapsed like a loose-jointed doll in Robert's arms. Annoyed, he freed himself and forced her to stand on her own two feet.

'It doesn't much matter now. First we have to get help for Stefan! Go in and ring right now, and I'll go back to him. And ring the clinic too, the ambulance has to come all the way from Uddevalla.'

He barked out his orders with the authority of a general, and Solveig reacted at once. She ran back to the house and, secure in the knowledge that help would soon be on the way, Robert hurried back to his brother.

When Dr Jacobsson arrived, none of them gave even a thought to the circumstances under which they had met earlier in the day. Robert backed away with relief, grateful that someone who knew what he was doing had now taken control of the situation. He waited tensely to hear the prognosis.

'He's alive, but we have to get to the hospital as soon as possible. The ambulance is on its way, I hear.'

'Yes,' said Robert in a faint voice.

'Go in and fetch a blanket.'

Robert was smart enough to understand that the doctor's request was more about giving him something to do than any real need for a blanket. But he was thankful to have a specific task to do and obeyed willingly. Robert had to squeeze past Solveig, who stood in the doorway to the shed crying silently and shaking. He didn't have enough strength left to offer her any comfort. He was fully occupied keeping himself together. She would have to manage as best she could. In the distance he heard sirens. Never before had he been so glad to see blue flashing lights glimmering among the trees.

For half an hour Laine sat in the room with Jacob. Patrik would have liked to press his ear to the wall, but he told himself to be patient. His foot jiggling up and down was the only thing that betrayed his eagerness. Both he and Gösta had gone into their respective offices to try and get some work done, but it was difficult. Patrik wished that he knew exactly what it was he hoped to get out of this whole charade, but he really had no idea. He only hoped that Laine would somehow press the right button to make Jacob talk. Although she might also make him close up even more. It could go either way. That was the thing. Weighing the risks against any possible gain often led to actions that in hindsight could not be explained logically.

It also annoyed him that it would take until morning for him to get an answer on the blood tests. He would gladly have worked all night examining evidence relating to Jenny, if only there had been any. Instead the blood samples were the only thing they had to go on at present. He had probably been counting on the likelihood that Jacob's sample would be a match more than he knew. Now that his whole theory had collapsed, he was staring at a blank piece of paper in front of him, and they were back where they'd started. Jenny was somewhere out there, but it felt as if they knew even less than before. The only tangible result so far was that they might have succeeded in breaking up a family and confirming a 24-year-old murder. Beyond that – nothing.

For the hundredth time he looked at the clock and in frustration played little drum solos with his pen on the desk. Maybe, just maybe, at this very moment Jacob was recounting details to his mother that would solve the whole case in one blow. Maybe . . .

Fifteen minutes later, he knew that all hope of gaining any leads from those two was lost. At the sound of the door to the interrogation room opening he jumped out of his chair and went out to meet them. He was met by two closed faces. Eyes as hard as stones glared at him defiantly, and he instantly knew that whatever Jacob was hiding, he was not going to reveal it voluntarily.

'You said that I could take my son with me,' said Laine in an icy, frosty voice.

'Yes,' said Patrik. There was nothing more to say.

Now they could do what he'd promised Gösta a while ago. They could go home and eat and get some sleep. Hopefully they would be able to come back to work with renewed energy tomorrow.

10

She was worried about how things would go for Mother who was sick. How would her father manage to take care of her all by himself? The hope that they would find her was slowly being worn down by the terror of now being alone in the dark. Without the other girl's soft skin the darkness seemed even blacker, if that were possible.

The smell bothered her too. The sweet, cloying smell of death pushed away all other smells. Even the smell of their excrement vanished in the disgusting sweetness, and she had vomited several times, acid eruptions of gall from the lack of food in her stomach. Now she began to feel a longing for death. It scared her more than anything else. It began to flirt with her, whisper to her, promising to take away the pain and torment.

She kept listening for footsteps from above. The sound of the hatch opening. The boards that were dragged away and then the footsteps again, slowly coming down the stairs. She knew that the next time she heard them, it would be the last. Her body couldn't stand any more pain, and like the other girl she would give in to the temptation of death.

As if on cue she heard the sounds she feared. With sorrow in her heart she prepared herself to die.

It had been wonderful to have Patrik home a little earlier this evening. But at the same time she hadn't expected it under the circumstances. With a baby of her own on the way, Erica for the first time could really understand a parent's worry, and she suffered along with Jenny Möller's parents.

All at once she felt a bit guilty because she had been feeling so content all day long. Since the guests had left, peace had descended over the house, which allowed her time to chat with the baby kicking inside, lie down, rest and read a good book. She had also puffed her way up Galärbacken to the market to buy something good to eat, along with a big bag of sweets. The latter was now making her feel a little guilty. The midwife had sternly pointed out that sugar was not a healthful element in a pregnant woman's diet. In large quantities it could even make the child turn into a little sugar addict. Of course she had muttered to herself that it would take very large quantities for that to happen, but nevertheless the midwife's words kept churning through Erica's head. There was a long list on the door of the fridge of things she couldn't eat. Sometimes it felt like an impossible task to deliver the baby with its health intact. Certain types of fish, for instance, she could not eat at all, while others were okay, but no more than once a week. Then there was the question of whether they were saltwater or freshwater fish . . . not to mention the cheese dilemma. Erica loved cheese in all its forms, and she had memorized which ones she could and could not eat. To her dismay, mouldy cheeses were on the forbidden list, and she was already having fantasies about how she would gorge on cheese and red wine as soon as she finished nursing.

She was so into her thoughts of food orgies that she didn't even hear Patrik come in the door, which startled her so much she almost jumped out of her skin. It took a long while before her heart rate was back to normal.

'Oh, good Lord, you gave me a fright!'

'Sorry, I didn't mean to. I thought you heard me coming.'

He plopped down on the living-room sofa beside her. She was shocked to see how he looked.

'Patrik, you're all grey in the face. Did something happen?' A thought occurred to her. 'Did you find her?' An ice-cold band of steel tightened round her heart.

Patrik shook his head. 'No.'

He didn't say another word, so she waited patiently. After a while he seemed able to continue.

'No, we didn't find her. And it feels like we lost a lot of ground today.'

He suddenly leaned forward and buried his face in his hands. Erica moved closer to him, put her arms round him and leaned her cheek on his shoulder. She felt him, rather than heard him, crying softly.

'Shit, she's only seventeen years old. Can you fathom that? Seventeen and some sick fuck thinks he can do whatever he wants with her. Who knows what she's having to endure while we're busy running about like incompetent bloody fools? We don't know shit about what we're doing. Why the hell did we think that we could handle an investigation like this on our own? We usually sit and investigate bicycle thefts and stuff like that. What sort of idiot – me! – allowed us to be in charge of this damned investigation?!' He threw out his hands in a helpless gesture.

'Nobody could have done it any better, Patrik. How do you think things would have gone if they sent in some group from Göteborg? What alternative did you have? They don't know the area, they don't know the people and they don't know the way things work here. They couldn't possibly have done a better job. It would have been even worse. And your team haven't really been working on this alone, even though I understand why you think so. Don't forget that Uddevalla sent a couple of men to work with you, to arrange search parties and such. You said yourself the other evening how well the joint effort was working out. Did you forget about that?'

Erica talked to him like a child, but without patronizing him. She just wanted to be very clear about what she meant. It seemed to be working, because Patrik grew calmer and she could feel his body beginning to relax.

'Yes, you're probably right,' he said reluctantly. 'We've done all we could do, but it all seems so hopeless. Time is ticking away and here I sit at home while Jenny may be dying at this very moment.'

The panic began to rise in his voice again, and Erica squeezed his shoulder.

'Shhh, you can't afford to think that way.' She let a little sharpness enter her voice. 'You can't fall apart now. If there's anything you owe her and her parents, it's to keep a cool head and just keep working.'

He sat quietly, but Erica could see that he was listening to what she said.

'Her parents rang me three times today,' Patrik said. 'Four times yesterday. Do you think that's because they're about to give up?'

'No, I don't,' Erica said. 'I just think they're counting on

343

you to do your job. And right now your job is to gather your forces for another day at work tomorrow. It will serve no good purpose for any of you to wear yourselves out completely.'

Patrik smiled wanly when he heard his own words to Gösta come like an echo from Erica. Maybe he did know what he was talking about sometimes.

He decided to listen to his wife's advice. Despite the fact that he couldn't even taste his food, he ate what was put on the table in front of him and then got some sleep, though he slept uneasily. In his dreams a young blonde girl kept running away from him. He came close enough that he should have been able to touch her, but when he reached out his hand to grab hold of her, she laughed teasingly and slipped away. When the alarm clock woke him, he was exhausted and in a cold sweat.

Next to him Erica had spent most of the night wide awake, worrying about her sister Anna. Earlier in the day she had firmly decided not to take the first step. She was equally certain in the grey hours of dawn that she would have to ring Anna as soon as it got light. Something was wrong. She could feel it.

The smell of the hospital frightened her. There was something final about that sterile odour, the colourless walls and the dreary artwork. After not being able to sleep a single minute during the night, she thought that everyone around her seemed to be moving in slow motion. The rustling of the staff's clothing was amplified so that in Solveig's ears it sounded very loud. She expected the world to come crashing down around her at any moment. Sometime near dawn, the doctor had told her that Stefan's life hung by a thin thread and she had already started to grieve. What else should she do? Everything she'd had in life had run through her fingers like fine grains of sand and been blown away with the wind.

Nothing she had ever tried to hold on to remained. Johannes, their life at Västergården, her sons' future – it had all faded to nothingness and driven her into a world of her own.

But now she could no longer flee. Not when reality was pressing in on her, taking the form of visions, sounds and smells. The reality that they were now cutting into Stefan's body was too palpable for her to flee from.

She had broken with God long ago, but now she prayed with all the fervour she could muster. She rattled off all the words she could remember from her childhood faith, made promises she would never be able to keep, hoping that they would be enough to give Stefan at least a tiny advantage that might keep him alive. Beside her sat Robert with a shocked expression which didn't change all night. Solveig wanted nothing more than to reach out and touch him, console him, be a mother. But so many years had passed that the chance of displaying any maternal feeling had vanished. Instead, they sat next to each other like strangers, united only by their love for the man who lay in the bed, both of them silent in their certainty that he was the best of all of them.

A familiar figure appeared at the end of the corridor. Linda slunk along the walls, unsure of how she would be received – but all desire to quarrel had been beaten out of Solveig and Robert, along with the blows that had been rained down on Stefan.

Linda sat down quietly next to Robert and waited a while before she dared ask, 'How's he doing? I heard from Pappa that you rang him this morning and told him about what happened.'

'Yes, I thought Gabriel ought to know,' said Solveig, still with her gaze fixed in the distance, 'because after all, blood is thicker than water. I just thought he should know . . .' She seemed to fade away and Linda merely nodded.

Solveig went on, 'They're still operating on him. We don't know much more than . . . than it's possible he might die.'

'But who did this?' said Linda, determined not to let her aunt escape into silence before she got an answer.

'We don't know,' said Robert. 'But whoever the bastard was, he's going to pay for this!'

He pounded his hand hard on the armrest and woke up from his state of shock. Solveig said nothing.

'What the hell are you doing here, anyway?' Robert said, only now realizing how odd it was that this cousin they had so little contact with had come to the hospital.

'I . . . we . . . I . . .' Linda stammered as she searched for words to describe what the relationship actually was between herself and Stefan. It surprised her that Robert didn't know about it. Stefan had told her that he hadn't said anything about their relationship to his brother, but she still thought he would have said something. The fact that Stefan had wanted to keep their relationship a secret was proof of how important it must have been for him, and the insight suddenly made her feel ashamed.

'We . . . we've been seeing a lot of each other, Stefan and I.' She scrutinized her perfectly manicured nails.

'What do you mean – seeing?' Robert gave her a look of astonishment. Then it dawned on him. 'Aha, so you've been . . . okay . . .' He laughed. 'Well, there you see. How about that? My little brother. What a stud.' Then the laughter stuck in his throat when he remembered why he was sitting there, and the shocked expression returned.

As the hours passed, all three of them silently sat in a row in the depressing waiting room. Every sound of footsteps in the corridor made them anxiously watch for a doctor in a white coat who would come and give them the news. Unknown to each other, they were all praying.

When Solveig rang early that morning Gabriel had been surprised at the sympathy he felt. The feud between the families had gone on for so long that hostility had become

346

second nature, but when he heard about Stefan's condition, all the old grudges were flushed away. Stefan was his brother's son, his own flesh and blood, and that was the only thing that counted. And yet it would not be entirely easy to go to the hospital. Somehow it felt like a hypocritical gesture, and he was thankful when Linda said that she would go. He had even paid the taxi fare to Uddevalla for her, even though under normal circumstances he regarded taking a taxi as the height of extravagance.

He was sitting at his big desk, at a loss what to do. The whole world seemed turned upside down, and things were just getting worse and worse. Everything seemed to have come to a head over the last twenty-four hours: Jacob taken in for interrogation, the search of Västergården, the whole family having to give blood samples, and now Stefan in hospital, hovering between life and death. The whole sense of security that he had spent his life creating was now crashing down before his eyes.

In the mirror hanging on the opposite wall, he saw his face as if for the first time. And it was, in a way. He saw for himself how he had aged over the past few days. The vitality in his eyes was gone, his face was lined with worry, and his usually well-groomed hair was dishevelled and dull. Gabriel had to admit that he was disappointed with himself. He had always considered himself a man who could cope with any difficulty, someone people could rely on in hard times. But instead it was Laine who had emerged as the stronger of the two of them. Maybe he had always known that was true. Maybe she had known it too, but allowed him to live in his illusions, since she knew that would make him happier. A warm feeling filled him. A quiet love. Something that had long been buried deep beneath his egocentric contempt, but which now had a chance to break out. Maybe something good could still come out of all this misery.

A knock on the door interrupted his meditations.

'Come in.'

Laine came in cautiously and he noticed once again what a transformation had taken place. Gone was the nervous expression on her face and the hands that fidgeted; she even looked taller, since now she stood up straight.

'Good morning, dear. Did you sleep well?' he asked.

She nodded and sat down in one of the two armchairs he kept in the office for visitors. Gabriel gave her a searching glance. The circles under her eyes contradicted her affirmative reply. And yet she had been asleep for more than twelve hours. Yesterday when she came home after collecting Jacob at the police station he could hardly get a word out of her. She had merely mumbled that she was tired and then went to lie down in her room. Something was brewing, he could feel that now. Laine hadn't looked at him even once since she came into the room. Instead she was studying her shoes with extreme care. He could feel his anxiety rising, but first he had to tell her about Stefan. She reacted with surprise and sympathy, but it was as though the words didn't really reach her. Something so monumental was occupying her thoughts that not even Stefan's beating could make her focus on anything else. Now all of Gabriel's warning lights were flashing at once.

'Has something happened? Did anything happen at the police station yesterday? I spoke with Marita last night, and she said that they'd released Jacob, so the police could hardly have . . .' He didn't know quite how to continue. His thoughts darted about in his head as he rejected one explanation after the other.

'No, Jacob has been freed of all suspicion,' Laine said.

'What? Well, that's fantastic!' Gabriel's face brightened. 'How . . . what is it that . . .'

Still the same grim expression, and Laine refused to look him in the eye.

'Before we get into that, there's something else you ought to know.' She hesitated. 'Johannes, he, he . . .'

Gabriel squirmed impatiently in his chair. 'Yes, what is it about Johannes? Is it about that unfortunate exhumation?'

'Yes, you could say that.' Another pause. Gabriel felt like shaking her to make her spit out what she was trying to say. Then Laine took a deep breath and everything spilled out so fast that he could hardly keep up with what she said.

'They told Jacob that they'd examined Johannes's remains and confirmed that he did not commit suicide. He was murdered.'

The pen Gabriel had been holding in his hand fell to the desk. He looked at Laine as if she'd lost her mind.

'Yes, I know it sounds utterly crazy,' she went on, 'but they're apparently quite certain. Somebody murdered Johannes.'

'Do they know who?' It was the only thing he could think of to say.

'Obviously not,' Laine snapped. 'They just discovered it, and since so many years have passed . . .' She threw out her hands.

'Well, that's some news, I must say. But tell me more about Jacob. Did the police apologize?' said Gabriel brusquely.

'As I said, he's no longer a suspect. They managed to prove what we already knew,' Laine snorted.

'That's hardly a surprise. It was only a matter of time. But how . . . ?'

'The blood samples they took from us yesterday. They compared his blood with some traces the killer left behind and it didn't match.'

'I could have told them that from the first. And I did, unless my memory deceives me,' Gabriel declared pompously, feeling that a huge knot was loosened. 'Why don't we have a little champagne to celebrate, Laine? I don't understand why you look so glum.'

Now she raised her head and looked him straight in the eye. 'Because they also managed to analyse your blood.'

'Well, it certainly couldn't have been a match,' said Gabriel with a laugh.

'No, not with the murderer's. But . . . it didn't match Jacob's, either.'

'What? What do you mean? Didn't match? In what way?'

'They could tell that you're not Jacob's father.'

The silence that followed was like an explosion. Gabriel again caught a glimpse of his own face in the mirror. This time he didn't even recognize himself. A stranger with a gaping mouth and wide eyes stared back at him. He couldn't look at himself and had to turn away.

Laine looked as if the cares of the world had fallen from her shoulders, and a radiance came over her face. He understood it was relief. He suddenly realized what a burden it must have been for her to bear such a secret all these years, but then his anger struck with full force.

'What the hell are you saying?' he roared, so loud that she jumped.

'They're right. You're not Jacob's father.'

'Who the hell is, then?'

Silence. Slowly the truth dawned on him. He fell back in his chair and whispered, 'Johannes.'

Laine didn't need to confirm it. Suddenly everything was clear as crystal to him, and he cursed his own stupidity. Imagine that he had not seen it earlier! The stolen glances, the feeling that someone was in his home when he wasn't there, Jacob's almost uncanny resemblance to his brother.

'But why . . . ?'

'Why did I have an affair with Johannes, you mean?' Laine's voice had taken on a cold, metallic undertone. 'Because he was everything that you were not. I was second choice for you, a wife chosen for practical reasons, someone who would know her place and see to it that your life would be the way you had always imagined, with the least possible aggravation. Everything would be organized, logical, rational – and lifeless!' Her voice softened. 'Johannes didn't do anything that he didn't want to do. He loved when he wanted to, hated when he wanted to, lived when he wanted to . . . Being with Johannes was like experiencing a force of nature. He really saw me, *saw* me. He didn't just pass me on the way to his next business meeting. Every time we made love it was like dying and being reborn.'

Gabriel trembled at the passion he heard in Laine's voice. Then her tone changed and she looked at him solemnly.

'I'm really sorry that I deceived you about Jacob for all these years. Believe me, I really am, and I apologize with all my heart. But I don't intend to beg forgiveness because I loved Johannes.'

Impulsively she leaned forward and placed her hands on Gabriel's. He resisted the urge to pull them away.

'You've had so many chances, Gabriel. I know that there is a lot of what defined Johannes in you as well, but you don't ever let it come out. We could have had many good years together, and I would have loved you. In a way I did come to love you, in spite of everything, but I also know you well enough to know that now you will never let me keep on loving you.'

Gabriel didn't say a word. He knew that she was right. All his life he had struggled against living in his brother's shadow. Laine's betrayal struck him in his most vulnerable spot.

He remembered the nights when he and Laine had kept watch together at their son's hospital bed. He remembered wishing that he'd been the only person there and that his son would see how unimportant all the others were, including Laine. In Gabriel's eyes he had been the only one that Jacob needed. It was the two of them against the world. It seemed ridiculous to think about it now, since *he* was actually the one who was superfluous in that connection. Johannes was the one who had had the right to sit at Jacob's side, hold his hand, tell him that everything would be all right. Along with Ephraim, who had saved Jacob's life. Ephraim and Johannes. The eternal duo that Gabriel could never join. Now they appeared invincible.

351

'And Linda?' He knew the answer but had to ask. If for no other reason than to needle Laine. She just snorted.

'Linda is your daughter. There's absolutely no doubt about that. Johannes is the only lover I had during the time we've been married, and now I'm going to have to take the consequences.'

Another question bothered him more.

'Does Jacob know?'

'Jacob knows.'

She stood up, giving Gabriel a sad look. Then she said quietly, 'I'll be packing today. I'll be gone by this evening.'

He didn't ask where she was going. It didn't make any difference. Nothing made any difference.

They had concealed their encroachment well. She and the children had hardly seen any signs that the police had been there. At the same time something had changed. Something she couldn't quite put her finger on, but it was there. A feeling that their home was no longer the safe place it had always been before. Everything in the house had been touched by the hands of strangers, turning things over and scrutinizing them. Searching for something evil – in their house! Naturally the Swedish police showed a great deal of consideration, but for the first time in her life Marita thought she could understand how life must be in one of those dictatorships or police states she'd seen on the TV news. She'd always shaken her head and felt sorry for the people who lived under the constant threat of incursions into their homes but had never really grasped how dirty a person would feel afterwards, or how great the fear would be about what might happen next.

She had missed Jacob in their bed at night. She had wanted to have him next to her, his hand in hers, reassuring her that everything would be the way it was before. But when she'd rung the station the police told her that his mother had come to collect him, so she assumed he was sleeping over at his parents' house instead. Of course he could have called her, but then she scolded herself for having such thoughts, telling herself that it was presumptuous. Jacob always did what was best for them. If she was upset that the police had been in her home, she couldn't even imagine how it must have been for her husband, locked up and bombarded with impossible questions.

Marita slowly cleared off the table after the children's breakfast. Hesitantly she picked up the phone and began to dial her in-laws' number, but changed her mind and put the receiver down. Jacob must be sleeping in today, and she didn't want to disturb him. Just then the telephone rang, and she jumped in surprise. On the caller ID she saw that it was from the manor and she picked up eagerly, expecting Jacob.

'Hi, Marita, it's Gabriel.'

She frowned. She hardly recognized her father-in-law's voice. He sounded like an old man.

'Hi, Gabriel. How are things with you two?'

Her cheerful tone masked her apprehension, but she waited tensely for him to continue. It suddenly occurred to her that something had happened to Jacob, but before she could ask Gabriel he said, 'Look, is Jacob at home by any chance?'

'Jacob? But Laine fetched him from the station yesterday. I was sure he was staying with you.'

'No, he hasn't been here. Laine dropped him off outside your house last night.' The panic in his voice coincided with what she was feeling.

'Good Lord, where is he then?' Marita clapped her hand to her mouth, struggling not to dissolve in her fear.

'He must have . . . he must be . . .' Gabriel couldn't finish his sentences, which only increased his anxiety. If Jacob wasn't at home and he wasn't at their house either, there weren't many other alternatives. A horrible thought occurred to him.

'Stefan is in hospital. He was attacked and beaten up at home yesterday,' Gabriel said.

'Oh, good heavens, how is he doing?'

'They don't even know whether he'll live. Linda is at the hospital, and she was going to ring when she knew more.'

Marita sat down heavily on one of the kitchen chairs. Her chest was cramping up, making it hard to breathe. Her throat felt as if it were in a noose.

'Do you think that . . .' she began.

Gabriel's voice was scarcely audible over the phone as he said, 'No, that's not possible. Who would . . .'

Then they both realized at once that all their worries had to do with the fact that a killer was on the loose. A heavy silence followed.

'Call the police, Marita,' said Gabriel. 'I'm coming over.' Then she heard the dial tone.

Perplexed, Patrik was once again sitting at his desk. He forced himself to try and find something to do rather than just sit and stare at the telephone. He was overwhelmed with impatience as he waited to get answers about the blood tests. The clock ticked relentlessly. He decided to try to catch up with some administrative matters and took out the relevant papers. Half an hour later he still hadn't done anything with them; he just sat and stared into space. The exhaustion from too little sleep was making itself felt. He took a swallow of coffee but pulled a face at once. It was cold. With the cup in hand he got up to refill it when the telephone rang. He threw himself on the receiver so fast that some of the cold coffee sloshed onto his desk.

'Patrik Hedström.'

'Jacob has disappeared!'

He had been so prepared to hear from Forensics that it took a second before his brain could switch gears.

'Pardon me?'

'This is Marita Hult. My husband has been missing since last night!'

'Missing?' He still wasn't quite with it. Fatigue was making his thoughts move sluggishly and reluctantly.

'He never came home last night. And he didn't sleep at his parents' house, either. Considering what happened to Stefan . . .'

Now he was really lost.

'Hold on, take it a little slower. What happened to Stefan?'

'He's in hospital in Uddevalla. He was beaten up and they don't know whether he'll live. Imagine if the same person attacked Jacob. He might be lying injured somewhere.'

The panic in Marita's voice rose, and now Patrik's mind finally caught up. They hadn't heard about the beating of Stefan Hult; their colleagues in Uddevalla must have taken the report. He had to get in touch with them right away, but the most important thing right now was to calm down Jacob's wife.

'Marita, I'm sure nothing has happened to Jacob. But I'll send someone over to talk to you, and I'll contact the police in Uddevalla and find out what they know about Stefan too. I'm not taking this matter lightly, but I don't think there's any reason to worry yet. We often see this kind of thing happen. For one reason or another, a person chooses to stay away from home for a night. And Jacob may have been upset after we spoke with him yesterday. Maybe he needed to be alone for a while.'

In frustration Marita said, 'Jacob would never stay away without telling me where he was. He's much too considerate for that.'

'I believe you, and I promise that we'll get busy on it at once. Someone will come out and talk with you, all right?

If you could call your in-laws and ask them to come over too, then we could talk with them at the same time.'

'It's probably easier if I go over to their house,' said Marita, who seemed relieved that concrete measures were being instigated at once.

'Then that's what we'll do,' said Patrik. He urged her again not to believe the worst, and hung up.

All of a sudden his previous passivity was gone. Despite what he'd told Marita, he was inclined to believe that there was something out of the ordinary behind Jacob's disappearance. And if Stefan had been subjected to a beating, or attempted murder or whatever it was, there was real reason for concern. Patrik started by ringing his colleagues in Uddevalla.

A couple of minutes later he had found out everything they knew about the attack, which wasn't much. Someone had beaten Stefan to within an inch of his life last night. Since Stefan himself was unable to tell them who did it, the police still had no leads. They had spoken with Solveig and Robert, but neither of them had seen anyone near the cabin. For an instant Patrik suspected Jacob, but the idea soon proved to be groundless. Stefan's beating had taken place at the same time they had Jacob under interrogation at the station.

Patrik wasn't sure how he should proceed. There were two tasks that demanded action. First, he wanted someone to drive to the hospital in Uddevalla and talk with Solveig and Robert to find out whether they knew anything. Second, he needed to send somebody to the manor to talk with Jacob's family. After a few moments of hesitation he decided to drive to Uddevalla himself and send Martin and Gösta to the manor. But just as he got up to leave, the phone rang again. This time it *was* Forensics.

With trepidation he steeled himself to listen to what the lab had to say. Maybe they would finally have the piece of the puzzle they were looking for. But never in Patrik's wildest imagination could he have predicted what he heard next.

By the time Martin and Gösta reached the manor they had spent the whole drive discussing what Patrik had told them. It didn't make sense to either of them. But more pressing matters prevented them from dwelling on the conundrum. The only thing they could do now was to put their heads down and plough stubbornly ahead.

At the foot of the stairs leading to the front door they had to climb over a couple of big suitcases. Martin wondered who was going on a trip. It looked like more luggage than Gabriel would need for a business trip, and the bags also had a feminine touch that made him guess they belonged to Laine.

This time they were not shown into the living room but led down a long hall to the kitchen at the other end of the house. It was a room that Martin liked immediately. The living room was beautiful, of course, but had a rather impersonal air about it. The kitchen overflowed with comfort, with a rustic simplicity that flouted the elegance that otherwise lay like a suffocating veil over the manor. In the living room Martin had felt like a yokel, but here he felt like rolling up his sleeves to start stirring the big pots with their steaming contents.

Marita sat at an enormous, rustic kitchen table, squeezed in at the end against the wall. It looked as though she were seeking security in a situation that was frightening and unexpected. From a distance Martin could hear the sound of children yelling, and when he craned his neck and looked out of the windows facing the garden he saw Jacob and Marita's two children running about and playing on the huge lawn.

Gösta and Martin merely nodded to the people in the kitchen. Then they sat down with Marita at the table. Martin thought a strange mood prevailed, but he couldn't put his finger on what it was. Gabriel and Laine had sat down as far

357

apart as they could get, and he noticed that they were both very careful not to look at each other. He thought about the luggage at the front door. Then he realized that Laine must have told Gabriel about her affair with Johannes, and what the result had been. No wonder the mood was so impenetrable. The only thing still keeping Laine at the manor was their shared concern over Jacob's disappearance.

'Let's start from the beginning,' said Martin. 'Which of you saw Jacob last?'

Laine gave a small wave of her hand. 'I did.'

'And when was that?' Gösta took up the questioning.

'Around eight o'clock. After I collected him from the station.' She nodded at the officers facing her at the table.

'And where did you drop him off?' said Martin.

'Just by the drive to Västergården. I offered to drive him all the way up, but he said that wouldn't be necessary. It's a little hard to turn round at the end of the drive, and it's only a couple of hundred metres to walk, so I didn't insist.'

'What was his mood like?' Martin continued.

She glanced furtively at Gabriel. They all knew what it was they were really talking about, but no one wanted to say it straight out. It struck Martin that Marita probably didn't know yet about Jacob's altered familial relationships. But unfortunately he couldn't make allowances for that now. They had to get all the facts and couldn't sit there worrying about niceties.

'He was . . .' Laine searched for the right word, 'pensive. I would even say that he seemed in a state of shock.'

Marita looked in bewilderment at Laine, and then at the police.

'What are you talking about? Why would Jacob be in shock? What did you do to him yesterday? Gabriel said that he was no longer a suspect, so why should he be upset?'

A slight twitch was visible on Laine's face, the only sign of the emotional storms whirling round inside her, but she calmly put her hand on Marita's.

'Jacob got some upsetting news yesterday, dear. I did something many, many years ago that I've been carrying around
inside for a long time. And thanks to the police,' she cast a
spiteful glance at Martin and Gösta, 'Jacob was told about it
last night. I'd always intended to tell him, but the years
rolled by so quickly and I suppose I was waiting for the right
moment.'

'The right moment for what?' asked Marita.

'To tell Jacob that Johannes, not Gabriel, is his father.'

At each word in the sentence Gabriel grimaced and
flinched, as if each syllable were a stab at his heart. But his
shocked expression was gone. His psyche had already begun
to process the information, and it was no longer as difficult
as hearing it for the first time.

'What are you saying?' Marita looked at Laine and Gabriel
with eyes wide. Then she collapsed. 'Oh good Lord, it must
have crushed him.'

Laine flinched as if she'd been slapped. 'What's done is
done,' she said. 'The important thing now is to find Jacob,
and then . . .' she paused, 'then we'll have to work out all
the rest.'

'Laine is right. No matter what the blood test showed, in
my heart Jacob remains my son,' said Gabriel, putting his
hand on his chest, 'and we have to find him.'

'We will find him,' said Gösta. 'It's not really so odd that
he might want to stay away and think things over for a
while.'

Martin was grateful for the reassuring tone that Gösta
could turn on when he wished. Right now it was perfectly
suited to calming everyone's nerves, and Martin calmly
resumed his questions.

'So Jacob never came home?'

'No,' said Marita. 'Laine rang me when they left the station,
so I knew he was on the way. But later, when he didn't show
up, I thought he must have driven home with her and slept

over there. That wasn't like him, of course, but on the other hand he and the whole family have been under such stress lately, so I thought he might need to spend some time with his parents.'

As she said the last word she cast a furtive glance at Gabriel, but he simply gave her a wan smile. It would take time before they could work out how to handle the new situation.

'How did you hear what happened to Stefan?' asked Martin.

'Solveig rang early this morning.'

'I thought that you'd . . . had a falling-out?' Martin enquired cautiously.

'Yes, you might call it that. But family is family, I suppose, and when the chips are down then . . .' Gabriel let the words die out. 'Linda is at the hospital. She and Stefan were closer than anyone imagined, it turns out.' Gabriel gave an odd, bitter little laugh.

'Have you heard anything more?' asked Laine.

Gösta shook his head. 'No, the last we heard was that his condition was unchanged. But Patrik Hedström is on his way to Uddevalla right now, so we'll see what he says. If anything happens, one way or the other, you'll hear about it as soon as we do. Linda will probably ring you direct, I mean.'

Martin stood up. 'Well, I think we have all the information we need.'

'Do you think the person who tried to kill Stefan was the same one who murdered that German girl?' Marita's lower lip quivered slightly. She didn't need to explain what she was really asking.

'There's no reason to believe that,' said Martin gently. 'I'm sure that we'll soon find out what happened. I mean, Stefan and Robert have moved a good deal in rather dubious circles, so it's more likely we'll find the assailant there.'

'What are you doing now to search for Jacob?' Marita continued stubbornly. 'Are you sending out search parties in the area, or what?'

'No, we probably won't start with that. I honestly think that he's sitting somewhere and thinking over the . . . situation. He'll probably show up at home at any moment. So the best thing you can do is to stay home, and then ring us directly and let us know when he comes home. Okay?'

No one said a word. Martin and Gösta took that to mean that they agreed. There was really not much the police could do as yet. But Martin had to admit that he didn't feel as confident as he had let on to Jacob's family. It was an odd coincidence that Jacob should vanish the same evening that his cousin, brother, or whatever they should call Stefan, was attacked.

In the car on the way back to the station Martin told his colleague Gösta what he was thinking. Gösta nodded in agreement. He also had a gut feeling that not everything was as it should be. Strange coincidences happened very rarely in real life; they were not something that a policeman could rely on. They hoped that Patrik could find out something more.

11

She woke up with a pounding headache and a cloying feeling in her mouth. Jenny didn't know where she was. The last thing she remembered was sitting in a car that had stopped to offer her a lift, and now she had suddenly been flung into some sort of strange, dark reality. At first she wasn't afraid at all. It felt like a dream, and at any moment she expected to wake up and discover that she was back in her family's caravan.

After a while the realization slowly sank in that this was not a dream she was going to wake up from. In panic she began to fumble about in the dark. At the far wall she felt wooden boards under her fingers. A staircase. She crawled up the stairs, feeling for each step. With a bang she hit her head. A ceiling stopped her from climbing more than a few steps. Her feeling of claustrophobia became acute. She estimated that she could stand up on the floor, although just barely because the ceiling was very low. Nor had it taken long to feel her way around the walls. The space couldn't be more than two metres across. Panicking, she knelt at the top of the steps and pressed upwards, feeling the boards give a little. But they were not about to budge. She heard a metallic rattling and guessed that there was probably a padlock on the other side.

After trying a couple more times to push up the hatch, she climbed back down in despair and sat on the earthen floor with her arms wrapped about her knees. The sound of footsteps above her head made her instinctively move as far away as possible.

When the man came down the stairs she pictured his face, although there was no light in the room. She had seen him when he picked her up in the car, and that fact scared her. Jenny could identify him, and she knew what sort of car he drove. That meant he would never let her out of here alive.

She started to scream, but he gently put his hand over her mouth and spoke soothingly. When he was convinced that she wouldn't scream any more, he took his hand from her mouth and carefully began to undress her. He stroked her limbs with pleasure, almost with love. She heard his breathing grow heavier. She closed her eyes to shut out the thought of what was to come.

Afterwards he apologized. Then the pain began.

The summer traffic was murderous. Patrik's irritation had grown as the kilometres piled up on the odometer, and when he turned into the car park at Uddevalla Hospital he forced himself to take a few deep breaths to calm down. He didn't normally get so worked up about caravans taking up the whole road or tourists driving slowly and pointing to everything they saw without caring about the queue of cars forming behind them. But his disappointment over the results of the blood analysis had contributed considerably to lowering his tolerance level.

He had hardly believed his ears. None of the samples matched the DNA in the semen taken from Tanja's body. He had been so convinced that they would know the identity of the murderer when the results were in that he still hadn't recovered from the shock. Someone related to Johannes Hult had murdered Tanja, that fact was inescapable. But it wasn't any of his known relatives.

Impatiently he dialled the number of the station. Annika had started work a little later than usual and he'd been waiting for her to arrive.

'Hi, it's Patrik. Pardon me for sounding stressed, but could you see if you can dig up some information ASAP on whether there are any other relatives of the Hult family in the area? I'm wondering mostly if there are any children of Johannes Hult born out of wedlock.'

He heard her writing it down and kept his fingers crossed. It was the last straw he could grasp, and he sincerely hoped that she would find something. If not, all he could do was sit here and scratch his head.

He had to admit that he liked the theory that popped into his head during the drive to Uddevalla. The idea that Johannes might have a son in the area that they didn't know about. With what they had learned about him, it didn't seem impossible. In fact it was quite likely, the more he thought about it. It might even be a motive for why Johannes was murdered, thought Patrik without really knowing how he was going to tie up all the loose ends. Jealousy was a superb motive for murder, and the way he'd been killed also fit in well with the theory. An impulsive, unpremeditated murder. An attack of rage and jealousy that ended up with Johannes dead.

But what did that have to do with the murders of Siv and Mona? That was the piece of the puzzle that he couldn't place yet, but maybe Annika's findings would help them in that respect too.

He slammed the car door and went towards the front entrance. After a little searching and help from friendly county council employees, he finally found the right department. In the waiting room he found the three people he was looking for. Like birds on a telephone line they were sitting next to each other, without speaking and looking straight ahead. But he saw a glint ignite in Solveig's eye when she caught sight of him. Slowly she got up and waddled over to meet him. She looked as if she hadn't slept a wink all night. Her clothes were wrinkled and rank with sweat. Her greasy hair was tangled, and there were dark circles under her eyes. Robert looked equally tired. Only Linda looked alert, with a clear gaze and neat appearance. She was still unaware that her family was breaking apart.

'Have you caught him?' Solveig pulled lightly on Patrik's sleeve.

'Unfortunately we don't have any new information. Have you heard anything from the doctors yet?'

Robert shook his head. 'No, but they're still in the operating room. There was something about pressure on the brain. I think they're opening up his whole skull. I'd be surprised if they actually find a brain in there.'

'Robert!' Solveig turned angrily and glowered at her son, but Patrik understood what he was trying to do. He wanted to conceal his worry and relieve the pressure by joking about it. It was a method that usually worked for him too.

Patrik sat down in one of the empty chairs. Solveig also sat down.

'Who would do this to my little boy?' She rocked back and forth in her chair. 'I saw how he looked when they carried him out. He looked like a stranger. There was nothing but blood everywhere.'

Linda winced and grimaced. Robert didn't react. When Patrik looked more closely at his black jeans and sweatshirt, he could see big splotches of Stefan's blood still on them.

'You didn't hear anything last night, or see anything either?'

'No,' said Robert, annoyed. 'We already told that to the other officers. How many times do we have to repeat it?'

'I beg your pardon, but I have to ask these questions. Bear with me for a moment, please.'

The sympathy in his voice was genuine. It was a hard job to be a cop sometimes, especially on occasions like this when he had to delve into the lives of people who had much more important things to think about. But he received unexpected help from Solveig.

'Robert, please co-operate. We should do everything we can to help them catch whoever did this to our Stefan, you know that.' She turned to Patrik.

'I thought I heard a sound, and a minute later Robert called for me. But we didn't see anyone, either before or after we found him.'

Patrik nodded. Then he said to Linda, 'Did you happen to see your brother Jacob last night?'

'No,' said Linda in surprise. 'I was staying over at the manor house. He was at home at Västergården, wasn't he? Why do you ask?'

'It seems he never came home last night, so I just thought you might have seen him.'

'No, as I said, I didn't. But check with Mamma and Pappa.'

'We've done that. They haven't seen him, either. Do you happen to know of somewhere else he might be?'

Now Linda was beginning to look nervous. 'No, where would that be?' Then an idea seemed to occur to her. 'Could he have driven to the farm at Bullaren and slept there? Of course he's never done that before, but . . .'

Patrik hit his thigh with his fist. It was crazy that they hadn't thought of Bullaren. He excused himself and went to ring Martin. He would have to drive out there immediately and check it out.

When he returned to the waiting room the mood had changed. While he was talking to Martin, Linda had called home on her mobile. Now she was looking at him with all the defiance of a teenager.

'What's going on, anyway? Pappa said that Marita called you and reported Jacob missing, and that those other two cops were out there asking a bunch of questions. Pappa sounded worried as hell.' She was standing in front of Patrik with her hands on her hips.

'There's no reason to worry yet,' he said, repeating the same mantra that Gösta and Martin had used at the manor.

'Your brother has probably gone off to be alone for a while, but we have to take all such reports seriously.'

Linda gave him a suspicious look, but seemed to be satisfied. Then she said in a low voice, 'Pappa also told us about Johannes. When were you planning to tell *them* about it?'

She tossed her head in the direction of Robert and Solveig. Patrik couldn't help watching in fascination the arc that her long blonde hair made in the air. Then he reminded himself of her age. He was shocked at the thought that all the upheaval involved in starting a family may have triggered a tendency to lechery in him.

He replied in the same low voice, 'We're waiting a bit on that. Now doesn't seem like a good time, considering Stefan's situation.'

'You're wrong about that,' said Linda calmly. 'Right now they could use some positive news. And believe me, I know Stefan well enough to say that the discovery that Johannes didn't take his own life would be welcome news in this family. So if you're not going to tell them, I will.'

What a cheeky person. But Patrik was inclined to admit that she was right. He may have already waited too long. They had a right to be told.

He nodded affirmatively to Linda and cleared his throat as he sat down.

'Solveig, Robert, I know that you had some objections to the fact that we opened Johannes's grave.'

Robert jumped up like a rocket from his chair. 'What the hell, are you crazy? Are you going to bring that up now? Don't we have enough to worry about right now?'

'Sit down, Robert,' Linda snapped. 'I know what he's going to say and believe me, you'll want to hear it.'

Shocked that his skinny cousin was giving him orders, Robert sat down and shut up. Patrik continued, as Solveig and Robert glared at him, reminded of the humiliation of seeing Johannes's coffin raised from the ground.

'We had a pathologist examine . . . uh . . . the body and he found something interesting.'

'Interesting,' Solveig snorted. 'Well, that's a nice choice of words.'

'Yes, you'll have to excuse me, but there's no good way to say this. Johannes did not take his own life. He was murdered.'

Solveig gasped for breath. Robert sat as if frozen to the spot, unable to move.

'What did you say?' Solveig grabbed for Robert's hand and he let her take it.

'You heard what I said. Johannes was murdered. He did not take his own life.'

Tears began running from Solveig's already red-rimmed eyes. Then her entire huge body began to shake, and Linda gave Patrik a triumphant look. They were tears of joy.

'I knew it,' Solveig said. 'I knew that he would never have done anything like that. And all those people who said that he committed suicide because he killed those girls. Now they'll have to eat their words. The same person who killed the girls must have murdered my Johannes. They'll have to crawl on their bare knees and beg us for forgiveness. All these years that we've – '

'Mamma, that's enough,' Robert interrupted her, sounding annoyed. It looked as though he hadn't really grasped what Patrik said. He probably needed the words to sink in.

'What are you going to do now to catch the person who murdered Johannes?' Solveig asked eagerly.

Patrik turned round to face her. 'Well, it's probably not going to be that easy. So many years have passed, and no evidence was preserved that might give us a lead. But naturally we're going to try, and we'll do the best we can. That's all I can promise you.'

Solveig snorted. 'Well, if you work as hard trying to catch Johannes's murderer as you did to put him in jail, then there shouldn't be any problem. And now I want an apology from the police even more!'

She wagged her finger at Patrik. He realized that it was probably time for him to be leaving before the situation deteriorated even further. He exchanged a glance with Linda, and she signalled discreetly for him to go. He had one last request for her. 'Linda, if you hear from Jacob, promise to ring us right away. But I should think you were right. He must be at Bullaren.'

She nodded, but the worry was still there in her eyes.

They were just turning into the car park at the police station when Patrik rang. Martin drove back out on the road in the direction of Bullaren. The heat had begun to creep up the thermometer again after a mercifully cool morning, and he turned up the fan a notch.

Gösta pulled at the collar of his short-sleeved shirt. 'If only this blasted heat would lay off for a while.'

'If you were out on the golf course you wouldn't be complaining,' Martin laughed.

'That's a completely different story,' Gösta said sourly. Golf and religion were two things nobody joked about in his world. For a brief second he wished he was working with Ernst again. It was certainly more productive to ride with Martin, but he had to admit that he liked the laziness of working with Ernst more than he'd previously thought. Ernst had his faults, of course, but he never protested if Gösta sneaked off for a couple of hours to hit a bucket of balls.

The next moment the photo of Jenny Möller appeared in his mind, and he was struck by an acute sense of guilt. In a brief instant of clarity he saw that he'd become a bitter and hostile old man, frightening like his father in his old age. If he kept on like this, sooner or later he'd be sitting alone in an old folks' home mumbling about imagined injustices like

371

his father; although without any children to look in on him now and then out of a guilty sense of duty.

'Do you think he's there?' he said to break off his unpleasant thoughts.

Martin hesitated for a moment, then he said, 'No, I'll be very surprised if he is. But it's still worth checking out.'

They swung into the yard and were amazed once again at the idyllic scene before them. The farm seemed eternally drenched in a mild sunlight that made the Falun red colour stand out in lovely contrast to the blue lake behind the house. As before, teenagers darted purposefully about, fully engaged in their activities. Words popped into Martin's mind: magnificent, healthful, clean, useful, Swedish, and the combination of those words infused him with a slight feeling of discomfort. Experience told him that if something looked too good to be true, it probably was.

'A slight Hitler Youth atmosphere about the place, don't you think?' said Gösta, putting words to Martin's discomfort.

'Yeah, maybe. Your choice of words is a bit strong, though. I wouldn't go bandying comments like that about too freely,' said Martin dryly.

Gösta looked offended. 'Excuse me,' he said grumpily, 'I didn't know you were the thought police. And by the way, they wouldn't take in boys like Kennedy if it was some fucking Nazi camp.'

Martin ignored the comment and headed for the front door. One of the female instructors at the farm opened it.

'Yes, what do you want?'

Jacob's grudge against the police had obviously rubbed off.

'We're looking for Jacob.' Gösta was still sulking, so Martin took the lead.

'He's not here. Try him at home.'

'Are you sure he's not here? We'd like to take a look for ourselves.'

Reluctantly the woman stepped aside and let in the two

policemen. 'Kennedy, the police are here again. They want to see Jacob's office.'

'We know the way,' said Martin.

The woman ignored him. With rapid steps Kennedy approached them. Martin wondered whether he was some sort of permanent guide at the farm. Or maybe he just liked showing people about.

Without a word he led Martin and Gösta down the corridor to Jacob's office. They thanked him politely and opened the door expectantly. No sign of Jacob. They entered and looked carefully for any trace that might indicate that Jacob might have spent the night there, a blanket on the sofa, an alarm clock, anything. But there was nothing. Disappointed, they left the office. Kennedy was calmly waiting for them. He raised his hand to push his hair back from his face, and Martin saw that his eyes were black and unfathomable.

'Nothing. Not a damned thing,' said Martin when the car was rolling in the direction of Tanumshede again.

'No,' said Gösta curtly. Martin rolled his eyes. He was evidently still sulking. Well, let him.

But Gösta's thoughts were occupied with a completely different matter. He had noticed something during their visit to the farm, but it kept eluding him. He tried to stop thinking about it and let his subconscious do the work, but it was as impossible as ignoring a grain of sand under his eyelid. There was something he'd seen – and should have remembered.

'How's it going, Annika? Did you find anything?'

She shook her head. Patrik's appearance worried her. Too little sleep, too little real food, and too much stress had stripped away the last of his suntan and left only a grey pallor behind. His body seemed to be sagging under the weight of something, and it didn't take a genius to work out what that burden could be. She wanted to tell him to separate his private emotions from his work, but she refrained. She too was feeling the pressure, and the last thing she saw before she closed her eyes each night was the desperate look on the faces of Jenny Möller's parents when they came in to report their daughter missing.

She decided to limit her comments to a brief: 'How are you doing?' She gave Patrik a sympathetic look over the rims of her glasses.

'As well as can be expected under the circumstances.' He impatiently ran his hands through his hair, making it stand straight up like a caricature of a mad professor.

'Like shit, I'm guessing,' Annika said frankly. She had never been much for glossing over things. If something was shit, it would still smell like shit even if you poured perfume all over it. That was her motto in life.

Patrik smiled. 'Yes, something like that. But enough about me. Did you find anything in the records?'

'No, unfortunately. There was nothing in the register of citizens about any other children of Johannes Hult, and there aren't very many other places to look.'

'Might there be children anyway, even though they're not registered?'

Annika looked at him as if he were a little slow in the head and snorted, 'Well, thank goodness there's no law that compels a mother to name the father of her children. There may be some children of his concealed under the heading "father unknown".'

'And let me guess, there are quite a few of them, right?'

'Not necessarily. It depends on how wide you want to extend the search geographically. But people have actually been surprisingly respectable in these parts. And you have to remember that it's not the Forties we're talking about here. Johannes would have been most active during the Sixties and Seventies. And by then it was no great shame to have a child out of wedlock. During certain periods in the Sixties it was probably considered almost an advantage.'

374

Patrik laughed. 'If you're talking about the Woodstock era, I really don't think that flower power and free love ever made it to Fjällbacka.'

'Don't say that. Even in the calmest waters . . .' said Annika, glad that she could lighten up the mood a bit. The station had felt like a funeral parlour the last few days. But Patrik quickly turned serious again.

'So theoretically you should be able to put together a list of the children within, say, Tanum county, who do not have a father registered?'

'Yes, I could do that not only theoretically, but also in practice. But it'll take a while,' Annika warned him.

'Just do it as fast as you can.'

'How are you going to use that list to find out who might be Johannes's offspring?'

'I intend to start by ringing round and asking. If that doesn't work, I'll think of something else.'

The door to the reception area opened and Martin and Gösta came in. Patrik thanked Annika for her help and went to meet them. Martin stopped, but Gösta fixed his eyes on the carpet and went into his office.

'Don't ask,' said Martin, shaking his head.

Patrik frowned. Friction among the personnel was the last thing he needed. It was bad enough with the way Ernst was acting up. Martin read his thoughts.

'It's nothing serious, don't worry about it.'

'Okay. Shall we have a cup of coffee in the lunchroom and compare notes?'

Martin nodded. They went in, poured themselves some coffee, and sat down facing each other at the table. Patrik said, 'Did you find any sign of Jacob at Bullaren?'

'No, not a thing. It doesn't look as though he's been there. How did it go for you?'

Patrik quickly told him about his visit to the hospital.

'Have you thought about why the blood analysis didn't

produce anything?' asked Martin. 'We know that the perp we're searching for is related to Johannes, but it's not Jacob, Gabriel, Stefan or Robert. And considering the nature of the sample, we can rule out the women at once. Do you have any ideas?'

'Yes, I've asked Annika to try to compile some data on whether Johannes had any children out of wedlock in the area.'

'That sounds smart. With a guy like him I'd be surprised if he didn't have any illegitimate kids scattered about.'

'What do you think of the theory that the same person who beat up Stefan is now after Jacob?' Patrik cautiously slurped a little coffee. It was freshly brewed and scalding hot.

'It would undeniably be a very odd coincidence. What do you think?'

'The same as you. That it would be a hell of an odd co-incidence if it's not the same person. It seems as if Jacob has completely vanished from the face of the earth. Nobody has seen him since last night. I have to admit I'm worried.'

'You've had a hunch the whole time that Jacob was hiding something. Could that be the reason something has happened to him?' Martin said hesitantly. 'Could somebody have heard that he was at the police station and thought he was going to blab about something, something that this person didn't want to come out?'

'Maybe,' Patrik said. 'But that's precisely the problem. Anything is possible right now, and all we have are a bunch of speculations.' He counted on his fingers. 'We have Siv and Mona murdered in '79; Johannes murdered in '79; Tanja murdered now, twenty-four years later; Jenny Möller abducted, presumably when hitchhiking; Stefan beaten up last night, and maybe even killed depending on the prognosis; and Jacob who has vanished without a trace. The whole time the Hult family seems to be the common denominator, and yet we have evidence that it's not one of them who is guilty of Tanja's death. And all indications are that whoever murdered Tanja also murdered Siv and Mona.' He threw out his hands in frustration. 'It's a mess, that's what it is. And we're standing in the middle of it all and can hardly tell our arse from our elbow.'

'You've been reading too much of that anti-police propaganda again,' Martin said with a laugh.

'So, what do we do now? I'm all out of ideas. Time must be running out for Jenny Möller, or it could already be too late.' He hastened to change the subject to drag himself up from his morose thoughts. 'Have you invited that girl out yet, by the way?'

'What girl?' said Martin, trying to force his face into a neutral expression.

'Don't even try. You know who I mean.'

'If it's Pia you're talking about, it wasn't anything like that. She helped us out with a little interpreting, that's all.'

'"She helped us out with a little interpreting, that's all",' Patrik mocked him in falsetto, wagging his head from side to side. 'Let go of the sideboards and get into the match now. I can tell when you talk about her that's what you're thinking. Although she may not be your type. Are you sure she doesn't already have a boyfriend?' Patrik smiled to take the sting out of his teasing.

Martin was collecting himself for a biting retort when Patrik's mobile rang.

With his ears pricked, Martin strained to hear who it might be on the phone. He heard something about the blood analyses, so it was probably someone from the lab. That much he could make out. He couldn't glean anything else from Patrik's end of the conversation:

'What do you mean by odd? Aha . . . I see. What the hell are you saying? But how can . . . Okay . . . '

Martin had to suppress a desire to scream. Patrik's changing expressions indicated that something big was brewing, but he stubbornly continued to give single-word replies to the person at the lab.

'So what you're saying is that you've precisely mapped the family relationships between them.' Patrik nodded to Martin to show that he was deliberately trying to share a little information from the conversation.

'But I still don't understand how that fits with . . . ? No, that's totally impossible. He's dead. There must be some other explanation. No, but for God's sake, you're the expert. Listen to what I'm saying and think about it. There *must* be another explanation.'

Patrik looked as if he was waiting tensely while the person on the other end was thinking.

Martin whispered, 'What's happening?'

Patrik held up a finger to shush him. Now he was obviously getting some sort of answer.

'It's not far-fetched at all. In this particular case it's actually completely plausible.'

Patrik's face lit up. Martin could see relief spreading like a wave through his colleague's body, while he himself was practically scratching long grooves in the table.

'Good Lord! Thanks! Thanks a lot!' Patrik slammed his mobile shut and turned to Martin, with relief still lighting up his face.

'I know who has Jenny Möller! And you're not going to believe your ears when you hear this . . .'

The operation was over. Stefan had been rolled in to the recovery room connected to all sorts of hoses and tubes, off in his own dark world. Robert sat next to the bed holding Stefan's hand. Solveig had reluctantly left them to go find the toilet, and he had his brother to himself for a while, since Linda had not been allowed in. They didn't want too many relatives in the room at one time.

The thick tube going into Stefan's mouth was connected

to a machine that made a wheezing sound. Robert had to force himself not to breathe in the same rhythm as the respirator. It was as if he wanted to help Stefan breathe, anything to take away the feeling of helplessness that threatened to overpower him.

He stroked Stefan's palm with his thumb. He thought he would try to look at his brother's lifeline, but he gave it up because he didn't know which of the three distinct lines was the lifeline. Stefan had two long lines and one short one. Robert hoped that the short one was his loveline.

The thought of a world without Stefan filled him with a dizzying sense of emptiness. He knew that he usually appeared to be the stronger of the two, the leader. But the truth was that without Stefan, he was nothing more than a little shit. There was a kindness in Stefan that Robert needed to retain his own sense of humanity. Any kindness he might have felt had vanished when he found his father's body. Without Stefan the harshness he felt inside would take over.

Robert continued to make promises as he sat next to his brother's hospital bed. The promise that everything would be different, if only Stefan were allowed to live. He promised never to steal again, to get a job, to try and use his life for something good; yes, he even promised to cut his hair.

The last promise he made with dread, but to his great surprise it seemed to be the one that made all the difference. He felt a feather-light trembling in Stefan's hand, a light movement of his index finger, as if he were trying to caress Robert's hand in return. It wasn't much, but it was all Robert needed. He waited eagerly for Solveig to come back. He longed to tell her that Stefan was going to be all right.

'Martin, there's a guy on the phone who says he has information about the beating of Stefan Hult.' Annika's head was sticking out the doorway and Martin stopped and turned round.

'Damn, I don't have time right now.'

'Should I ask him to call back?'

'No, damn it, no, I'll take it.' Martin rushed into Annika's office and took the phone from her. After listening intently for a while and asking some more questions, he hung up and ran out the door.

'Annika, Patrik and I have to go. Can you get hold of Gösta and ask him to ring me on my mobile right away? And where's Ernst?'

'Gösta and Ernst left to go to lunch, but I'll call them on the mobile.'

'Good.' He took off.

A few seconds later Patrik rushed in.

'Did you get hold of Uddevalla, Annika?'

She gave him the thumbs up. 'All clear, they're on their way!'

'Great!' He turned to go but stopped. 'I forgot to tell you, you don't have to do any more work on that list of fatherless children.'

Then she watched him disappear too, hurrying down the corridor. The energy at the station had risen to a level that was almost palpable. Patrik had told her in haste what had happened, and she could feel excitement tingling in her hands and feet. It was a relief to finally get a breakthrough in the investigation, and right now every minute counted. She waved to Patrik and Martin as they passed her window and left the station. 'Good luck!' she called, not sure if they heard her. She quickly dialled Gösta's number.

'Yeah, it's really the pits, Gösta. Here the two of us sit while the young cocks strut.' Ernst was getting into his favourite topic, and Gösta had to admit that it was starting to wear on his nerves. Even though he'd railed against Martin before, it was mostly bitterness over being reprimanded by someone not even half his age. Afterwards he realized that it wasn't that big a deal.

380

They had taken the car to Grebbestad and were sitting at the Telegrafen restaurant having lunch. The choice of eating establishments in Tanum was not great, and they'd tired of them pretty quickly. And Grebbestad was only ten minutes away on the coast.

Gösta's telephone was lying on the table. When it rang, they both saw from the display that it was the station calling.

'Damn, don't answer it. You have the right to eat your lunch in peace and quiet.' Ernst reached out to turn off Gösta's phone, but a look from his colleague stopped him.

It was the height of the lunchtime rush. Some of the patrons glowered angrily at the sight of someone bold enough to take a phone call in the middle of the restaurant. Gösta glared back and talked extra loud. When he finished he placed a banknote on the table, stood up and motioned to Ernst to do the same.

'We've got a job to do.'

'Can't it wait? I haven't even had a bite yet.'

'You can have something at the station later. Right now we have to bring a guy in.'

For the second time that day Gösta was headed towards Bullaren; this time he was behind the wheel. He told Ernst what Annika had reported. When they arrived half an hour later, they found a teenage boy waiting for them by the road, just as she had said, a short distance from the farm.

They stopped the car and climbed out.

'Are you Lelle?' said Gösta.

The boy nodded. He was big and husky, with a wrestler's neck and enormous hands. As if born to be a bouncer, Gösta thought. Or a henchman, as in this case. But a henchman with a conscience, or so it seemed.

'You rang us, so start talking,' said Gösta.

'Yes, let's hear it. Come on, start talking,' said Ernst aggressively, and Gösta shot him a warning glance. This assignment wouldn't demand any macho displays on his part.

381

'Well, as I told the girl at the station, Kennedy and I did something dumb yesterday.'

Something dumb, Gösta thought. The boy was certainly inclined to understatement.

'Yes?'

'We beat up that guy a little, the one who's related to Jacob.'

'Stefan Hult?'

'Yeah, I think Stefan's his name.' His voice turned shrill. 'I swear, I didn't know that Kennedy would go off on him so damn hard. He said he was just going to have a talk with him. Just to threaten him a little. Nothing heavy.'

'But that's not what happened.' Gösta tried to sound fatherly, but wasn't very successful.

'No, Kennedy flipped out. He kept saying a bunch of stuff about how fucking good Jacob is and that he, Stefan I mean, had fucked him over somehow and lied about something that Kennedy wanted him to take back, and when Stefan said no, then Kennedy really lost it and started beating the shit out of him.'

Here the boy had to stop and catch his breath. Gösta thought he'd followed most of the account, but he wasn't entirely sure. Kids these days didn't seem to speak the same language.

'And what were you doing in the meantime? Messing about in the garden?' said Ernst scornfully. He got another dark look from Gösta.

'I was holding the guy,' Lelle said quietly. 'I held him by the arms so he couldn't hit back, but I didn't know that Kennedy was going to go fucking crazy. How would I know that?' He looked from Gösta to Ernst and back. 'What's going to happen now? Can I keep staying here? Am I going to prison?'

The big tough guy was almost in tears. He looked like a scared little boy, and Gösta no longer had to make an effort to sound fatherly; now it came naturally.

'We'll talk about that later. We'll work it out. Right now the most important thing is for us to talk to Kennedy. You can either wait here while we drive over and collect him, or wait in the car. Take your pick.'

'I'll wait in the car,' said Lelle in a low voice. 'The others are going to find out anyway that I was the one who ratted out Kennedy.'

'All right, let's go.'

They drove the last hundred metres up to the farm. The same woman who had opened the door for Gösta and Martin that morning opened it again. Her irritation had risen another notch.

'What do you want now? We're going to have to put in a swinging door for the police. I swear, I've never seen anything like it. After all the co-operation we've shown the police over the years – '

Gösta interrupted her by holding up his hand. He looked as solemn as the grave when he said, 'We don't have time for any discussion. We need to talk to Kennedy. Now.'

The woman heard the gravity in his voice and immediately called Kennedy. When she spoke again her tone was softer.

'What do you want with Kennedy? Has he done something?'

'You'll hear all the details later,' Ernst said brusquely. 'Right now our only job is to take the boy to the station and have a talk with him there. We're taking in that big boy, Lelle, too.'

Kennedy stepped out of the shadows. He wore dark trousers and a white shirt. And with his hair neatly combed he looked like a boy from an English boarding school, not a former offender at a reform school. All that disturbed the image were the big scrapes on his knuckles. Gösta swore to himself. That's what he'd noticed earlier. He should have remembered.

'May I help you gentlemen?' Kennedy's tone of voice was well modulated, but perhaps a touch overdone. They could hear that he took great pains to speak correctly, which deadened the whole effect.

'We've talked to Lelle. So you're going to have to come with us to the station.'

Kennedy bent his head in silent acquiescence. If there was anything Jacob had taught him, it was that a person had to suffer the consequences of his actions to be worthy in the sight of God.

He took one last regretful look around. He was going to miss the farm.

They sat silently facing each other. Marita had taken the children with her and gone down to Västergården to wait for Jacob. Outside the summer birds were chirping, but indoors it was quiet. The luggage was still standing at the bottom of the front steps. Laine couldn't leave before she knew that Jacob wasn't hurt.

'Have you heard anything from Linda?' she asked in an uncertain voice, afraid to disturb the delicate temporary cease-fire between herself and Gabriel.

'No, not yet. Poor Solveig,' said Gabriel.

Laine thought about all the years of extortion, but said nothing. A mother cannot but feel sympathy for another mother whose child has been injured.

'Do you think that Jacob also . . . ?' The words stuck in her throat.

In an unexpected gesture Gabriel put his hand on hers. 'No, I don't think so. You heard what the police said. He's no doubt somewhere trying to think things through. He has a lot to think about.'

'Yes, he certainly does,' said Laine bitterly.

Gabriel said nothing, but kept his hand on hers. It was astonishing how comforting it felt, and she suddenly realized

384

that it was the first time in all these years that Gabriel had shown her such tenderness. A warm feeling spread through her body, but at the same time it was mixed with the pain of parting. She didn't wish to leave him. She had taken the initiative to save him the humiliation of throwing her out, but all at once she was unsure whether she had done the right thing. Then he removed his hand and the moment passed.

'You know, in hindsight I can say that I always felt that Jacob was more like Johannes than me. I saw it as a scornful trick of fate. Outwardly it may have seemed that Ephraim and I were closer to each other than he and Johannes were. Father lived here with us, and I inherited the manor and all that. But it wasn't true. The reason they fought so much was that they were basically so alike. Sometimes it seemed that Ephraim and Johannes were actually one and the same person. I was always on the outside. Until Jacob was born and I saw so much of both my father and my brother in him. It felt like a possibility had opened up for me to join the community. If I could bind my son strongly to me and get to know him inside and out, then it would be like getting to know Ephraim and Johannes at the same time. I would become a part of their community.'

'I know,' Laine said softly, but Gabriel didn't seem to hear her. He was looking out of the window into the distance as he went on.

'I envied Johannes. He actually believed Father's lies that we could heal people. Imagine what power that faith gave him! To look at your hands and know that they were the tools of God. To see people stand up and walk, to make the blind see and know that you were the one who made it possible. I myself saw only the spectacle. I saw my father standing in the wings, guiding and directing, and I detested every minute of it. Johannes saw only the sick before him. He saw only his direct channel to God. What sorrow he must have felt when it was closed. And I offered him no sympathy. Instead I was overjoyed. Finally we could be normal boys, Johannes and I. Finally we could be equals. But that never happened. Johannes continued to spellbind people, while I, I . . .' His voice caught.

'You have all the power that Johannes had. But you don't dare use it, Gabriel. That's the difference between you two. But believe me, it's there.'

For the first time in all their years together she saw tears in his eyes. Not even when Jacob's illness was at its worst had he dared let go. She took his hand and he gripped hers hard.

Gabriel said, 'I can't promise forgiveness. But I can promise to try.'

'I know. Believe me, Gabriel, I know.' She placed his hand on her cheek.

Erica's worry was growing with each hour that passed. She had a grinding pain in the small of her back, and she massaged the spot absentmindedly with her fingertips. All morning she had tried to ring Anna, at home and on her mobile, but she got no answer. From Information she'd got hold of Gustav's mobile, but he could tell her only that he'd sailed Anna and the children down to Uddevalla the day before and then they'd taken the train from there. They should have arrived in Stockholm that evening. It bothered Erica that he didn't sound a bit worried. He calmly came up with a bunch of logical explanations: they may have been tired and unplugged the jack, the battery in the mobile had run down, or, he laughed, maybe Anna hadn't paid her telephone bill. That comment made Erica boil, and she simply hung up on him. If she hadn't been worried enough before, she certainly was now.

She tried to ring Patrik to ask his advice, or at least receive some support, but he didn't answer either his mobile or his office phone. She rang the switchboard and Annika said that he was out on a call and she didn't know when he'd be back.

Frantically Erica kept making calls. The grinding feeling wouldn't go away. Just as she was about to give up someone answered Anna's mobile.

'Hello?' A kid's voice. Must be Emma, Erica thought.

'Hi darling, it's your aunt. Tell me, where are you?'

'In Stockholm,' Emma lisped. 'Did the baby come yet?'

Erica smiled. 'No, not yet. Look, Emma, could I talk to your mamma?'

Emma ignored the question. Now that she was lucky enough to have her mamma's telephone and even answer a call, she didn't intend to give it up so easily.

'You know wha-a-a-t?' said Emma.

'No, I don't,' said Erica, 'but darling, we can talk about it later. I'd really like to talk to your mamma now.' Her patience was running out.

'You know wha-a-a-t?' Emma repeated stubbornly.

'No, what?' Erica sighed wearily.

'We moved!'

'Yes, I know, you did that a while ago.'

'No, today!' Emma said triumphantly.

'Today?'

'Yes, we moved back home with Pappa,' Emma announced.

The room started to spin before Erica's eyes. But before she could say anything else she heard Emma say, 'Bye, I have to go play now.' Then the connection was cut.

With a sinking feeling in her heart Erica hung up.

Patrik knocked loudly on the door at Västergården. Marita opened it.

'Hello, Marita. We have a warrant to search your house.'

'But you've already done that,' she said, looking puzzled.

'We've uncovered some new information. I have a team with me, but I've asked them to wait a short distance away

387

until you've had a chance to take the children with you. It's not necessary for them to see all the police and be frightened.'

She nodded mutely. Worrying about Jacob had used up all her strength, and she had no energy left to object. She turned to go and fetch the children, but Patrik stopped her with another question.

'Are there any other buildings on the grounds than the ones we can see in this area?'

She shook her head. 'No, just the house, the barn, the tool shed and the playhouse. That's all.'

Patrik nodded and let her go.

Fifteen minutes later the house was empty. They could start their search. Patrik gave some brief instructions in the living room.

'We've been here once before without finding anything, but this time we're going to do a more thorough job. Search everywhere, and I mean everywhere. If you need to tear up boards in the floor or from the walls, then do it. If you need to break up furniture then do that too. Understood?'

They all nodded. There was a sense that they were about to do something fateful, but everyone was ready to go to work. Before they went in, Patrik had given them a brief rundown of developments in the case. Now they wanted nothing more than to get started.

After they had worked for an hour with no results, the house looked like a disaster zone. Everything had been torn up and hauled outside. But there were still no leads. Patrik was helping out in the living room when Gösta and Ernst came in the door and looked around wide-eyed.

'What the hell is going on here?' said Ernst.

Patrik ignored the question. 'Did it go well with Kennedy?'

'Yep, he confessed without beating about the bush, and he's now behind bars. Damned snot-nosed kid.'

Stressed, Patrik merely nodded.

'So what's happening here? It feels like we're the only

ones who are in the dark. Annika wouldn't tell us anything. She just said that we were supposed to come out here and you would fill us in.'

'I can't explain everything to you right now,' Patrik said impatiently. 'For the time being you should know that all indications point to Jacob as the one who kidnapped Jenny Möller. We have to find something that tells us where she is.'

'But then he wasn't the one who killed the German,' said Gösta. 'Because the blood test showed . . .' He looked bewildered.

With growing irritation Patrik said, 'No, he probably *was* the one who killed Tanja.'

'Then who murdered the other girls? He was too young back then . . .'

'It wasn't him. But we'll go over all that later. Now lend us a hand here!'

'What are we looking for?' said Ernst.

'The search warrant is on the kitchen table. There's a description of the things we're interested in finding.' Then Patrik turned and continued searching the bookshelf.

Another hour passed without anyone finding anything of interest. Patrik began to lose heart. Imagine if they didn't find anything. He had moved on from the living room and was searching the home office, with no result. Now he stood with his hands on his hips, forced himself to take a few deep breaths and let his eyes wander around the room. The office was small but neat. Shelves with binders and folders, all neatly labelled. No papers lay loose on top of the big antique bureau, and in the drawers everything was in order. Pensively Patrik let his gaze wander back to the bureau. He frowned. An antique. Having never missed a single episode of *Antiques Roadshow* on TV, his thoughts turned naturally to secret compartments when he looked at the old piece of furniture. He should have thought of that before. He started in the part above the writing surface, the part that had numerous small drawers. He pulled them out one by one and cautiously stuck his finger in the holes behind them. When he came to the last drawer he felt something. A little metal object was sticking up, and it moved when he pressed on it. With a clack the wall of the cavity behind it fell away and a secret compartment was revealed. His pulse quickened. Inside he found an old notebook in black leather. He pulled on some plastic gloves and carefully lifted out the book. With rising horror he read the contents. There was no time to lose in finding Jenny.

He remembered a paper he'd seen when he was searching through the drawers of the secretary. He pulled out the correct drawer and found it after leafing through some other documents. A county council routing stamp in one corner showed who the sender was. Patrik skimmed the few lines and read the name at the bottom. Then he took out his mobile and rang the station.

'Annika, it's Patrik. Listen, I want you to check on something for me.' He explained briefly. 'The one you should ask for is Dr Zoltan Czaba. In the cancer unit, yes. Ring me back as soon as you know something.'

The days had stretched interminably before them. Several times a day Kerstin and Bo Möller would ring the police station in the hope of hearing some news, but in vain. When Jenny's face appeared on flyers, their mobile phones began ringing almost non-stop. Friends, relatives, acquaintances. Everyone voiced dismay, but in the midst of their own worry they tried to infuse hope in Jenny's parents. Several had offered to come to Grebbestad to be with them, but the Möllers had declined politely but firmly. They thought it would make the situation seem even worse; they would be unable to forget that something was terribly wrong. If they simply stayed here in the caravan and waited, sitting across from each other at the little table, sooner or later Jenny would walk through the door and everything would go back to normal.

So there they sat, day after day, cloaked in their own anxiety. This day had been, if possible, more excruciating than any before. All night Kerstin had had horrible dreams. Sweating, she had tossed and turned in her sleep as images that were hard to decipher flickered inside her eyelids. She saw Jenny several times. Mostly as a little girl. At home on the front lawn. On a bathing beach at a campground. But the images were always replaced by dark, strange shapes, and she couldn't make any sense of them. It was cold and dark, and something was brooding at the periphery of her vision. She could never quite see it, even though in her dream she reached out for the shadow, time after time.

When she awoke in the morning she had a sinking feeling in her breast. As the hours passed and the temperature climbed inside the little caravan, she sat quietly facing Bo, trying desperately to conjure up the feeling of Jenny's infant body in her arms. But exactly as in the dream, it seemed just beyond her reach. She remembered the sensation, which had been so strong the whole time Jenny had been missing, but she could no longer feel it. Slowly the realization dawned on her. She raised her eyes from the tabletop and looked at her husband.

Then she said, 'She's gone now.'

He didn't question what she said. As soon as she said the words he felt inside himself that it was true.

12

The days merged into one another as if in a haze. She was tortured in a way that she never thought possible, and she couldn't stop cursing herself. If only she hadn't been so stupid as to hitchhike, this would never have happened. Mamma and Pappa had told her so many times never to get into a strange car, but she had felt invulnerable.

It seemed like so long ago. Jenny tried to conjure that feeling again, wanting to enjoy it again, even if only for a brief moment. The feeling that nothing in the world could get the better of her, that bad things might befall others but not her. Whatever happened now, she would never get back that feeling.

She lay on her side, scratching her fingers in the dirt. Her other arm was unusable, but she forced herself to move the healthier one to keep her circulation going. She dreamt that like a heroine in a film she would cast herself upon him and overpower him the next time he came down here. She would leave him unconscious on the floor and escape out to the waiting crowd, which had been searching for her everywhere. It was a magnificent but impossible dream. Her legs were no longer any good for walking.

Life was slowly trickling out of her. She had an image of her life

393

running into the ground beneath her and giving sustenance to the organisms below. Worms and larvae greedily sucking up her vital energy.

As the last of her strength ebbed away she saw that she would never get a chance to ask her parents' forgiveness for being so impossible during the past few weeks. She hoped they would understand.

He had been sitting with her in his arms all night. She had gradually grown colder and colder. A dense darkness surrounded them. He hoped that she had found the darkness as safe and comforting as he had. It was like a big black blanket enfolding him.

For a second Jacob saw the children before him. But that image reminded him too much of reality, and he pushed it aside.

Johannes had shown the way. Johannes and Ephraim and himself. They were a trinity; he had always known that. They possessed a gift that Gabriel could never share. That's why he would never understand. Johannes and Ephraim and himself. They were unique. They stood closer to God than anyone else. They were special. That's what Johannes had written in his book.

It was no accident that he had found Johannes's black notebook. Something had led him to it, drawing him like a magnet towards what he saw as Johannes's bequest to him. He had been moved by the sacrifice that Johannes had been ready to make to save his life. He, as much as anyone could, understood what Johannes had wanted to achieve. Imagine the irony that it had turned out to be unnecessary. Grandpa

Ephraim was the one who came to save him. It pained him that Johannes had failed. It was a shame that the girls had died. But he had more time at his disposal than Johannes ever had. He would not fail. He would try over and over again until he found the key to his inner light. The light that Grandpa Ephraim had told him that he also possessed, hidden deep within. Just like Johannes, his father.

Regretfully Jacob stroked the girl's cold arm. It wasn't that he didn't mourn her death. But she was an ordinary person, and God would give her a special place because she had sacrificed herself for one of God's chosen. A thought occurred to Jacob: perhaps it was that God expected a certain number of sacrifices before He would allow him to have the key. Perhaps it had been that way for Johannes too. It wasn't that they had failed, it was only that the Lord expected further proof of their faith before He would show them the way.

That idea brightened Jacob's mood. That must be the answer. He had always believed more in the God of the Old Testament. The God who demanded blood sacrifice.

One thing still gnawed at his conscience, however. How forgiving would God be that he hadn't been able to resist the lust of the flesh? Johannes had been stronger. He had never been tempted, and Jacob admired him for that. Jacob himself had felt the soft, smooth skin against his, and something deep inside him had awoken. For a brief time the Devil had overpowered him and he had given in. But he had deeply regretted it afterwards, and surely God must have noticed this. He who could see straight into his heart must be able to see that his remorse was righteous and grant him the forgiveness that He bestowed on all sinners.

Jacob rocked the girl in his arms. He brushed away a lock of hair that had fallen in her face. She was beautiful. As soon as he'd seen her by the road, her thumb stuck out for a lift, he had known she was the right one. The first girl had been the sign he'd been waiting for. For years he had read with fascination Johannes's words in the book. When the girl showed up at his door asking about her mother, the same day that he himself had received the Judgement, he realized that it was a sign.

He wasn't disheartened by the fact that he hadn't been able to find the power with her help. Johannes had been unsuccessful with her mother, too. The important thing was that, with that first girl, Jacob had set out on the path that had been determined for him. To follow in his father's footsteps.

Placing the girls together in the King's Cleft had been a way to demonstrate this to the world. A proclamation that he was now continuing what Johannes had started. He didn't think that anyone else would understand. It was enough that God understood and found it good.

If Jacob had needed any final proof of that, he received it last night. When they began talking about the results of the blood tests, he was sure that he would be locked up as a criminal. He had forgotten that the Devil had also made him leave traces on the body.

But he had laughed the Devil right in the face. To his great surprise the police had told him that the tests exonerated him. That was the final proof he needed to be convinced that he was on the right path and that nobody could stop him. He was special. He was protected. He was blessed.

Slowly he stroked the girl's hair once more. He would have to find a new one.

It took only ten minutes before Annika called back.

'It was like you said. Jacob has cancer again. But this time it isn't leukaemia, but a big tumour in his brain. He's been informed that there's nothing they can do, it's too far advanced.'

'When did he get the news?'

Annika looked at the notes she had jotted down. 'The same day that Tanja went missing.'

Patrik sank down on the sofa in the living room. He knew it, yet had a hard time believing it was true. The house breathed such peace, such calm. There was not a trace of the evil for which he held the proof in his hands. Only deceptive normality. Flowers in a vase, children's toys spread across the floor, a half-read book on the coffee table. No skulls, no blood-spattered clothes, no black candles burning.

Over the mantelpiece there was even a painting of Jesus, on his way up to Heaven after the resurrection, with a halo round his head and people praying on the ground before him, looking up.

How could anyone justify the most evil of actions with the thought that he had carte blanche from God? Although perhaps it wasn't so strange after all. Down through the ages millions of people had been murdered in God's name. There was something tempting about that power, something that intoxicated human beings and misled them.

Patrik wrenched himself out of his theological musings and found that the team was now standing around looking at him, waiting for more instructions. He had shown them what he'd found, and every one of them was now struggling not to think of the horrors that Jenny might be going through at that very moment.

The problem was that they had no idea where she could be. During the time Patrik was waiting for Annika to call back, they had continued an even more feverish search through the house. At the same time he had rung the manor and asked Marita, Gabriel and Laine whether there was anywhere they thought Jacob might go. He brusquely brushed off their counter-questions. There was no time for that right now.

He ruffled his hair, which was already standing on end. 'Where the hell can he be? We can't keep searching the whole county, centimetre by centimetre. He could be hiding her near the farm in Bullaren instead, or somewhere in

398

between. What the hell are we going to do?' he said in frustration.

Martin felt the same impotence but said nothing. Patrik hadn't meant it as a question. Then an idea occurred to him.

'It must be here around Västergården somewhere. Think of the trail of the fertilizer. My guess is that Jacob is using the same place that Johannes used. And what would be more logical than somewhere around here?'

'You're right, but both Marita and her in-laws say that there aren't any other buildings on the property. Of course it could be a cave or something like that, but do you know how large the Hult family property is? It's like looking for a needle in a haystack.'

'Yes, but what about Solveig and her boys? Have you asked them? They lived here before. They might know something about the place that Marita doesn't know.'

'That's a hell of a good idea. Isn't there a list of numbers in the kitchen by the telephone? Linda has her mobile with her, so maybe I can reach them on that.'

Martin went and checked. He came back with a list on which Linda's name was neatly written. Impatiently Patrik let it ring. After what seemed like an eternity Linda answered.

'Linda, this is Patrik Hedström. I need to talk to Solveig or Robert.'

'They're in with Stefan. He woke up!' Linda said, sounding elated. With a heavy heart Patrik realized that the joy would soon disappear from her voice.

'Get one of them now, this is important!'

'Okay, which would you prefer?'

He thought a moment. Who would know the area around the house where he lived better than a child? The choice was easy. 'Robert.'

He heard her put down the phone and go to fetch him. She probably couldn't take the mobile into the hospital room because it might disturb the equipment. Patrik just managed to think of that before he heard Robert's sombre voice on the line.

'Yes, this is Robert.'

'Hello, it's Patrik Hedström. I wonder whether you could help us with something. It's extremely important,' he hastened to add.

'Yes, okay, what is it?' said Robert hesitantly.

'I wonder if you know of any buildings on the grounds around Västergården besides the ones located near the house. It doesn't even have to be a building, actually. More a good place to hide, if you know what I mean. But it has to be fairly big. There has to be room for more than one person.'

Patrik could clearly sense the question marks piling up in Robert's brain, but to his relief Robert didn't challenge the reason for his questions. Instead, after thinking for a moment, he said, 'Well, the only thing I can come up with is the old bomb shelter. It's located a good bit up in the woods. We used to play there when we were little, Stefan and I.'

'And Jacob,' said Patrik, 'did he know about it?'

'Yes, we made the mistake of showing it to him once. But then he ran straight to Pappa. They came back and told us never to play there again. It was dangerous, Pappa said. So that was the end of our fun. Jacob has always been a little too proper for his own good,' Robert said sourly as he remembered his childhood disappointment. Patrik thought that proper was perhaps not the word that would come to be associated with Jacob in future.

He thanked him hastily after getting directions and hung up.

'I think I know where they are, Martin. Gather everybody out in the yard.'

Five minutes later, eight solemn officers were standing in the blazing sunshine outside. Four from Tanumshede, four from Uddevalla.

'We have reason to believe that Jacob Hult is hiding nearby in the woods, in an old bomb shelter. He probably has Jenny

Möller there, and we don't know whether she's dead or alive. So we have to act as though she's alive and use the utmost caution in handling the situation. We'll move forward carefully until we find the shelter, then we'll surround it. In silence,' Patrik said sharply, letting his gaze wander over them all but resting a bit longer on Ernst. 'We'll have weapons drawn, but nobody does anything without an express order from me. Is that clear?'

Everyone nodded, their faces solemn.

'An ambulance is on its way from Uddevalla, but they won't be arriving with blue lights on. They'll stop just outside the drive into Västergården. Sound travels far in the woods, and we don't want him to hear that something is going down. As soon as we have the situation under control we'll call in the EMTs.'

'Shouldn't we have some medics with us up front?' asked one of the officers from Uddevalla. 'It might be urgent by the time we find her.'

Patrik nodded. 'You're right in principle, but we don't have time to wait for them. Right now it's more important to locate her quickly, and hopefully the EMTs will have arrived in the meantime. Okay, let's move out.'

Robert had described where they should go in the woods behind the house. A hundred metres farther away they would come to the path leading to the bomb shelter. The path was almost invisible if you didn't know it was there, and Patrik almost missed it at first. They advanced slowly towards the goal and after about a kilometre he thought he could see something glinting through the foliage. Without a word he turned round and directed the men behind him to move forward. They spread out as quietly as possible and encircled the shelter, but it wasn't possible to avoid a bit of rustling. Patrik grimaced at every sound and hoped the thick concrete walls would filter out any noise Jacob might overhear.

He drew his weapon and out of the corner of his eye saw

Martin do the same. They crept forward and cautiously tried the door. It was locked. Damn, what were they going to do now? They had no equipment with them to get it open and the only alternative was to urge Jacob to come out voluntarily. In trepidation Patrik knocked on the door and moved quickly to the side.

'Jacob. We know you're in there. We want you to come out!'

No answer. He tried again.

'Jacob, I know that you didn't mean to hurt those girls. You were just doing what Johannes did. Come out and let's talk about it.'

He could hear how lame his words sounded. Maybe he should have taken a course in hostage negotiation, or at least brought along a psychologist. Lacking that, he would have to rely on his own instincts about how to talk a psychopath out of a bomb shelter.

To his great surprise he heard the lock click a moment later. The door opened slowly. Martin and Patrik, standing on either side of the door, exchanged a glance. Both of them were holding their weapons in front of their faces and tensed their bodies to be ready. Jacob stepped out through the door. In his arms he was carrying Jenny. There was no doubt that she was dead, and Patrik could almost feel the disappointment and sorrow sweeping through the hearts of the policemen, who now stood fully visible with their weapons aimed at Jacob.

He ignored them. Instead he was looking up and speaking into the air.

'I don't understand. I was chosen. You were supposed to protect me.' He looked as confused as if the world were suddenly turned upside down. 'Why did You save me yesterday if I'm not in Your grace today?'

Patrik and Martin looked at each other. Jacob seemed completely out of it. But that made him all the more dangerous.

There was no way to tell what he was going to do next. They kept their weapons steadily aimed at him.

'Put down the girl,' said Patrik.

Jacob kept his eyes on Heaven, talking to his invisible God. 'I know that You would have let me have the gift, but I need more time. Why do You turn away from me now?'

'Put down the girl and get your hands in the air!' said Patrik with more sharpness in his voice. Still no reaction from Jacob. He was holding the girl in his arms and didn't seem to have any weapon on him. Patrik wondered whether he should tackle him to break the stand-off. There was no reason to worry about injuring the girl. It was too late for that.

He had scarcely finished his thought when a tall figure came flying forward from the left. Patrik was so startled that his finger shook on the trigger, and he almost put a bullet into either Jacob or Martin. He watched with horror as Ernst's lanky body flew through the air straight at Jacob, who dropped to the ground with a thud. Jenny fell out of his arms and landed right in front of him with a nasty hollow sound, like a sack of flour flung to the ground.

With a triumphant expression Ernst twisted Jacob's hands behind his back. He didn't try to resist, but he still had the same astonished look on his face.

'That's how it's done,' said Ernst and looked up to receive the cheers of the crowd. They all stood as if frozen, and when Ernst saw the dark look on Patrik's face he realized that once again he had acted without thinking.

Patrik was still shaking after coming so close to shooting Martin. He had to control himself to keep from putting his hands round Ernst's skinny neck and slowly throttling him. But they would deal with that later. Now the most important thing was to take Jacob into custody.

Gösta got out a pair of handcuffs and went over to Jacob and fastened them round his wrists. Together with Martin he brusquely helped Jacob to his feet and then shot a questioning look at Patrik, who turned to two of the officers from Uddevalla.

'Take him back to Västergården. I'll be there right away. See to it that the ambulance crew come out here too and tell them to bring a stretcher.'

They started to leave with Jacob, but Patrik stopped them. 'Wait a minute, I just want to look him in the eyes. I want to see what somebody who can do this really looks like.' He motioned towards Jenny's lifeless body.

Jacob met his gaze without remorse, but still with the same bewildered expression. He looked at Patrik and said, 'Isn't it strange? Last night to save me, God performed a miracle, and then today He lets me get caught?'

Patrik tried to see in the man's eyes whether he was serious, or whether all this was a game to try and save himself from the consequences of his own actions. The look that met him was as blank as a mirror; he was looking into the face of madness.

Wearily he said, 'It wasn't God. It was Ephraim. You passed the blood test because Ephraim donated his bone marrow to you when you were sick. That meant that you received his blood and his DNA in your blood. That's why your blood sample didn't match the DNA test we took on the . . . evidence . . . you left on Tanja. We didn't understand it until the experts at the lab mapped the relationships of your family. According to your blood test you were supposedly the father of Johannes and Gabriel.'

Jacob simply nodded. Then he said gently, 'But isn't that a miracle?' Then he was led off through the woods.

Martin, Gösta and Patrik remained standing by Jenny's body. Ernst had hastily slunk away with the police from Uddevalla, and he would probably do his best to keep a low profile for a while.

All three of them wished they had a jacket to cover her

with. Her nakedness was so vulnerable, so degrading. They saw the wounds on her body. Wounds that were identical to those Tanja had suffered. And probably the same as Siv and Mona had when they died.

Despite his impulsive temperament Johannes had been a methodical man. His notebook showed how he had precisely recorded the wounds he inflicted on his victims, and then how he had tried to heal them. He kept records of it all like a scientist. The same wounds on both, in the same order. Perhaps to convince himself that it had some semblance of being a scientific experiment. An experiment in which they were unfortunate but necessary sacrifices. Necessary so that God would give him back the gift of healing that he'd had as a boy. The gift he had longed for his whole adult life and which became so acutely necessary to resurrect when Jacob, his first-born son, fell ill.

It was an unhappy inheritance that Ephraim had left to his son and his grandson. Jacob's imagination had been set in motion by Ephraim's accounts of the healing Gabriel and Johannes had done during their boyhood years. For the sake of effect Ephraim had said that he saw the same gift in his grandson. That had engendered ideas which over the years were exaggerated by the illness that brought Jacob so close to death. Then he had found Johannes's notebook, and judging by how dog-eared the pages were, he had returned to it time after time. It was a tragic coincidence that Tanja showed up at Västergården asking about her mother on the same day that Jacob received his terminal prognosis. All of these factors combined had led up to this moment, as the police officers stood looking at a dead girl.

When Jacob dropped Jenny she had fallen on her side. It almost looked as though she were huddled up in the foetal position. In surprise Martin and Patrik saw Gösta unbutton his short-sleeved shirt and take it off. He exposed a chalk-white, hairless chest, and without a word he spread the shirt over Jenny and tried to hide as much as possible of her nakedness.

'Don't just stand there staring at the girl when she doesn't have a stitch of clothing on,' he said gruffly, crossing his arms to ward off the raw dampness in the shade of the trees.

Patrik knelt down and spontaneously took Jenny's cold hand in his. She had died alone, but she would not have to wait alone.

A couple of days later the worst of the commotion had settled down. Patrik sat in front of Mellberg, wanting only to get it over with. The boss had demanded a full review of the case. Patrik knew that the chief's motive was to learn enough so that he could tell tall tales for years to come about his participation in the Hult case. But that didn't particularly bother Patrik. After personally delivering the news to Jenny's parents, he had a hard time seeing either honour or fame in connection with the investigation. He gladly turned over that aspect to Mellberg.

'I still don't understand that part about the blood,' Mellberg said.

Patrik sighed and started explaining for the third time, speaking even more slowly.

'When Jacob was sick with leukaemia, he received a bone marrow transplant from his grandfather Ephraim. That meant that the blood produced inside Jacob after the transplant had the same DNA as the donor, that is, Ephraim. In other words, Jacob then had the DNA of two people in his body. His grandfather's DNA in his blood and his own in the other parts of his body. That's why we got Ephraim's DNA profile when we analysed Jacob's blood sample. Since the DNA that Jacob left on his victim was in the form of semen, that sample retained his original DNA profile. So the two profiles didn't match. According to SCL, the statistical probability for something like this happening is so small that it's highly implausible. But not impossible . . .'

Mellberg finally seemed to grasp the facts. He shook his head in amazement. 'What bloody science fiction. We've heard just about everything now, Hedström, haven't we? I must say that we did a damned good job on this case. The chief of police in Göteborg rang me personally yesterday and thanked us for our excellent handling of the case, and I couldn't agree more.'

Patrik had a hard time seeing what was excellent about it all, since they hadn't succeeded in saving the girl's life, but he chose not to comment. Sometimes things happened in spite of their best efforts. And there wasn't much one could do about it.

The past few days had been depressing. In a way it had been a grieving process. He was still sleeping poorly, haunted by images conjured up by the sketches and notes in Johannes's book. Erica had restlessly hovered round him, and he had noticed that she too lay tossing and turning next to him at night. But somehow he hadn't had the energy to reach out towards her. He had to work through this by himself.

Not even feeling the baby's movements in her belly could awaken the sense of wellbeing it had always given him before. It was as though he was suddenly reminded of how dangerous the world was, and how evil and crazy people could be. How would he be able to protect a child from all that? The result was that he pulled away from Erica and the baby. Away from the risk of someday having to go through the pain he had seen in Bo and Kerstin Möller's faces when he stood before them and with a sob in his throat informed them that unfortunately Jenny was dead. How could anyone survive such pain?

In the darker hours of the night he had even considered running away. Just clear out, bag and baggage. Away from all responsibility and duty. Away from the risk that his love for their child would become a weapon pressed to his temple, the trigger slowly pulled. He had always been dedication personified, yet for the first time in his life he seriously considered taking the coward's way out. At the same time he knew that Erica needed his support now more than ever. Hearing that Anna and the children had moved back in with Lucas had made her despair. He knew that, but he still couldn't reach out to her.

He looked at Mellberg sitting in front of him. The chief's mouth kept moving. 'Yes, I don't see any reason why we shouldn't see an increase in our share in the next budget round, considering the goodwill we've built up . . .'

Blah, blah, blah, thought Patrik. Words that gushed forth, devoid of meaning. Money and honour, a bigger budget and commendations from superiors. Worthless measurements of success. He had an urge to take his cup of coffee and slowly pour the hot liquid over Mellberg's bird's nest of hair. Just to shut him up.

'Yes, and your contribution will be noted, of course,' Mellberg said. 'As a matter of fact I was saying to the chief of police that I had great support in the investigation from you. But please don't remind me that I said that when it comes time to talk about salary,' Mellberg chuckled and winked at Patrik. 'The only thing that concerns me is the part about Johannes Hult's death. You still don't have any idea who murdered him?'

Patrik shook his head. They had talked to Jacob about it, but he honestly seemed to be as much in the dark as they were. The murder was still marked unsolved and it appeared likely to remain so.

'It would certainly be the icing on the cake if you could sew up that part too. It wouldn't hurt to get a little gold star next to your commendation, would it?' Then Mellberg's expression turned serious. 'And naturally I've noted your criticism of Ernst's actions, but considering his many years on the force I think we ought to be magnanimous and draw a line through that little episode. I mean, everything turned out all right in the end.'

Patrik remembered the feeling of his finger quivering on the trigger with Martin and Jacob in his line of fire. Now his hand holding the coffee cup began to shake. As if of its own accord, the hand began to raise the cup and slowly move towards Mellberg's barely covered pate. The cup stopped abruptly when there was a knock at the door. It was Annika.

'Patrik, there's a call for you.'

'Can't you see that we're busy?' Mellberg hissed.

'I really think he'll want to take this call,' she said, giving Patrik an insistent look.

Puzzled, Patrik stared at her but she refused to say anything. When they got to her office she pointed at the receiver lying on the desk and discreetly stepped out in the corridor.

Patrik put the phone to his ear.

'Why the hell don't you have your mobile turned on?'

He looked at his phone hanging in its case on his belt and realized it needed charging.

'The battery's dead. Why?' He didn't understand why Erica was getting so worked up. She could still reach him through the switchboard.

'Because it's starting! And you didn't answer your land-line and then you didn't answer your mobile either and then – '

He interrupted, confused. 'What do you mean, it's starting? What's starting?'

'Labour, you idiot. The pains have started and my waters broke! You have to come get me, we have to leave right now!'

'But I thought you weren't due for three weeks?' He still felt confused.

'The baby obviously doesn't know that, it's coming now!' Then he heard only the dial tone.

Patrik stood transfixed with the phone in his hand. A goofy grin began to play over his lips. His baby was on the way. His and Erica's baby.

On trembling legs he ran out to the car and yanked at the door handle a couple of times in confusion. Somebody tapped him on the shoulder. Behind him stood Annika with the car keys dangling in her hand.

'It would probably be quicker if you unlocked the car first.'

He snatched the keys from her hand and waved a hasty goodbye as he stomped the gas pedal to the floor and zoomed off towards Fjällbacka. Annika looked at the black tyre marks he left on the asphalt. Laughing she went back to her place at the reception desk.

13

Ephraim was worried. Gabriel was still stubbornly claiming that it was Johannes he'd seen with the missing girl. He refused to believe it, but at the same time he knew that his son was the last person who would ever lie. For Gabriel, truth and order were more important even than his own brother, and that's why Ephraim was having such a hard time dismissing the claim. He kept thinking that maybe Gabriel had simply been mistaken. The twilight could have made his eyes deceive him, or else he was fooled by the formation of shadows, or something like that. Ephraim could hear for himself how far-fetched that sounded. But he also knew Johannes. His carefree, irresponsible son who played his way through life. Would he really be capable of taking someone's life?

Leaning on his cane Ephraim walked along the path from the farm over to Västergården. He really didn't need the cane because by his own estimation his physical condition was as good as a twenty-year-old's. But he thought it looked stylish. A cane and hat gave him a look befitting a landowner, and he made use of that image as often as he could.

It bothered Ephraim that Gabriel was making the distance between them get worse with each year that passed. He knew that Gabriel

411

believed that he favoured Johannes, and to be honest, he supposed he did. It was only that Johannes was so much easier to deal with. His charm and his openness made it possible to treat him with a kind indulgence, which made Ephraim feel like a patriarch in the true sense of the word. Johannes was someone he could reprimand harshly, someone who made him feel needed, if for nothing other than keeping his son's feet on the ground with all the womenfolk who were always running after him. With Gabriel it was different. He always regarded his father with a contempt that made Ephraim respond with a demeanour of cool superiority. He knew that in many respects the fault was his own. While Johannes had bounced with joy each time Ephraim held a worship service in which the boys had a chance to be useful, Gabriel had shrunk back and grown increasingly sullen. Ephraim noticed this and took full blame upon himself, but after all he had done it for their own good. After Ragnhild died, the family had to depend on his charm and his gift of the gab to put food on the table and clothes on their backs. It was a lucky accident that he proved to be such a natural talent that the dotty widow Dybling ended up leaving him her estate and her fortune. Gabriel probably should have paid more attention to the end result, instead of constantly bothering him with reproaches about his 'terrible' childhood. The truth was that if Ephraim hadn't had the brilliant idea of using the boys in his worship services, they wouldn't have had everything they owned today. Nobody had been able to resist those two delightful little boys, who through God's providence had received the gift of healing the sick and the lame. Combined with Ephraim's own charisma and gift for speaking, they had been unbeatable. He knew that he was still a legendary preacher within the world of the free church, and it afforded him boundless amusement. He also loved the fact that in popular parlance he had been given the nickname of The Preacher.

But it had surprised him to see how distressed Johannes was to receive the news that he had grown out of his gift. For Ephraim it had been a simple way to conclude the deception, and for Gabriel it had also come as a great relief. But Johannes had mourned.

Ephraim had always intended to tell the boys that it was all a trick on his part and that the people they had 'healed' were in fact perfectly healthy. He had given them a coin so that they would play along with the spectacle. But as the years passed he began to have doubts. Sometimes Johannes seemed so fragile. That's why Ephraim was so worried about this whole thing with the police and their interrogation of Johannes. He was more vulnerable than he seemed, and Ephraim wasn't sure how it would affect him. That's why he'd decided to take a walk over to Västergården and have a talk with his son. Get a feeling for how he seemed to be handling the situation.

A smile passed over Ephraim's lips. Jacob had come home from hospital a week earlier and was spending hours up in his grandfather's room. He loved the boy. He had saved Jacob's life, which forever united them with a special bond. On the other hand Ephraim wasn't as gullible as they all thought. It was possible that Gabriel believed Jacob to be his son, but Ephraim had seen what was going on. Jacob was probably Johannes's son, he could see it in Johannes's eyes. Well, he wasn't going to get involved with that. But the boy was the pride and joy of his old age. Of course he also liked Robert and Stefan, but they were still so young. What Ephraim liked most about Jacob was how wise he could sound and how fervently he listened to his grandfather's stories. Jacob loved to hear the stories about when Gabriel and Johannes were little and travelled around with their preacher father. 'The healer stories,' he called them. 'Grandpa, tell me the healer stories,' Jacob would say every time he came upstairs to say hello. Ephraim had nothing against reliving those times, because they had certainly been fun. And it didn't do the boy any harm if he embellished the stories a little extra. He had made it a habit to conclude the stories with a dramatic pause and then point with his knotty finger to Jacob's chest and say, 'Oh, you Jacob, you also have the gift within you. Somewhere deep inside it's waiting to be coaxed out.' The boy used to sit at his feet with his eyes wide and his mouth hanging open. Ephraim loved to see how fascinated the boy was.

He knocked on the door of the house. No answer. Everything was quiet. Solveig and the boys didn't seem to be at home, either. He could usually hear the boys from several kilometres away. There was a sound from the barn, and he went over to have a look. Johannes stood there doing something with the combine harvester and didn't notice that his father had come in until Ephraim was standing right behind him. He jumped.

'Plenty to do, I see.'

'Yep, there's always something to keep me busy on the farm.'

'I heard that you'd been to see the police again,' Ephraim said. He normally got straight to the point.

'Yep,' said Johannes.

'What did they want to know now?'

'It was more questions about Gabriel's testimony, of course.' Johannes kept working on the combine and didn't look at Ephraim.

'You know that Gabriel doesn't mean to hurt you.'

'I know that. It's just the way he is. But the result is still the same.'

'How true, how true.' Ephraim stood rocking on his heels, unsure of how to go on.

'It's great to see little Jacob on his feet again, isn't it?' he said, looking for a neutral topic. A smile spread across Johannes's face.

'It's wonderful. It's like he was never sick.' He straightened up and looked his father in the eye. 'I'm eternally thankful to you for that, Pappa.'

Ephraim simply nodded and stroked his moustache, feeling pleased.

Johannes went on, cautiously, 'Pappa, if you couldn't have saved Jacob . . . Do you think that . . . ' He hesitated, but then continued in a firm voice as if trying to overcome his embarrassment. 'Do you think that I could have found the gift again? To be able to heal Jacob, I mean?'

The question made Ephraim step back in astonishment. He was shocked to realize that he had created a bigger illusion than he'd intended. His regret and guilt ignited a defensive spark of rage, and he lashed out fiercely at Johannes.

'How stupid are you anyway, boy? I thought that sooner or later you'd grow up enough to see the truth, but I suppose I should have written it on your nose. None of that was for real! None of the people you and Gabriel ' "healed" ' – he made the quotation marks with his fingers – 'were really sick. They were paid! By me!' He shrieked out the words, making spittle spray out of his mouth. The next second he regretted what he had said. All colour had vanished from Johannes's face. He wobbled back and forth like a drunkard, and for a moment Ephraim wondered whether his son was having an attack of some sort. Then Johannes whispered, so quietly that he could hardly hear it:

'Then I killed those girls for nothing.'

All the anxiety, all the guilt, all the regret exploded inside Ephraim and pulled him into a dark black hole, where he had no choice but to get rid of the pain of this confession somehow. His fist lashed out and struck Johannes in the chin with full force. In slow motion he saw Johannes fall backwards with a look of shock towards the metal of the combine. A dull thud echoed through the barn when the back of Johannes's head struck the hard surface. Ephraim stared in horror at Johannes lying lifeless on the ground. He knelt down and tried desperately to find a pulse. Nothing. He put his ear to his son's mouth, hoping to hear even the faintest sound of his breathing. Still nothing. Slowly he realized that Johannes was dead. Felled by his own father's hand.

His first impulse had been to run and ring for help. Then his survival instinct took over. And if there was anything that could be said about Ephraim, it was that he was a survivor. If he called for help he'd be forced to explain why he hit Johannes, and that must never come out at any price. The girls were dead and so was Johannes. In some biblical way, justice had been done. Nor did Ephraim have any desire to spend his last days in prison. It would be punishment enough to live the rest of his life with the knowledge that he had killed Johannes. Decisively he set about the task of concealing his crime. Thank goodness he had a number of favours he could call in.

Jacob felt that he was getting on quite well with his life. The doctors had given him six months at most, and at least he could spend those months in peace and quiet. Naturally he missed Marita and the children, but they were allowed to come and visit once a week, and the rest of his time he spent in prayer. He had already forgiven God for abandoning him at the end. Even Jesus had stood in the garden of Gethsemane and shouted to Heaven, asking his Father why He had forsaken him, the night before God sacrificed His only son. If Jesus could forgive, so could Jacob.

The garden at the hospital was the place where he spent most of his time. He knew that the other prisoners were avoiding him. They were all serving sentences for something, mostly for murder, but for some reason the others viewed him as dangerous. They didn't understand. He hadn't enjoyed killing the girls. He hadn't done it for his own sake. He did it because it was his duty. Ephraim had explained that he, just like Johannes, was special. Chosen. It was his obligation to make use of his inheritance and not let himself waste away with a disease that was stubbornly trying to exterminate him.

And he wouldn't give up yet. He couldn't give up. The past

weeks he had come to the understanding that he and Johannes may have chosen the wrong way to proceed. They had tried to find a practical method to reclaim the gift, but perhaps that was not how to do it. Perhaps they should have begun by searching inward instead. The prayers and the silence here had helped him to focus. Gradually he had become better and better at achieving the meditative state in which he felt he was approaching God's original plan. He could feel the energy beginning to fill him. On those occasions he tingled all over with anticipation. Soon he would be able to start harvesting the fruits of his newfound knowledge. Of course he regretted even more that lives had been wasted unnecessarily, but there was a war raging between good and evil, and from that perspective the girls were necessary sacrifices.

The afternoon sun warmed him as he sat on the park bench. Today's prayer session had been especially powerful, and he felt as though he were competing with the sun for radiance. When he looked at his hand he saw a thin band of light surrounding it. Jacob smiled. It had begun.

Next to the bench he caught sight of a dead pigeon. It was lying on its side, and nature had already begun to reclaim the body and convert it to earth. Stiff and dirty, it lay with eyes that had taken on the milky membrane of death. Excited, Jacob leaned forward to study the bird. It was a sign.

He got up from the bench and squatted down next to the pigeon. Tenderly he studied its body. His hand was now glowing as if a fire were burning inside his limbs. Trembling he reached out the index finger of his right hand to the pigeon and let it rest lightly on the ruffled plumage. Nothing happened. Disappointment threatened to wash over him, but he forced himself to remain in the place where the prayers usually led him. After a while the pigeon twitched. One of its stiff legs began to shake. Then everything happened at once. The pigeon's feathers regained their lustre, the white

418

membrane covering the bird's eyes vanished. It got to its feet and with a powerful flap of its wings the bird took off towards Heaven. Jacob smiled, content.

By a window facing the garden, Dr Stig Holbrand stood watching Jacob together with Fredrik Nydin, a resident physician who was doing part of his practice in criminal psychiatry.

'That's Jacob Hult. He's a bit of a special case here. He tortured two girls while attempting to heal them. They died of their wounds and he was convicted of murder. But he didn't pass the criminal psychiatric examination, and he also has an inoperable brain tumour.'

'How long does he have left?' asked the resident. He understood the tragic nature of the case, but at the same time couldn't help thinking that it was enormously interesting.

'About six months. He claims that he'll be able to heal himself, and he spends large parts of his days in meditation. We let him have his way. He isn't hurting anyone.'

'But what is he doing now?'

'Well, that's not to say that he doesn't behave oddly sometimes.' Dr Holbrand squinted through the window and shaded his eyes with his hand to see better.

'I think he's throwing a pigeon up in the air. At least *that* poor creature was already dead,' he said dryly.

They moved on to the next patient.

Acknowledgements

Once again I would like to thank my husband Micke, who true to form always puts my writing first and is still my biggest supporter. Without him it would have been impossible to manage both the baby and the writing.

A big thank you also to my agent Mikael Nordin, along with Bengt and Jenny at the Bengt Nordin Agency, who all worked, and continue to work, indefatigably to get my books out to a broader public.

The officers at Tanumshede police station and their chief Folke Åberg deserve a special mention, since they took the time to read the material and offer suggestions. They also showed immeasurable equanimity when I placed a couple of apparently incompetent officers at their workplace. In this case reality does not resemble fiction!

One person who was invaluable during the work on *The Preacher* is my editor and publisher Karin Linge Nordh, who with greater exactitude than I could ever muster scrutinized the manuscript and offered judicious advice. She has also taught me the essential expression, 'When in doubt – delete'. Everyone at my new publishing house, Forum, has made me feel welcome.

Other people who have been a big help to me during the

work on this book, as well as the first one, include Gunilla Sandin and Ingrid Kampås. And Martin and Helena Persson, my mother-in-law Gunnel Läckberg, and Åsa Bohman all willingly read and commented on the manuscript.

Finally I would also like to give a special thanks to Berith and Anders Torevi, who not only marketed *The Ice Princess* in an enthusiastic manner but also took the time to read and comment on the manuscript of *The Preacher*.

All characters and events are fictitious. Fjällbacka and its environs are described accurately, although sometimes I have taken liberties with the geography.

Enskede, 11 February 2004
Camilla Läckberg
www.camillalackberg.com

The Ice Princess

Camilla Läckberg

'Heart-stopping and heart-warming . . . a masterclass in Scandinavian crime writing'   Val McDermid

Returning to her hometown after the funeral of her parents, writer Erica Falck finds a community on the brink of tragedy. The death of her childhood friend, Alex, is just the beginning. Her wrists slashed, her body frozen in an ice cold bath, it seems that she has taken her own life.

Erica conceives a memoir about the beautiful but remote Alex, one that will answer questions about their lost friendship. While her interest grows to an obsession, local detective Patrik Hedstrom is following his own suspicions about the case. But it is only when they start working together that the truth begins to emerge about the small town with a deeply disturbing past.

'A top-class Scandinavian crime writer'   *The Times*

ISBN: 978-0-00-725392-0

The Stonecutter

Camilla Läckberg

The remote resort of Fjällbacka has seen its share of tragedy, though perhaps none worse than that of the little girl found in a fisherman's net. But the post-mortem reveals that this is no accidental drowning . . .

Local detective Patrik Hedström has just become a father. It is his grim task to discover who could be behind the methodical murder of a child both he and his partner, Erica, knew well.

He knows the solution lies with finding a motive for this terrible crime. What he does not know is how this case will reach into the dark heart of Fjällbacka and tear aside its idyllic façade, perhaps forever.

'Camilla Läckberg is a more than welcome addition to the growing ranks of Scandinavian crime writing'

Peter Robinson

ISBN: 978-0-00-730593-3

Audio book available on CD and download